"No," Stefan said. "*I* don't understand. He's evil, Elena. He kills for pleasure; he has no conscience at all—"

"Right now he's being more cooperative than you are," Elena said. "Stefan, do you really want to be mortal enemies with your brother forever?"

"Do you really think *he* wants anything else?"

Elena didn't answer for a minute, and when she did it was very quietly.

"He stopped me from killing you."

Elena felt the flare of Stefan's defensive anger, then felt it slowly fade. "Then you do agree?" she said quietly.

"Yes. I . . . agree."

"And *I* agree," said Damon, extending his hand with exaggerated courtesy. "In fact, we all seem to be in a frenzy of pure agreement."

Don't, Elena thought, but at that moment, standing in the cool twilight of the choir loft, she felt that it was true, that they were all three connected, and in accord, and strong.

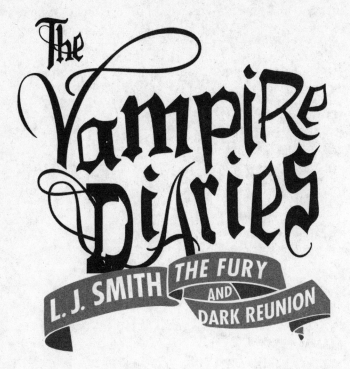

The Vampire Diaries

L. J. SMITH

THE FURY
AND
DARK REUNION

HARPERTEEN
An Imprint of HarperCollins*Publishers*

HarperTeen is an imprint of HarperCollins Publishers.

Library of Congress Catalog Card Number: 2007926265
ISBN 978-0-06-114098-3

Typography by Jennifer Heuer
❖
First HarperTeen paperback edition, 2007
09 10 11 12 13 CG/RRDH 20 19 18 17 16 15 14

To my aunt Margie, and in memory
of my aunt Agnes and Aunt Eleanore,
for fostering creativity

CONTENTS

Elena stepped into the clearing.

Beneath her feet tatters of autumn leaves were freezing into the slush. Dusk had fallen, and although the storm was dying away the woods were getting colder. Elena didn't feel the cold.

Neither did she mind the dark. Her pupils opened wide, gathering up tiny particles of light that would have been invisible to a human. She could see the two figures struggling beneath the great oak tree quite clearly.

One had thick dark hair, which the wind had churned into a tumbled sea of waves. He was slightly taller than the other, and although Elena couldn't see his face she somehow knew his eyes were green.

The other had a shock of dark hair as well, but his was fine and straight, almost like the pelt of an animal. His lips were drawn back from his teeth in fury, and the lounging grace of his body was gathered into a predator's crouch. His eyes were black.

Elena watched them for several minutes without moving. She'd forgotten why she had come here, why she'd been pulled here by the echoes of their battle in her mind. This close the clamor of their anger and hatred and pain was almost deafening, like silent shouts coming from the fighters. They were locked in a death match.

I wonder which of them will win, she thought. They were both wounded and bleeding, and the taller one's left arm hung at an unnatural angle. Still, he had just slammed the other against the gnarled trunk of an oak tree. His fury was so strong that Elena could feel and taste it as well as hear it, and she knew it was giving him impossible strength.

And then Elena remembered why she had come. How could she have forgotten? *He* was hurt. *His* mind had summoned her here, battering her with shock waves of rage and pain. She had come to help him because she belonged to him.

The two figures were down on the icy ground now, fighting like wolves, snarling. Swiftly and silently Elena went to them. The one with the wavy hair and green eyes—*Stefan*, a voice in her mind whispered—was on top, fingers scrabbling at the other's throat. Anger washed through Elena, anger and protectiveness. She reached between the two of them to grab that choking hand, to pry the fingers up.

It didn't occur to her that she shouldn't be strong enough to do this. She *was* strong enough; that was all. She threw her weight to the side, wrenching her captive away from his opponent. For good measure, she bore down hard on his wounded arm, knocking him flat on his face in the leaf-strewn slush. Then she began to choke him from behind.

Her attack had taken him by surprise, but he was far from beaten. He struck back at her, his good hand fumbling for her throat. His thumb dug into her windpipe.

Elena found herself lunging at the hand, going for it with her teeth. Her mind could not understand it, but her body knew what to do. Her teeth were a weapon, and they slashed into flesh, drawing blood.

But he was stronger than she was. With a jerk of his shoulders, he broke her hold on him and twisted in her grasp, flinging her down. And then he was above her, his face contorted with animal fury. She hissed at him and went for his eyes with her nails, but he knocked her hand away.

He was going to kill her. Even wounded, he was by far the stronger. His lips had drawn back to show teeth already stained with scarlet. Like a cobra, he was ready to strike.

Then he stopped, hovering over her, his face changing.

Elena saw the green eyes widen. The pupils, which had been contracted to vicious dots, sprang open. He was staring down at her as if truly seeing her for the first time.

Why was he looking at her that way? Why didn't he just get it over with? But now the iron hand on her shoulder was releasing her. The animal snarl had disappeared, replaced by a look of bewilderment and wonder. He sat back, helping her to sit up, all the while gazing into her face.

"Elena," he whispered. His voice was cracked. "Elena, it's you."

Is that who I am? she thought. Elena?

It didn't really matter. She cast a glance toward the old oak tree. *He* was still there, standing between the upthrust roots, panting, supporting himself against it with one hand. *He* was looking at her with his endlessly black eyes, his brows drawn together in a frown.

Don't worry, she thought. I can take care of this one. He's stupid. Then she flung herself on the green-eyed one again.

"Elena!" he cried as she knocked him backward. His good hand pushed at her shoulder, holding her up. "Elena, it's me, Stefan! Elena, look at me!"

She was looking. All she could see was the exposed patch of skin at his neck. She hissed again, upper lip drawing back, showing him her teeth.

He froze.

She felt the shock reverberate through his body, saw his gaze shatter. His face went as white as if someone had struck him a blow in the stomach. He shook his head slightly on the muddy ground.

"No," he whispered. "Oh, no . . ."

He seemed to be saying it to himself, as if he didn't expect her to hear him. He reached a hand toward her cheek, and she snapped at it.

"Oh, Elena . . ." he whispered.

The last traces of fury, of animal bloodlust, had disappeared from his face. His eyes were dazed and stricken and grieving.

And vulnerable. Elena took advantage of the moment to dive for the bare skin at his neck. His arm came up to fend her off, to push her away, but then it dropped again.

He stared at her a moment, the pain in his eyes reaching a peak, and then he simply gave up. He stopped fighting completely.

She could feel it happen, feel the resistance leave his body. He lay on the icy ground with scraps of oak leaves in his hair, staring up past her at the black and clouded sky.

Finish it, his weary voice said in her mind.

Elena hesitated for an instant. There was something about those eyes that called up memories inside her.

Standing in the moonlight, sitting in an attic room . . . But the memories were too vague. She couldn't get a grasp on them, and the effort made her dizzy and sick.

And this one had to die, this green-eyed one called Stefan. Because he'd hurt *him*, the other one, the one Elena had been born to be with. No one could hurt *him* and live.

She clamped her teeth into his throat and bit deep.

She realized at once that she wasn't doing it quite right. She hadn't hit an artery or vein. She worried at the throat, angry at her own inexperience. It felt good to bite something, but not much blood was coming. Frustrated, she lifted up and bit again, feeling his body jerk in pain.

Much better. She'd found a vein this time, but she hadn't torn it deeply enough. A little scratch like that wouldn't do. What she needed was to rip it right across, to let the rich hot blood stream out.

Her victim shuddered as she worked to do this, teeth raking and gnawing. She was just feeling the flesh give way when hands pulled at her, lifting her from behind.

Elena snarled without letting go of the throat. The hands were insistent though. An arm looped about her waist, fingers twined in her hair. She fought, clinging with teeth and nails to her prey.

Let go of him. Leave him!

The voice was sharp and commanding, like a blast

from a cold wind. Elena recognized it and stopped struggling with the hands that pulled her away. As they
deposited her on the ground and she looked up to see
him, a name came into her mind. Damon. *His* name was
Damon. She stared at him sulkily, resentful of being
yanked away from her kill, but obedient.

Stefan was sitting up, his neck red with blood. It was
running onto his shirt. Elena licked her lips, feeling a
throb like a hunger pang that seemed to come from every
fiber of her being. She was dizzy again.

"I thought," Damon said aloud, "that you said she was
dead."

He was looking at Stefan, who was even paler than
before, if that was possible. That white face filled with
infinite hopelessness.

"Look at her" was all he said.

A hand cupped Elena's chin, tilting her face up. She
met Damon's narrowed dark eyes directly. Then long,
slender fingers touched her lips, probing between them.
Instinctively Elena tried to bite, but not very hard.
Damon's finger found the sharp curve of a canine tooth,
and Elena did bite now, giving it a nip like a kitten's.

Damon's face was expressionless, his eyes hard.

"Do you know where you are?" he said.

Elena glanced around. Trees. "In the woods," she said
craftily, looking back at him.

"And who is that?"

She followed his pointing finger. "Stefan," she said indifferently. "Your brother."

"And who am I? Do you know who I am?"

She smiled up at him, showing him her pointed teeth. "Of course I do. You're Damon, and I love you."

2

Stefan's voice was quietly savage. "That's what you wanted, wasn't it, Damon? And now you've got it. You had to make her like us, like you. It wasn't enough just to kill her."

Damon didn't glance back at him. He was looking at Elena intently through those hooded eyes, still kneeling there holding her chin. "That's the third time you've said that, and I'm getting a little tired of it," he commented softly. Disheveled, still slightly out of breath, he was yet self-composed, in control. "Elena, did I kill you?"

"Of course not," Elena said, winding her fingers in those of his free hand. She was getting impatient. What were they talking about anyway? Nobody had been killed.

"I never thought you were a liar," Stefan said to

Damon, the bitterness in his voice unchanged. "Just about everything else, but not that. I've never heard you try to cover up for yourself before."

"In another minute," said Damon, "I'm going to lose my temper."

What more can you possibly do to me? Stefan returned. *Killing me would be a mercy.*

"I ran out of mercy for you a century ago," Damon said aloud. He let go, finally, of Elena's chin. "What do you remember about today?" he asked her.

Elena spoke tiredly, like a child reciting a hated lesson. "Today was the Founders' Day celebration." Flexing her fingers in his, she looked up at Damon. That was as far as she could get on her own, but it wasn't enough. Nettled, she tried to remember something else.

"There was someone in the cafeteria. . . . Caroline." She offered the name to him, pleased. "She was going to read my diary in front of everyone, and that was bad because . . ." Elena fumbled with the memory and lost it. "I don't remember why. But we tricked her." She smiled at him warmly, conspiratorially.

"Oh, 'we' did, did we?"

"Yes. You got it away from her. You did it for me." The fingers of her free hand crept under his jacket, searching for the square-cornered hardness of the little book. "Because you love me," she said, finding it and scratching at it lightly. "You do love me, don't you?"

There was a faint sound from the center of the clearing. Elena looked and saw that Stefan had turned his face away.

"Elena. What happened next?" Damon's voice called her back.

"Next? Next Aunt Judith started arguing with me." Elena pondered this a moment and at last shrugged. "Over . . . something. I got angry. She's not my mother. She can't tell me what to do."

Damon's voice was dry. "I don't think that's going to be a problem anymore. What next?"

Elena sighed heavily. "Next I went and got Matt's car. Matt." She said the name reflectively, flicking her tongue over her canine teeth. In her mind's eye, she saw a handsome face, blond hair, sturdy shoulders. "Matt."

"And where did you go in Matt's car?"

"To Wickery Bridge," Stefan said, turning back toward them. His eyes were desolate.

"No, to the boardinghouse," Elena corrected, irritated. "To wait for . . . mm . . . I forget. Anyway, I waited there. Then . . . then the storm started. Wind, rain, all that. I didn't like it. I got in the car. But something came after me."

"*Someone* came after you," said Stefan, looking at Damon.

"Some *thing*," Elena insisted. She had had enough of his interruptions. "Let's go away somewhere, just us," she said to Damon, kneeling up so that her face was close to his.

"In a minute," he said. "What kind of thing came after you?"

She settled back, exasperated. "I don't know what kind of thing! It was like nothing I've ever seen. Not like you and Stefan. It was . . ." Images rippled through her mind. Mist flowing along the ground. The wind shrieking. A shape, white, enormous, looking as if it were made out of mist itself. Gaining on her like a wind-driven cloud.

"Maybe it was just part of the storm," she said. "But I thought it wanted to hurt me. I got away though." Fiddling with the zipper to Damon's leather jacket, she smiled secretly and looked up at him through her lashes.

For the first time, Damon's face showed emotion. His lips twisted in a grimace. "You got away."

"Yes. I remembered what . . . someone . . . told me about running water. Evil things can't cross it. So I drove toward Drowning Creek, toward the bridge. And then . . ." She hesitated, frowning, trying to find a solid memory in the new confusion. Water. She remembered water. And someone screaming. But nothing else. "And then I crossed it," she concluded finally, brightly. "I must have, because here I am. And that's all. Can we go now?"

Damon didn't answer her.

"The car's still in the river," said Stefan. He and Damon were looking at each other like two adults having a discussion over the head of an uncomprehending child, their hostilities suspended for the moment. Elena felt a surge of annoyance. She opened her mouth, but Stefan was continuing. "Bonnie and Meredith and I found it. I went underwater and got her, but by then . . ."

By then, what? Elena frowned.

Damon's lips were curved mockingly. "And you gave up on her? You, of all people, should have suspected what might happen. Or was the idea so repugnant to you that you couldn't even consider it? Would you rather she were really dead?"

"She had no pulse, no respiration!" Stefan flared. "And she'd never had enough blood to change her!" His eyes hardened. "Not from *me* anyway."

Elena opened her mouth again, but Damon laid two fingers on it to keep her quiet. He said smoothly, "And that's the problem now—or are you too blind to see that, too? You told me to look at her; look at her yourself. She's in shock, irrational. Oh, yes, even I admit that." He paused for a blinding smile before going on. "It's more than just the normal confusion after changing. She'll need blood, human blood, or her body won't have the strength to finish the change. She'll die."

What do you mean irrational? Elena thought indignantly. "I'm fine," she said around Damon's fingers. "I'm tired, that's all. I was going to sleep when I heard you two fighting, and I came to help you. And then you wouldn't even let me kill him," she finished, disgusted.

"Yes, why didn't you?" said Stefan. He was staring at Damon as if he could bore holes through him with his eyes. Any trace of cooperation on his part was gone. "It would have been the easiest thing to do."

Damon stared back at him, suddenly furious, his own animosity flooding up to meet Stefan's. He was breathing quickly and lightly. "Maybe I don't like things easy," he hissed. Then he seemed to regain control of himself once more. His lips curled in mockery, and he added, "Put it this way, dear brother: if anyone's going to have the satisfaction of killing you, it will be me. No one else. I plan to take care of the job personally. And it's something I'm very good at; I promise you."

"You've shown us that," Stefan said quietly, as if each word sickened him.

"But this one," Damon said, turning to Elena with glittering eyes, "I *didn't* kill. Why should I? I could have changed her any time I liked."

"Maybe because she had just gotten engaged to marry someone else."

Damon lifted Elena's hand, still twined with his. On

the third finger a gold ring glittered, set with one deep blue stone. Elena frowned at it, vaguely remembering having seen it before. Then she shrugged and leaned against Damon wearily.

"Well, now," Damon said, looking down at her, "that doesn't seem to be much of a problem, does it? I think she may have been glad to forget you." He looked up at Stefan with an unpleasant smile. "But we'll find out once she's herself again. We can ask her then which of us she chooses. Agreed?"

Stefan shook his head. "How can you even suggest that? After what happened . . ." His voice trailed off.

"With Katherine? I can say it, if you can't. Katherine made a foolish choice, and she paid the price for it. Elena is different; she knows her own mind. But it doesn't matter if you agree," he added, overriding Stefan's new protests. "The fact is that she's weak now, and she needs blood. I'm going to see that she gets it, and then I'm going to find who did this to her. You can come or not. Suit yourself."

He stood, drawing Elena up with him. "Let's go."

Elena came willingly, pleased to be moving. The woods were interesting at night; she'd never noticed that before. Owls were sending their mournful, haunting cries through the trees, and deer mice scuttled away from her gliding feet. The air was colder in patches, as it froze first in the hollows and dips of the wood. She found it was easy to move silently beside Damon through the leaf litter; it was just a matter of being careful where she stepped. She didn't look back to see if Stefan was following them.

She recognized the place where they left the wood. She had been there earlier today. Now, however, there was some sort of frenzied activity going on: red and blue lights flashing on cars, spotlights framing the dark huddled shapes of people. Elena looked at them curiously. Several were familiar. That woman, for instance, with the thin harrowed face and the anxious eyes—Aunt Judith? And the tall man beside her—Aunt Judith's fiancé, Robert?

There should be someone else with them, Elena thought. A child with hair as pale as Elena's own. But try as she might, she could not conjure up a name.

The two girls with their arms around each other, standing in a circle of officials, *those* two she remembered though. The little red-haired one who was crying was Bonnie. The taller one with the sweep of dark hair, Meredith.

"But she's not *in* the water," Bonnie was saying to a man in a uniform. Her voice trembled on the edge of hysteria. "We saw Stefan get her out. I've told you and told you."

"And you left him here with her?"

"We had to. The storm was getting worse, and there was something coming—"

"Never mind that," Meredith broke in. She sounded only slightly calmer than Bonnie. "Stefan said that if he—had to leave her, he'd leave her lying under the willow trees."

"And just where is Stefan now?" another uniformed man asked.

"We don't know. We went back to get help. He probably followed us. But as for what happened to—to Elena . . ." Bonnie turned back and buried her face in Meredith's shoulder.

They're upset about *me*, Elena realized. How silly of them. I can clear that up, anyway. She started forward into the light, but Damon pulled her back. She looked at him, wounded.

"Not like that. Pick the ones you want, and we'll draw them out," he said.

"Want for what?"

"For feeding, Elena. You're a hunter now. Those are your prey."

Elena pushed her tongue against a canine tooth doubtfully. Nothing out there looked like food to her. Still, because Damon said so, she was inclined to give him the benefit of the doubt. "Whichever you think," she said obligingly.

Damon tilted his head back, eyes narrowed, scanning the scene like an expert evaluating a famous painting. "Well, how about a couple of nice paramedics?"

"*No,*" said a voice behind them.

Damon barely glanced over his shoulder at Stefan. "Why not?"

"Because there've been enough attacks. She may need human blood, but she doesn't have to hunt for it." Stefan's face was shut and hostile, but there was an air of grim determination about him.

"There's another way?" Damon asked ironically.

"You know there is. Find someone who's willing—or who can be influenced to be willing. Someone who would do it for Elena and who is strong enough to deal with this, mentally."

"And I suppose you know where we can find such a paragon of virtue?"

"Bring her to the school. I'll meet you there," Stefan said, and disappeared.

They left the activity still bustling, lights flashing, people milling. As they went, Elena noticed a strange thing. In the middle of the river, illuminated by the spotlights, was an automobile. It was completely submerged except for the front fender, which stuck out of the water.

What a stupid place to park a car, she thought, and followed Damon back into the woods.

* * *

Stefan was beginning to feel again.

It hurt. He'd thought he was through with hurting, through with feeling anything. When he'd pulled Elena's lifeless body out of the dark water, he'd thought that nothing could ever hurt again because nothing could match that moment.

He'd been wrong.

He stopped and stood with his good hand braced against a tree, head down, breathing deeply. When the red mists cleared and he could see again, he went on, but the burning ache in his chest continued undiminished. Stop thinking about her, he told himself, knowing that it was useless.

But she wasn't truly dead. Didn't that count for something? He'd thought he would never hear her voice again, never feel her touch. . . .

And now, when she touched him, she wanted to kill him.

He stopped again, doubling over, afraid he was going to be sick.

Seeing her like this was worse torture than seeing her lying cold and dead. Maybe that was why Damon had let him live. Maybe this was Damon's revenge.

And maybe Stefan should just do what he'd planned to do after killing Damon. Wait until dawn and take off the silver ring that protected him from sunlight. Stand bathing in the fiery embrace of those rays until they burned the flesh from his bones and stopped the pain once and for all.

But he knew he wouldn't. As long as Elena walked the earth, he would never leave her. Even if she hated him, even if she hunted him. He would do anything he could to keep her safe.

Stefan detoured toward the boardinghouse. He needed to clean up before he could let humans see him. In his room, he washed the blood from his face and neck and examined his arm. The healing process had already begun, and with concentration he could accelerate it still further. He was burning up his Powers fast; the fight with his brother had already weakened him. But this was important. Not because of the pain—he scarcely noticed that—but because he needed to be fit.

Damon and Elena were waiting outside the school. He could feel his brother's impatience and Elena's wild new presence there in the dark.

"This had better work," Damon said.

Stefan said nothing. The school auditorium was another center of commotion. People ought to have been enjoying the Founders' Day dance; in fact, those who had remained through the storm were pacing around or gathered in small groups talking. Stefan looked in the open door, searching with his mind for one particular presence.

He found it. A blond head was bent over a table in the corner.

Matt.

Matt straightened and looked around, puzzled. Stefan willed him to come outside. *You need some fresh air,* he thought, insinuating the suggestion into Matt's subconscious. *You feel like just stepping out for a moment.*

To Damon, standing invisible just beyond the light, he said, *Take her into the school, to the photography room. She knows where it is. Don't show yourselves until I say.* Then he backed away and waited for Matt to appear.

Matt came out, his drawn face turned up to the moonless sky. He started violently when Stefan spoke to him.

"Stefan! You're here!" Desperation, hope, and horror struggled for dominance on his face. He hurried over to Stefan. "Did they—bring her back yet? Is there any news?"

"What have *you* heard?"

Matt stared at him a moment before answering. "Bonnie and Meredith came in saying that Elena had gone off of Wickery Bridge in my car. They said that she . . ." He paused and swallowed. "Stefan, it's not true, is it?" His eyes were pleading.

Stefan looked away.

"Oh, God," Matt said hoarsely. He turned his back on

Stefan, pressing the heels of his hands into his eyes. "I don't believe it; I *don't*. It can't be true."

"Matt . . ." He touched the other boy's shoulder.

"I'm sorry." Matt's voice was rough and ragged. "You must be going through hell, and here I am making it worse."

More than you know, thought Stefan, his hand falling away. He'd come with the intention of using his Powers to persuade Matt. Now that seemed an impossibility. He couldn't do it, not to the first—and only—human friend he'd had in this place.

His only other option was to tell Matt the truth. Let Matt make his own choice, knowing everything.

"If there were something you could do for Elena right now," he said, "would you do it?"

Matt was too lost in emotion to ask what kind of idiotic question that was. "Anything," he said almost angrily, rubbing a sleeve over his eyes. "I'd do anything for her." He looked at Stefan with something like defiance, his breathing shaky.

Congratulations, Stefan thought, feeling the sudden yawning pit in his stomach. You've just won yourself a trip to the Twilight Zone.

"Come with me," he said. "I've got something to show you."

lena and Damon were waiting in the darkroom. Stefan could sense their presence in the small annex as he pushed the door to the photography room open and led Matt inside.

"These doors are supposed to be locked," Matt said as Stefan flipped on the light switch.

"They were," said Stefan. He didn't know what else to say to prepare Matt for what was coming. He'd never deliberately revealed himself to a human before.

He stood, quietly, until Matt turned and looked at him. The classroom was cold and silent, and the air seemed to hang heavily. As the moment stretched out, he saw Matt's expression slowly change from grief-numbed bewilderment to uneasiness.

"I don't understand," Matt said.

"I know you don't." He went on looking at Matt, purposefully dropping the barriers that concealed his Powers from human perception. He saw the reaction in Matt's face as uneasiness coalesced into fear. Matt blinked and shook his head, his breath coming quicker.

"What—?" he began, his voice gravelly.

"There are probably a lot of things you've wondered about me," Stefan said. "Why I wear sunglasses in strong light. Why I don't eat. Why my reflexes are so fast."

Matt had his back to the darkroom now. His throat jerked as if he were trying to swallow. Stefan, with his predator's senses, could hear Matt's heart thudding dully.

"No," Matt said.

"You *must* have wondered, must have asked yourself what makes me so different from everybody else."

"No. I mean—I don't care. I keep out of things that aren't my business." Matt was edging toward the door, his eyes darting toward it in a barely perceptible movement.

"Don't, Matt. I don't want to hurt you, but I can't let you leave now." He could feel barely leashed need emanating from Elena in her concealment. *Wait*, he told her.

Matt went still, giving up any attempt to move away. "If you want to scare me, you have," he said in a low voice. "What else do you want?"

Now, Stefan told Elena. He said to Matt, "Turn around."

Matt turned. And stifled a cry.

Elena stood there, but not the Elena of that afternoon, when Matt had last seen her. Now her feet were bare beneath the hem of her long dress. The thin folds of white muslin that clung to her were caked with ice crystals that sparkled in the light. Her skin, always fair, had a strange wintry luster to it, and her pale gold hair seemed overlaid with a silvery sheen. But the real difference was in her face. Those deep blue eyes were heavy-lidded, almost sleepy looking, and yet unnaturally awake. And a look of sensual anticipation and hunger curled about her lips. She was more beautiful than she had been in life, but it was a frightening beauty.

As Matt stared, paralyzed, Elena's pink tongue came out and licked her lips.

"Matt," she said, lingering over the first consonant of the name. Then she smiled.

Stefan heard Matt's indrawn breath of disbelief, and the near sob he gave as he finally backed away from her.

It's all right, he said, sending the thought to Matt on a surge of Power. As Matt jerked toward him, eyes wide with shock, he added, "So now you know."

Matt's expression said that he didn't want to know, and Stefan could see the denial in his face. But Damon stepped out beside Elena and moved a little to the right, adding his presence to the charged atmosphere of the room.

Matt was surrounded. The three of them closed in on him, inhumanly beautiful, innately menacing.

Stefan could smell Matt's fear. It was the helpless fear of the rabbit for the fox, the mouse for the owl. And Matt was right to be afraid. They were the hunting species; he was the hunted. Their job in life was to kill him.

And just now instincts were getting out of control. Matt's instinct was to panic and run, and it was triggering reflexes in Stefan's head. When the prey ran, the predator gave chase; it was as simple as that. All three of the predators here were keyed up, on edge, and Stefan felt he couldn't be responsible for the consequences if Matt bolted.

We don't want to harm you, he told Matt. *It's Elena who needs you, and what she needs won't leave you permanently damaged. It doesn't even have to hurt, Matt.* But Matt's muscles were still tensed to flee, and Stefan realized that the three of them were stalking him, moving closer, ready to cut off any escape.

You said you would do anything for Elena, he reminded Matt desperately and saw him make his choice.

Matt released his breath, the tension draining from his body. "You're right; I did," he whispered. He visibly braced himself before he continued. "What does she need?"

Elena leaned forward and put a finger on Matt's neck, tracing the yielding ridge of an artery.

"Not that one," Stefan said quickly. "You don't want to kill him. Tell her, Damon." He added, when Damon made no effort to do so, *Tell her*.

"Try here, or here." Damon pointed with clinical efficiency, holding Matt's chin up. He was strong enough that Matt couldn't break the grip, and Stefan felt Matt's panic surge up again.

Trust me, Matt. He moved in behind the human boy. *But it has to be your choice*, he finished, suddenly washed with compassion. *You can change your mind*.

Matt hesitated and then spoke through clenched teeth. "No. I still want to help. I want to help you, Elena."

"Matt," she whispered, her heavy-lashed jewel blue eyes fixed on his. Then they trailed down to his throat and her lips parted hungrily. There was no sign of the uncertainty she'd shown when Damon suggested feeding off the paramedics. "Matt." She smiled again, and then she struck, swift as a hunting bird.

Stefan put a flattened hand against Matt's back to give him support. For a moment, as Elena's teeth pierced his skin, Matt tried to recoil, but Stefan thought swiftly, *Don't fight it; that's what causes the pain*.

As Matt tried to relax, unexpected help came from Elena, who was radiating the warm happy thoughts of a wolf cub being fed. She had gotten the biting technique right on the first try this time, and she was filled with

innocent pride and growing satisfaction as the sharp pangs
of hunger eased. And with appreciation for Matt, Stefan
realized, with a sudden shock of jealousy. She didn't hate
Matt or want to kill him, because he posed no threat to
Damon. She was fond of Matt.

Stefan let her take as much as was safe and then intervened. *That's enough, Elena. You don't want to injure him.*
But it took the combined efforts of him, Damon, and a
rather groggy Matt to pry her off.

"She needs to rest now," Damon said. "I'm taking her
someplace where she can do it safely." He wasn't asking
Stefan; he was telling him.

As they left, his mental voice added, for Stefan's ears
alone, *I haven't forgotten the way you attacked me, brother.
We'll talk about that later.*

Stefan stared after them. He'd noted how Elena's eyes
remained locked on Damon, how she followed him without question. But she was out of danger now; Matt's blood
had given her the strength she needed. That was all
Stefan had to hang on to, and he told himself it was all
that mattered.

He turned to take in Matt's dazed expression. The
human boy had sunk into one of the plastic chairs and was
gazing straight ahead.

Then his eyes lifted to Stefan's, and they regarded
each other grimly.

"So," Matt said. "Now I know." He shook his head, turning away slightly. "But I still can't believe it," he muttered. His fingers pressed gingerly at the side of his neck, and he winced. "Except for this." Then he frowned. "That guy—Damon. Who is he?"

"My older brother," Stefan said without emotion. "How do you know his name?"

"He was at Elena's house last week. The kitten spat at him." Matt paused, clearly remembering something else. "And Bonnie had some kind of psychic fit."

"She had a precognition? What did she say?"

"She said—she said that Death was in the house."

Stefan looked at the door Damon and Elena had passed through. "She was right."

"Stefan, what's going on?" A note of appeal had entered Matt's voice. "I still don't understand. What's happened to Elena? Is she going to be like this forever? Isn't there anything we can do?"

"Be like what?" Stefan said brutally. "Disoriented? A vampire?"

Matt looked away. "Both."

"As for the first, she may become more rational now that she's fed. That's what Damon thinks anyway. As for the other, there's only one thing you can do to change her condition." As Matt's eyes lit with hope, Stefan continued. "You can get a wooden stake and hammer it through her heart. Then she won't be a vampire anymore. She'll just be dead."

Matt got up and went to the window.

"You wouldn't be killing her, though, because that's already been done. She drowned in the river, Matt. But because she'd had enough blood from me"—he paused to steady his voice—"and, it seems, from my brother, she changed instead of simply dying. She woke up a hunter, like us. That's what she'll be from now on."

With his back still turned, Matt answered. "I always knew there was something about you. I told myself it was just because you were from another country." He shook his head again self-deprecatingly. "But deep down I knew it was more than that. And something still kept telling me I could trust you, and I did."

"Like when you went with me to get the vervain."

"Yeah. Like that." He added, "Can you tell me what the hell it was for, now?"

"For Elena's protection. I wanted to keep Damon away from her. But it looks as if that's not what *she* wanted after all." He couldn't help the bitterness, the raw betrayal, in his voice.

Matt turned. "Don't judge her before you know all the facts, Stefan. That's one thing I've learned."

Stefan was startled; then, he gave a small humorless smile. As Elena's exes, he and Matt were in the same position now. He wondered if he would be as gracious about it as Matt had been. Take his defeat like a gentleman.

He didn't think so.

Outside, a noise had begun. It was inaudible to human ears, and Stefan almost ignored it—until the words penetrated his consciousness.

Then he remembered what he had done in this very school only a few hours ago. Until that moment, he'd forgotten all about Tyler Smallwood and his tough friends.

Now that memory had returned; shame and horror closed his throat. He'd been out of his mind with grief over Elena, and his reason had snapped under the pressure. But that was no excuse for what he had done. Were they all dead? Had he, who had sworn so long ago never to kill, killed six people today?

"Stefan, wait. Where are you going?" When he didn't answer, Matt followed him, half running to keep up, out of the main school building and onto the blacktop. On the far side of the field, Mr. Shelby stood by the Quonset hut.

The janitor's face was gray and furrowed with lines of horror. He seemed to be trying to shout, but only small hoarse gasps came out of his mouth. Elbowing past him, Stefan looked into the room and felt a curious sense of déjà vu.

It looked like the Mad Slasher room from the Haunted

House fund-raiser. Except that this was no tableau set up for visitors. This was real.

Bodies were sprawled everywhere, amid shards of wood and glass from the shattered window. Every visible surface was spattered with blood, red-brown and sinister as it dried. And one look at the bodies revealed why: each one had a pair of livid purple wounds in the neck. Except Caroline: her neck was unmarked, but her eyes were blank and staring.

Behind Stefan, Matt was hyperventilating. "Stefan, Elena didn't—she didn't—"

"Be quiet," Stefan answered tersely. He glanced back at Mr. Shelby, but the janitor had stumbled over to his cart of brooms and mops and was leaning against it. Glass grated under Stefan's feet as he crossed the floor to kneel by Tyler.

Not dead. Relief exploded over Stefan at the realization. Tyler's chest moved feebly, and when Stefan lifted the boy's head his eyes opened a slit, glazed and unfocused.

You don't remember anything, Stefan told him mentally. Even as he did it, he wondered why he was bothering. He should just leave Fell's Church, cut out now and never come back.

But he wouldn't. Not as long as Elena was here.

He gathered the unconscious minds of the other victims into his mental grasp and told them the same thing, feeding it deep into their brains. *You don't remember who attacked you. The whole afternoon is a blank.*

As he did, he felt his mental Powers tremble like over-fatigued muscles. He was close to burnout.

Outside, Mr. Shelby had found his voice at last and was shouting. Wearily, Stefan let Tyler's head slip back through his fingers to the floor and turned around.

Matt's lips were peeled back, his nostrils flared, as if he had just smelled something disgusting. His eyes were the eyes of a stranger. "Elena didn't," he whispered. *"You did."*

Be quiet! Stefan pushed past him into the thankful coolness of the night, putting distance between him and that room, feeling the icy air on his hot skin. Running footsteps from the vicinity of the cafeteria told him that some humans had heard the janitor's cries at last.

"You did it, didn't you?" Matt had followed Stefan out to the field. His voice said he was trying to understand.

Stefan rounded on him. "Yes, I did it," he snarled. He stared Matt down, concealing none of the angry menace in his face. "I told you, Matt, we're hunters. Killers. You're the sheep; we're the wolves. And Tyler has been asking for it every day since I came here."

"Asking for a punch in the nose, sure. Like you gave him before. But—that?" Matt closed in on him, standing eye to eye, unafraid. He had physical courage; Stefan had to give him that. "And you're not even sorry? You don't even regret it?"

"Why should I?" said Stefan coldly, emptily. "Do you regret it when you eat too much steak? Feel sorry for the cow?" He saw Matt's look of sick disbelief and pressed on, driving the pain in his chest deeper. It was better that Matt stay away from him from now on, far away. Or Matt might end up like those bodies in the Quonset hut. "I am what I am, Matt. And if you can't handle it, you'd better steer clear of me."

Matt stared at him a moment longer, the sick disbelief transforming slowly into sick disillusionment. The muscles around his jaw stood out. Then, without a word, he turned on his heel and walked away.

Elena was in the graveyard.

Damon had left her there, exhorting her to stay until he came back. She didn't want to sit still, though. She felt tired but not really sleepy, and the new blood was affecting her like a jolt of caffeine. She wanted to go exploring.

The graveyard was full of activity although there wasn't a human in sight. A fox slunk through the shadows toward the river path. Small rodents tunneled under the long lank grass around the headstones, squeaking and scurrying. A barn owl flew almost silently toward the ruined church, where it alighted on the belfry with an eerie cry.

Elena got up and followed it. This was much better than hiding in the grass like a mouse or vole. She looked around the ruined church interestedly, using her sharpened senses to examine it. Most of the roof had fallen in, and only three walls were standing, but the belfry stood up like a lonely monument in the rubble.

At one side was the tomb of Thomas and Honoria Fell, like a large stone box or coffin. Elena gazed earnestly down into the white marble faces of their statues on the lid. They lay in tranquil repose, their eyes shut, their hands folded on their breasts. Thomas Fell looked serious and a little stern, but Honoria looked merely sad. Elena thought absently of her own parents, lying side by side down in the modern cemetery.

I'll go home; that's where I'll go, she thought. She had just remembered about home. She could picture it now: her pretty bedroom with blue curtains and cherrywood furniture and her little fireplace. And something important under the floorboards in the closet.

She found her way to Maple Street by instincts that ran deeper than memory, letting her feet guide her there. It was an old, old house, with a big front porch and floor-to-ceiling windows in front. Robert's car was parked in the driveway.

Elena started for the front door and then stopped.

There was a reason people shouldn't see her, although she couldn't remember what it was right now. She hesitated and then nimbly climbed the quince tree up to her bedroom window.

But she wasn't going to be able to get in here without being noticed. A woman was sitting on the bed with Elena's red silk kimono in her lap, staring down at it. Aunt Judith. Robert was standing by the dresser, talking to her. Elena found that she could pick up the murmur of his voice even through the glass.

". . . out again tomorrow," he was saying. "As long as it doesn't storm. They'll go over every inch of those woods, and they'll find her, Judith. You'll see." Aunt Judith said nothing, and he went on, sounding more desperate. "We can't give up hope, no matter what the girls say—"

"It's no good, Bob." Aunt Judith had raised her head at last, and her eyes were red-rimmed but dry. "It's no use."

"The rescue effort? I won't have you talking that way." He came over to stand beside her.

"No, not just that . . . although I know, in my heart, that we're not going to find her alive. I mean . . . everything. Us. What happened today is our fault—"

"That's not true. It was a freak accident."

"Yes, but we made it happen. If we hadn't been so harsh with her, she would never have driven off alone and been caught in the storm. No, Bob, don't try to shut me up; I want you to listen." Aunt Judith took a deep breath and continued. "It wasn't just today, either. Elena's been having problems for a long time, ever since school started, and somehow I've let the signs slip right past me. Because I've been too involved with myself—with *us*—to pay attention to them. I can see that now. And now that Elena's . . . gone . . . I don't want the same thing to happen with Margaret."

"What are you saying?"

"I'm saying that I can't marry you, not as soon as we planned. Maybe not ever." Without looking at him, she spoke softly. "Margaret has lost too much already. I don't want her to feel she's losing me, too."

"She won't be losing you. If anything, she'll be gaining someone, because I'll be here more often. You know how I feel about her."

"I'm sorry, Bob; I just don't see it that way."

"You can't be serious. After all the time I've spent here—after all I've done . . ."

Aunt Judith's voice was drained and implacable. "I *am* serious."

From her perch outside the window, Elena eyed Robert curiously. A vein throbbed in his forehead, and his face had flushed red.

"You'll feel differently tomorrow," he said.

"No, I won't."

"You don't mean it—"

"I *do* mean it. Don't tell me that I'm going to change my mind, because I'm not."

For an instant, Robert looked around in helpless frustration; then, his expression darkened. When he spoke, his voice was flat and cold. "I see. Well, if that's your final answer, I'd better leave right now."

"Bob." Aunt Judith turned, startled, but he was already outside the door. She stood up, wavering, as if she were unsure whether or not to go after him. Her fingers kneaded at the red material she was holding. "Bob!" she called again, more urgently, and she turned to drop the kimono on Elena's bed before following him.

But as she turned she gasped, a hand flying to her mouth. Her whole body stiffened. Her eyes stared into Elena's through the silvery pane of glass. For a long moment, they stared at each other that way, neither moving. Then Aunt Judith's hand came away from her mouth, and she began to shriek.

omething yanked Elena out of the tree and, yowling a protest, she fell and landed on her feet like a cat. Her knees hit the ground a second later and got bruised.

She reared back, fingers hooked into claws to attack whoever had done it. Damon slapped her hand away.

"Why did you grab me?" she demanded.

"Why didn't you stay where I put you?" he snapped.

They glared at each other, equally furious. Then Elena was distracted. The shrieking was still going on upstairs, augmented now by rattling and banging at the window. Damon nudged her against the house, where they couldn't be seen from above.

"Let's get away from this noise," he said fastidiously, looking up. Without waiting for a response, he caught her arm. Elena resisted.

"I have to go in there!"

"You can't." He gave her a wolfish smile. "I mean that literally. You *can't* go in that house. You haven't been invited."

Momentarily nonplussed, Elena let him tow her a few steps. Then she dug her heels in again.

"But I need my diary!"

"What?"

"It's in the closet, under the floorboards. And I need it. I can't go to sleep without my diary." Elena didn't know why she was making such a fuss, but it seemed important.

Damon looked exasperated; then, his face cleared. "Here," he said calmly, eyes glinting. He withdrew something from his jacket. "Take it."

Elena eyed his offering doubtfully.

"It's your diary, isn't it?"

"Yes, but it's my old one. I want my new one."

"This one will have to do, because this one is all you're getting. Come on before they wake up the whole neighborhood." His voice had turned cold and commanding again.

Elena considered the book he held. It was small, with a blue velvet cover and a brass lock. Not the newest edition perhaps, but it was familiar to her. She decided it was acceptable.

She let Damon lead her out into the night.

She didn't ask where they were going. She didn't much care. But she recognized the house on Magnolia Avenue; it was where Alaric Saltzman was staying.

And it was Alaric who opened the front door, beckoning Elena and Damon inside. The history teacher looked strange, though, and didn't really seem to see them. His eyes were glassy and he moved like an automaton.

Elena licked her lips.

"No," Damon said shortly. "This one's not for biting. There's something fishy about him, but you should be safe enough in the house. I've slept here before. Up here." He led her up a flight of stairs to an attic with one small window. It was crowded with stored objects: sleds, skis, a hammock. At the far end, an old mattress lay on the floor.

"He won't even know you're here in the morning. Lie down." Elena obeyed, assuming a position that seemed natural to her. She lay on her back, hands folded over the diary that she held to her breast.

Damon dropped a piece of oilcloth over her, covering her bare feet.

"Go to sleep, Elena," he said.

He bent over her, and for a moment she thought he was going to . . . do something. Her thoughts were too muddled. But his night black eyes filled her vision. Then he pulled back, and she could breathe again. The gloom of the attic settled in on her. Her eyes drifted shut and she slept.

She woke slowly, assembling information about where she was, piece by piece. Somebody's attic from the looks of it. What was she doing here?

Rats or mice were scuffling somewhere among the piles of oilcloth-draped objects, but the sound didn't bother her. The faintest trace of pale light showed around the edges of the shuttered window. Elena pushed her makeshift blanket off and got up to investigate.

It was definitely someone's attic, and not that of anyone she knew. She felt as if she had been sick for a long time and had just woken up from her illness. What day is it? she wondered.

She could hear voices below her. Downstairs. Something told her to be careful and quiet. She felt afraid of making any kind of disturbance. She eased the attic door open without a sound and cautiously descended to the landing. Looking down, she could see a living room. She recognized it; she'd sat on that ottoman when Alaric Saltzman had given a party. She was in the Ramsey house.

And Alaric Saltzman was down there; she could see the top of his sandy head. His voice puzzled her. After a moment she realized it was because he didn't sound fatuous or inane or any of the ways Alaric usually sounded in class. He wasn't spouting psycho-babble, either. He was speaking coolly and decisively to two other men.

"She might be anywhere, even right under our noses. More likely outside town, though. Maybe in the woods."

"Why the woods?" said one of the men. Elena knew that voice, too, and that bald head. It was Mr. Newcastle, the high school principal.

"Remember, the first two victims were found near the woods," said the other man. Is that Dr. Feinberg? Elena thought. What's he doing here? What am *I* doing here?

"No, it's more than that," Alaric was saying. The other men were listening to him with respect, even with deference. "The woods are tied up in this. They may have a hiding place out there, a lair where they can go to earth if they're discovered. If there is one, I'll find it."

"Are you sure?" said Dr. Feinberg.

"I'm sure," Alaric said briefly.

"And that's where you think Elena is," said the principal. "But will she stay there? Or will she come back into town?"

"I don't know." Alaric paced a few steps and picked up a book from the coffee table, running his thumbs over it absently. "One way to find out is to watch her friends. Bonnie McCullough and that dark-haired girl, Meredith. Chances are they'll be the first ones to see her. That's how it usually happens."

"And once we do track her down?" Dr. Feinberg asked.

"Leave that to me," Alaric said quietly and grimly. He shut the book and dropped it on the coffee table with a disturbingly conclusive sound.

The principal glanced at his watch. "I'd better get moving; the service starts at ten o'clock. I presume you'll both be there?" He paused on his way to the door and looked back, his manner irresolute. "Alaric, I hope you can take care of this. When I called you in, things hadn't gone this far. Now I'm beginning to wonder—"

"I *can* take care of it, Brian. I told you; leave it to me. Would you rather have Robert E. Lee in all the papers, not just as the scene of a tragedy but also as 'The Haunted High School of Boone County'? A gathering place for ghouls? The school where the undead walk? Is that the kind of publicity you want?"

Mr. Newcastle hesitated, chewing his lip, then nodded, still looking unhappy. "All right, Alaric. But make it quick and clean. I'll see you at the church." He left and Dr. Feinberg followed him.

Alaric stood there for some time, apparently staring into space. At last he nodded once and went out the front door himself.

Elena slowly trailed back up the stairs.

Now what had all that been about? She felt confused,

as if she were floating loose in time and space. She needed to know what day it was, why she was here, and why she felt so frightened. Why she felt so intensely that no one must see her or hear her or notice her at all.

Looking around the attic, she saw nothing that would give her any help. Where she had been lying there were only the mattress and the oilcloth—and a little blue book.

Her diary! Eagerly, she snatched it up and opened it, skipping through the entries. They stopped with October 17; they were no help to discovering today's date. But as she looked at the writing, images formed in her mind, stringing up like pearls to make memories. Fascinated, she slowly sat down on the mattress. She leafed back to the beginning and began to read about the life of Elena Gilbert.

When she finished, she was weak with fear and horror. Bright spots danced and shimmered before her eyes. There was so much pain in these pages. So many schemes, so many secrets, so much need. It was the story of a girl who'd felt lost in her own hometown, in her own family. Who'd been looking for . . . something, something she could never quite reach. But that wasn't what caused this throbbing panic in her chest that drained all the energy from her body. That wasn't why she felt as if she were falling even when she sat as still as she could get. What caused the panic was that she *remembered*.

She remembered everything now.

The bridge, the rushing water. The terror as the air left her lungs and there was nothing but liquid to breathe. The way it had hurt. And the final instant when it had stopped hurting, when everything had stopped. When everything . . . stopped.

Oh, Stefan, I was so frightened, she thought. And the same fear was inside her now. In the woods, how could she have behaved like that to Stefan? How could she have forgotten him, everything he meant to her? What had made her act that way?

But she knew. At the center of her consciousness, she knew. Nobody got up and walked away from a drowning like that. Nobody got up and walked away alive.

Slowly, she rose and went to look at the shuttered window. The darkened pane of glass acted as a mirror, throwing her reflection back at her.

It was not the reflection she'd seen in her dream, where she had run down a hall of mirrors that seemed to have a life of their own. There was nothing sly or cruel about this face. Just the same, it was subtly different from what she was used to seeing. There was a pale glow to her skin and a telling hollowness about the eyes. Elena touched fingertips to her neck, on either side. This was where Stefan and Damon had each taken her blood. Had it really been enough times, and had she really taken enough of theirs in return?

It must have been. And now, for the rest of her life, for the rest of her existence, she would have to feed as Stefan did. She would have to . . .

She sank to her knees, pressing her forehead against the bare wood of a wall. I can't, she thought. Oh, please, I can't; I can't.

She had never been very religious. But from that deep place inside, her terror was welling up, and every particle of her being joined in the cry for aid. Oh, please, she thought. Oh, please, please, help me. She didn't ask for anything specific; she couldn't gather her thoughts that far. Only: Oh, please help me, oh, please, *please*.

After a while she got up again.

Her face was still pale but eerily beautiful, like fine porcelain lit from within. Her eyes were still smudged with shadows. But there was a resolve in them.

She had to find Stefan. If there was any help for her, he would know of it. And if there wasn't . . . well, she needed him all the more. There was nowhere else she wanted to be except with him.

She shut the door of the attic carefully behind her as she went out. Alaric Saltzman mustn't discover her hiding place. On the wall, she saw a calendar with the days up to December 4 crossed off. Four days since last Saturday night. She'd slept for four days.

When she reached the front door, she cringed from the daylight outside. It hurt. Even though the sky was so overcast that rain or snow looked imminent, it hurt her eyes. She had to force herself to leave the safety of the house, and then she felt a gnawing paranoia about being out in the open. She slunk along beside fences, staying close to trees, ready to melt into the shadows. She felt like a shadow herself—or a ghost, in Honoria Fell's long white gown. She would frighten the wits out of anyone who saw her.

But all her circumspection seemed to be wasted. There was no one on the streets to see her; the town might have been abandoned. She went by seemingly deserted houses, forsaken yards, closed stores. Presently she saw parked cars lining the street, but they were empty, too.

And then she saw a shape against the sky that stopped her in her tracks. A steeple, white against the thick dark clouds. Elena's legs trembled as she made herself creep closer to the building. She'd known this church all her life; she'd seen the cross inscribed on that wall a thousand times. But now she edged toward it as if it were a caged animal that might break loose and bite her. She pressed one hand to the stone wall and slid it nearer and nearer to the carved symbol.

When her outspread fingers touched the arm of the cross, her eyes filled and her throat ached. She let her hand glide along it until it gently covered the engraving. Then she leaned against the wall and let the tears come.

I'm not evil, she thought. I did things I shouldn't have. I thought about myself too much; I never thanked Matt and Bonnie and Meredith for all they did for me. I should have played more with Margaret and been nicer to Aunt Judith. But I'm not evil. I'm not damned.

When she could see again, she looked up at the building. Mr. Newcastle had said something about the church. Was it this one he meant?

She avoided the front of the church and the main doorway. There was a side door that led to the choir loft, and she slipped up the stairs noiselessly and looked down from the gallery.

She saw at once why the streets had been so empty. It seemed as if everyone in Fell's Church was here, every seat in every pew filled, and the back of the church packed solid with people standing. Staring at the front rows, Elena realized that she recognized every face; they were members of the senior class, and neighbors, and friends of Aunt Judith. Aunt Judith was there, too, wearing the black dress she'd worn to Elena's parents' funeral.

Oh, my God, Elena thought. Her fingers gripped the railing. Until now she'd been too busy looking to listen, but the quiet monotone of Reverend Bethea's voice suddenly resolved into words.

". . . share our remembrances of this very special girl," he said, and he moved aside.

Elena watched what happened after with the unearthly feeling that she had a loge seat at a play. She was not at all involved in the events down there on stage; she was only a spectator, but it was *her* life she was watching.

Mr. Carson, Sue Carson's father, came up and talked about her. The Carsons had known her since she was born, and he talked about the days she and Sue had played in their front yard in the summer. He talked about the beautiful and accomplished young lady she had become. He got a frog in his throat and had to stop and take off his glasses.

Sue Carson went up. She and Elena hadn't been close friends since elementary school, but they'd remained on good terms. Sue had been one of the few girls who'd stayed on Elena's side after Stefan had come under suspicion for Mr. Tanner's murder. But now Sue was crying as if she'd lost a sister.

"A lot of people weren't nice to Elena after Halloween," she said, wiping her eyes and going on. "And I know that hurt her. But Elena was *strong*. She never changed just to conform to what other people thought she should be. And I respected her for that, so much . . ." Sue's voice wobbled. "When I was up for Homecoming Queen, I wanted to be chosen, but I knew I wouldn't be and that was all right. Because if Robert E. Lee ever had a queen, it was Elena. And I think she always will be now, because that's how we'll all remember her. And I think that for years to come the girls who will go to our school might remember her and think about how she stuck by what she thought was right. . . ." This time Sue couldn't steady her voice and the reverend helped her back to her seat.

The girls in the senior class, even the ones that had been nastiest and most spiteful, were crying and holding hands. Girls Elena knew for a fact hated her were sniffling. Suddenly she was everybody's best friend.

There were boys crying, too. Shocked, Elena huddled closer to the railing. She couldn't stop watching, even though it was the most horrible thing she had ever seen.

Frances Decatur got up, her plain face plainer than ever with grief. "She went out of her way to be nice to me," she said huskily. "She let me eat lunch with her." Rubbish, Elena thought. I only spoke to you in the first place because you were useful in finding out information about Stefan. But it was the same with each person who went up to the pulpit; no one could find enough words to praise Elena.

"I always admired her. . . ."

"She was a role model to me. . . ."

"One of my favorite students . . ."

When Meredith rose, Elena's whole body stiffened. She didn't know if she could deal with this. But the dark-haired girl was one of the few people in the church who wasn't crying, although her face had a grave, sad look that reminded Elena of Honoria Fell as she looked on her tomb.

"When I think about Elena, I think about the good times we had together," she said, speaking quietly and with her customary self-control. "Elena always had ideas, and she could make the most boring work into fun. I never told her that, and now I wish I had. I wish that I could talk to her one more time, just so she would know. And if Elena could hear me now"—Meredith looked around the church and drew a long breath, apparently to calm herself—"if she could hear me now, I would tell her how much those good times meant to me, and how much I wish that we could still have them. Like the Thursday nights we used to sit together in her room, practicing for the debate team. I wish we could do that just once more like we used to." Meredith took another long breath and shook her head. "But I know we can't, and that hurts."

What are you talking about? Elena thought, her misery interrupted by bewilderment. We used to practice for the debate team on *Wednesday* nights, not Thursdays. And it wasn't in my bedroom; it was in yours. And it was no fun at all; in fact, we ended up quitting because we both hated it. . . .

Suddenly, watching Meredith's carefully composed face, so calm on the outside to conceal the tension within, Elena felt her heart begin to pound.

Meredith was sending a message, a message only Elena could be expected to understand. Which meant that Meredith expected Elena to be able to hear it.

Meredith knew.

Had Stefan told her? Elena scanned the rows of mourners below, realizing for the first time that Stefan wasn't among them. Neither was Matt. No, it didn't seem likely that Stefan would have told Meredith, or that Meredith would choose this way of getting a message to her if he had. Then Elena remembered the way Meredith had looked at her the night they had rescued Stefan from the well, when Elena had asked to be left alone with Stefan. She remembered those keen dark eyes studying her face more than once in the last months, and the way Meredith had seemed to grow quieter and more thoughtful each time Elena came up with some odd request.

Meredith had guessed then. Elena wondered just how much of the truth she'd put together.

Bonnie was coming up now, crying in earnest. That was surprising; if Meredith knew, why hadn't she told Bonnie? But maybe Meredith had only a suspicion, something she didn't want to share with Bonnie in case it turned out to be a false hope.

Bonnie's speech was as emotional as Meredith's had been collected. Her voice kept breaking and she kept having to brush tears off her cheeks. Finally Reverend Bethea crossed over and gave her something white, a handkerchief or some tissue.

"Thank you," Bonnie said, wiping her streaming eyes. She tilted her head back to look at the ceiling, either to regain her poise or to get inspiration. As she did, Elena saw something that no one else could see: she saw Bonnie's face drain of color and of expression, not like somebody about to faint, but in a way that was all too familiar.

A chill crawled up Elena's backbone. Not here. Oh, God, of all times and places, not here.

But it was already happening. Bonnie's chin had lowered; she was looking at the congregation again. Except that this time she didn't seem to see them at all, and the voice that came from Bonnie's throat was not Bonnie's voice.

"No one is what they appear. Remember that. *No one is what they appear*." Then she just stood there, unmoving, staring straight ahead with blank eyes.

People began to shuffle and look at one another. There was a murmur of worry.

"Remember that—remember—no one is what they seem . . ." Bonnie swayed suddenly, and Reverend

Bethea ran to her while another man hastened up from the other side. The second man had a bald head that was now shining with sweat—Mr. Newcastle, Elena realized. And there at the back of the church, striding up the nave, was Alaric Saltzman. He reached Bonnie just as she fainted, and Elena heard a step behind her on the stair.

5

r. Feinberg, Elena thought wildly, trying to twist around to look and simultaneously press herself into the shadows. But it wasn't the small, hawk-nosed visage of the doctor that met her eyes. It was a face with features as fine as those on a Roman coin or medallion, and haunted green eyes. Time caught for a moment, and then Elena was in his arms.

"Oh, Stefan. Stefan . . ."

She felt his body go still with shock. He was holding her mechanically, lightly, as if she were a stranger who'd mistaken him for someone else.

"*Stefan,*" she said desperately, burrowing her face into his shoulder, trying to get some response. She couldn't bear it if he rejected her; if he hated her now she would *die.* . . .

With a moan, she tried to get even closer to him, wanting to merge with him completely, to disappear inside him. Oh, please, she thought, oh, please, oh, please. . . .

"Elena. Elena, it's all right; I've got you." He went on talking to her, repeating silly nonsense meant to soothe, stroking her hair. And she could feel the change as his arms tightened around her. He knew who he was holding now. For the first time since she'd awakened that day, she felt safe. Still, it was a long while before she could relax her grip on him even slightly. She wasn't crying; she was gasping in panic.

At last she felt the world start to settle into place around her. She didn't let go, though, not yet. She simply stood for endless minutes with her head on his shoulder, drinking in the comfort and security of his nearness.

Then she raised her head to look into his eyes.

When she'd thought of Stefan earlier that day, she'd thought of how he might help her. She'd meant to ask him, to beg him, to save her from this nightmare, to make her the way she had been before. But now, as she looked at him, she felt a strange despairing resignation flow through her.

"There's nothing to be done about it, is there?" she said very softly.

He didn't pretend to misunderstand. "No," he said, equally soft.

Elena felt as if she had taken some final step over an invisible line and that there was no returning. When she could speak again, she said, "I'm sorry for the way I acted toward you in the woods. I don't know why I did those things. I remember doing them, but I can't remember *why*."

"*You're* sorry?" His voice shook. "Elena, after all I've done to you, all that's happened to you because of me . . ." He couldn't finish, and they clung to each other.

"Very touching," said a voice from the stairway. "Do you want me to imitate a violin?"

Elena's calm shattered, and fear snaked through her bloodstream. She'd forgotten Damon's hypnotic intensity and his burning dark eyes.

"How did you get here?" said Stefan.

"The same way you did, I presume. Attracted by the blazing beacon of the fair Elena's distress." Damon was really angry; Elena could tell. Not just annoyed or discommoded but in a white heat of rage and hostility.

But he'd been decent to her when she'd been confused and irrational. He'd taken her to shelter; he'd kept her safe. And he hadn't kissed her while she'd been in that horrifyingly vulnerable state. He'd been . . . kind to her.

"Incidentally, there's something going on down there," Damon said.

"I know; it's Bonnie again," said Elena, releasing Stefan and moving back.

"That's not what I meant. This is outside."

Startled, Elena followed him down to the first bend in the stairs, where there was a window overlooking the parking lot. She felt Stefan behind her as she looked down at the scene below.

A crowd of people had come out of the church, but they were standing in a solid phalanx at the edge of the lot, not going any farther. Opposite them, in the parking lot itself, was an equally large assembly of dogs.

It looked like two armies facing each other. What was eerie, though, was that both groups were absolutely motionless. The people seemed to be paralyzed by uneasiness, and the dogs seemed to be waiting for something.

Elena saw the dogs first as different breeds. There were small dogs like sharp-faced corgis and brown-and-black silky terriers and a Lhasa apso with long golden hair. There were medium-sized dogs like springer spaniels and Airedales and one beautiful snow white Samoyed. And there were the big dogs: a barrel-chested rottweiler with a cropped tail, a panting gray wolfhound, and a giant schnauzer, pure black. Then Elena began to recognize individuals.

"That's Mr. Grunbaum's boxer and the Sullivans'

German shepherd. But what's going on with them?"

The people, originally uneasy, now looked frightened. They stood shoulder to shoulder, no one wanting to break out of the front line and move any closer to the animals.

And yet the dogs weren't *doing* anything, just sitting or standing, some with their tongues lolling gently out. Strange, though, how still they were, Elena thought. Every tiny motion, such as the slightest twitch of tail or ears, seemed vastly exaggerated. And there were no wagging tails, no signs of friendliness. Just . . . waiting.

Robert was toward the back of the crowd. Elena was surprised at seeing him, but for a moment she couldn't think of why. Then she realized it was because he hadn't been in the church. As she watched, he drew farther apart from the group, disappearing under the overhang below Elena.

"Chelsea! Chelsea . . ."

Someone had moved out of the front line at last. It was Douglas Carson, Elena realized, Sue Carson's married older brother. He'd stepped into the no-man's-land between the dogs and the people, one hand slightly extended.

A springer spaniel with long ears like brown satin turned her head. Her white stump of a tail quivered slightly, questioningly, and her brown-and-white muzzle lifted. But she didn't come to the young man.

Doug Carson took another step. "Chelsea . . . good girl. Come here, Chelsea. Come!" He snapped his fingers.

"What do you sense from those dogs down there?" Damon murmured.

Stefan shook his head without looking away from the window. "Nothing," he said shortly.

"Neither do I." Damon's eyes were narrowed, his head tilted back appraisingly, but his slightly bared teeth reminded Elena of the wolfhound. "But we *should* be able to, you know. They ought to have some emotions we can pick up on. Instead, every time I try to probe them it's like running into a blank white wall."

Elena wished she knew what they were talking about. "What do you mean 'probe them'?" she said. "They're animals."

"Appearances can be deceiving," Damon said ironically, and Elena thought about the rainbow lights in the feathers of the crow that had followed her since the first day of school. If she looked closely, she could see those same rainbow lights in Damon's silky hair. "But animals have emotions, in any case. If your Powers are strong enough, you can examine their minds."

And my Powers aren't, thought Elena. She was startled by the twinge of envy that went through her. Just a few minutes ago she'd been clinging to Stefan, frantic to get rid of any Powers she had, to change herself *back*. And now, she wished she were stronger. Damon always had an odd effect on her.

"I may not be able to probe Chelsea, but I don't think Doug should go any closer," she said aloud.

Stefan had been staring fixedly out the window, his eyebrows drawn together. Now he nodded fractionally, but with a sudden sense of urgency. "I don't either," he said.

"C'mon, Chelsea, be a good girl. Come here." Doug Carson had almost reached the first row of dogs. All eyes, human and canine, were fixed on him, and even such tiny movements as twitches had stopped. If Elena hadn't seen the sides of one or two dogs hollow and fill with their breathing, she might have thought the whole group was some giant museum display.

Doug had come to a halt. Chelsea was watching him from behind the corgi and the Samoyed. Doug clucked his tongue. He stretched out his hand, hesitated, and then stretched it out farther.

"No," Elena said. She was staring at the rottweiler's glossy flanks. Hollow and fill, hollow and fill. "Stefan, influence him. Get him out of there."

"Yes." She could see his gaze unfocus with concentration; then, he shook his head, exhaling like a person who's tried to lift something too heavy. "It's no good; I'm burnt out. I can't do it from here."

Below, Chelsea's lips skinned back from her teeth. The red-gold Airedale rose to her feet in one beautifully smooth movement, as if pulled by strings. The hindquarters of the rottweiler bunched.

And then they sprang. Elena couldn't see which of the dogs was the first; they seemed to move together like a great wave. Half a dozen hit Doug Carson with enough force to knock him backward, and he disappeared under their massed bodies.

The air was full of hellish noise, from a metallic baying that set the church rafters ringing and gave Elena an instant headache, to a deep-throated continuous growl that she felt rather than heard. Dogs were tearing at clothing, snarling, lunging, while the crowd scattered and screamed.

Elena caught sight of Alaric Saltzman at the edge of the parking lot, the only one who wasn't running. He was standing stiffly, and she thought she could see his lips moving, and his hands.

Everywhere else was pandemonium. Someone had gotten a hose and was turning it into the thick of the pack, but it was having no effect. The dogs seemed to have gone mad. When Chelsea raised her brown-and-white muzzle from her master's body, it was tinged with red.

Elena's heart was pounding so that she could barely breathe. "They need help!" she said, just as Stefan broke away from the window and went down the stairs, taking them two and three at a time. Elena was halfway down the stairs herself when she realized two things: Damon wasn't following her, and she couldn't let herself be seen.

She *couldn't*. The hysteria it would cause, the questions, the fear and hatred once the questions were answered. Something that ran deeper than compassion or sympathy or the need to help wrenched her back, flattening her against the wall.

In the dim, cool interior of the church, she glimpsed a boiling pocket of activity. People were dashing back and forth, shouting. Dr. Feinberg, Mr. McCullough, Reverend Bethea. The still point of the circle was Bonnie lying on a pew with Meredith and Aunt Judith and Mrs. McCullough bent over her. "Something evil," she was moaning, and then Aunt Judith's head came up, turning in Elena's direction.

Elena scuttled up the stairs as quickly as she could, praying Aunt Judith hadn't seen her. Damon was at the window.

"I can't go down there. They think I'm dead!"

"Oh, you've remembered that. Good for you."

"If Dr. Feinberg examines me, he'll know something's wrong. Well, won't he?" she demanded fiercely.

"He'll think you're an interesting specimen, all right."

"Then I can't go. But you can. Why don't you *do* something?"

Damon continued to look out the window, eyebrows hiking up. "Why?"

"*Why?*" Elena's alarm and overexcitement reached flash point and she almost slapped him. "Because they need help! Because you *can* help. Don't you care about anything besides yourself?"

Damon was wearing his most impenetrable mask, the expression of polite inquiry he'd worn when he invited himself to her house for dinner. But she knew that beneath it he was angry, angry at finding her and Stefan together. He was baiting her on purpose and with savage enjoyment.

And she couldn't help her reaction, her frustrated, impotent rage. She started for him, and he caught her wrists and held her off, his eyes boring into hers. She was startled to hear the sound that came from her lips then; it was a hiss that sounded more feline than human. She realized her fingers were hooked into claws.

What am I doing? Attacking him because he won't defend people against the dogs that are attacking *them*? What kind of sense does that make? Breathing hard, she relaxed her hands and wet her lips. She stepped back and he let her.

There was a long moment while they stared at each other.

"I'm going down," Elena said quietly and turned.

"No."

"They need help."

"All right, then, damn you." She'd never heard Damon's voice so low, or so furious. "I'll—" he broke off and Elena, turning back quickly, saw him slam a fist into the windowsill, rattling the glass. But his attention was outside and his voice perfectly composed again when he said dryly, "Help has arrived."

It was the fire department. Their hoses were much more powerful than the garden hose, and the jet streams of water drove the lunging dogs off with sheer force. Elena saw a sheriff with a gun and bit the inside of her cheek as he aimed and sighted. There was a crack, and the giant schnauzer went down. The sheriff aimed again.

It ended quickly after that. Several dogs were already running from the barrage of water, and with the second crack of the pistol more broke from the pack and headed for the edges of the parking lot. It was as if the purpose that had driven them had released them all at once. Elena felt a rush of relief as she saw Stefan standing unharmed in the middle of the rout, shoving a dazed-looking golden retriever away from Doug Carson's form. Chelsea took a skulking step toward her master and looked into his face, head and tail drooping.

"It's all over," Damon said. He sounded only mildly interested, but Elena glanced at him sharply. All right then, damn you, I'll *what?* she thought. What had he been about to say? He wasn't in any mood to tell her, but she was in a mood to push.

"Damon . . ." She put a hand on his arm.

He stiffened, then turned. "Well?"

For a second they stood looking at each other, and then there was a step on the stair. Stefan had returned.

"Stefan . . . you're hurt," she said, blinking, suddenly disoriented.

"I'm all right." He wiped blood off his cheek with a tattered sleeve.

"What about Doug?" Elena asked, swallowing.

"I don't know. He *is* hurt. A lot of people are. That was the strangest thing I've ever seen."

Elena moved away from Damon, up the stairs into the choir loft. She felt that she had to think, but her head was pounding. The strangest thing Stefan had ever seen . . . that was saying a lot. Something strange in Fell's Church.

She reached the wall behind the last row of seats and put a hand against it, sliding down to sit on the floor. Things seemed at once confused and frighteningly clear. Something strange in Fell's Church. The day of the founders' celebration she would have sworn she didn't care anything about Fell's Church or the people in it. But now she knew differently. Looking down on the memorial service, she had begun to think perhaps she *did* care. And then, when the dogs had attacked outside, she'd known it. She felt somehow responsible for the town, in a way she had never felt before.

Her earlier sense of desolation and loneliness had been pushed aside for the moment. There was something more important than her own problems now. And she clung to that something, because the truth was that she really couldn't deal with her own situation, no, she really, really couldn't. . . .

She heard the gasping half sob she gave then and looked up to see both Stefan and Damon in the choir loft, looking at her. She shook her head slightly, putting a hand to it, feeling as if she were coming out of a dream.

"Elena . . . ?"

It was Stefan who spoke, but Elena addressed herself to the other one.

"Damon," she said shakily, "if I ask you something, will you tell me the truth? I know you didn't chase me off Wickery Bridge. I could *feel* whatever it was, and it was different. But I want to ask you this: was it you who dumped Stefan in the old Francher well a month ago?"

"In a *well?*" Damon leaned back against the opposite wall, arms crossed over his chest. He looked politely incredulous.

"On Halloween night, the night Mr. Tanner was killed. After you showed yourself for the first time to Stefan in the woods. He told me he left you in the clearing and started to walk to his car but that someone attacked him before he reached it. When he woke up, he was trapped in the well, and he would have died there if Bonnie hadn't led us to him. I always assumed you were the one who attacked him. *He* always assumed you were the one. But were you?"

Damon's lip curled, as if he didn't like the demanding intensity of her question. He looked from her to Stefan with hooded, deriding eyes. The moment stretched out until Elena had to dig her fingernails into her palms with tension. Then Damon gave a small shrug and looked off at a middle distance.

"As a matter of fact, no," he said.

Elena let out her breath.

"You can't believe that!" Stefan exploded. "You can't believe anything he says."

"Why should I lie?" Damon returned, clearly enjoying Stefan's loss of control. "I admit freely to killing Tanner. I drank his blood until he shriveled like a prune. And I wouldn't mind doing the same thing to *you*, brother. But a *well*? It's hardly my style."

"I believe you," Elena said. Her mind was rushing ahead. She turned to Stefan. "Don't you feel it? There's something else here in Fell's Church, something that may not even be human—may never have been human, I mean. Something that chased me, forced my car off the bridge. Something that made those dogs attack people. Some terrible force that's here, something evil . . ." Her voice trailed off, and she looked over toward the interior of the church where she had seen Bonnie lying. "Something evil . . ." she repeated softly. A cold wind seemed to blow inside her, and she huddled into herself, feeling vulnerable and alone.

"If you're looking for evil," Stefan said harshly, "you don't have to look far."

"Don't be any more stupid than you can help," said Damon. "I told you four days ago that someone else had killed Elena. And I said that I was going to find that someone and deal with him. And I am." He uncrossed his arms and straightened up. "You two can continue that private conversation you were having when I interrupted."

"Damon, wait." Elena hadn't been able to help the shudder that tore through her when he said *killed*. I can't have been killed; I'm still here, she thought wildly, feeling panic swell up in her again. But now she pushed the panic aside to speak to Damon.

"Whatever this thing is, it's strong," she said. "I felt it when it was after me, and it seemed to fill the whole sky. I don't think any of us would stand a chance against it alone."

"So?"

"So . . ." Elena hadn't had time to gather her thoughts

this far. She was running purely on instinct, on intuition. And intuition told her not to let Damon go. "So . . . I think we three ought to stick together. I think we have a much better chance of finding it and dealing with it together than separately. And maybe we can stop it before it hurts or—or kills—anyone else."

"Frankly, my dear, I don't give a damn about anyone else," Damon said charmingly. Then he gave one of his ice-cold lightning smiles. "But are you suggesting that this is your choice? Remember, we agreed that when you were more rational you would make one."

Elena stared at him. Of course it wasn't her choice, if he meant romantically. She was wearing the ring Stefan had given her; she and Stefan belonged together.

But then she remembered something else, just a flash: looking up at Damon's face in the woods and feeling such—such excitement, such affinity with him. As if he understood the flame that burned inside her as nobody else ever could. As if together they could do anything they liked, conquer the world or destroy it; as if they were better than anyone else who had ever lived.

I was out of my mind, irrational, she told herself, but that little flash of memory wouldn't go away.

And then she remembered something else: how Damon had acted later that night, how he'd kept her safe, even been gentle with her.

Stefan was looking at her, and his expression had changed from belligerence to bitter anger and fear. Part of her wanted to reassure him completely, to throw her arms around him and tell him that she was his and always would be and that nothing else mattered. Not the town, not Damon, not anything.

But she wasn't doing it. Because another part of her was saying that the town *did* matter. And because still another part was just terribly, terribly confused. So confused . . .

She felt a trembling begin deep inside her, and then she found she couldn't make it stop. Emotional overload, she thought, and put her head in her hands.

6

"She's already made her choice. You saw it your-self when you 'interrupted' us. You've already chosen, haven't you, Elena?" Stefan said it not smugly, or as a demand, but with a kind of desperate bravado.

"I . . ." Elena looked up. "Stefan, I love you. But don't you understand, if I have a choice right now I have to choose for all of us to stay together. Just for now. *Do* you understand?" Seeing only stoniness in Stefan's face, she turned to Damon. "Do you?"

"I think so." He gave her a secret, possessive smile. "I told Stefan from the beginning that he was selfish not to share you. Brothers should share things, you know."

"That's not what I meant."

"Isn't it?" Damon smiled again.

"No," Stefan said. "*I* don't understand, and I don't see how you can ask me to work with *him*. He's evil, Elena. He kills for pleasure; he has no conscience at all. He doesn't care about Fell's Church; he said that himself. He's a monster—"

"Right now he's being more cooperative than you are," Elena said. She reached for Stefan's hand, searching for some way to get through to him. "Stefan, I *need* you. And we both need him. Can't you try to accept that?" When he didn't answer she added, "Stefan, do you really want to be mortal enemies with your brother forever?"

"Do you really think *he* wants anything else?"

Elena stared down at their joined hands, looking at the planes and curves and shadows. She didn't answer for a minute, and when she did it was very quietly.

"He stopped me from killing you," she said.

She felt the flare of Stefan's defensive anger, then felt it slowly fade. Something like defeat crept through him, and he bowed his head.

"That's true," he said. "And, anyway, who am I to call him evil? What's he done that I haven't done myself?"

We need to talk, Elena thought, hating this self-hatred of his. But this wasn't the time or place.

"Then you do agree?" she said hesitantly. "Stefan, tell me what you're thinking."

"Right now I'm thinking that you always get your way. Because you always do, don't you, Elena?"

Elena looked into his eyes, noticing how the pupils were dilated, so that only a ring of green iris showed around the edge. There was no longer anger there, but the tiredness and the bitterness remained.

But I'm not just doing it for myself, she thought, thrusting out of her mind the sudden surge of self-doubt. I'll prove that to you, Stefan; you'll see. For once I'm not doing something for my own convenience.

"Then you agree?" she said quietly.

"Yes. I . . . agree."

"And *I* agree," said Damon, extending his own hand with exaggerated courtesy. He captured Elena's before she could say anything. "In fact, we all seem to be in a frenzy of pure agreement."

Don't, Elena thought, but at that moment, standing in the cool twilight of the choir loft, she felt that it was true, that they were all three connected, and in accord, and strong.

Then Stefan pulled his hand away. In the silence that followed, Elena could hear the sounds outside and in the church below. There was still crying and the occasional shout, but the overall urgency was gone. Looking out the window, she saw people picking their way across the wet parking lot between the little groups that huddled over wounded victims. Dr. Feinberg was moving from island to island, apparently dispensing medical advice. The victims looked like survivors of a hurricane or earthquake.

"No one is what they seem," Elena said.

"What?"

"That's what Bonnie said during the memorial service. She had another one of her fits. I think it might be important." She tried to put her thoughts in order. "I think there are people in town that we ought to look out for. Like Alaric Saltzman." She told them, briefly, what she had overheard earlier that day in Alaric's house. "*He's* not what he seems, but I don't know exactly what he is. I think we should watch him. And since I obviously can't appear in public, you two are going to have to do it. But you can't let him suspect you know—" Elena broke off as Damon held up a hand swiftly.

Down at the base of the stairs, a voice was calling. "Stefan? Are you up there?" And then, to someone else, "I thought I saw him go up here."

It sounded like Mr. Carson. "Go," Elena hissed almost inaudibly to Stefan. "You have to be as normal as possible so you can stay here in Fell's Church. I'll be all right."

"But where will *you* go?"

"To Meredith's. I'll explain later. Go on."

Stefan hesitated, and then started down the stairs, calling, "I'm coming." Then he pulled back. "I'm not leaving you with *him*," he said flatly.

Elena threw her hands up in exasperation. "Then both of you go. You just agreed to work together; are you going to go back on your word now?" she added to Damon, who was looking unyielding himself.

He gave another of his little shrugs. "All right. Just one thing—are you hungry?"

"I—no." Stomach lurching, Elena realized what he was asking. "No, not at all."

"That's good. But later on, you will be. Remember that." He crowded Stefan down the stairs, earning himself a searing look. But Elena heard Stefan's voice in her mind as they both disappeared.

I'll come for you later. Wait for me.

She wished she could answer with her own thoughts. She also noticed something. Stefan's mental voice was much weaker than it had been four days ago when he had been fighting his brother. Come to think of it, he hadn't been able to speak with his mind at all before the Founders' Day celebration. She'd been so confused when she woke up by the river that it hadn't occurred to her, but now she wondered. What had happened to make him so strong? And why was his strength fading now?

Elena had time to think about it as she sat there in the deserted choir loft, while below the people left the church and outside the overcast skies slowly grew darker. She thought about Stefan, and about Damon, and she wondered if she had made the right choice. She'd vowed never to let them fight over her, but that vow was broken already. Was she crazy to try and make them live under a truce, even a temporary one?

When the sky outside was uniformly black, she ventured down the stairs. The church was empty and echoing. She hadn't thought about how she would get out, but fortunately the side door was bolted only from the inside. She slipped out into the night gratefully.

She hadn't realized how good it was to be outside and in the dark. Being inside buildings made her feel trapped, and daylight hurt her eyes. This was best, free and unfettered—and unseen. Her own senses rejoiced at the lush world around her. With the air so still, scents hung in the air for a long time, and she could smell a whole plethora of nocturnal creatures. A fox was scavenging in somebody's trash. Brown rats were chewing something in the bushes. Night moths were calling to one another with scent.

She found it wasn't hard to get to Meredith's house undetected; people seemed to be staying inside. But once she got there, she stood looking up at the graceful farm-house with the screened porch in dismay. She couldn't just walk up to the front door and knock. Was Meredith really expecting her? Wouldn't she be waiting outside if she were?

Meredith was about to get a terrible shock if she *weren't*, Elena reflected, eyeing the distance to the roof of the porch. Meredith's bedroom window was above it and just around the corner. It would be a bit of a reach, but Elena thought she could make it.

Getting onto the roof was easy; her fingers and bare toes found holds between the bricks and sent her sailing up. But leaning around the corner to look into Meredith's window was a strain. She blinked against the light that flooded out.

Meredith was sitting on the edge of her bed, elbows on knees, staring at nothing. Every so often she ran a hand through her dark hair. A clock on the nightstand said 6:43.

Elena tapped on the window glass with her fingernails.

Meredith jumped and looked the wrong way, toward the door. She stood up in a defensive crouch, clutching a throw pillow in one hand. When the door didn't open, she sidled a pace or two toward it, still in a defensive posture. "Who is it?" she said.

Elena tapped on the glass again.

Meredith spun to face the window, her breath coming fast.

"Let me in," said Elena. She didn't know if Meredith could hear her, so she mouthed it clearly. "Open the window."

Meredith, panting, looked around the room as if she expected someone to appear and help her. When no one did, she approached the window as if it were a dangerous animal. But she didn't open it.

"Let me *in*," Elena said again. Then she added impatiently, "If you didn't want me to come, why did you make an appointment with me?"

She saw the change as Meredith's shoulders relaxed slightly. Slowly, with fingers that were unusually clumsy, Meredith opened the window and stood back.

"Now ask me to come inside. Otherwise I can't."

"Come . . ." Meredith's voice failed and she had to try again. "Come in," she said. When Elena, wincing, had boosted herself over the sill and was flexing her cramped fingers, Meredith added almost dazedly, "It's got to be you. Nobody else gives orders like that."

"It's me," Elena said. She stopped wringing out the cramps and looked into the eyes of her friend. "It really is me, Meredith," she said.

Meredith nodded and swallowed visibly. Right then what Elena would have liked most in the world would have been for the other girl to give her a hug. But Meredith wasn't much of the hugging type, and right now she was backing slowly away to sit on the bed again.

"Sit down," she said in an artificially calm voice. Elena pulled out the desk chair and unthinkingly took up the same position Meredith had been in before, elbows on knees, head down. Then she looked up. "How did you know?"

"I . . ." Meredith just stared at her for a moment, then shook herself. "Well. You—your body was never found, of course. That was strange. And then those attacks on the old man and Vickie and Tanner—and Stefan and little things I'd put together about him—but I didn't *know*. Not for sure. Not until now." She ended almost in a whisper.

"Well, it was a good guess," Elena said. She was trying to behave normally, but what was normal in this situation? Meredith was acting as if she could scarcely bear to look at her. It made Elena feel more lonely, more alone, than she could ever remember being in her life.

A doorbell rang downstairs. Elena heard it, but she could tell Meredith didn't. "Who's coming?" she said. "There's someone at the door."

"I asked Bonnie to come over at seven o'clock, if her mother would let her. It's probably her. I'll go see." Meredith seemed almost indecently eager to get away.

"Wait. Does *she* know?"

"No. . . . Oh, you mean I should break it to her gently." Meredith looked around the room again uncertainly, and Elena snapped on the little reading light by the bed.

"Turn the room light off. It hurts my eyes anyway," she said quietly. When Meredith did, the bedroom was dim enough that she could conceal herself in the shadows.

Waiting for Meredith to return with Bonnie, she stood in a corner, hugging her elbows with her hands. Maybe it was a bad idea trying to get Meredith and Bonnie involved. If imperturbable Meredith couldn't handle the situation, what would Bonnie do?

Meredith heralded their arrival by muttering over and over, "Don't scream now; *don't scream*," as she bundled Bonnie across the threshold.

"What's *wrong* with you? What are you *doing*?" Bonnie was gasping in return. "Let go of me. Do you know what I had to do to get my mother to let me out of the house tonight? She wants to take me to the hospital at Roanoke."

Meredith kicked the door shut. "Okay," she said to Bonnie. "Now, you're going to see something that will . . . well, it's going to be a shock. But you can't scream, do you understand me? I'll let go of you if you promise."

"It's too dark to see anything, and you're scaring me. What's *wrong* with you, Meredith? Oh, all right, I promise, but what are you talking—"

"Elena," said Meredith. Elena took it as an invitation and stepped forward.

Bonnie's reaction wasn't what she expected. She frowned and leaned forward, peering in the dim light. When she saw Elena's form, she gasped. But then, as she stared at Elena's face, she clapped her hands together with a shriek of joy.

"I knew it! I knew they were wrong! So there, Meredith—and you and Stefan thought you knew so much about drowning and all that. But I knew you were wrong! Oh, Elena, I missed you! Everyone's going to be so—"

"Be *quiet*, Bonnie! Be quiet!" Meredith said urgently. "I told you not to scream. Listen, you idiot, do you think if Elena were really all right she'd be *here* in the middle of the night without anybody knowing about it?"

"But she *is* all right; look at her. She's standing there. It is you, isn't it, Elena?" Bonnie started toward her, but Meredith grabbed her again.

"Yes, it's me." Elena had the strange feeling she'd wandered into a surreal comedy, maybe one written by Kafka, only she didn't know her lines. She didn't know what to say to Bonnie, who was looking rapturous.

"It's me, but . . . I'm not exactly all right," she said awkwardly, sitting down again. Meredith nudged Bonnie to sit down on the bed.

"What are you two being so mysterious for? She's here,

but she's not all right. What's that supposed to mean?"

Elena didn't know whether to laugh or cry. "Look, Bonnie . . . oh, I don't know how to say this. Bonnie, did your psychic grandmother ever talk to you about vampires?"

Silence fell, heavy as an ax. The minutes ticked by. Impossibly, Bonnie's eyes widened still further; then, they slid toward Meredith. There were several more minutes of silence, and then Bonnie shifted her weight toward the door. "Uh, look, you guys," she said softly, "this is getting really weird. I mean, really, really, really . . ."

Elena cast about in her mind. "You can look at my teeth," she said. She pulled her upper lip back, poking at a canine with her finger. She felt the reflexive lengthening and sharpening, like a cat's claw lazily extending.

Meredith came forward and looked and then looked away quickly. "I get the point," she said, but in her voice there was none of the old wry pleasure in her own wit. "Bonnie, look," she said.

All the elation, all the excitement had drained out of Bonnie. She looked as if she were going to be sick. "No. I don't want to."

"You have to. You have to believe it, or we'll never get anywhere." Meredith grappled a stiff and resisting Bonnie forward. "Open your eyes, you little twit. You're the one who loves all this supernatural stuff."

"I've changed my *mind*," Bonnie said, almost sobbing. There was genuine hysteria in her tone. "Leave me *alone*, Meredith; I don't *want* to look." She wrenched herself away.

"You don't have to," Elena whispered, stunned. Dismay pooled inside her, and tears flooded her eyes. "This was a bad idea, Meredith. I'll go away."

"*No*. Oh, don't." Bonnie turned back as quickly as she'd whirled away and precipitated herself into Elena's arms. "I'm sorry, Elena; I'm sorry. I don't care what you are; I'm just glad you're back. It's been terrible without you." She was sobbing now in earnest.

The tears that wouldn't come when Elena had been with Stefan came now. She cried, holding on to Bonnie, feeling Meredith's arms go around both of them. They were all crying—Meredith silently, Bonnie noisily, and Elena herself with passionate intensity. She felt as if she were crying for everything that had happened to her, for everything she had lost, for all the loneliness and the fear and the pain.

Eventually, they all ended up sitting on the floor, knee to knee, the way they had when they were kids at a sleepover making secret plans.

"You're so brave," Bonnie said to Elena, sniffling. "I

don't see how you can be so brave about it."

"You don't know how I'm feeling inside. I'm not brave at all. But I've got to deal with it somehow, because I don't know what else to do."

"Your hands aren't cold." Meredith squeezed Elena's fingers. "Just sort of cool. I thought they'd be colder."

"Stefan's hands aren't cold either," Elena said, and she was about to go on, but Bonnie squeaked: *"Stefan?"*

Meredith and Elena looked at her.

"Be sensible, Bonnie. You don't get to be a vampire by yourself. Somebody has to make you one."

"But you mean *Stefan* . . . ? You mean he's a . . . ?" Bonnie's voice choked off.

"I think," said Meredith, "that maybe this is the time to tell us the whole story, Elena. Like all those minor details you left out the last time we asked you for the whole story."

Elena nodded. "You're right. It's hard to explain, but I'll try." She took a deep breath. "Bonnie, do you remember the first day of school? It was the first time I ever heard you make a prophecy. You looked into my palm and said I'd meet a boy, a dark boy, a stranger. And that he wasn't tall but that he *had* been once. Well"—she looked at Bonnie and then at Meredith—"Stefan's not really tall now. But he was once . . . compared to other people in the fifteenth century."

Meredith nodded, but Bonnie made a faint sound and swayed backward, looking shell-shocked. "You mean—"

"I mean he lived in Renaissance Italy, and the average person was shorter then. So Stefan looked taller by comparison. And, wait, before you pass out, here's something else you should know. Damon's his brother."

Meredith nodded again. "I figured something like that. But then why has Damon been saying he's a college student?"

"They don't get along very well. For a long time, Stefan didn't even know Damon was in Fell's Church." Elena faltered. She was verging on Stefan's private history, which she'd always felt was *his* secret to tell. But Meredith had been right; it was time to come out with the whole story. "Listen, it was like this," she said. "Stefan and Damon were both in love with the same girl back in Renaissance Italy. She was from Germany, and her name was Katherine. The reason Stefan was avoiding me at the beginning of school was that I reminded him of her; she had blond hair and blue eyes, too. Oh, and this was her ring." Elena let go of Meredith's hand and showed them the intricately carved golden circlet set with a single stone of lapis lazuli.

"And the thing was that Katherine was a vampire. A

guy named Klaus had made her one back in her village in Germany to save her from dying of her last illness. Stefan and Damon both knew this, but they didn't care. They asked her to choose between them the one she wanted to marry." Elena stopped and gave a lopsided smile, thinking that Mr. Tanner had been right; history did repeat itself. She only hoped her story didn't end like Katherine's. "But she chose *both* of them. She exchanged blood with both of them, and she said they could all three be companions through eternity."

"Sounds kinky," murmured Bonnie.

"Sounds *dumb*," said Meredith.

"You got it," Elena told her. "Katherine was sweet but not very bright. Stefan and Damon already didn't like each other. They told her she *had* to choose, that they wouldn't even think of sharing her. And she ran off crying. The next day—well, they found her body, or what was left of it. See, a vampire needs a talisman like this ring to go out in the sun without being killed. And Katherine went out in the sun and took hers off. She thought if she were out of the way, Damon and Stefan would be reconciled."

"Oh, my God, how ro—"

"No, it *isn't*," Elena cut Bonnie off savagely. "It's not romantic at all. Stefan's been living with the guilt ever since, and I think Damon has, too, although you'd never get him to admit it. And the immediate result was that they got a couple of swords and killed each other. Yes, *killed*. That's why they're vampires now, and that's why they hate each other so much. And that's why I'm probably crazy trying to get them to cooperate now."

"To cooperate at what?" Meredith asked.

"I'll explain about that later. But first I want to know what's been going on in town since I—left."

"Well, hysteria mostly," Meredith said, raising an eyebrow. "Your aunt Judith's been pretty badly off. She hallucinated that she saw you—only it wasn't a hallucination, was it? And she and Robert have sort of broken up."

"I know," Elena said grimly. "Go on."

"Everybody at school is upset. I wanted to talk to Stefan, especially when I began to suspect you weren't really dead, but he hasn't been at school. Matt *has* been, but there's something wrong with him. He looks like a zombie, and he won't talk to anyone. I wanted to explain to him that there was a chance you might not be gone forever;

I thought that would cheer him up. But he wouldn't listen. He was acting totally out of character, and at one point I thought he was going to hit me. He wouldn't listen to a word."

"Oh, God—Matt." Something terrible was stirring at the bottom of Elena's mind, some memory too disturbing to be let loose. She couldn't cope with anything more just now, she *couldn't*, she thought, and slam dunked the memory back down.

Meredith was going on. "It's clear, though, that some other people are suspicious about your 'death.' That's why I said what I did in the memorial service; I was afraid if I said the real day and place that Alaric Saltzman would end up ambushing you outside the house. He's been asking all sorts of questions, and it's a good thing Bonnie didn't know anything she could blab."

"That isn't fair," Bonnie protested. "Alaric's just interested, that's all, and he wants to help us through the trauma, like before. He's an Aquarius—"

"He's a spy," said Elena, "and maybe more than that. But we'll talk about that later. What about Tyler Smallwood? I didn't see him at the service."

Meredith looked nonplussed. "You mean you don't know?"

"I don't know *anything*; I've been asleep for four days in an attic."

"Well . . ." Meredith paused uneasily. "Tyler just got back from the hospital. Same with Dick Carter and those four tough guys they had along with them on Founders' Day. They were attacked in the Quonset hut that evening and they lost a lot of blood."

"*Oh.*" The mystery of why Stefan's Powers had been so much stronger that night was explained. And why they'd been getting weaker ever since. He probably hadn't eaten since then. "Meredith, is Stefan a suspect?"

"Well, Tyler's father tried to make him one, but the police couldn't make the times work out. They know approximately when Tyler was attacked because he was supposed to meet Mr. Smallwood, and he didn't show up. And Bonnie and I can alibi Stefan for that time because we'd just left him by the river with your body. So he *couldn't* have gotten back to the Quonset hut to attack Tyler—at least no normal human could. And so far the police aren't thinking about anything supernatural."

"I see." Elena felt relieved on that score at least.

"Tyler and those guys can't identify the attacker because they can't remember a thing about that afternoon," Meredith added.

"Neither can Caroline."

"*Caroline* was in there?"

"Yes, but she wasn't bitten. Just in shock. In spite of everything she's done, I almost feel sorry for her." Meredith shrugged and added, "She looks pretty pathetic these days."

"And I don't think anyone will ever suspect Stefan after what happened with those dogs at church today," Bonnie put in. "My dad says that a big dog could have broken the window in the Quonset hut, and the wounds in Tyler's throat looked sort of like animal wounds. I think a lot of people believe it was a dog or a pack of dogs that did it."

"It's a convenient explanation," Meredith said dryly. "It means they don't have to think any more about it."

"But that's ridiculous," said Elena. "Normal dogs don't behave that way. Aren't people wondering about *why* their dogs would suddenly go mad and turn on them?"

"Lots of people are just getting rid of them. Oh, and I heard someone talk about mandatory rabies testing," Meredith said. "But it's not just rabies, is it, Elena?"

"No, I don't think so. And neither do Stefan or Damon. And that's what I came over to talk to you about." Elena explained, as clearly as she could, what she had been thinking about the Other Power in Fell's Church. She told about the force that had chased her off the bridge and about the feeling she'd had with the dogs and about everything she and Stefan and Damon had discussed. She finished with, "And Bonnie said it herself in church today: 'Something evil.' I think that's what's here in Fell's Church, something nobody knows about, something completely evil. I don't suppose *you* know what you meant by that, Bonnie."

But Bonnie's mind was running on another track. "So Damon didn't *necessarily* do all those awful things you said he did," she said shrewdly. "Like killing Yangtze and hurting Vickie and murdering Mr. Tanner, and all. I told you nobody that gorgeous could be a psycho killer."

"I think," said Meredith with a glance at Elena, "that you had better forget about Damon as a love interest."

"Yes," said Elena emphatically. "He *did* kill Mr. Tanner, Bonnie. And it stands to reason he did the other attacks, too; I'll ask him about that. And I'm having enough trouble dealing with him myself. You don't want to mess with him, Bonnie, believe me."

"I'm supposed to leave Damon alone; I'm supposed to leave Alaric alone. . . . Are there any guys I'm *not* supposed to leave alone? And meanwhile Elena gets them all. It's not fair."

"*Life* isn't fair," Meredith told her callously. "But listen, Elena, even if this Other Power exists, what sort of power do you think it is? What does it look like?"

"I don't know. Something tremendously strong—but it could be shielding itself so that we can't sense it. It could look like an ordinary person. And that's why I came for your help, because it could be anybody in Fell's Church. It's like what Bonnie said during the service today: 'Nobody is what they seem.'"

Bonnie looked forlorn. "I don't remember saying that."

"You said it, all right. 'Nobody is what they seem,'" Elena quoted again weightily. *"Nobody."* She glanced at Meredith, but the dark eyes under the elegantly arched eyebrows were calm and distant.

"Well, that would seem to make *everybody* a suspect," Meredith said in her most unruffled voice. "Right?"

"Right," said Elena. "But we'd better get a note pad and pencil and make a list of the most important ones. Damon and Stefan have already agreed to help investigate, and if you'll help, too, we'll stand an even better chance of finding it." She was hitting her stride with this; she'd always been good at organizing things, from schemes to get boys to fund-raising events. This was just a more serious version of the old plan A and plan B.

Meredith gave the pencil and paper to Bonnie, who looked at it, and then at Meredith, and then at Elena. "Fine," she said, "but who goes *on* the list?"

"Well, anyone we have reason to suspect of being the Other Power. Anyone who might have done the things we know it did: seal Stefan in the well, chase me, set those dogs on people. Anyone we've noticed behaving oddly."

"Matt," said Bonnie, writing busily. "And Vickie. And Robert."

"Bonnie!" exclaimed Elena and Meredith simultaneously.

Bonnie looked up. "Well, Matt *has* been acting oddly, and so has Vickie, for months now. And Robert was hanging around outside the church before the service, but he never came in—"

"Oh, Bonnie, honestly," Meredith said. "Vickie's a *victim*, not a suspect. And if Matt's an evil Power, I'm the hunchback of Notre Dame. And as for Robert—"

"Fine, I've crossed it all out," said Bonnie coldly. "Now let's hear *your* ideas."

"No, wait," Elena said. "Bonnie, wait a moment." She was thinking about something, something that had been nagging at her for quite a while, ever since— "Ever since the church," she said aloud, remembering it. "Do you know, I saw Robert outside the church, too, when I was hidden in the choir loft. It was just before the dogs attacked, and he was sort of backing away like he knew what was going to happen."

"Oh, but Elena—"

"No, listen, Meredith. And I saw him before, on Saturday night, with Aunt Judith. When she told him she wouldn't marry him there was something in his face. . . . I don't know. But I think you'd better put him back on the list, Bonnie."

Soberly, after a moment's hesitation, Bonnie did. "Who else?" she said.

"Well, Alaric, I'm afraid," Elena said. "I'm sorry,

Bonnie, but he's practically number one." She told what she had overheard that morning between Alaric and the principal. "He isn't a normal history teacher; they called him here for some reason. He knows I'm a vampire, and he's looking for me. And today, while the dogs were attacking, he was standing there on the sidelines making some kind of weird gestures. He's definitely not what he seems, and the only question is: what *is* he? Are you listening, Meredith?"

"Yes. You know, I think you should put Mrs. Flowers on that list. Remember the way she stood at the window of the boardinghouse when we were bringing Stefan back from the well? But she wouldn't come downstairs to open the door for us? That's odd behavior."

Elena nodded. "Yes, and how she kept hanging up on me when I called him. And she certainly keeps to herself in that old house. She may just be a dotty old lady, but put her down anyway, Bonnie." She ran a hand through her hair, lifting it off the back of her neck. She was hot. Or— not hot exactly, but uncomfortable in some way that was similar to being overheated. She felt parched.

"All right, we'll go by the boardinghouse tomorrow before school," Meredith said. "Meanwhile, what else can we be doing? Let's have a look at that list, Bonnie."

Bonnie held the list out so they could see it, and Elena and Meredith leaned forward and read:

~~Matt Honeycutt~~
~~Vickie Bennett~~
Robert Maxwell—What was he doing at the church when the dogs attacked? And what was going on that night with Elena's aunt?
Alaric Saltzman—Why does he ask so many questions? What was he called to Fell's Church to do?
Mrs. Flowers—Why does she act so strange? Why didn't she let us in the night Stefan was wounded?

"Good," Elena said. "I guess we could also find out whose dogs were at the church today. And you can watch Alaric at school tomorrow."

"*I'll* watch Alaric," Bonnie said firmly. "And I'll get him cleared of suspicion; you see if I don't."

"Fine, you do that. You can be assigned to him. And Meredith can investigate Mrs. Flowers, and I can take Robert. And as for Stefan and Damon—well, they can be assigned to *everyone*, because they can use their Powers to probe people's minds. Besides, that list is by no means complete. I'm going to ask them to scout around town searching for any signs of Power, or anything else weird going on. They're more likely than I am to recognize it."

Sitting back, Elena wet her lips absently. She *was* parched. She noticed something she'd never noticed before: the fine tracery of veins on Bonnie's inner wrist.

Bonnie was still holding the note pad out, and the skin of her wrist was so translucent that the teal blue veins showed clearly through. Elena wished she'd listened when they'd studied human anatomy at school; now what was the name for this vein, the big one that branched like a fork in a tree . . . ?

"Elena. Elena!"

Startled, Elena looked up to see Meredith's wary dark eyes and Bonnie's alarmed expression. It was only then that she realized she was crouched close to Bonnie's wrist, rubbing the biggest vein with her finger.

"Sorry," she murmured, sitting back. But she could feel the extra length and sharpness of her canine teeth. It was something like wearing braces; she could clearly feel the difference in weight. She realized her reassuring smile at Bonnie was not having the desired effect. Bonnie was looking scared, which was silly. Bonnie ought to know that Elena would never hurt her. And Elena wasn't *very* hungry tonight; Elena had always been a light eater. She could get all she needed from this tiny vein here in the wrist. . . .

Elena jumped to her feet and spun toward the window, leaning against the casing, feeling the cool night air blowing on her skin. She felt dizzy, and she couldn't seem to get her breath.

What had she been *doing*? She turned around to see Bonnie huddled close to Meredith, both of them looking sick with fear. She hated having them look at her that way.

"I'm sorry," she said. "I didn't mean to, Bonnie. Look, I'm not coming any closer. I should have eaten before I came here. Damon said I'd get hungry later."

Bonnie swallowed, looking even sicker. "Eaten?"

"Yes, of course," Elena said tartly. Her veins were burning; that was what this feeling was. Stefan had described it before, but she'd never really understood; she'd never realized what he was going through when the need for blood was on him. It was terrible, irresistible. "What do you think I eat these days, air?" she added defiantly. "I'm a hunter now, and I'd better go out hunting."

Bonnie and Meredith were trying to cope; she could tell they were, but she could also see the revulsion in their eyes. She concentrated on using her new senses, in opening herself to the night and searching for Stefan's or Damon's presence. It was difficult, because neither of them was projecting with his mind as he had been the night they'd been fighting in the woods, but she thought she could sense a glimmer of Power out there in the town.

But she had no way to communicate with it, and frustration made the scorching in her veins even worse. She'd just decided that she might have to go without them when the curtains whipped back into her face, flapping in a burst of wind. Bonnie lurched up with a gasp, knocking the reading lamp off the nightstand and plunging the room into darkness. Cursing, Meredith worked to get it righted again. The curtains fluttered madly in the flickering light that emerged, and Bonnie seemed to be trying to scream.

When the bulb was finally screwed back in, it revealed Damon sitting casually but precariously on the sill of the open window, one knee up. He was smiling one of his wildest smiles.

"Do you mind?" he said. "This is uncomfortable."

Elena glanced back at Bonnie and Meredith, who were braced against the closet, looking horrified and hypnotized at once. She herself shook her head, exasperated.

"And I thought *I* liked to make a dramatic entrance," she said. "Very funny, Damon. Now let's go."

"With two such beautiful friends of yours right here?" Damon smiled again at Bonnie and Meredith. "Besides, I only just got here. Won't somebody be polite and ask me in?"

Bonnie's brown eyes, fixed helplessly on his face, softened a bit. Her lips, which had been parted in horror, parted further. Elena recognized the signs of imminent meltdown.

"No, they *won't*," she said. She put herself directly between Damon and the other girls. "Nobody here is for you, Damon—not now, not ever." Seeing the flare of challenge in his eyes, she added archly, "And anyway, I'm leaving. I don't know about *you*, but I'm going hunting." She was reassured to sense Stefan's presence nearby, on the roof probably, and to hear his instant amendment: *We're going hunting, Damon. You can sit there all night if you want.*

Damon gave in with good grace, shooting one last amused glance toward Bonnie before disappearing from the window. Bonnie and Meredith both started forward in alarm as he did, obviously concerned that he had just fallen to his death.

"He's fine," said Elena, shaking her head again. "And don't worry, I won't let him come back. I'll meet you at the same time tomorrow. Good-bye."

"But—Elena—" Meredith stopped. "I mean, I was going to ask you if you wanted to change your clothes."

Elena regarded herself. The nineteenth-century heirloom dress was tattered and bedraggled, the thin white muslin shredded in some places. But there was no time to change it; she had to feed *now.*

"It'll have to wait," she said. "See you tomorrow." And she boosted herself out of the window the way Damon had. The last she saw of them, Meredith and Bonnie were staring after her dazedly.

She was getting better at landings; this time she didn't bruise her knees. Stefan was there, and he wrapped something dark and warm around her.

"Your cloak," she said, pleased. For a moment they smiled at each other, remembering the first time he had given her the cloak, after he'd saved her from Tyler in the graveyard and taken her back to his room to clean up. He'd been afraid to touch her then. But, Elena thought, smiling up into his eyes, she had taken care of that fear rather quickly.

"I thought we were hunting," Damon said.

Elena turned the smile on him, without unlinking her hand from Stefan's. "We are," she said. "Where should we go?"

"Any house on this street," Damon suggested.

"The woods," Stefan said.

"The woods," Elena decided. "We don't touch humans, and we don't kill. Isn't that how it goes, Stefan?"

He returned the pressure of her fingers. "That's how it goes," he said quietly.

Damon's lip curled fastidiously. "And just what are we looking for in the woods, or don't I want to know? Muskrat? Skunk? Termites?" His eyes moved to Elena and his voice dropped. "Come with me, and I'll show you some real hunting."

"We can go through the graveyard," Elena said, ignoring him.

"White-tailed deer feed all night in the open areas," Stefan told her, "but we'll have to be careful stalking them; they can hear almost as well as we can."

Another time, then, Damon's voice said in Elena's mind.

8

"**W**ho—? Oh, it's you!" Bonnie said, starting at the touch on her elbow. "You scared me. I didn't hear you come up."

He'd have to be more careful, Stefan realized. In the few days he'd been away from school, he'd gotten out of the habit of walking and moving like a human and fallen back into the noiseless, perfectly controlled stride of the hunter. "Sorry," he said, as they walked side by side down the corridor.

"S'okay," said Bonnie with a brave attempt at nonchalance. But her brown eyes were wide and rather fixed. "So what are you doing here today? Meredith and I came by the boardinghouse this morning to check on Mrs. Flowers, but nobody answered the door. And I didn't see you in biology."

"I came this afternoon. I'm back at school. For as long as it takes to find what we're looking for anyway."

"To spy on Alaric, you mean," Bonnie muttered. "I told Elena yesterday just to leave him to me. Oops," she added, as a couple of passing juniors stared at her. She rolled her eyes at Stefan. By mutual consent, they turned off into a side corridor and made for an empty stairwell. Bonnie leaned against the wall with a groan of relief.

"I've got to remember not to say her name," she said pathetically, "but it's so *hard*. My mother asked me how I felt this morning and I almost told her, 'fine,' since I saw Elena last night. I don't know how you two kept—you know what—a secret so long."

Stefan felt a grin tugging at his lips in spite of himself. Bonnie was like a six-week-old kitten, all charm and no inhibitions. She always said exactly what she was thinking at the moment, even if it completely contradicted what she'd just said the moment before, but everything she did came from the heart. "You're standing in a deserted hallway with a you-know-what right now," he reminded her devilishly.

"Ohhh." Her eyes widened again. "But you wouldn't, would you?" she added, relieved. "'Because Elena would *kill* you. . . . Oh, dear." Searching for another topic, she gulped and said, "So—so how did things go last night?"

Stefan's mood darkened immediately. "Not so good. Oh, Elena's all right; she's sleeping safely." Before he could go on, his ears picked up footfalls at the end of the corridor. Three senior girls were passing by, and one broke away from the group at the sight of Stefan and Bonnie. Sue Carson's face was pale and her eyes were red-rimmed, but she smiled at them.

Bonnie was full of concern. "Sue, how are you? How's Doug?"

"I'm okay. He's okay, too, or at least he's going to be. Stefan, I wanted to talk to you," she added in a rush. "I know my dad thanked you yesterday for helping Doug the way you did, but I wanted to thank you, too. I mean, I know that people in town have been pretty horrible to you and—well, I'm just surprised you cared enough to help at all. But I'm glad. My mom says you saved Doug's life. And so, I just wanted to thank you, and to say I'm sorry—about everything."

Her voice was shaking by the end of the speech. Bonnie sniffed and groped in her backpack for a tissue, and for a moment it looked as if Stefan was going to be caught on the stairwell with two sobbing females. Dismayed, he racked his brains for a distraction.

"That's all right," he said. "How's Chelsea today?"

"She's at the pound. They're holding the dogs in quarantine there, all the ones they could round up." Sue blotted her eyes and straightened, and Stefan relaxed, seeing that the danger was over. An awkward silence descended.

"Well," said Bonnie to Sue at last, "have you heard what the school board decided about the Snow Dance?"

"I heard they met this morning and they've pretty much decided to let us have it. Somebody said they were talking about a police guard, though. Oh, there's the late bell. We'd better get to history before Alaric hands us all demerits."

"We're coming in a minute," Stefan said. He added casually, "When is this Snow Dance?"

"It's the thirteenth; Friday night, you know," Sue said, and then winced. "Oh my God, Friday the thirteenth. I didn't even think about that. But it reminds me that there was one other thing I wanted to tell you. This morning I took my name out of the running for snow queen. It—it just seemed right, somehow. That's all." Sue hurried away, almost running.

Stefan's mind was racing. "Bonnie, *what* is this Snow Dance?"

"Well, it's the Christmas dance really, only we have a snow queen instead of a Christmas queen. After what happened at Founders' Day, they were thinking of canceling it, and then with the dogs yesterday—but it sounds like they're going to have it after all."

"On Friday the thirteenth," Stefan said grimly.

"Yes." Bonnie was looking scared again, making herself small and inconspicuous. "Stefan, don't look that way; you're frightening me. What's wrong? What do you think will happen at the dance?"

"I don't know." But something would, Stefan was thinking. Fell's Church hadn't had one public celebration that had escaped being visited by the Other Power, and this would probably be the last festivity of the year. But there was no point in talking about it now. "Come on," he said. "We're really late."

He was right. Alaric Saltzman was at the chalkboard when they walked in, as he had been the first day he'd appeared in the history classroom. If he was surprised at seeing them late, or at all, he covered it faultlessly, giving one of his friendliest smiles.

So you're the one who's hunting the hunter, Stefan thought, taking his seat and studying the man before him. But are you anything more than that? Elena's Other Power maybe?

On the face of it, nothing seemed more unlikely. Alaric's sandy hair, worn just a little too long for a teacher, his boyish smile, his stubborn cheerfulness, all contributed to an impression of harmlessness. But Stefan had been wary from the beginning of what was under that inoffensive exterior. Still, it didn't seem very likely that Alaric Saltzman was behind the attack on Elena or the incident with the dogs. No disguise could be that perfect.

Elena. Stefan's hand clenched under his desk, and a slow ache woke in his chest. He hadn't meant to think about her. The only way he had gotten through the last five days was by keeping her at the edge of his mind, not letting her image any closer. But then of course the effort of holding her away at a safe distance took up most of his time and energy. And this was the worst place of all to be, in a classroom where he couldn't care less about what was being taught. There was nothing to do *but* think here.

He made himself breathe slowly, calmly. She was well; that was the important thing. Nothing else really mattered. But even as he told himself this, jealousy bit into him like the thongs of a whip. Because whenever he thought about Elena now, he had to think about *him*.

About Damon, who was free to come and go as he liked. Who might even be with Elena this minute.

Anger burned in Stefan's mind, bright and cold, mingling with the hot ache in his chest. He still wasn't convinced that Damon wasn't the one who had casually thrown him, bleeding and unconscious, into an abandoned well shaft to die. And he would take Elena's idea about the Other Power much more seriously if he was completely sure that Damon hadn't chased Elena to her death. Damon was evil; he had no mercy and no scruples. . . .

And what's he done that I haven't done? Stefan asked himself heavily, for the hundredth time. Nothing.

Except kill.

Stefan had tried to kill. He'd meant to kill Tyler. At the

memory, the cold fire of his anger toward Damon was doused, and he glanced instead toward a desk at the back of the room.

It was empty. Though Tyler had gotten out of the hospital the day before, he hadn't returned to school. Still, there should be no danger of his remembering anything from that grisly afternoon. The subliminal suggestion to forget should hold for quite a while, as long as no one messed with Tyler's mind.

He suddenly became aware that he was staring at Tyler's empty desk with narrow, brooding eyes. As he looked away, he caught the glance of someone who'd been watching him do it.

Matt turned quickly and bent over his history book, but not before Stefan saw his expression.

Don't think about it. Don't think about anything, Stefan told himself, and he tried to concentrate on Alaric Saltzman's lecture about the Wars of the Roses.

December 5—I don't know what time, probably early
afternoon.

Dear Diary,
    Damon got you back for me this morning.
Stefan said he didn't want me going into Alaric's
attic again. This is Stefan's pen I'm using. I don't

own anything anymore, or at least I can't get at any of my own things, and most of them Aunt Judith would miss if I took them. I'm sitting right now in a barn behind the boardinghouse. I can't go where people sleep, you know, unless I've been invited in. I guess animals don't count, because there are some rats sleeping here under the hay and an owl in the rafters. At the moment, we're ignoring each other.

I'm trying very hard not to have hysterics.

I thought writing might help. Something normal, something familiar. Except that nothing in my life is normal anymore.

Damon says I'll get used to it faster if I throw my old life away and embrace the new one. He seems to think it's inevitable that I turn out like him. He says I was born to be a hunter and there's no point in doing things halfway.

I hunted a deer last night. A stag, because it was making the most noise, clashing its antlers against tree branches, challenging other males. I drank its blood.

When I look over this diary, all I can see is that I was searching for something, for someplace to belong. But this isn't it. This new life isn't it. I'm afraid of what I'll become if I do start to belong here.

Oh, God, I'm frightened.

The barn owl is almost pure white, especially when it spreads its wings so you can see the underside. From the back it looks more gold. It has just a little gold around the face. It's staring at me right now because I'm making noises, trying not to cry.

It's funny that I can still cry. I guess it's witches that can't.

It's started snowing outside. I'm pulling my cloak up around me.

Elena tucked the little book close to her body and drew the soft dark velvet of the cloak up to her chin. The barn was utterly silent, except for the minute breathing of the animals that slept there. Outside the snow drifted down just as soundlessly, blanketing the world in muffling stillness. Elena stared at it with unseeing eyes, scarcely noticing the tears that ran down her cheeks.

"And could Bonnie McCullough and Caroline Forbes please stay after class a moment," Alaric said as the last bell rang.

Stefan frowned, a frown that deepened as he saw Vickie Bennett hovering outside the open door of the history room, her eyes shy and frightened. "I'll be right outside," he said meaningfully to Bonnie, who nodded. He added a warning lift of his eyebrows, and she responded with a virtuous look. Catch *me* saying anything I'm not supposed to, the look said.

Going out, Stefan only hoped she could stick to it.

Vickie Bennett was entering as he exited, and he had to step out of her way. But that took him right into the path of Matt, who'd come out the other door and was trying to get down the corridor as fast as possible.

Stefan grabbed his arm without thinking. "Matt, wait."

"Let go of me." Matt's fist came up. He looked at it in apparent surprise, as if not sure what he should be so mad about. But every muscle in his body was fighting Stefan's grip.

"I just want to talk to you. Just for a minute, all right?"

"I don't have a minute," Matt said, and at last his eyes, a lighter, less complicated blue than Elena's, met Stefan's. But there was a blankness in the depths of them that reminded Stefan of the look of someone who'd been hypnotized, or who was under the influence of some Power.

Only it was no Power except Matt's own mind, he realized abruptly. This was what the human brain did to itself when faced with something it simply couldn't deal with. Matt had shut down, turned off.

Testing, Stefan said, "About what happened Saturday night—"

"I don't know what you're talking about. Look, I said I had to go, damn it." Denial was like a fortress behind

Matt's eyes. But Stefan had to try again.

"I don't blame you for being mad. If I were you, I'd be furious. And I know what it's like not to want to think, especially when thinking can drive you crazy." Matt was shaking his head, and Stefan looked around the hallway. It was almost empty, and desperation made him willing to take a risk. He lowered his voice. "But maybe you'd at least like to know that Elena's awake, and she's much—"

"Elena's dead!" Matt shouted, drawing the attention of everyone in the corridor. "And I told you to let go of me!" he added, oblivious of their audience, and shoved Stefan hard. It was so unexpected that Stefan stumbled back against the lockers, almost ending up sprawled on the ground. He stared at Matt, but Matt never even glanced back as he took off down the hallway.

Stefan spent the rest of the time until Bonnie emerged just staring at the wall. There was a poster there for the Snow Dance, and he knew every inch of it by the time the girls came out.

Despite everything Caroline had tried to do to him and Elena, Stefan found he couldn't summon up any hatred of her. Her auburn hair looked faded, her face pinched. Instead of being willowy, her posture just looked wilted, he thought, watching her go.

"Everything okay?" he said to Bonnie, as they fell into step with each other.

"Yes, of course. Alaric just knows we three—Vickie, Caroline, and I—have been through a lot, and he wants *us* to know that he supports us," Bonnie said, but even her dogged optimism about the history teacher sounded a little forced. "None of us told him about anything, though. He's having another get-together at his house next week," she added brightly.

Wonderful, thought Stefan. Normally he might have said something about it, but at that moment he was distracted. "There's Meredith," he said.

"She must be waiting for us—no, she's going down the history wing," Bonnie said. "That's funny, I told her I'd meet her out here."

It was more than funny, thought Stefan. He'd caught only a glimpse of her as she turned the corner, but that glimpse stuck in his mind. The expression on Meredith's face had been calculating, watchful, and her step had been stealthy. As if she were trying to do something without being seen.

"She'll come back in a minute when she sees we're not down there," Bonnie said, but Meredith didn't come back in a minute, or two, or three. In fact, it was almost ten minutes before she appeared, and then she looked startled to see Stefan and Bonnie waiting for her.

"Sorry, I got held up," she said coolly, and Stefan had to admire her self-possession. But he wondered what was behind it, and only Bonnie was in a mood to chat as the three of them left school.

"But last time you used fire," Elena said.

"That was because we were looking for Stefan, for a specific person," Bonnie replied. "This time we're trying to predict the future. If it was just *your* personal future I was trying to predict, I'd look in your palm, but we're trying to find out something general."

Meredith entered the room, carefully balancing a china bowl full to the brim with water. In her other hand, she held a candle. "I've got the stuff," she said.

"Water was sacred to the druids," Bonnie explained, as Meredith placed the dish on the floor and the three girls sat around it.

"Apparently, *everything* was sacred to the druids," said Meredith.

"Shh. Now, put the candle in the candlestick and light it. Then I'm going to pour melted wax into the water, and the shapes it makes will tell me the answers to your questions. My grandmother used melted lead, and she said *her* grandmother used melted silver, but she told me wax would do." When Meredith had lit the candle, Bonnie glanced at it sideways and took a deep breath. "I'm getting scareder and scareder to do this," she said.

"You don't have to," Elena said softly.

"I know. But I want to—this once. Besides, it's not these kind of rituals that scare me; it's getting taken over that's so awful. I *hate* it. It's like somebody else getting into my body."

Elena frowned and opened her mouth, but Bonnie was continuing.

"Anyway, here goes. Turn down the lights, Meredith. Give me a minute to get attuned and then ask your questions."

In the silence of the dim room Elena watched the candlelight flickering over Bonnie's lowered eyelashes and Meredith's sober face. She looked down at her own hands in her lap, pale against the blackness of the sweater and leggings Meredith had lent her. Then she looked at the dancing flame.

"All right," Bonnie said softly and took the candle.

Elena's fingers twined together, clenching hard, but she spoke in a low voice so as not to break the atmosphere. "Who is the Other Power in Fell's Church?"

Bonnie tilted the candle so that the flame licked up its sides. Hot wax streamed down like water into the bowl and formed round globules there.

"I was afraid of that," Bonnie murmured. "That's no answer, nothing. Try a different question."

Disappointed, Elena sat back, fingernails biting into her palms. It was Meredith who spoke.

"Can *we* find this Other Power if we look? And can we defeat it?"

"That's two questions," Bonnie said under her breath as she tilted the candle again. This time the wax formed a circle, a lumpy white ring.

"That's unity! The symbol for people joining hands. It means we can do it if we stick together."

Elena's head jerked up. Those were almost the same words she'd said to Stefan and Damon. Bonnie's eyes were shining with excitement, and they smiled at each other.

"Watch out! You're still pouring," Meredith said.

Bonnie quickly righted the candle, looking into the bowl again. The last spill of wax had formed a thin, straight line.

"That's a sword," she said slowly. "It means sacrifice. We can do it if we stick together, but not without sacrifice."

"What kind of sacrifice?" asked Elena.

"I don't know," Bonnie said, her face troubled. "That's all I can tell you this time." She stuck the candle back in the candleholder.

"Whew," said Meredith, as she got up to turn on the lights. Elena stood, too.

"Well, at least we know we can beat it," she said, tugging up the leggings, which were too long for her. She caught a glimpse of herself in Meredith's mirror. She certainly didn't look like Elena Gilbert the high school fashion plate anymore. Dressed all in black like this, she looked pale and dangerous, like a sheathed sword. Her hair fell haphazardly around her shoulders.

"They wouldn't know me at school," she murmured, with a pang. It was strange that she should care about going to school, but she did. It was because she *couldn't* go, she guessed. And because she'd been queen there so long, she'd run things for so long, that it was almost unbelievable that she could never set foot there again.

"You could go somewhere else," Bonnie suggested. "I mean, after this is all over, you could finish the school year someplace where nobody knows you. Like Stefan did."

"No, I don't think so." Elena was in a strange mood tonight, after spending the day alone in the barn watching the snow. "Bonnie," she said abruptly, "would you look at my palm again? I want you to tell *my* future, my personal future."

"I don't even know if I remember all the stuff my grandmother taught me . . . but, all right, I'll try," Bonnie relented. "There'd just better be no *more* dark strangers on the way, that's all. You've already got all you can handle." She giggled as she took Elena's outstretched hand. "Remember when Caroline asked what you could do with two? I guess you're finding out now, huh?"

"Just read my palm, will you?"

"All right, this is your life line—" Bonnie's stream of patter broke off almost before it was started. She stared at Elena's hand, fear and apprehension in her face. "It should go all the way down to here," she said. "But it's cut off so short. . . ."

She and Elena looked at each other without speaking for a moment, while Elena felt that same apprehension solidify inside herself. Then Meredith broke in.

"Well, naturally it's short," she said. "It just means what happened already, when Elena drowned."

"Yes, of course, that must be it," Bonnie murmured. She let go of Elena's hand and Elena slowly drew back. "That's it, all right," Bonnie said in a stronger voice.

Elena was gazing into the mirror again. The girl who gazed back was beautiful, but there was a sad wisdom about her eyes that the old Elena Gilbert had never had. She realized that Bonnie and Meredith were looking at her.

"That must be it," she said lightly, but her smile didn't touch her eyes.

9

"Well, at least I didn't get taken over," Bonnie said. "But I'm sick of this psychic stuff anyway; I'm tired of the whole thing. That was the last time, absolutely the last."

"All right," said Elena, turning away from the mirror, "let's talk about something else. Did you find anything out today?"

"I talked with Alaric, and he's having another get-together next week," Bonnie replied. "He asked Caroline and Vickie and me if we wanted to be hypnotized to help us deal with what's been happening. But I'm sure he isn't the Other Power, Elena. He's too nice."

Elena nodded. She'd had second thoughts about her suspicions of Alaric herself. Not because he was nice, but because she had spent four days in his attic asleep. Would the Other Power really have let her stay there unharmed? Of course, Damon had said he'd influenced Alaric to forget that she was up there, but would the Other Power have succumbed to Damon's influence? Shouldn't it be far too strong?

Unless its Powers had temporarily burned out, she thought suddenly. The way Stefan's were burning out now. Or unless it had only been *pretending* to be influenced.

"Well, we won't cross him off the list just yet," she said. "We've got to be careful. What about Mrs. Flowers? Did you find out anything about her?"

"No luck," said Meredith. "We went to the boardinghouse this morning, but she didn't answer the door. Stefan said he'd try to track her down in the afternoon."

"If somebody would only invite me *in* there, I could watch her, too," Elena said. "I feel like I'm the only one not doing anything. I think . . ." She paused a moment, considering, and then said, "I think I'll go by home—by Aunt Judith's, I mean. Maybe I'll find Robert hanging around in the bushes or something."

"We'll go with you," Meredith said.

"No, it's better for me to do it alone. Really, it is. I can be very inconspicuous these days."

"Then take your own advice and be careful. It's still snowing hard."

Elena nodded and dropped over the windowsill.

As she approached her house, she saw that a car was just pulling out of the driveway. She melted into the shadows and watched. The headlights illuminated an eerie winter sight: the neighbors' black locust tree, like a bare-branched silhouette, with a white owl sitting in it.

As the car roared past, Elena recognized it. Robert's blue Oldsmobile.

Now, *that* was interesting. She had an urge to follow him, but a stronger urge to check the house, make sure everything was all right. She circled it stealthily, examining windows.

The yellow chintz curtains at the kitchen window were looped back, revealing a bright section of kitchen inside. Aunt Judith was closing the dishwasher. Had Robert come to dinner? Elena wondered.

Aunt Judith moved toward the front hallway and Elena moved with her, circling the house again. She found a slit in the living room curtains and cautiously applied her eye to the thick, wavery old glass of the window. She heard the front door open and shut, and then lock, and then Aunt Judith came into the living room and sat on the couch. She switched on the TV and began flipping through channels idly.

Elena wished she could see more than just her aunt's profile in the flickering light of the TV. It gave her a strange feeling to look at this room, knowing that she could *only* look and not go in. How long had it been since she realized what a nice room it was? The old mahogany whatnot, crowded with china and glassware, the Tiffany lamp on the table next to Aunt Judith, the needlepoint pillows on the couch, all seemed precious to her now. Standing outside, feeling the feathery caress of the snow on the back of her neck, she wished she could go in just for a moment, just for a little while.

Aunt Judith's head was tilting back, her eyes shutting. Elena leaned her forehead against the window, then slowly turned away.

She climbed the quince tree outside her own bedroom, but to her disappointment the curtains were shut tight. The maple tree outside Margaret's room was fragile and harder to climb, but once she got up she had a good view; these curtains were wide open. Margaret was asleep with the bedcovers drawn up to her chin, her mouth open, her pale hair spread out like a fan on the pillow.

Hello, baby, Elena thought and swallowed back tears. It was such a sweetly innocent scene: the nightlight, the little girl in bed, the stuffed animals on the shelves keeping watch over her. And here came a little white kitten padding through the open door to complete the picture, Elena thought.

Snowball jumped onto Margaret's bed. The kitten

yawned, showing a tiny pink tongue, and stretched, displaying miniature claws. Then it walked daintily over to stand on Margaret's chest.

Something tingled at the roots of Elena's hair.

She didn't know if it was some new hunter's sense or sheer intuition, but suddenly she was afraid. There was danger in that room. Margaret was in danger.

The kitten was still standing there, tail swishing back and forth. And all at once Elena realized what it looked like. The dogs. It looked the way Chelsea had looked at Doug Carson before she lunged at him. Oh, God, the town had quarantined the dogs, but nobody had thought about the cats.

Elena's mind was working at top speed, but it wasn't helping her. It was only flashing pictures of what a cat could do with curved claws and needle-sharp teeth. And Margaret just lay there breathing softly, oblivious to any danger.

The fur on Snowball's back was rising, her tail swelling like a bottle brush. Her ears flattened and she opened her mouth in a silent hiss. Her eyes were fixed on Margaret's face just the way Chelsea's had been on Doug Carson's.

"No!" Elena looked around desperately for something to throw at the window, something to make noise. She couldn't get any closer; the outer branches of the tree wouldn't support her weight. "Margaret, wake up!"

But the snow, settling like a blanket around her, seemed to deaden the words into nothingness. A low, discordant wail was started in Snowball's throat as it flicked its eyes toward the window and then back to Margaret's face.

"Margaret, wake up!" Elena shouted. Then, just as the kitten pulled back a curved paw, she threw herself at the window.

She never knew, later, how she managed to hang on. There was no room to kneel on the sill, but her fingernails sank into the soft old wood of the casing, and the toe of one boot jammed into a foothold below. She banged against the window with her body weight, shouting.

"Get away from her! Wake up, Margaret!"

Margaret's eyes flew open and she sat up, throwing Snowball backward. The kitten's claws caught in the eyelet bedspread as it scrambled to right itself. Elena shouted again.

"Margaret, get off the bed! Open the window, quick!"

Margaret's four-year-old face was full of sleepy surprise, but no fear. She got up and stumbled toward the window while Elena gritted her teeth.

"That's it. Good girl . . . now say, 'Come in.' Quick, say it!"

"Come in," Margaret said obediently, blinking and stepping back.

The kitten sprang out as Elena fell in. She made a grab

for it, but it was too fast. Once outside it glided across the maple branches with taunting ease and leaped down into the snow, disappearing.

A small hand was tugging at Elena's sweater. "You came back!" Margaret said, hugging Elena's hips. "I missed you."

"Oh, Margaret, I missed *you*—" Elena began, and then froze. Aunt Judith's voice sounded from the top of the stairs.

"Margaret, are you awake? What's going on in there?"

Elena had only an instant to make her decision. "Don't tell her I'm here," she whispered, dropping to her knees. "It's a secret; do you understand? Say you let the kitty out, but don't tell her I'm here." There wasn't time for any more; Elena dived under the bed and prayed.

From under the dust ruffle, she watched Aunt Judith's stocking feet come into the room. She pressed her face into the floorboards, not breathing.

"Margaret! What are you doing up? Come on, let's get you back in bed," Aunt Judith's voice said, and then the bed creaked with Margaret's weight and Elena heard the noises of Aunt Judith's fussing with the covers. "Your hands are freezing. What on earth is the window doing open?"

"I opened it and Snowball went out," Margaret said. Elena let out her breath.

"And now there's snow all over the floor. I can't believe this. . . . Don't you open it up again, do you hear me?" A little more bustling and the stocking feet went out again. The door shut.

Elena squirmed out.

"Good girl," she whispered as Margaret sat up. "I'm proud of you. Now tomorrow you tell Aunt Judith that you have to give your kitty away. Tell her it scared you. I know you don't want to"—she put up a hand to stop the wail that was gathering on Margaret's lips—"but you have to. Because I'm telling you that kitty will hurt you if you keep it. You don't want to get hurt, do you?"

"No," said Margaret, her blue eyes filling. "But—"

"And you don't want the kitty to hurt Aunt Judith, either, do you? You tell Aunt Judith you can't have a kitten or a puppy or even a bird until—well, for a while. Don't tell her that I said so; that's still our secret. Tell her you're scared because of what happened with the dogs at church." It was better, Elena reasoned grimly, to give the little girl nightmares than to have a nightmare play out in this bedroom.

Margaret's mouth drooped sadly. "Okay."

"I'm sorry, sweetie." Elena sat down and hugged her. "But that's the way it has to be."

"You're cold," Margaret said. Then she looked up into Elena's face. "Are you an angel?"

"Uh . . . not exactly." Just the opposite, Elena thought ironically.

"Aunt Judith said you went to be with Mommy and Daddy. Did you see them yet?"

"I—it's sort of hard to explain, Margaret. I haven't seen them yet, no. And I'm not an angel, but I'm going to be like your guardian angel anyway, all right? I'll watch over you, even when you can't see me. Okay?"

"Okay." Margaret played with her fingers. "Does that mean you can't live here anymore?"

Elena looked around the pink-and-white bedroom, at the stuffed animals on the shelves and the little writing desk and the rocking horse that had once been hers in the corner. "That's what it means," she said softly.

"When they said you went to be with Mommy and Daddy, I said I wanted to go, too."

Elena blinked hard. "Oh, baby. It's not time for you to go, so you can't. And Aunt Judith loves you very much, and she'd be lonely without you."

Margaret nodded, her eyelids drooping. But as Elena eased her down and pulled the bedspread over her, Margaret asked one more question. "But don't *you* love me?"

"Oh, of course I do. I love you so much—I never even knew how much until now. But I'll be all right, and Aunt Judith needs you more. And . . ." Elena had to take a breath to steady herself, and when she looked down she saw Margaret's eyes were shut, her breathing regular. She was asleep.

Oh, stupid, *stupid*, Elena thought, forging through the banked snow to the other side of Maple Street. She'd missed her chance to ask Margaret whether Robert had been at dinner. It was too late now.

Robert. Her eyes narrowed suddenly. At the church, Robert had been outside and then the dogs had gone mad. And tonight Margaret's kitten had gone feral—just a little while after Robert's car had pulled out of the driveway.

Robert has a lot to answer for, she thought.

But melancholy was pulling at her, tugging her thoughts away. Her mind kept returning to the bright house she'd just left, going over the things she'd never see again. All her clothes and knickknacks and jewelry— what would Aunt Judith do with them? I don't own anything anymore, she thought. I'm a pauper.

Elena?

With relief, Elena recognized the mental voice and the distinctive shadow at the end of the street. She hurried toward Stefan, who took his hands out of his jacket pockets and held hers to warm them.

"Meredith told me where you'd gone."

"I went home," Elena said. That was all she could say,

but as she leaned against him for comfort, she knew that he understood.

"Let's find someplace we can sit down," he said, and stopped in frustration. All the places they used to go were either too dangerous or closed to Elena. The police still had Stefan's car.

Eventually they just went to the high school where they could sit under the overhang of a roof and watch the snow sift down. Elena told him what had happened in Margaret's room.

"I'm going to have Meredith and Bonnie spread it around town that cats can attack, too. People should know that. And I think somebody ought to be watching Robert," she concluded.

"We'll tail him," Stefan said, and she couldn't help smiling.

"It's funny how much more American you've gotten," she said. "I hadn't thought about it in a long time, but when you first came you were a lot more foreign. Now nobody would know you hadn't lived here all your life."

"We adapt quickly. We have to," Stefan said. "There are always new countries, new decades, new situations. You'll adapt, too."

"Will I?" Elena's eyes remained on the glitter of falling snowflakes. "I don't know. . . ."

"You'll learn, in time. If there is anything . . . good . . .

about what we are, it's time. We have plenty of it, as much as we want. Forever."

"'Joyous companions forever.' Isn't that what Katherine said to you and Damon?" Elena murmured.

She could feel Stefan's stiffening, his withdrawal. "She was talking about all three of us," he said. "I wasn't."

"Oh, Stefan, please don't, not now. I wasn't even thinking about Damon, only about forever. It scares me. Everything about this scares me, and sometimes I think I just want to go to sleep and never wake up again. . . ."

In the shelter of his arms she felt safer, and she found her new senses were just as amazing close up as they were at a distance. She could hear each separate pulse of Stefan's heart, and the rush of blood through his veins. And she could smell his own distinctive scent mingled with the scent of his jacket, and the snow, and the wool of his clothes.

"Please trust me," she whispered. "I know you're angry with Damon, but try to give him a chance. I think there's more to him than there seems to be. And I want his help in finding the Other Power, and that's *all* I want from him."

At that moment it was completely true. Elena wanted nothing to do with the hunter's life tonight; the darkness held no appeal for her. She wished she could be at home sitting in front of a fire.

But it was sweet just to be held like this, even if she and Stefan had to sit in the snow to do it. Stefan's breath was warm as he kissed the back of her neck, and she sensed no further withdrawal in Stefan's body.

No hunger, either, or at least not the kind she was used to sensing when they were close like this. Now that she was a hunter like he, the need was different, a need for togetherness rather than for sustenance. It didn't matter. They had lost something, but they had gained something, too. She *understood* Stefan in a way she never had before. And her understanding brought them closer, until their minds were touching, almost meshing with each other's. It wasn't the noisy chatter of mental voices; it was a deep and wordless communion. As if their spirits were united.

"I love you," Stefan said against her neck, and she held on tighter. She understood now why he'd been afraid to say it for so long. When the thought of tomorrow scared you sick, it was hard to make a commitment. Because you didn't want to drag someone else down with you.

Particularly someone you loved. "I love you, too," she made herself say and sat back, her peaceful mood broken. "And will you try to give Damon a chance, for my sake? Try to work with him?"

"I'll work with him, but I won't trust him. I can't. I know him too well."

"I sometimes wonder if anybody knows him at all. All

right, then, do what you can. Maybe we can ask him to follow Robert tomorrow."

"I followed Mrs. Flowers today." Stefan's lip quirked.
"All afternoon and evening. And you know what she
did?"

"What?"

"Three loads of wash—in an ancient machine that
looked like it was going to explode any minute. No
clothes dryer, just a wringer. It's all down in the basement.
Then she went outside and filled about two dozen bird
feeders. Then back to the basement to wipe off jars of
preserves. She spends most of her time down there. She
talks to herself."

"Just like a dotty old lady," said Elena. "All right;
maybe Meredith's wrong and that's all she is." She
noticed his change of expression at Meredith's name and
added, "What?"

"Well, Meredith may have some explaining to do herself. I didn't ask her about it; I thought maybe it was better coming from you. But she went to talk to Alaric
Saltzman after school today. And she didn't want anyone
to know where she was going."

Disquiet uncoiled in Elena's middle. "So what?"

"So she lied about it afterward—or at least she evaded
the issue. I tried to probe her mind, but my Powers are
just about burnt out. And she's strong-willed."

"And you had no right! Stefan, listen to me. Meredith would never do anything to hurt us or betray us. Whatever she's keeping from us—"

"So you do admit that she's hiding something."

"Yes," Elena said reluctantly. "But it's nothing that will hurt us, I'm sure. Meredith has been my friend since the first grade. . . ." Without knowing it, Elena let the sentence slip away from her. She was thinking of another friend, one who'd been close to her since kindergarten. Caroline. Who last week had tried to destroy Stefan and humiliate Elena in front of the entire town.

And what was it Caroline's diary had said about Meredith? *Meredith doesn't* do *anything; she just watches. It's as if she can't act, she can only react to things. Besides, I've heard my parents talking about her family—no wonder she never mentions them.*

Elena's eyes left the snowy landscape to seek Stefan's waiting face. "It doesn't matter," she said quietly. "I know Meredith, and I trust her. I'll trust her to the end."

"I hope she's worthy of it, Elena," he said. "I really do."

10

December 12, Thursday morning

ear Diary,
So after a week of work, what have we accomplished?

Well, between us we've managed to follow our three suspects just about continuously for the last six or seven days. Results: reports on Robert's movements for the last week, which he spent acting like any normal businessman. Reports on Alaric, who hasn't been doing anything unusual for a history teacher. Reports on Mrs. Flowers, who apparently spends most of her time in the basement. But we haven't really learned anything.

Stefan says that Alaric met with the principal a

couple times, but he couldn't get close enough to hear what they were talking about.

Meredith and Bonnie spread the news about other pets besides dogs being dangerous. They didn't need to work very hard at it; it seems as if everybody in town is on the verge of hysteria already. Since then there've been several other animal attacks reported, but it's hard to know which ones to take seriously. Some kids were teasing a squirrel and it bit them. The Massases' pet rabbit scratched their littlest boy. Old Mrs. Coomber saw copperhead snakes in her yard, when all the snakes should be hibernating.

The only one I'm sure about is the attack on the vet who was keeping the dogs in quarantine. A bunch of them bit him and most of them escaped from the holding pens. After that they just disappeared. People are saying good riddance and hoping they'll starve in the woods, but I wonder.

And it's been snowing all the time. Not storming but not stopping, either. I've never seen so much snow.

Stefan's worried about the dance tomorrow night.

Which brings us back to: what have we learned so far? What do we know? None of our suspects

were anywhere near the Massases' or Mrs.
Coomber's or the vet's when the attacks happened.
We're no closer to finding the Other Power than we
were when we started.

Alaric's little get-together is tonight. Meredith
thinks we should go to it. I don't know what else
there is to do.

Damon stretched out his long legs and spoke lazily, looking around the barn. "No, I don't think it's dangerous,
particularly. But I don't see what you expect to accomplish."

"Neither do I, exactly," Elena admitted. "But I don't
have any better ideas. Do you?"

"What, you mean about other ways to spend the time?
Yes, I do. Do you want me to tell you about them?" Elena
waved him to silence and he subsided.

"I mean about useful things we can do at this point.
Robert's out of town, Mrs. Flowers is down—"

"In the basement," chorused several voices.

"And we're all just sitting here. *Does* anybody have a
better idea?"

Meredith broke the silence. "If you're worried about
its being dangerous for me and Bonnie, why don't you *all*
come? I don't mean you have to show yourselves. You
could come and hide in the attic. Then if anything happened, we could scream for help and you would hear us."

"I don't see why anybody's going to be screaming," said Bonnie. "Nothing's going to happen there."

"Well, maybe not, but it doesn't hurt to be safe," Meredith said. "What do you think?"

Elena nodded slowly. "It makes sense." She looked around for objections, but Stefan just shrugged, and Damon murmured something that made Bonnie laugh.

"All right, then, it's decided. Let's go."

The inevitable snow greeted them as they stepped outside the barn.

"Bonnie and I can go in my car," Meredith said. "And you three—"

"Oh, we'll find our own way," Damon said with his wolfish smile. Meredith nodded, not impressed. Funny, Elena thought as the other girls walked away; Meredith never *was* impressed with Damon. His charm seemed to have no effect on her.

She was about to mention that she was hungry when Stefan turned to Damon.

"Are you willing to stay with Elena the entire time you're over there? Every minute?" he said.

"Try and stop me," Damon said cheerfully. He dropped the smile. "Why?"

"Because if you are, the two of you can go over alone, and I'll meet you later. I've got something to do, but it won't take long."

Elena felt a wave of warmth. He was trying to trust his brother. She smiled at Stefan in approval as he drew her aside.

"What is it?"

"I got a note from Caroline today. She asked if I would meet her at the school before Alaric's party. She said she wanted to apologize."

Elena opened her mouth to make a sharp remark, and then shut it again. From what she'd heard, Caroline was a sorry sight these days. And maybe it would make Stefan feel better to talk to her.

"Well, *you* don't have anything to apologize for," she told him. "Everything that happened to her was her own fault. You don't think she's dangerous at all?"

"No; I've got that much of my Powers left anyway. She's all right. I'll meet her, and she and I can go to Alaric's together."

"Be careful," Elena said as he started off into the snow.

The attic was as she remembered it, dark and dusty and full of mysterious oilcloth-covered shapes. Damon, who had come in more conventionally through the front door, had had to take the shutters off to let her in through the window. After that they sat side by side on the old mattress and listened to the voices that came up through the ducts.

"I could think of more romantic settings," Damon

murmured, fastidiously pulling a cobweb off his sleeve. "Are you sure you wouldn't rather—"

"Yes," said Elena. "Now hush."

It was like a game, listening to the bits and pieces of conversations and trying to put them together, trying to match each voice to a face.

"And then I said, I don't care how long you've had the parakeet; get rid of it or I'm going to the Snow Dance with Mike Feldman. And he said—"

"—rumor going around that Mr. Tanner's grave was dug up last night—"

"—you hear that everybody but Caroline has dropped out of the snow queen competition? Don't you think—"

"—dead, but I'm telling you I *saw* her. And no, I wasn't dreaming; she was wearing a sort of silvery dress and her hair was all golden and blowing—"

Elena raised her eyebrows at Damon, then looked meaningfully down at her sensible black attire. He grinned.

"Romanticism," he said. "Myself, I like you in black."

"Well, you would, wouldn't you?" she murmured. It was strange how much more comfortable she felt with Damon these days. She sat quietly, letting the conversations drift around her, almost losing track of time. Then she caught a familiar voice, cross, and closer than the rest.

"Okay, okay, I'm *going*. Okay."

Elena and Damon exchanged a glance and rose to their

feet as the handle on the attic door turned. Bonnie peered around the edge.

"Meredith told me to come up here. I don't know why. She's hogging Alaric and it's a rotten party. Achoo!"

She sat down on the mattress, and after a few minutes Elena sat back down beside her. She was beginning to wish that Stefan would get here. By the time the door opened again and Meredith came in, she was sure of it.

"Meredith, what's going on?"

"Nothing, or at least nothing to worry about. Where's Stefan?" Meredith's cheeks were unusually flushed, and there was an odd look about her eyes, as if she were holding something tightly under control.

"He's coming later—" Elena began, but Damon interrupted.

"Never mind where he is. Who's coming up the stairs?"

"What do you mean, 'who's coming up the stairs?'" said Bonnie, rising.

"Everybody just stay *calm*," Meredith said, taking up a position in front of the window as if guarding it. She didn't look overly calm herself, Elena thought. "All right," she called, and the door opened and Alaric Saltzman came in.

Damon's motion was so smooth that even Elena's eyes couldn't follow it; in one movement he caught Elena's wrist and pulled her behind him, at the same time moving to face Alaric directly. He ended in a predator's crouch, every muscle drawn taut and ready for the attack.

"Oh, don't," cried Bonnie wildly. She flung herself at Alaric, who had already begun to recoil a step from Damon. Alaric nearly lost his balance and groped behind himself for the door. His other hand was groping at his belt.

"Stop it! Stop it!" Meredith said. Elena saw the shape beneath Alaric's jacket and realized it was a gun.

Again, she couldn't quite follow what happened next. Damon let go of her wrist and took hold of Alaric's. And then Alaric was sitting on the floor, wearing a dazed expression, and Damon was emptying the gun of cartridges, one by one.

"I *told* you that was stupid and you wouldn't need it," Meredith said. Elena realized she was holding the dark-haired girl by the arms. She must have done it to keep Meredith from interfering with Damon, but she didn't remember.

"These wood-tipped things are nasty; they might hurt somebody," Damon said, mildly chiding. He replaced one of the cartridges and snapped the clip back in, aiming thoughtfully at Alaric.

"Stop it," said Meredith intensely. She turned to Elena. "Make him stop, Elena; he's only doing more harm. Alaric won't hurt you; I promise. I've spent all week convincing him that *you* won't hurt *him*."

"And now I think my wrist is broken," Alaric said, rather calmly. His sandy hair was falling into his eyes in front.

"You've got no one but yourself to blame," Meredith returned bitterly. Bonnie, who had been clutching solicitously at Alaric's shoulders, looked up at the familiarity of Meredith's tone, and then backed away a few paces and sat down.

"I can't wait to hear the explanation for *this*," she said.

"Please trust me," Meredith said to Elena.

Elena looked into the dark eyes. She did trust Meredith; she'd said so. And the words stirred another memory, her own voice asking for Stefan's trust. She nodded.

"Damon?" she said. He flipped the gun away casually and then smiled around at all of them, making it abundantly clear that he didn't need any such artificial weapons.

"Now if everybody will just listen, you'll all understand," Meredith said.

"Oh, I'm *sure*," Bonnie said.

Elena walked toward Alaric Saltzman. She wasn't afraid of him, but by the way he looked only at her, slowly, starting from the feet and then continuing up, he was afraid of her.

She stopped when she was a yard from where he sat on the ground and knelt there, looking into his face.

"Hello," she said.

He was still holding his wrist. "Hello," he said, and gulped.

Elena glanced back at Meredith and then looked at Alaric again. Yes, he was scared. And with his hair in his eyes that way, he looked young. Maybe four years older than Elena, maybe five. No more than that.

"We're not going to hurt you," she said.

"That's what I've been telling him," Meredith said quietly. "I explained that whatever he's seen before, whatever stories he's heard, you're different. I told him what you told me about Stefan, how he's been fighting his nature all those years. I told him about what you've been going through, Elena, and how you never asked for this."

But *why* did you tell him so much? Elena thought. She said to Alaric, "All right, you know about us. But all we know about you is that you're not a history teacher."

"He's a hunter," Damon said softly, menacingly. "A vampire hunter."

"*No,*" said Alaric. "Or at least, not in the sense that you mean it." He seemed to come to some decision. "All right. From what I know of you three—" He broke off, looking around the dark room as if suddenly realizing something. "Where's Stefan?"

"He's coming. In fact, he should be here by now. He was going to stop by the school and bring Caroline," Elena said. She was unprepared for Alaric's reaction.

"Caroline Forbes?" he said sharply, sitting up. His voice sounded the way it had when she'd overheard him talking with Dr. Feinberg and the principal, hard-edged and decisive.

"Yes. She sent him a note today, said she wanted to apologize or something. She wanted to meet him at school before the party."

"He can't go. You've got to stop him." Alaric scrambled to his feet and repeated urgently, "You've got to stop him."

"He's gone already. Why? Why shouldn't he?" Elena demanded.

"Because I hypnotized Caroline two days ago. I'd tried it earlier with Tyler, with no luck. But Caroline's a good subject, and she remembered a little of what happened in the Quonset hut. And she identified Stefan Salvatore as the attacker."

The shocked silence lasted only a fraction of a second. Then Bonnie said, "But what can Caroline do? She can't hurt him—"

"Don't you understand? You're not just dealing with high school students anymore," Alaric said. "It's gone too far. Caroline's father knows about it, and Tyler's father.

They're concerned for the safety of the town—"

"Hush! Be quiet!" Elena was casting about with her mind, trying to pick up some hint of Stefan's presence. He's let himself get weak, she thought, with the part of her that was icy calm amid the whirling fear and panic. At last she sensed something, just a trace, but she thought it was Stefan. And it was in distress.

"Something's wrong," Damon confirmed, and she realized he must have been searching, too, with a mind much more powerful than hers. "Let's go."

"Wait, let's talk first. Don't just go jumping into this." But Alaric might as well have been talking to the wind, trying to rein in its destructive power with words. Damon was already at the window, and the next moment Elena let herself drop out, landing neatly by Damon in the snow. Alaric's voice followed them from above.

"We're coming, too. *Wait* for us there. Let me talk to them first. I can take care of it. . . ."

Elena scarcely heard him. Her mind was burning with one purpose, one thought. To hurt the people who wanted to hurt Stefan. It's gone too far, all right, she thought. And now *I'm* going to go as far as it takes. If they dare to touch him . . . images flashed through her mind, too quickly to count, of what she would do to them. At another time, she might have been shocked at the rush of adrenaline, of excitement, that coursed up at the thoughts.

She could sense Damon's mind beside her as they raced over the snow; it was like a blaze of red light and fury. The fierceness inside Elena welcomed it, glad to feel it so near. But then something else occurred to her.

"I'm slowing you down," she said. She was scarcely out of breath, even from running through unbroken snow, and they were making extraordinary time. But nothing on two legs, or even four, could match the speed of a bird's wings. "Go on," she said. "Get there as fast as you can. I'll meet you."

She didn't stay to watch the blur and shudder of the air, or the swirling darkness that ended in the rush of beating wings. But she glanced up at the crow that soared up and she heard Damon's mental voice.

Good hunting, it said, and the winged black shape arrowed toward the school.

Good hunting, Elena thought after him, meaning it. She redoubled her speed, her mind fixed all the while on that glimmer of Stefan's presence.

Stefan lay on his back, wishing his vision wasn't so blurred or that he had more than a tentative hold on consciousness. The blur was partly pain and partly snow, but there was also a trickle of blood from the three-inch wound in his scalp.

He'd been stupid, of course, not to look around the

school; if he had he would have seen the darkened cars parked on the other side. He'd been stupid to come here in the first place. And now he was going to pay for that stupidity.

If only he could collect his thoughts enough to call for help . . . but the weakness that had allowed these men to overcome him so easily prevented that, too. He'd scarcely fed since the night he'd attacked Tyler. That was ironic, somehow. His own guilt was responsible for the mess he was in.

I should never have tried to change my nature, he thought. Damon had it right after all. Everyone's the same—Alaric, Caroline, everyone. Everyone will betray you. I should have hunted them all and enjoyed it.

He hoped Damon would take care of Elena. She'd be safe with him; Damon was strong and ruthless. Damon would teach her to survive. He was glad of that.

But something inside him was crying.

The crow's sharp eyes spotted the crossing shafts of headlight below and dropped. But Damon didn't need the confirmation of sight; he was homing in on the faint pulsation that was Stefan's life-force. Faint because Stefan was weak and because he'd all but given up.

You never learn, do you, brother? Damon thought to him. *I ought to just leave you where you are.* But even as he skimmed the ground, he was changing, taking a shape that would do more damage than a crow.

The black wolf leaped into the knot of men surrounding Stefan, aiming precisely for the one holding the sharpened cylinder of wood above Stefan's chest. The force of the blow knocked the man ten feet backward, and the stake went skittering across the grass. Damon restrained his impulse—all the stronger because it fit the instincts of the shape he was wearing—to lock his teeth in the man's throat. He twisted around and went back for the other men who were still standing.

His second rush scattered them, but one of them reached the edge of the light and turned, lifting something to his shoulder. Rifle, thought Damon. And probably loaded with the same specially treated bullets as Alaric's handgun had been. There was no way to reach the man before he could get a shot off. The wolf growled and crouched for a leap anyway. The man's fleshy face creased in a smile.

Quick as a striking snake, a white hand reached out of the darkness and knocked the rifle away. The man looked around frantically, bewildered, and the wolf let its jaws fall open in a grin. Elena had arrived.

11

lena watched Mr. Smallwood's rifle bounce across the grass. She enjoyed the expression on his face as he spun around, looking for what had grabbed it. And she felt the flare of Damon's approval from across the pool of light, fierce and hot like the pride of a wolf for its cub's first kill. But when she glimpsed Stefan lying on the ground, she forgot everything else. White fury took her breath away, and she started toward him.

"Everybody stop! Just stop everything, right where you are!"

The shout was borne toward them along with the sound of tires squealing. Alaric Saltzman's car nearly spun out as it turned into the staff parking lot and screeched to a halt, and Alaric leaped from the car almost before it stopped moving.

"What's going on here?" he demanded, striding toward the men.

At the shout, Elena had pulled back automatically into the shadows. Now, she looked at the men's faces as they turned toward him. Besides Mr. Smallwood, she recognized Mr. Forbes and Mr. Bennett, Vickie Bennett's father. The others must be the fathers of the other guys who'd been with Tyler in the Quonset hut, she thought.

It was one of the strangers who answered the question, in a drawl that couldn't quite hide the nervousness underneath. "Well now, we just got a little tired of waiting any longer. We decided to speed things up a bit."

The wolf growled, a low rumbling that rose to a chainsaw snarl. All the men flinched back, and Alaric's eyes showed white as he noticed the animal for the first time.

There was another sound, softer and continuous, coming from a figure huddled next to one of the cars. Caroline Forbes was whimpering over and over, "They said they just wanted to talk to him. They didn't tell me what they were going to do."

Alaric, with one eye on the wolf, gestured toward her. "And you were going to let her see *this*? A young girl? Do you realize the psychological damage that could do?"

"What about the psychological damage when her throat gets ripped out?" Mr. Forbes returned, and there were shouts of agreement. "That's what *we're* worried about."

"Then you'd better worry about getting the right man," Alaric said. "Caroline," he added, turning toward the girl, "I want you to think, Caroline. We didn't get to finish your sessions. I know when we left off you thought you recognized Stefan. But, are you absolutely positive it was him? Could it have been somebody else, somebody who resembled him?"

Caroline straightened, bracing herself against the car and raising a tear-stained face. She looked at Stefan, who was just sitting up, and then at Alaric. "I . . ."

"Think, Caroline. You have to be absolutely certain. Is there someone else it could have been, like—"

"Like that guy who calls himself Damon Smith," came Meredith's voice. She was standing beside Alaric's car, a slim shadow. "You remember him, Caroline? He came to Alaric's first party. He looks like Stefan in some ways."

Tension held Elena in perfect suspension as Caroline stared, uncomprehending. Then, slowly, the auburn-haired girl began to nod.

"Yes . . . it could have been, I suppose. Everything happened so fast . . . but it could have been."

"And you really can't be sure which it was?" Alaric said.

"No . . . not absolutely sure."

"There," said Alaric. "I told you she needed more sessions, that we couldn't be certain of anything yet. She's still very confused." He was walking, carefully, toward

Stefan. Elena realized that the wolf had withdrawn back into the shadows. She could see it, but the men probably couldn't.

Its disappearance made them more aggressive. "What are you talking about? Who is this Smith? I've never seen him."

"But your daughter Vickie probably has, Mr. Bennett," Alaric said. "That may come out in my next session with her. We'll talk about it tomorrow; it can wait that long. Right now I think I'd better take Stefan to a hospital." There was discomforted shifting among some of the men.

"Oh, certainly, and while we're waiting anything could happen," began Mr. Smallwood. "Anytime, anywhere—"

"So you're just going to take the law into your own hands, then?" Alaric said. His voice sharpened. "Whether you've got the right suspect or not. Where's your evidence this boy has supernatural powers? What's your proof? How much of a fight did he even put up?"

"There's a wolf around somewhere who put up plenty of fight," Mr. Smallwood said, red-faced. "Maybe they're in it together."

"I don't see any wolf. I saw a dog. Maybe one of the dogs that got out of quarantine. But what's that got to do with it? I'm telling you that in my professional opinion you've got the wrong man."

The men were wavering, but there was still some

doubt in their faces. Meredith spoke up.

"I think you should know that there've been vampire attacks in this county before," she said. "A long time before Stefan came here. My grandfather was a victim. Maybe some of you have heard about that." She looked across at Caroline.

That was the end of it. Elena could see the men exchanging uneasy glances and backing toward their cars. Suddenly they all seemed eager to be somewhere else.

Mr. Smallwood was one who stayed behind to say, "You said we'd talk about this tomorrow, Saltzman. I want to hear what my son says the next time *he's* hypnotized."

Caroline's father collected her and got in his car fast, muttering something about this all being a mistake and nobody taking it too seriously.

As the last car pulled away, Elena ran to Stefan.

"Are you all right? Did they hurt you?"

He moved away from Alaric's supporting arm. "Somebody hit me from behind while I was talking to Caroline. I'll be all right—now." He shot a glance at Alaric. "Thanks. Why?"

"He's on our side," said Bonnie, joining them. "I told you. Oh, Stefan, are you really okay? I thought I was going to faint there for a minute. They weren't serious. I mean, they couldn't really have been *serious*. . . ."

"Serious or not, I don't think we should stay here," said

Meredith. "Does Stefan really need a hospital?"

"No," Stefan said, as Elena anxiously examined the cut on his head. "I just need rest. Somewhere to sit down."

"I've got my keys. Let's go to the history room," Alaric said.

Bonnie was looking around the shadows apprehensively. "The wolf, too?" she said, and then jumped as a shadow coalesced and became Damon.

"What wolf?" he said. Stefan turned slightly, wincing.

"Thank you, too," he said unemotionally. But Stefan's eyes lingered on his brother with something like puzzlement as they walked to the school building.

In the hallway, Elena pulled him aside. "Stefan, *why* didn't you notice them coming up behind you? Why were you so weak?"

Stefan shook his head evasively, and she added, "When did you feed last? Stefan, *when*? You always make some excuse when I'm around. What are you trying to do to yourself?"

"I'm all right," he said. "Really, Elena. I'll hunt later."

"Do you *promise*?"

"I promise."

It didn't occur to Elena at the moment that they hadn't agreed on what "later" meant. She allowed him to lead her on down the hall.

The history room looked different at night to Elena's eyes. There was a strange atmosphere about it, as if the lights were too bright. Just now all the students' desks were shoved out of the way, and five chairs were pulled up to Alaric's desk. Alaric, who'd just finished arranging the furniture, urged Stefan into his own padded chair.

"Okay, why don't the rest of you take a seat."

They just looked at him. After a moment Bonnie sank down into a chair, but Elena stood by Stefan, Damon continued to lounge halfway between the group and the door, and Meredith pushed some papers to the center of Alaric's desk and perched on the corner.

The teacher look faded from Alaric's eyes. "All right," he said and sat down in one of the students' chairs himself. "Well."

"Well," said Elena.

Everyone looked at everyone else. Elena picked up a piece of cotton from the first-aid kit she'd grabbed at the door and began dabbing Stefan's head with it.

"I think it's time for that explanation," she said.

"Right. Yes. Well, you all seemed to have guessed I'm not a history teacher. . . ."

"In the first five minutes," Stefan said. His voice was quiet and dangerous, and with a jolt Elena realized it reminded her of Damon's. "So what are you?"

Alaric made an apologetic gesture and said almost

diffidently, "A psychologist. Not the couch kind," he added hastily as the rest of them exchanged looks. "I'm a researcher, an experimental psychologist. From Duke University. You know, where the ESP experiments were started."

"The ones where they make you guess what's on the card without looking at it?" Bonnie asked.

"Yes, well, it's gone a bit beyond that now, of course. Not that I wouldn't love to test you with Rhine cards, especially when you're in one of those trances." Alaric's face lit with scientific inquiry. Then he cleared his throat and went on. "But—ah—as I was saying. It started a couple of years ago when I did a paper on parapsychology. I wasn't trying to prove supernatural powers existed, I just wanted to study what their psychological effect is on the people who have them. Bonnie, here, is a case in point." Alaric's voice took on a lecturer's tone. "What does it do to her, mentally, emotionally, to have to deal with these powers?"

"It's awful," Bonnie interrupted vehemently. "I don't want them anymore. I *hate* them."

"Well, there you see," Alaric said. "You'd have made a great case study. My problem was that I couldn't find anybody with real psychic powers to examine. There were plenty of fakers, all right—crystal healers, dowsers, channelers, you name it. But I couldn't find anything genuine until I got a tip from a friend in the police department.

"There was this woman down in South Carolina who claimed she'd been bitten by a vampire, and since then she was having psychic nightmares. By that time I was so used to fakes I expected her to turn out to be one, too. But she wasn't, at least not about being bitten. I never could prove she was really psychic."

"How could you be sure she'd been bitten?" Elena asked.

"There was medical evidence. Traces of saliva in her wounds that were similar to human saliva—but not quite the same. It contained an anticoagulatory agent similar to that found in the saliva of leeches. . . ." Alaric caught himself and hurried on. "Anyway, I was sure. And that was how it started. Once I was convinced something had really happened to the woman, I started to look up other cases like hers. There weren't a lot of them, but they were out there. People who'd encountered vampires.

"I dropped all my other studies and concentrated on finding victims of vampires and examining them. And if I say so myself, I've become the foremost expert in the field," Alaric concluded modestly. "I've written a number of papers—"

"But you've never actually seen a vampire," Elena interrupted. "Until now, I mean. Is that right?"

"Well—no. Not in the flesh, as it were. But I've written

monographs . . . and things." His voice trailed off.

Elena bit her lip. "What were you doing with the dogs?" she asked. "At the church, when you were waving your hands at them."

"Oh . . ." Alaric looked embarrassed. "I've picked up a few things here and there, you know. That was a spell an old mountain man showed me for fending off evil. I thought it might work."

"You've got a lot to learn," said Damon.

"Obviously," Alaric said stiffly. Then he grimaced. "Actually, I figured that out right after I got here. Your principal, Brian Newcastle, had heard of me. He knew about the studies I do. When Tanner was killed and Dr. Feinberg found no blood in the body and lacerations made by teeth in the neck . . . well, they gave me a call. I thought it could be a big break for me—a case with the vampire still in the area. The only problem was that once I got here I realized they expected *me* to take care of the vampire. They didn't know I'd dealt only with the victims before. And . . . well, maybe I was in over my head. But I did my best to justify their confidence—"

"You faked it," Elena accused. "That was what you were doing when I heard you talking to them at your house about finding our supposed lair and all that. You were just winging it."

"Well, not *completely*," Alaric said. "Theoretically, I *am* an expert." Then he did a double take. "What do you mean, when you heard me talking to them?"

"While you were out searching for a lair, she was sleeping in your attic," Damon informed him dryly. Alaric opened his mouth and then shut it again.

"What I'd like to know is how Meredith comes into all this," Stefan said. He wasn't smiling.

Meredith, who had been gazing thoughtfully at the jumble of papers on Alaric's desk during all this, looked up. She spoke evenly, without emotion.

"I recognized him, you see. I couldn't remember where I'd seen him at first, because it was almost three years ago. Then I realized it was at Granddad's hospital. What I told those men was the truth, Stefan. My grandfather was attacked by a vampire."

There was a little silence and then Meredith went on. "It happened a long time ago, before I was born. He wasn't badly hurt by it, but he never really got well. He became . . . well, sort of like Vickie, only more violent. It got so that they were afraid he'd harm himself, or somebody else. So they took him to a hospital, a place he'd be safe."

"A mental institution," Elena said. She felt a pang of sympathy for the dark-haired girl. "Oh, Meredith. But why didn't you say anything? You could have told us."

"I know. I could have . . . but I couldn't. The family's

kept it a secret so long—or tried anyway. From what Caroline wrote in her diary, she'd obviously heard. The thing is, nobody ever believed Granddad's stories about the vampire. They just thought it was another of his delusions, and he had a lot of them. Even I didn't believe them . . . until Stefan came. And then—I don't know, my mind started to put little things together. But I didn't really *believe* what I was thinking until you came back, Elena."

"I'm surprised you didn't hate me," Elena said softly.

"How could I? I *know* you, and I know Stefan. I know you're not evil." Meredith didn't glance at Damon; he might as well not have been present for all the acknowledgment she gave him. "But when I remembered seeing Alaric talking to Granddad at the hospital I knew *he* wasn't, either. I just didn't know exactly how to get all of you together to prove it."

"I didn't recognize you, either," Alaric said. "The old man had a different name—he's your mother's father, right? And I may have seen you hanging around the waiting room sometime, but you were just a kid with skinny legs then. You've changed," he added appreciatively.

Bonnie coughed, a pointed sound.

Elena was trying to arrange things in her mind. "So what were those men doing out there with a stake if you didn't tell them to be?"

"I had to ask Caroline's parents for permission to hypnotize her, of course. And I reported what I found to them. But if you're thinking I had anything to do with what happened tonight, you're wrong. I didn't even know about it."

"I've told him about what we've been doing, how we've been looking for the Other Power," Meredith said. "And he wants to help."

"I said I *might* help," Alaric said cautiously.

"Wrong," said Stefan. "You're either with us or against us. I'm grateful for what you did out there, talking to those men, but the fact remains that you started a lot of this trouble in the first place. Now you have to decide: are you on our side—or theirs?"

Alaric looked around at each of them, at Meredith's steady gaze and Bonnie's raised eyebrows, at Elena kneeling on the floor and at Stefan's already-healing scalp. Then he turned to glance at Damon, who was leaning against the wall, dark and saturnine. "I'll help," he said at last. "Hell, it's the ultimate case study."

"All right, then," Elena said. "You're in. Now, what about Mr. Smallwood tomorrow? What if he wants you to hypnotize Tyler again?"

"I'll stall him," Alaric said. "It won't work forever, but it'll buy some time. I'll tell him I've got to help with the dance—"

"Wait," said Stefan. "There shouldn't *be* a dance, not if there's any way to prevent it. You're on good terms with the principal; you can talk to the school board. Make them cancel it."

Alaric looked startled. "You think something's going to happen?"

"Yes," Stefan said. "Not just because of what's happened at the other public functions, but because something's building up. It's been building up all week; I can feel it."

"So can I," Elena said. She hadn't realized it until that moment, but the tension she felt, the sense of urgency, was not just from inside her. It was outside, all around. It thickened the air. "Something's going to happen, Alaric."

Alaric let out his breath in a soft whistle. "Well, I can try to convince them, but—I don't know. Your principal is dead set on keeping everything looking normal. And it isn't as if I can give any rational explanation for wanting to shut it down."

"Try *hard*," Elena said.

"I will. And meanwhile, maybe you should think about protecting yourself. If what Meredith says is right, then most of the attacks have been on you and people close to you. *Your* boyfriend got dropped in a well; your car got chased into the river; your memorial service was broken up. Meredith says even your little sister was threatened.

If something's going to happen tomorrow, you might want to leave town."

It was Elena's turn to be startled. She had never thought of the attacks in that way, but it was true. She heard Stefan's indrawn breath and felt his fingers tighten on hers.

"He's right," Stefan said. "You should leave, Elena. I can stay here until—"

"*No.* I'm not going without you. And," Elena continued, slowly, thinking it out, "I'm not going *anywhere* until we find the Other Power and stop it." She looked up at him earnestly, speaking quickly now. "Oh, Stefan, don't you see, nobody else even has a chance against it. Mr. Smallwood and his friends don't have a clue. Alaric thinks you can fight it by waving your hands at it. *None* of them know what they're up against. We're the only ones who can help."

She could see the resistance in Stefan's eyes and feel it in the tenor of his muscles. But as she kept on looking straight at him, she saw his objections fall one by one. For the simple reason that it was the truth, and Stefan hated lying.

"All right," he said at last, painfully. "But as soon as this is all over, we're leaving. I'm not having you stay in a town where vigilantes run around with stakes."

"Yes." Elena returned the pressure of his fingers with

hers. "Once this is all over, we'll go."

Stefan turned to Alaric. "And if there's no way to talk them out of having the dance tomorrow, I think we should keep an eye on it. If something does happen, we may be able to stop it before it gets out of hand."

"That's a good idea," Alaric said, perking up. "We could meet tomorrow after dark here in the history room. Nobody comes here. We could keep up a watch all night."

Elena tilted a doubtful eye toward Bonnie.

"Well . . . it would mean missing the dance itself—for those of us who could have gone, I mean."

Bonnie drew herself up. "Oh, who cares about missing a *dance*?" she said indignantly. "What on earth does a *dance* matter to anyone?"

"Right," said Stefan gravely. "Then it's settled." A spasm of pain seemed to overtake him and he winced, looking down. Elena was immediately concerned.

"You need to get home and rest," she said. "Alaric, can you drive us? It's not that far."

Stefan protested that he was perfectly able to walk, but in the end he gave in. At the boardinghouse, after Stefan and Damon had gotten out of the car, Elena leaned in Alaric's window for one last question. It had been gnawing at her mind ever since Alaric had told them his story.

"About those people who'd encountered vampires," she said. "Just what were the psychological effects? I mean, did they all go crazy or have nightmares? Were any of them okay?"

"It depends on the individual," Alaric said. "And with how many contacts they'd had, and what kind of contacts they were. But mostly just with the personality of the victim, with how well the individual mind can cope."

Elena nodded, and said nothing until the lights of Alaric's car had been swallowed by the snowy air. Then she turned to Stefan.

"Matt."

12

tefan looked at Elena, snow crystals dusting his dark hair. "What about Matt?"

"I remember—something. It's not clear. But that first night, when I wasn't myself—did I see Matt then? Did I—?"

Fear and a sick sense of dismay swelled her throat and cut her words off. But she didn't need to finish, and Stefan didn't need to answer. She saw it in his eyes.

"It was the only way, Elena," he said then. "You would have died without human blood. Would you rather have attacked somebody unwilling, hurt them, maybe killed them? The need can drive you to that. Is that what you would have wanted?"

"*No,*" Elena said violently. "But did it have to be Matt? Oh, don't answer that; I can't think of anybody else, either." She took a shaky breath. "But now I'm worried about him, Stefan. I haven't seen him since that night. Is he okay? What has he said to you?"

"Not much," said Stefan, looking away. "'Leave me alone' was about the gist of it. He also denied that anything happened that night, and said that you were dead."

"Sounds like one of those individuals who can't cope," Damon commented.

"Oh, shut up!" said Elena. "You keep out of this, and while you're at it, you might think about poor Vickie Bennett. How d'you think *she's* coping these days?"

"It might help if I knew who this Vickie Bennett is. You keep talking about her, but I've never met the girl."

"Yes, you have. Don't play games with me, Damon—the cemetery, remember? The ruined church? The girl you left wandering around there in her slip?"

"Sorry, no. And I usually *do* remember girls I leave wandering in their slips."

"I suppose Stefan did it, then," Elena said sarcastically.

Anger flashed to the surface of Damon's eyes, covered quickly with a disturbing smile. "Maybe he did. Maybe *you* did. It's all the same to me, except that I'm getting a little tired of accusations. And now—"

"Wait," said Stefan, with surprising mildness. "Don't go yet. We should talk—"

"I'm afraid I have a previous engagement." There was a flurry of wings, and Stefan and Elena were alone.

Elena put a knuckle to her lips. "Damn. I didn't mean to make him angry. After he was really almost civilized all evening."

"Never mind," said Stefan. "He likes to be angry. What were you saying about Matt?"

Elena saw the weariness in Stefan's face and put an arm around him. "We won't talk about it now, but I think tomorrow maybe we should go see him. To tell him . . ." Elena lifted her other hand helplessly. She didn't know what she wanted to tell Matt; she only knew that she needed to do *something*.

"I think," said Stefan slowly, "that *you* had better go see him. I tried to talk to him, but he didn't want to listen to me. I can understand that, but maybe you'll do better. And I think"—he paused and then went on resolutely— "I think you'd do better alone with him. You could go now."

Elena looked at him hard. "Are you sure?"

"Yes."

"But—will you be all right? I should stay with you—"

"I'll be fine, Elena," Stefan said gently. "Go on."

Elena hesitated, then nodded. "I won't be long," she promised him.

* * *

Unseen, Elena slipped around the side of the frame house with the peeling paint and the crooked mailbox labeled *Honeycutt.* Matt's window was unlocked. Careless boy, she thought reprovingly. Don't you know something might come creeping in? She eased it open, but of course that was as far as she could go. An invisible barrier that felt like a soft wall of thickened air blocked her way.

"Matt," she whispered. The room was dark, but she could see a vague shape on the bed. A digital clock with pale green numbers showed that it was 12:15. "Matt," she whispered again.

The figure stirred. "Uh?"

"Matt, I don't want to frighten, you." She made her voice soothing, trying to wake him gently rather than startle him out of his wits. "But it's me, Elena, and I wanted to talk. Only you've got to ask me in first. Can you ask me in?"

"Uh. C'mon in." Elena was amazed at the lack of surprise in his voice. It was only after she'd gotten over the sill that she realized he was still asleep.

"Matt. *Matt*," she whispered, afraid to go too close. The room was stifling and overheated, the radiator going full blast. She could see a bare foot sticking out of the mound of blankets on the bed and blond hair at the top.

"Matt?" Tentatively, she leaned over and touched him.

That got a response. With an explosive grunt, Matt sat

bolt upright, whipping around. When his eyes met hers, they were wide and staring.

Elena found herself trying to look small and harmless, nonthreatening. She backed away against the wall. "I didn't mean to frighten you. I know it's a shock. But will you talk to me?"

He simply went on staring at her. His yellow hair was sweaty and ruffled up like wet chicken feathers. She could see his pulse pounding in his bare neck. She was afraid he was going to get up and dash out of the room.

Then his shoulders relaxed, slumping, and he slowly shut his eyes. He was breathing deeply but raggedly, "Elena."

"Yes," she whispered.

"You're dead."

"No. I'm here."

"Dead people don't come back. My dad didn't come back."

"I didn't really die. I just changed." Matt's eyes were still shut in repudiation, and Elena felt a cold wave of hopelessness wash over her. "But you wish I had died, don't you? I'll leave now," she whispered.

Matt's face cracked and he started to cry.

"No. Oh, no. Oh, don't, Matt, please."

She found herself cradling him, fighting not to cry herself. "Matt, I'm sorry; I shouldn't even have come here."

"Don't leave," he sobbed. "Don't go away."

"I won't." Elena lost the fight, and tears fell onto Matt's damp hair. "I didn't mean to hurt you, ever," she said. "Not *ever*, Matt. All those times, all those things I did—I never wanted to hurt you. Truly . . ." Then she stopped talking and just held him.

After a while his breathing quieted and he sat back, swiping his face with a fistful of sheet. His eyes avoided hers. There was a look on his face, not just of embarrassment, but of distrust, as if he were bracing himself for something he dreaded.

"Okay, so you're here. You're alive," he said roughly. "So what do you want?"

Elena was dumbfounded.

"Come on, there must be something. What is it?"

New tears welled up, but Elena gulped them back. "I guess I deserve that. I *know* I do. But for once, Matt, I want absolutely nothing. I came to apologize, to say that I'm sorry for using you—not just that one night, but always. I care about you, and I care if you hurt. I thought maybe I could make things better." After a heavy silence, she added, "I guess I *will* leave now."

"No, wait. Wait a second." Matt scrubbed at his face with the sheet again. "Listen. That was stupid, and I'm a jerk—"

"That was the truth and you're a gentleman. Or you'd've

told me to go take a hike a long time ago."

"No, I'm a stupid jerk. I should be banging my head against the wall with joy because you're not dead. I will in a minute. Listen." He grabbed her wrist and Elena looked at it in mild surprise. "I don't care if you're the Creature from the Black Lagoon, It, Godzilla, and Frankenstein all rolled up into one. I just—"

"Matt." Panicked, Elena put her free hand over his mouth.

"I know. You're engaged to the guy in the black cape. Don't worry; I remember him. I even like him, though God knows why." Matt took a breath and seemed to calm down. "Look, I don't know if Stefan told you. He said a bunch of stuff to me—about being evil, about not being sorry for what he did to Tyler. You know what I'm talking about?"

Elena shut her eyes. "He's scarcely eaten since that night. I think he's hunted once. Tonight he almost got himself killed because he's so weak."

Matt nodded. "So it was your basic crap. I should have known."

"Well, it is and it isn't. The need is strong, stronger than you can imagine." It was dawning on Elena that *she* hadn't fed today and that she'd been hungry before they'd set out for Alaric's. "In fact—Matt, I'd better go. Just one thing—if there's a dance tomorrow night, don't go. Something's going to happen then, something bad.

We're going to try to guard it, but I don't know what we can do."

"Who's 'we'?" Matt said sharply.

"Stefan and Damon—I think Damon—and me. And Meredith and Bonnie . . . and Alaric Saltzman. Don't ask about Alaric. It's a long story."

"But what are you guarding *against*?"

"I forgot; you don't know. *That's* a long story, too, but . . . well, the short answer is, whatever killed me. Whatever made those dogs attack people at my memorial service. It's something bad, Matt, that's been around Fell's Church for a while now. And we're going to try to stop it from doing anything tomorrow night." She tried not to squirm. "Look, I'm sorry, but I really should leave." Her eyes drifted, despite herself, to the broad blue vein in his neck.

When she managed to tear her gaze away and look at his face, she saw shock giving way to sudden understanding. Then to something incredible: acceptance. "It's okay," Matt said.

She wasn't sure she'd heard correctly. "Matt?"

"I said, it's okay. It didn't hurt me before."

"No. No, Matt, really. I didn't *come* here for that—"

"I know. That's why I want to. I want to give you something you *didn't* ask for." After a moment he said, "For old friends' sake."

Stefan, Elena was thinking. But Stefan had told her to come, and come alone. Stefan had known, she realized. And it was all right. It was his gift to Matt—and to her.

But I'm coming back to *you*, Stefan, she thought.

As she leaned toward him, Matt said, "I'm going to come and help you tomorrow, you know. Even if I'm not invited."

Then her lips touched his throat.

December 13, Friday

Dear Diary,

Tonight's the night.

I know I've written that before, or thought it at least. But tonight is the night, the big one, when everything is going to happen. This is it.

Stefan feels it, too. He came back from school today to tell me that the dance is still on—Mr. Newcastle didn't want to cause a panic by canceling it or something. What they're going to do is have "security" outside, which means the police, I guess. And maybe Mr. Smallwood and some of his friends with rifles. Whatever's going to happen, I don't think they can stop it.

I don't know if we can, either.

It's been snowing all day. The pass is blocked, which means nothing gets in or out of town on wheels. Until the snowplow gets up there, which won't be until morning, which will be too late.

And the air has a funny feeling to it. Not just snow. It's as if something even colder than that is waiting. It's pulled back the way the ocean pulls back before a tidal wave. When it lets go . . .

I thought about my other diary today, the one under the floorboards of my bedroom closet. If I own anything anymore, I own that diary. I thought about getting it out, but I don't want to go home again. I don't think I could cope, and I know Aunt Judith couldn't if she saw me.

I'm surprised anybody's *been able to cope. Meredith, Bonnie—especially Bonnie. Well, Meredith, too, considering what her family has been through. Matt.*

They're good and loyal friends. It's funny, I used to think that without a whole galaxy of friends and admirers I wouldn't survive. Now I'm perfectly happy with three, thank you. Because they're real friends.

I didn't know how much I cared about them before. Or about Margaret, or Aunt Judith even. And everybody at school . . . I know a few weeks ago I was saying that I didn't care if the entire population of Robert E. Lee dropped dead, but that isn't true. Tonight I'm going to do my best to protect them.

I know I'm jumping from subject to subject, but I'm just talking about things that are important to me. Kind of gathering them together in my mind. Just in case.

Well, it's time. Stefan is waiting. I'm going to finish this last line and then go.

I think we're going to win. I hope so.

We're going to try.

The history room was warm and brightly lit. On the other side of the school building, the cafeteria was even brighter, shining with Christmas lights and decorations. Upon arriving, Elena had scrutinized it from a cautious distance, watching the couples arrive for the dance and pass by the sheriff's officers at the door. Feeling Damon's silent presence behind her, she had pointed out a girl with long, light brown hair.

"Vickie Bennett," she said.

"I'll take your word for it," he replied.

Now, she looked around their makeshift headquarters for the night. Alaric's desk had been cleared, and he was bent over a rough map of the school. Meredith leaned in beside him, her dark hair sweeping his sleeve. Matt and Bonnie were out mingling with the dancegoers in the parking lot, and Stefan and Damon were prowling the perimeter of the school grounds. They were going to take turns.

"You'd better stay inside," Alaric had told Elena. "All we need is for somebody to see you and start chasing you with a stake."

"I've been walking around town all week," Elena said, amused. "If I don't want to be seen, you don't see me." But she agreed to stay in the history room and coordinate.

It's like a castle, she thought as she watched Alaric plot out the positions of sheriff's officers and other men on the map. And we're defending it. Me and my loyal knights.

The round, flat-faced clock on the wall ticked the minutes by. Elena watched it as she let people in the door and let them out again. She poured hot coffee out of a Thermos for those who wanted it. She listened to the reports come in.

"Everything's quiet on the north side of the school."

"Caroline just got crowned snow queen. Big surprise."

"Some rowdy kids in the parking lot—the sheriff just rounded them up. . . ."

Midnight came and went.

"Maybe we were wrong," Stefan said an hour or so later. It was the first time they'd all been inside together since the beginning of the evening.

"Maybe it's happening somewhere else," said Bonnie, emptying out a boot and peering into it.

"There's no way to know where it's going to happen,"

Elena said firmly. "But we weren't wrong about it happening."

"Maybe," said Alaric thoughtfully, "there *is* a way. To find out where it's going to happen, I mean." As heads raised questioningly, he said, "We need a precognition."

All eyes turned to Bonnie.

"Oh, no," Bonnie said. "I'm through with all that. I *hate* it."

"It's a great gift—" began Alaric.

"It's a great big pain. Look, you don't understand. The ordinary predictions are bad enough. It seems like most of the time I'm finding out things I don't want to know. But getting taken over—that's *awful*. And afterward I don't even remember what I've said. It's horrible."

"Getting taken over?" Alaric repeated. "What's that?"

Bonnie sighed. "It's what happened to me in the church," she said patiently. "I can do other kinds of predictions, like divining with water or reading palms"—she glanced at Elena, and then away—"and stuff like that. But then there are times when—someone—takes me over and just uses me to talk for them. It's like having somebody else in my body."

"Like in the graveyard, when you said there was something there waiting for me," said Elena. "Or when you warned me not to go near the bridge. Or when you came to dinner and said that Death, my death, was in the house." She looked automatically around at Damon, who returned her gaze impassively. Still, that had been wrong, she thought. Damon hadn't been her death. So what had the prophecy meant? For just an instant something glimmered in her mind, but before she could get a grasp on it, Meredith interrupted.

"It's like another voice that speaks through Bonnie," Meredith explained to Alaric. "She even looks different. Maybe you weren't close enough in the church to see."

"But why didn't you tell me about this?" Alaric was excited. "This could be important. This—entity—whatever it is—could give us vital information. It could clear up the mystery of the Other Power, or at least give us a clue how to fight it."

Bonnie was shaking her head. "No. It isn't something I can just whistle up, and it doesn't answer questions. It just *happens* to me. And I hate it."

"You mean you can't think of anything that tends to set it off? Anything that's led to it happening before?"

Elena and Meredith, who knew very well what could set it off, looked at each other. Elena bit the inside of her cheek. It was Bonnie's choice. It had to be Bonnie's choice.

Bonnie, who was holding her head in her hands, shot a sideways glance through red curls at Elena. Then she shut her eyes and moaned.

"Candles," she said.

"What?"

"*Candles*. A candle flame might do it. I can't be sure, you understand; I'm not promising *anything*—"

"Somebody go ransack the science lab," said Alaric.

It was a scene reminiscent of the day Alaric had come to school, when he'd asked them all to put their chairs in a circle. Elena looked at the circle of faces lit eerily from below by the candle's flame. There was Matt, with his jaw set. Beside him, Meredith, her dark lashes throwing shadows upward. And Alaric, leaning forward in his eagerness. Then Damon, light and shadow dancing over the planes of his face. And Stefan, high cheekbones looking too sharply defined to Elena's eyes. And finally, Bonnie, looking fragile and pale even in the golden light of the candle.

We're connected, Elena thought, overcome by the same feeling that she'd had in the church, when she had taken Stefan's and Damon's hands. She remembered a thin white circle of wax floating in a dish of water. *We can do it if we stick together.*

"I'm just going to look into the candle," Bonnie said, her voice quivering slightly. "And not think of anything. I'm going to try to—leave myself open to it." She began to breathe deeply, gazing into the candle flame.

And then it happened, just as it had before. Bonnie's

face smoothed out, all expression draining away. Her eyes went blank as the stone cherub's in the graveyard.

She didn't say a word.

That was when Elena realized they hadn't agreed on what to ask. She groped through her mind to find a question before Bonnie lost contact. "Where can we find the Other Power?" she said, just as Alaric blurted out, "Who are you?" Their voices mingled, their questions intertwining.

Bonnie's blank face turned, sweeping the circle with sightless eyes. Then the voice that wasn't Bonnie's voice said, "Come and see."

"Wait a minute," Matt said, as Bonnie stood up, still entranced, and made for the door. "Where's she going?"

Meredith grabbed for her coat. "Are we going with her?"

"Don't touch her!" said Alaric, jumping up as Bonnie went out the door.

Elena looked at Stefan, and then at Damon. With one accord, they followed, trailing Bonnie down the empty, echoing hall.

"Where are we going? Which question is she answering?" Matt demanded. Elena could only shake her head. Alaric was jogging to keep up with Bonnie's gliding pace.

She slowed down as they emerged into the snow, and to Elena's surprise, walked up to Alaric's car in the staff parking lot and stood beside it.

"We can't all fit; I'll follow with Matt," Meredith said

swiftly. Elena, her skin chilled with apprehension as well as cold air, got in the back of Alaric's car when he opened it for her, with Damon and Stefan on either side. Bonnie sat up front. She was looking straight ahead, and she didn't speak. But as Alaric pulled out of the parking lot, she lifted one white hand and pointed. Right on Lee Street and then left on Arbor Green. Straight out toward Elena's house and then right on Thunderbird. Heading toward Old Creek Road.

It was then that Elena realized where they were going.

They took the other bridge to the cemetery, the one everyone always called "the new bridge" to distinguish it from Wickery Bridge, which was now gone. They were approaching from the gate side, the side Tyler had driven up when he took Elena to the ruined church.

Alaric's car stopped just where Tyler's had stopped. Meredith pulled up behind them.

With a terrible sense of déjà vu, Elena made the trek up the hill and through the gate, following Bonnie to where the ruined church stood with its belfry pointing like a finger to the stormy sky. At the empty hole that had once been the doorway, she balked.

"Where are you taking us?" she said. "*Listen* to me. Will you just tell us which question you're answering?"

"Come and see."

Helplessly, Elena looked at the others. Then she

stepped over the threshold. Bonnie walked slowly to the white marble tomb, and stopped.

Elena looked at it, and then at Bonnie's ghostly face. Every hair on her arms and the back of her neck was standing up. "Oh, no . . ." she whispered. "Not that."

"Elena, what are you talking about?" Meredith said.

Dizzy, Elena looked down at the marble countenances of Thomas and Honoria Fell, lying on the stone lid of their tomb. "This thing opens," she whispered.

13

"Dou think we're supposed to—look inside?" Matt said.

"I don't know," Elena said miserably. She didn't want to see what was inside that tomb now any more than she had when Tyler had suggested opening it to vandalize it. "Maybe we won't be able to *get* it open," she added. "Tyler and Dick couldn't. It started to slide only when I leaned on it."

"Lean on it now; maybe there's some sort of hidden spring mechanism," Alaric suggested, and when Elena did, with no results, he said, "All right, let's all get a grip, and brace ourselves—like this. Come on, now—"

From his crouch, he looked up at Damon, who was standing motionless next to the tomb, looking faintly amused. "Excuse me," Damon said, and Alaric stepped back, frowning. Damon and Stefan each gripped an end of the stone lid and lifted.

The lid came away, making a grinding sound as Damon and Stefan slid it to the ground on one side of the tomb.

Elena couldn't bring herself to move closer.

Instead, fighting nausea, she concentrated on Stefan's expression. It would tell her what was to be found in there. Pictures crashed through her mind, of parchment-colored mummified bodies, of rotting corpses, of grinning skulls. If Stefan looked horrified or sickened, disgusted . . .

But as Stefan looked into the open tomb, his face registered only disconcerted surprise.

Elena couldn't stand it any longer. "What is it?"

He gave her a crooked smile and said with a glance at Bonnie, "Come and see."

Elena inched up to the tomb and looked down. Then her head flew up, and she regarded Stefan in astonishment.

"What is it?"

"I don't know," he replied. He turned to Meredith and Alaric. "Does either of you have a flashlight? Or some rope?"

After a look inside the stone box, they both headed for their cars. Elena remained where she was, staring down, straining her night vision. She still couldn't believe it.

The tomb was not a tomb, but a doorway.

Now she understood why she had felt a cold wind blow from it when it had shifted beneath her hand that night. She was looking down into a kind of vault or cellar in the ground. She could see only one wall, the one that dropped straight down below her, and that one had iron rungs driven into the stone, like a ladder.

"Here you go," Meredith said to Stefan, returning. "Alaric's got a flashlight, and here's mine. And here's the rope Elena put in my car when we went looking for you."

The narrow beam of Meredith's flashlight swept the dark room below. "I can't see very far inside, but it looks empty," Stefan said. "I'll go down first."

"Go *down*?" said Matt. "Look, are you sure we're *supposed* to go down? Bonnie, how about it?"

Bonnie hadn't moved. She was still standing there with that utterly abstracted expression on her face, as if she saw nothing around her. Without a word, she swung a leg over the edge of the tomb, twisted, and began to descend.

"Whoa," said Stefan. He tucked the flashlight in his jacket pocket, put a hand on the tomb's foot, and jumped.

Elena had no time to enjoy Alaric's expression; she leaned down and shouted, "Are you okay?"

"Fine." The flashlight winked at her from below. "Bonnie will be all right, too. The rungs go all the way down. Better bring the rope anyway."

Elena looked at Matt, who was closest. His blue eyes

met hers with helplessness and a certain resignation, and he nodded. She took a deep breath and put a hand on the foot of the tomb as Stefan had. Another hand suddenly clamped on her wrist.

"I've just thought of something," Meredith said grimly. "What if Bonnie's entity *is* the Other Power?"

"I thought of that a long time ago," Elena said. She patted Meredith's hand, pried it off, and jumped.

She stood up into Stefan's supporting arm and looked around. "My God . . ."

It was a strange place. The walls were faced with stone. They were smooth and almost polished-looking. Driven into them at intervals were iron candelabra, some of which had the remains of wax candles in them. Elena could not see the other end of the room, but the flashlight showed a wrought-iron gate quite close, like the gate in some churches used to screen off an altar.

Bonnie was just reaching the bottom of the rung ladder. She waited silently while the others descended, first Matt, then Meredith, then Alaric with the other flashlight.

Elena looked up. "Damon?"

She could see his silhouette against the lighter black rectangle that was the tomb's opening to the sky. "Well?"

"Are you with us?" she asked. Not "Are you *coming* with us?" She knew he would understand the difference.

She waited five heartbeats in the silence that followed.

Six, seven, eight . . .

There was a rush of air, and Damon landed neatly. But he didn't look at Elena. His eyes were oddly distant, and she could read nothing in his face.

"It's a crypt," Alaric was saying in wonder, as his flashlight scythed through the darkness. "An underground chamber beneath a church, used as a burial place. They're usually built under larger churches."

Bonnie walked straight up to the scrolled gate and placed one small white hand on it, opening it. It swung away from her.

Elena's heartbeats were coming too quickly to count now. Somehow she forced her legs to move forward, to follow Bonnie. Her sharpened senses were almost painfully acute, but they could tell her nothing about what she was walking into. The beam from Stefan's flashlight was so narrow, and it showed only the rock floor ahead, and Bonnie's enigmatic form.

Bonnie stopped.

This is it, thought Elena, her breath catching in her throat. Oh, my God, this is it; this is really it. She had the sudden intense sensation of being in the middle of a lucid dream, one where she knew she was dreaming but couldn't change anything or wake up. Her muscles deadlocked.

She could smell fear from the others, and she could feel the sharp edge of it from Stefan beside her. His flashlight skimmed over objects beyond Bonnie, but at first Elena's eyes could make no sense of them. She saw angles, planes, contours, and then something leaped into focus. A dead-white face, hanging grotesquely sideways . . .

The scream never got out of her throat. It was only a statue, and the features were familiar. They were the same as on the lid of the tomb above. This tomb was the twin of the one they had come through. Except that this one had been ravaged, the stone lid broken in two and flung against the wall of the crypt. Something was scattered about the floor like fragile ivory sticks. Bits of marble, Elena told her brain desperately; it's only marble, bits of marble.

They were human bones, splintered and crushed.

Bonnie turned around.

Her heart-shaped face swung as if those fixed blank eyes were surveying the group. She ended directly facing Elena.

Then, with a shudder, she stumbled and pitched violently forward like a marionette whose strings have been cut.

Elena barely caught her, half falling herself. "Bonnie? Bonnie?" The brown eyes that looked up at her, dilated and disoriented, were Bonnie's own frightened eyes. "But what happened?" Elena demanded. "Where did it go?"

"I am here."

Above the plundered tomb, a hazy light was showing. No, not a light, Elena thought. She was sensing it with her eyes, but it was not light in the normal spectrum. This was something stranger than infrared or ultraviolet, something human senses had not been built to see. It was being revealed to her, forced on her brain, by some outside Power.

"The Other Power," she whispered, her blood freezing.

"No, Elena."

The voice was not sound, in the same way that the vision was not light. It was quiet as star shine, and sad. It reminded her of something.

Mother? she thought wildly. But it wasn't her mother's voice. The glow above the tomb seemed to swirl and eddy, and for a moment Elena glimpsed in it a face, a gentle, sad face. And then she knew.

"I've been waiting for you," Honoria Fell's voice said softly. "Here I can speak to you at last in my own form, and not through Bonnie's lips. Listen to me. Your time is short, and the danger is very great."

Elena found her tongue. "But what is this room? Why did you bring us here?"

"You asked me to. I couldn't show you until you asked. This is your battleground."

"I don't understand."

"This crypt was built for me by the people of Fell's Church. A resting place for my body. A secret place for one who had secret powers in life. Like Bonnie, I knew things no one else could know. I saw things no one else could see."

"You were psychic," Bonnie whispered huskily.

"In those days, they called it witchery. But I never used my powers for harm, and when I died they built me this monument so that my husband and I could lie in peace. But then, after many years, our peace was disturbed."

The eldritch light ebbed and flowed, Honoria's form wavering. "Another Power came to Fell's Church, full of hatred and destruction. It defiled my resting place and scattered my bones. It made its home here. It went out to work evil against my town. I woke.

"I have tried to warn you against it from the beginning, Elena. It lives here below the graveyard. It has been waiting for you, watching you. Sometimes in the form of an owl—"

An owl. Elena's mind raced ahead. An owl, like the owl she had seen nesting in the belfry of the church. Like the owl that had been in the barn, like the owl in the black locust tree by her house.

White owl . . . hunting bird . . . flesh eater . . . she

thought. And then she remembered great white wings that seemed to stretch to the horizon on either side. A great bird made of mist or snow, coming after her, focused on her, full of bloodlust and animal hate . . .

"No!" she cried, memory engulfing her.

She felt Stefan's hands on her shoulders, his fingers digging in almost painfully. It brought her back to reality. Honoria Fell was still speaking.

"And you, Stefan, it has been watching you. It hated you before it hated Elena. It has been tormenting you and playing with you like a cat with a mouse. It hates those you love. It is full of poisoned love itself."

Elena looked involuntarily behind her. She saw Meredith, Alaric, and Matt standing frozen. Bonnie and Stefan were next to her. But Damon . . . where was Damon?

"Its hatred has grown so great that any death will do, any blood spilled will give it pleasure. Right now, the animals it controls are slinking out of the woods. They are moving toward the town, toward the lights."

"The Snow Dance!" Meredith said sharply.

"Yes. And this time they will kill until the last of them is killed."

"We have to warn those people," Matt said. "Everyone at that dance—"

"You will never be safe until the mind that controls

them is destroyed. The killing will go on. You must destroy the Power that hates; that is why I have brought you here."

There was another flux in the light; it seemed to be receding. "You have the courage, if you can find it. Be strong. This is the only help I can give you."

"Wait—please—" Elena began.

The voice continued relentlessly, taking no heed of her. "Bonnie, you have a choice. Your secret powers are a responsibility. They are also a gift, and one that can be taken away. Do you choose to relinquish them?"

"I—" Bonnie shook her head, frightened. "I don't know. I need time. . . ."

"There is no time. Choose." The light was dwindling, caving in on itself.

Bonnie's eyes were bewildered and uncertain as she searched Elena's face for help. "It's *your* choice," Elena whispered. "You have to decide for yourself."

Slowly, the uncertainty left Bonnie's face, and she nodded. She stood away from Elena, without support, turning back to the light. "I'll keep them," she said huskily. "I'll deal with them somehow. My grandmother did."

There was a flicker of something like amusement from the light. "You've chosen wisely. May you use them as well. This is the last time I will speak to you."

"But—"

"I have earned my rest. The fight is yours." And the glow faded, like the last embers of a dying fire.

With it gone, Elena could feel the pressure all around her. Something was going to happen. Some crushing force was coming toward them, or hanging over them. "Stefan—"

Stefan felt it too; she could tell. "Come on," Bonnie said, her voice panicked. "We have to get out of here."

"We have to get to the dance," Matt gasped. His face was white. "We have to help them—"

"Fire," cried Bonnie, looking startled, as if the thought had just come to her. "Fire won't kill them, but it will hold them off—"

"Didn't you listen? We have to face the Other Power. And it's *here*, right here, right now. We can't go!" Elena cried. Her mind was filled with turmoil. Images, memories, and a dreadful foreboding. Bloodlust . . . she could feel it. . . .

"Alaric." Stefan spoke with the ring of command. "You go back. Take the others; do what you can. I'll stay—"

"I think we all should leave!" Alaric shouted. He had to shout to be heard over the deafening noise surrounding them.

His weaving flashlight showed Elena something she hadn't noticed before. In the wall next to her was a gaping hole, as if the stone facing had been ripped away. And beyond was a tunnel into the raw earth, black and endless.

Where does it go? Elena wondered, but the thought was lost among the tumult of her fear. White owl . . . hunting bird . . . flesh eater . . . *crow*, she thought, and suddenly she knew with blinding clarity what she was afraid of.

"Where's Damon?" she screamed, dragging Stefan around as she turned, looking. "Where's Damon?"

"Get *out*!" cried Bonnie, her voice shrill with terror. She threw herself toward the gate just as the sound split the darkness.

It was a snarl, but not a dog's snarl. It could never be mistaken for that. It was so much deeper, heavier, more, resonant. It was a *huge* sound, and it reeked of the jungle, of the hunting bloodlust. It reverberated in Elena's chest, jarred her bones.

It paralyzed her.

The sound came again, hungry and savage, but somehow almost lazy. That confident. And with it came heavy footfalls from the tunnel.

Bonnie was trying to scream, making only a thin whistling sound. In the blackness of the tunnel, something was coming. A shape that moved with a rangy feline swing. Elena recognized the snarl now. It was the sound of the largest of the hunting cats, larger than a lion. The tiger's eyes showed yellow as it reached the end of the tunnel.

And then everything happened at once.

Elena felt Stefan try to pull her backward to get her out of the way. But her own petrified muscles were a hindrance to him, and she knew that it was too late.

The tiger's leap was grace itself, powerful muscles launching it into the air. In that instant, she saw it as if caught in the light of a flashbulb, and her mind noted the lean shining flanks and the supple backbone. But her voice screamed out on its own.

"Damon, no!"

It was only as the black wolf sprang out of the darkness to meet it that she realized the tiger was white.

The great cat's rush was thrown off by the wolf, and Elena felt Stefan wrench her out of the way, pulling her sideways to safety. Her muscles had melted like snowflakes, and she yielded numbly as he put her against the wall. The lid of the tomb was between her and the snarling white shape now, but the gate was on the other side of the fight.

Elena's own weakness was part terror and part bewilderment. She didn't understand anything; confusion roared in her ears. A moment ago she had been certain Damon had been playing with them all this time, that he had been the Other Power all along. But the malice and the bloodlust that emanated from the tiger were unmistakable. This was what had chased her in the graveyard, and from the boardinghouse to the river and her death. This white Power that the wolf was fighting to kill.

It was an impossible match. The black wolf, vicious and aggressive though it might be, didn't stand a chance. One swipe of the tiger's huge claws laid the wolf's shoulder open to the bone. Its jaws snarled open as it tried to get a bone-cracking grip on the wolf's neck.

But then Stefan was there, training the blaze of the flashlight into the cat's eyes, thrusting the wounded wolf out of the way. Elena wished she could scream, wished she could do something to release this rushing ache inside her. She didn't understand; she didn't understand anything. Stefan was in danger. But she couldn't move.

"Get out!" Stefan was shouting to the others. "Do it now; get out!"

Faster than any human, he darted out of the way of a white paw, keeping the light in the tiger's eyes. Meredith was on the other side of the gate now. Matt was half carrying and half dragging Bonnie. Alaric was through.

The tiger lunged and the gate crashed shut. Stefan fell to the side, slipping as he tried to scramble up again.

"We won't leave you—" Alaric cried.

"Go!" shouted Stefan. "Get to the dance; do what you can! *Go!*"

The wolf was attacking again, despite the bleeding wounds in its head, and its shoulder where muscle and tendon lay exposed and shining. The tiger fought back. The animal sounds rose to a volume that Elena couldn't stand. Meredith and the others were gone; Alaric's flashlight had disappeared.

"Stefan!" she screamed, seeing him poised to jump into the fight again.

If he died, she would die, too. And if she had to die, she wanted it to be with him.

The paralysis left her, and she stumbled toward him, sobbing, reaching out to clutch him tightly. She felt his arm around her as he held her with his body between her and the noise and violence. But she was stubborn, as stubborn as he was. She twisted, and then they faced it together.

The wolf was down. It was lying on its back, and although its fur was too dark to show the blood, a red pool gathered beneath it. The white cat stood above it, jaws gaping inches from the vulnerable black throat.

But the death-dealing bite to the neck didn't come. Instead the tiger raised its head to look at Stefan and Elena.

With a strange calmness, Elena found herself noticing tiny details of its appearance.

The whiskers were straight and slender, like silver wires. Its fur was pure white, striped with faint marks like unburnished gold. White and gold, she thought, remembering the owl in the barn. And that stirred another memory . . . of something she'd seen . . . or something she'd heard about. . . .

With a heavy swipe, the cat sent the flashlight flying out of Stefan's hand. Elena heard him hiss in pain, but she could no longer see anything in the blackness. Where there was no light at all, even a hunter was blind. Clinging to him, she waited for the pain of the killing blow.

But suddenly her head was reeling; it was full of gray and spinning fog and she couldn't hold on to Stefan. She couldn't think; she couldn't speak. The floor seemed to be dropping away from her. Dimly, she realized that Power was being used against her, that it was overwhelming her mind.

She felt Stefan's body giving, slumping, falling away from her, and she could no longer resist the fog. She fell forever and never knew when she hit the ground.

14

hite owl . . . hunting bird . . . hunter . . . tiger. Playing with you like a cat with a mouse. Like a cat . . . a great cat . . . a kitten. A white kitten.

Death is in the house.

And the kitten, the kitten had run from Damon. Not out of fear, but out of the fear of being discovered. Like when it had stood on Margaret's chest and wailed at the sight of Elena outside the window.

Elena moaned and almost surfaced from unconsciousness, but the gray fog dragged her back under before she could open her eyes. Her thoughts seethed around her again.

Poisoned love . . . Stefan, it hated you before it hated Elena. . . . White and gold . . . something white . . . *some-*

thing white under the tree . . .

This time, when she struggled to open her eyes, she succeeded. And even before she could focus in the dim and shifting light, she knew. She finally knew.

The figure in the trailing white dress turned from the candle she was lighting, and Elena saw what might have been her own face on its shoulders. But it was a subtly distorted face, pale and beautiful as an ice sculpture, but *wrong*. It was like the endless reflections of herself Elena had seen in her dream of the hall of mirrors. Twisted and hungry, and mocking.

"Hello, Katherine," she whispered.

Katherine smiled, a sly and predatory smile. "You're not as stupid as I thought," she said.

Her voice was light and sweet—silvery, Elena thought. Like her eyelashes. There were silvery lights in her dress when she moved, too. But her hair was gold, almost as pale a gold as Elena's own. Her eyes were like the kitten's eyes: round and jewel blue. At her throat she wore a necklace with a stone of the same vivid color.

Elena's own throat was sore, as if she had been screaming. It felt dry as well. When she turned her head slowly to the side, even that little motion hurt.

Stefan was beside her, slumped forward, bound by his arms to the wrought-iron pickets of the gate. His head sagged against his chest, but what she could see of his face was deathly white. His throat was torn, and blood had dripped onto his collar and dried.

Elena turned back to Katherine so quickly that her head spun. "Why? Why did you do that?"

Katherine smiled, showing pointed white teeth. "Because I *love* him," she said in a childish singsong. "Don't you love him, too?"

It was only then that Elena fully realized why she couldn't move, and why her arms hurt. She was tied up like Stefan, lashed securely to the closed gate. A painful turning of her head to the other side revealed Damon.

He was in worse shape than his brother. His jacket and arm were ripped open, and the sight of the wound made Elena sick. His shirt hung in tatters, and Elena could see the tiny movement of his ribs as he breathed. If it hadn't been for that, she would have thought he was dead. Blood matted his hair and ran into his closed eyes.

"Which one do you like better?" Katherine asked, in an intimate, confiding tone. "You can tell me. Which one do you think is best?"

Elena looked at her, sickened. "Katherine," she whispered. "Please. Please listen to me. . . ."

"Tell me. Go on." Those jewel blue eyes filled Elena's vision as Katherine leaned in close, her lips almost touching Elena's. "*I* think they're both fun. Do you like fun, Elena?"

Revolted, Elena shut her eyes and turned her face away. If only her head would stop spinning.

Katherine stepped back with a clear laugh. "I know, it's so hard to choose." She did a little pirouette, and Elena saw that what she had vaguely taken for the train to Katherine's dress was Katherine's hair. It flowed like molten gold down her back to spill over the floor, trailing behind her.

"It all depends on your taste," Katherine continued, doing a few graceful dance steps and ending up in front of Damon. She looked over at Elena impishly. "But then I have such a sweet tooth." She grasped Damon by the hair, and, yanking his head up, sank her teeth into his neck.

"No! Don't do that; don't hurt him any more. . . ." Elena tried to surge forward, but she was tied too tightly. The gate was solid iron, set in stone, and the ropes were sturdy. Katherine was making animal sounds, gnawing and chewing at the flesh, and Damon moaned even in unconsciousness. Elena saw his body jerk reflexively with pain.

"Please stop; oh, please stop—"

Katherine lifted her head. Blood was running down her chin. "But I'm hungry and he's so *good*," she said. She reared back and struck again, and Damon's body spasmed. Elena cried out.

I was like that, she thought. In the beginning, that first

night in the woods, I was like that. I hurt Stefan like that, I wanted to kill him. . . .

Darkness swept up around her, and she gave in to it gratefully.

Alaric's car skewed on a patch of ice as it reached the school, and Meredith almost ran into it. She and Matt jumped out of her car, leaving the doors open. Ahead, Alaric and Bonnie did the same.

"What about the rest of the town?" Meredith shouted, running toward them. The wind was rising, and her face burned with frost.

"Just Elena's family—Aunt Judith and Margaret," Bonnie cried. Her voice was shrill and frightened, but there was a look of concentration in her eyes. She leaned her head back as if trying to remember something, and said, "Yes, that's it. They're the other ones the dogs will be after. Make them go somewhere—like the cellar. Keep them there!"

"I'll do it. You three take the dance!"

Bonnie turned to run after Alaric. Meredith raced back to her car.

The dance was in the last stages of breaking up. As many couples were outside as inside, starting toward the parking lot. Alaric shouted at them as he and Matt and Bonnie came pounding up.

"Go back in! Get everybody inside and shut the doors!" he yelled at the sheriff's officers.

But there wasn't time. He reached the cafeteria just as the first lurking shape in the darkness did. One officer went down without a sound or a chance to fire his gun.

Another was quicker, and a gunshot rang out, amplified by the concrete courtyard. Students screamed and began to run away from it, into the parking lot. Alaric went after them, yelling, trying to herd them back.

Other shapes came out of the darkness, from between parked cars, from all sides. Panic ensued. Alaric kept shouting, kept trying to gather the terrified students toward the building. Out here they were easy prey.

In the courtyard, Bonnie turned to Matt. "We need fire!" she said. Matt darted into the cafeteria and came out with a box half-full of dance programs. He threw it to the ground, groping in his pockets for one of the matches they'd used to light the candle before.

The paper caught and burned brightly. It formed an island of safety. Matt continued to wave people into the cafeteria doors behind it. Bonnie plunged inside, to find a scene just as riotous as outside.

She looked around for someone in authority but couldn't see any adults, only panicked kids. Then the red and green crepe paper decorations caught her eye.

The noise was thunderous; even a shout couldn't be heard in here. Struggling past the people trying to get out, she made it to the far side of the room. Caroline was there, looking pale without her summer tan, and wearing the snow queen tiara. Bonnie towed her to the microphone.

"You're good at talking. Tell them to get inside and *stay* in! Tell them to start taking down the decorations. We need anything that'll burn—wood chairs, stuff in garbage cans, *anything*. Tell them it's our only chance!" She added, as Caroline stared at her, frightened and uncomprehending: "You've got the crown on now—so *do* something with it!"

She didn't wait to see Caroline obey. She plunged again into the furor of the room. A moment later she heard Caroline's voice, first hesitant and then urgent, on the loudspeakers.

It was dead quiet when Elena opened her eyes again.

"Elena?"

At the hoarse whisper, she tried to focus and found herself looking into pain-filled green eyes.

"Stefan," she said. She leaned toward him yearningly, wishing she could move. It didn't make sense, but she felt that if they could only hold each other it wouldn't be so bad.

There was a childish laugh. Elena didn't turn toward it,

but Stefan did. Elena saw his reaction, saw the sequence of expressions passing across his face almost too quickly to identify. Blank shock, disbelief, dawning joy—and then horror. A horror that finally turned his eyes blind and opaque.

"Katherine," he said. "But that's impossible. It can't be. You're dead. . . ."

"Stefan . . ." Elena said, but he didn't respond.

Katherine put a hand in front of her mouth and giggled behind it.

"You wake up, too," she said, looking on the other side of Elena. Elena felt a surge of Power. After a moment Damon's head lifted slowly, and he blinked.

There was no astonishment in his face. He leaned his head back, eyes wearily narrowed, and looked for a minute or so at his captor. Then he smiled, a faint and painful smile, but recognizable.

"Our sweet little white kitten," he whispered. "I should have known."

"You didn't know, though, did you?" Katherine said, as eager as a child playing a game. "Even you didn't guess. I fooled everyone." She laughed again. "It was so much fun, watching you while you were watching Stefan, and neither of you knew I was there. I even scratched you once!" Hooking her fingers into claws, she mimicked a kitten's slash.

"At Elena's house. Yes, I remember," Damon said slowly. He didn't seem so much angry as vaguely, whimsically amused. "Well, you're certainly a hunter. The lady *and* the tiger, as it were."

"And I put Stefan in that well," Katherine bragged. "I saw you two fighting; I liked that. I followed Stefan to the edge of the woods, and then—" She clapped her cupped hands together, like someone catching a moth. Opening them slowly, she peered down into them as if she really had something there, and giggled secretly. "I was going to keep him to play with," she confided. Then her lower lip thrust out and she looked at Elena balefully. "But you took him. That was mean, Elena. You shouldn't have done that."

The dreadful childish slyness was gone from her face, and for a moment Elena glimpsed the searing hatred of a woman.

"Greedy girls get punished," Katherine said, moving toward her, "and you're a greedy girl."

"Katherine!" Stefan had woken from his daze, and he spoke quickly. "Don't you want to tell us what else you've done?"

Distracted, Katherine stepped back. She looked surprised, then flattered.

"Well—if you really want me to," she said. She hugged her elbows with her hands and pirouetted again, her golden hair twisting on the floor. "No," she said gleefully, turning back and pointing at them. "You guess. You guess and I'll tell you 'right' or 'wrong.' Go on!"

Elena swallowed, casting a covert glance at Stefan. She didn't see the point of stalling Katherine; it was all going to come out the same in the end. But some instinct told her to hang on to life as long as she could.

"You attacked Vickie," she said carefully. Her own voice sounded winded to her ears, but she was positive now. "The girl in the ruined church that night."

"Good! Yes," Katherine cried. She made another kitten swipe with clawed fingers. "Well, after all, she was in my church," she added reasonably. "And what she and that boy were doing—well! You don't do that in church. So, I *scratched* her!" Katherine drew out the word, demonstrating, like somebody telling a story to a young child. "And . . . I licked the blood up!" She licked pale pink lips with her tongue. Then she pointed at Stefan. "Next guess!"

"You've been hounding her ever since," Stefan said. He wasn't playing the game; he was making a sickened observation.

"Yes, we're done with that! Go on to something else," Katherine said sharply. But then she fiddled with the buttons at the neck of her dress, her fingers twinkling. And Elena thought of Vickie, with her startled-fawn eyes, undressing in the cafeteria in front of everyone. "I made her do silly things." Katherine laughed. "She was fun to play with."

Elena's arms were numb and cramped. She realized that she was reflexively straining against the ropes, so offended by Katherine's words that she couldn't hold still. She made herself stop, trying instead to lean back and get a little feeling into her deadened hands. What she was going to do if she got free she didn't know, but she had to try.

"Next *guess*," Katherine was saying dangerously.

"Why do you say it's your church?" Damon asked. His voice was still distantly amused, as if none of this affected him at all. "What about Honoria Fell?"

"Oh, that old spook!" Katherine said maliciously. She peered around behind Elena, her mouth pursed, her eyes glaring. Elena realized for the first time that they were facing the entrance to the crypt, with the ransacked tomb behind them. Maybe Honoria would help them. . . .

But then she remembered that quiet, fading voice. *This is the only help I can give you.* And she knew that no further aid would come.

As if she'd read Elena's thoughts, Katherine was saying, "She can't do *anything*. She's just a pack of old bones." The graceful hands made gestures as if Katherine were breaking those bones. "All she can do is talk, and lots of times I stopped you from hearing her." Katherine's expression was dark again, and Elena felt an acid twinge of fear.

"You killed Bonnie's dog, Yangtze," she said. It was a random guess, thrown out to divert Katherine, but it worked.

"Yes! That was funny. You all came running out of the house and started moaning and crying. . . ." Katherine evoked the scene in pantomime: the little dog lying in front of Bonnie's house, the girls rushing out to find his body. "He tasted bad, but it was worth it. I followed Damon there when he was a crow. I used to follow him a lot. If I wanted I could have grabbed that crow, and . . ." She made a sharp wringing motion.

Bonnie's dream, thought Elena, icy revelation sweeping over her. She didn't even realize she'd spoken aloud until she saw Stefan and Katherine looking at her. "Bonnie dreamed about you," she whispered. "But she thought it was me. She told me that she saw me standing under a tree with the wind blowing. And she was afraid of me. She said I looked different, pale but almost glowing. And a crow flew by and I grabbed it and wrung its neck." Bile was rising in Elena's throat, and she gulped it down. "But it was you," she said.

Katherine looked delighted, as if Elena had somehow proved her point. "People dream about me a lot," she said smugly. "Your aunt—she's dreamed about me. I tell her it was her fault you died. She thinks it's you telling her."

"Oh, God . . ."

"I wish you *had* died," Katherine went on, her face turning spiteful. "You *should* have died. I kept you in the river long enough. But you were such a tramp, getting blood from both of them, that you came back. Oh, well." She gave a furtive smile. "Now I can play with you longer. I lost my temper that day, because I saw Stefan had given you my ring. My ring!" Her voice rose. "Mine, that I left for them to remember me by. And he gave it to *you*. That was when I knew I wasn't just going to play with him. I had to kill him."

Stefan's eyes were stricken, confounded. "But I thought you were dead," he said. "You *were* dead, five hundred years ago. Katherine . . ."

"Oh, that was the first time I fooled you," Katherine said, but there was no glee in her tone now. It was sullen. "I arranged it all with Gudren, my maid. The two of you wouldn't accept my choice," she burst out, looking from Stefan to Damon angrily. "I wanted us all to be happy; I loved you. I loved you both. But that wasn't good enough for you."

Katherine's face had changed again, and Elena saw in it the hurt child of five centuries ago. That must have been what Katherine looked like *then*, she thought wonderingly. The wide blue eyes were actually filling with tears.

"I wanted you to love each other," Katherine went on, sounding bewildered, "but you wouldn't. And I felt awful. I thought if you thought I'd died, that you *would* love each other. And I knew I had to go away, anyway, before Papa started to suspect what I was.

"So Gudren and I arranged it," she said softly, lost in memory. "I had another talisman against the sun made, and I gave her my ring. And she took my white dress—my best white dress—and ashes from the fireplace. We burned fat there so the ashes would smell right. And she put them out in the sun, where you would find them, along with my note. I wasn't sure you'd be fooled, but you were.

"But then"—Katherine's face twisted in grief—"you did everything all *wrong*. You were supposed to be sorry, and cry, and comfort each other. I did it for *you*. But instead you ran and got swords. Why did you *do* that?" It was a cry from the heart. "Why didn't you *take* my gift? You treated it like garbage. I told you in the note that I wanted you to be reconciled with each other. But you didn't listen and you got swords. You killed each other. *Why* did you do it?"

Tears were slipping down Katherine's cheeks, and Stefan's face was wet, too. "We were stupid," he said, as caught up in the memory of the past as she was. "We blamed each other for your death, and we were so stupid. . . . Katherine, listen to me. It was my fault; I was the one who attacked first. And I've been sorry—you don't know how sorry I've been ever since. You don't know how many times I've thought about it and wished there was something I could do to change it. I'd have given anything to take it back—*anything*. I killed my brother. . . ." His voice cracked, and tears spilled from his eyes. Elena, her heart breaking with grief, turned helplessly to Damon and saw that he wasn't even aware of her. The look of amusement was gone, and his eyes were fixed on Stefan in utter concentration, riveted.

"Katherine, please listen to me," Stefan said shakily, regaining his voice. "We've all hurt one another enough. Please let us go now. Or keep me, if you want, but let them leave. I'm the one that's to blame. Keep me, and I'll do whatever you want. . . ."

Katherine's jewel-like eyes were liquid and impossibly blue, filled with an endless sorrow. Elena didn't dare to breathe, afraid to break the spell as the slender girl moved toward Stefan, her face softened and yearning.

But then the ice inside Katherine crept out again, freezing the tears on her cheeks. "You should have thought of that a long time ago," she said. "I might have listened to you then. I was sorry you'd killed each other at first. I ran away, without even Gudren, back to my home. But then I didn't have *anything*, not even a new dress, and I was hungry and cold. I might have starved if Klaus hadn't found me."

Klaus. Through her dismay, Elena remembered something Stefan had told her. Klaus was the man who'd made Katherine a vampire, the man the villagers said was evil.

"*Klaus* taught me the truth," Katherine said. "He showed me how the world really is. You have to be strong, and take the things you want. You have to think only of yourself. And I'm the strongest of all now. I am. You know how I got that way?" She answered the question without even waiting for them to respond. "Lives. So many lives. Humans and vampires, and they're all inside *me* now. I killed Klaus after a century or two. He was *surprised*. He didn't know how much I'd learned.

"I was so happy, taking lives, filling myself up with them. But then I would remember *you*, you two, and what you did. How you treated my gift. And I knew I had to punish you. I finally figured out how to do it.

"I brought you here, both of you. I put the thought in your mind, Stefan, the way you put thoughts into a human's. I guided you to this place. And then I made sure Damon followed you. Elena was here. I think she must be related to me somehow; she looks like me. I knew you'd see her and feel guilty. But you weren't supposed to fall in love with her!" The resentfulness in Katherine's voice gave way to fury again. "You weren't supposed to forget me! You weren't supposed to give her my ring!"

"Katherine . . ."

Katherine swept on. "Oh, you made me so angry. And now I'm going to make you sorry, really sorry. I know who I hate most now, and it's you, Stefan. Because I loved you best." She seemed to regain control of herself, wiping the last traces of tears from her face and drawing herself up with exaggerated dignity.

"I don't hate Damon as much," she said. "I might even let him live." Her eyes narrowed, and then widened with an idea. "Listen, Damon," she said secretly. "You're not as stupid as Stefan is. You know the way things really are. I've heard you say it. I've seen things you've done." She leaned forward. "I've been lonely since Klaus died. You could keep me company. All you have to do is say you love me best. Then after I kill them we'll go away. You can even kill the girl if you want. I'd let you. What do you think?"

Oh, God, thought Elena, sickened again. Damon's eyes were on Katherine's wide blue ones; he seemed to be searching her face. And the whimsical amusement was back in his expression. Oh, God, no, Elena thought. Please, no . . .

Slowly, Damon smiled.

15

Elena watched Damon with mute dread. She knew that disturbing smile too well. But even as her heart sank, her mind threw a mocking question at her. What difference did it make? She and Stefan were going to die anyway. It only made sense for Damon to save himself. And it was wrong to expect him to go against his nature.

She watched that beautiful, capricious smile with a feeling of sorrow for what Damon might have been.

Katherine smiled back at him, enchanted. "We'll be so happy together. Once they're dead, I'll let you go. I didn't mean to hurt you, not really. I just got angry." She put out a slender hand and stroked his cheek. "I'm sorry."

"Katherine," he said. He was still smiling.

"Yes." She leaned closer.

"Katherine . . ."

"Yes, Damon?"

"Go to hell."

Elena flinched from what happened next before it happened, feeling the violent upsurge of Power, of malevolent, unbridled Power. She screamed at the change in Katherine. That lovely face was twisting, mutating into something that was neither human nor animal. A red light blazed in Katherine's eyes as she fell on Damon, her fangs sinking into his throat.

Talons sprang from her fingertips, and she raked Damon's already-bleeding chest with it, tearing into his skin while the blood flowed. Elena kept screaming, realizing dimly that the pain in her arms was from fighting the ropes that held her. She heard Stefan shouting, too, but above everything she heard the deafening shriek of Katherine's mental voice.

Now you'll be sorry! Now I'm going to make you sorry! I'll kill you! I'll kill you! I'll kill you! I'll kill you!

The words themselves hurt, like daggers stabbing into Elena's mind. The sheer Power of it stupefied her, rocking her back against the iron pickets. But there was no way to get away from it. It seemed to echo from all around her, hammering in her skull.

Kill you! Kill you! Kill you!

Elena fainted.

* * *

Meredith, crouched beside Aunt Judith in the utility room, shifted her weight, straining to interpret the sounds outside the door. The dogs had gotten into the cellar; she wasn't sure how, but from the bloody muzzles of some of them, she thought they had broken through the ground-level windows. Now they were outside the utility room, but Meredith couldn't tell what they were doing. It was too quiet out there.

Margaret, huddled on Robert's lap, whimpered once.

"Hush," Robert whispered quickly. "It's all right, sweetheart. Everything's going to be all right."

Meredith met his frightened, determined eyes over Margaret's tow head. We almost had you pegged for the Other Power, she thought. But there was no time to regret it now.

"Where's Elena? Elena said she'd watch over me," Margaret said, her eyes large and solemn. "She said she'd take care of me." Aunt Judith put a hand to her mouth.

"She is taking care of you," Meredith whispered. "She just sent me to do it, that's all. It's the *truth*," she added fiercely, and saw Robert's look of reproach melt into per-plexity.

Outside, the silence had given way to scratching and gnawing sounds. The dogs were at work on the door.

Robert cradled Margaret's head closer to his chest.

* * *

Bonnie didn't know how long they had been working. Hours, certainly. Forever, it seemed like. The dogs had gotten in through the kitchen and the old wooden side doors. So far, though, only about a dozen had gotten past the fires lit like barricades in front of these openings. And the men with guns had taken care of most of those.

But Mr. Smallwood and his friends were now holding empty rifles. And they were running out of things to burn.

Vickie had gotten hysterical a little while ago, screaming and holding her head as if something was hurting her. They'd been looking for ways to restrain her when she finally passed out.

Bonnie went up to Matt, who was looking out over the fire through the demolished side door. He wasn't looking for dogs, she knew, but for something else much farther away. Something you couldn't see from here.

"You had to go, Matt," she said. "There was nothing else you could do." He didn't answer or turn around.

"It's almost dawn," she said. "Maybe when that comes, the dogs will leave." But even as she said it, she knew it wasn't true.

Matt didn't answer. She touched his shoulder. "Stefan's with her. Stefan's there."

At last, Matt gave some response. He nodded. "Stefan's there," he said.

Brown and snarling, another shape charged out of the dark.

It was much later when Elena came gradually to consciousness. She knew because she could see, not just by the handful of candles Katherine had lit but also by the cold gray dimness that filtered down from the crypt's opening.

She could see Damon, too. He was lying on the floor, his bonds slashed along with his clothes. There was enough light now to see the full extent of his wounds, and Elena wondered if he was still alive. He was motionless enough to be dead.

Damon? she thought. It was only after she had done it that she realized the word had not been spoken. Somehow, Katherine's shrieking had closed a circuit in her mind, or maybe it had awakened something sleeping. And Matt's blood had undoubtedly helped, giving her the strength to finally find her mental voice.

She turned her head the other way. *Stefan?*

His face was haggard with pain, but aware. Too aware. Elena almost wished that he were as insensible as Damon to what was happening to them.

Elena, he returned.

Where is she? Elena said, her eyes moving slowly around the room.

Stefan looked toward the opening of the crypt. *She went up there a while ago. Maybe to check on how the dogs are doing.*

Elena had thought she'd reached the limit of fear and dread, but it wasn't true. She hadn't remembered the others then.

Elena, I'm sorry. Stefan's face was filled with what no words could express.

It's not your fault, Stefan. You didn't do this to her. She did it to herself. Or—it just happened to her, because of what she is. What we are. Running beneath Elena's thoughts was the memory of how she had attacked Stefan in the woods, and how she had felt when she was racing toward Mr. Smallwood, planning her revenge. *It could have been me*, she said.

No! You could never become like that.

Elena didn't answer. If she had the Power now, what would she do to Katherine? What *wouldn't* she do to her? But she knew it would only upset Stefan more to talk about it.

I thought Damon was going to betray us, she said.

I did, too, said Stefan queerly. He was looking at his brother with an odd expression.

Do you still hate him?

Stefan's gaze darkened. *No*, he said quietly. *No, I don't hate him anymore.*

Elena nodded. It was important, somehow. Then she

started, her nerves hyper-alert, as something shadowed the entrance to the crypt. Stefan tensed, too.

She's coming. Elena—

I love you, Stefan, Elena said hopelessly, as the misty white shape hurtled down.

Katherine took form in front of them.

"I don't know what's happening," she said, looking annoyed. "You're blocking my tunnel." She peered behind Elena again, toward the broken tomb and the hole in the wall. "That's what I use for getting around," she went on, seemingly unaware of Damon's body at her feet. "It goes beneath the river. So I don't have to cross over running water, you see. Instead, I cross *under* it." She looked at them as if waiting for their appreciation of the joke.

Of course, thought Elena. How could I have been so stupid? Damon rode with us in Alaric's car over the river. He crossed running water then, and probably lots of other times. He couldn't have been the Other Power.

It was strange how she could think even though she was so frightened. It was as if one part of her mind stood watching from a distance.

"I'm going to kill you now," Katherine said conversationally. "Then I'm going under the river to kill your friends. I don't think the dogs have done it yet. But I'll take care of it myself."

"Let Elena go," said Stefan. His voice was quenched but compelling all the same.

"I haven't decided how to do it," said Katherine, ignoring him. "I might roast you. There's almost enough light for that now. And I've got these." She reached down the front of her gown and brought her closed hand out. "One—two—three!" she said, dropping two silver rings and a gold one onto the ground. Their stones shone blue as Katherine's eyes, blue as the stone in the necklace at Katherine's throat.

Elena's hands twisted frantically and she felt the smooth bareness of her ring finger. It was true. She wouldn't have believed how naked she felt without that circlet of metal. It was necessary to her life, to her survival. Without it—

"Without these you'll die," Katherine said, scuffing the rings carelessly with the toe of one foot. "But I don't know if that's *slow* enough." She paced back almost to the far wall of the crypt, her silver dress shimmering in the dim light.

It was then that the idea came to Elena.

She could move her hands. Enough to feel one with the other, enough to know that they weren't numb anymore. The ropes were looser.

But Katherine was strong. Unbelievably strong. And faster than Elena, too. Even if Elena got free she would have time for only one quick act.

She rotated one wrist, feeling the ropes give.

"There are other ways," Katherine said. "I could cut you and watch you bleed. I like watching."

Gritting her teeth, Elena exerted pressure against the rope. Her hand was bent at an excruciating angle, but she continued to press. She felt the burn of the rope slipping aside.

"Or rats," Katherine was saying pensively. "Rats could be fun. I could tell them when to start and when to stop."

Working the other hand free was much easier. Elena tried to give no sign of what was going on behind her back. She would have liked to call to Stefan with her mind, but she didn't dare. Not if there was any chance Katherine might hear.

Katherine's pacing had taken her right up to Stefan. "I think I'll start with you," she said, pushing her face close to his. "I'm hungry again. And you're so sweet, Stefan. I forgot how sweet you were."

There was a rectangle of gray light on the floor. Dawn light. It was coming in through the crypt's opening. Katherine had already been out in that light. But . . .

Katherine smiled suddenly, her blue eyes sparkling. "I know! I'll drink you almost up and make you watch while I kill *her*! I'll leave you just enough strength so you see her die before you do. Doesn't that sound like a good plan?"

Blithely, she clapped her hands and pirouetted again, dancing away.

Just one more step, thought Elena. She saw Katherine approach the rectangle of light. Just one more step . . .

Katherine took the step. "That's it, then!" She started to turn around. "What a good—"

Now!

Yanking her cramped arms out of the last loops of rope, Elena rushed her. It was like the rush of a hunting cat. One desperate sprint to reach the prey. One chance. One hope.

She struck Katherine with her full weight. The impact knocked them both into the rectangle of light. She felt Katherine's head crack against the stone floor.

And felt the searing pain, as if her own body had been plunged into poison. It was a feeling like the burning dryness of hunger, only stronger. A thousand times stronger. It was unbearable.

"*Elena!*" Stefan screamed, with mind and voice.

Stefan, she thought. Beneath her Power surged as Katherine's stunned eyes focused. Her mouth twisted with rage, fangs bursting forth. They were so long they cut into the lower lip. That distorted mouth opened in a howl.

Elena's clumsy hand fumbled at Katherine's throat. Her fingers closed on the cool metal of Katherine's blue necklace. With all her strength, she wrenched and felt the chain give way. She tried to clasp it, but her fingers felt thick and uncoordinated and Katherine's clawing hand scrabbled at it wildly. It spun away into the shadows.

"Elena!" Stefan called again in that dreadful voice.

She felt as if her body were filled with light. As if she were transparent. Only, light was pain. Beneath her, Katherine's warped face was looking up directly into the winter sky. Instead of a howl, there was a shrieking that went up and up.

Elena tried to lift herself off, but she didn't have the strength. Katherine's face was rifting, cracking open. Lines of fire opened in it. The screaming reached a crescendo. Katherine's hair was aflame, her skin was blackening. Elena felt fire from both above and below.

Then she felt something grab her, seize her shoulders and yank her away. The coolness of the shadows was like ice water. Something was turning her, cradling her.

She saw Stefan's arms, red where they had been exposed to the sun and bleeding where he had torn free of his ropes. She saw his face, saw the stricken horror and grief. Then her eyes blurred and she saw nothing.

Meredith and Robert, striking at the blood-soaked muzzles that thrust through the hole in the door, paused in confusion. The teeth had stopped snapping and tearing.

One muzzle jerked and slid out of the way. Edging sideways to look at the other, Meredith saw that the dog's eyes were glazed and milky. They didn't move. She looked at Robert, who stood panting.

There was no more noise from the cellar. Everything was silent.

But they didn't dare to hope.

Vickie's demented shrieking stopped as if it had been cut with a knife. The dog, which had sunk its teeth into Matt's thigh, stiffened and gave a convulsive shudder; then, its jaws released him. Gasping for breath, Bonnie swung to look beyond the dying fire. There was just enough light to see bodies of other dogs lying where they had fallen outside.

She and Matt leaned on each other, looking around, bewildered.

It had finally stopped snowing.

Slowly, Elena opened her eyes.

Everything was very clear and calm.

She was glad the shrieking was over. That had been bad; it had hurt. Now, nothing hurt. She felt as if her body were filled with light again, but this time there was no pain. It was as if she were floating, very high and easy, on wafts of air. She almost felt she didn't have a body at all.

She smiled.

Turning her head didn't hurt, although it increased the loose, floating feeling. She saw, in the oblong of pale light on the floor, the smoldering remains of a silvery dress. Katherine's lie of five hundred years ago had become the truth.

That was that, then. Elena looked away. She didn't wish anyone harm now, and she didn't want to waste time on Katherine. There were so many more important things.

"Stefan," she said and sighed, and smiled. Oh, this was nice. This must be how a bird felt.

"I didn't mean for things to turn out this way," she said, softly rueful. His green eyes were wet. They filled again, but he returned her smile.

"I know," he said. "I know, Elena."

He understood. That was good; that was important. It was easy to see the things that were really important now. And Stefan's understanding meant more to her than all the world.

It seemed to her that it had been a long while since she'd really looked at him. Since she'd taken time to appreciate how beautiful he was, with his dark hair and his eyes as green as oak leaves. But she saw it now, and she saw his soul shining through those eyes. It was worth it, she thought. I didn't want to die; I don't want to now. But I'd do it all over again if I had to.

"I love you," she whispered.

"I love you," he said, squeezing their joined hands.

The strange, languorous lightness cradled her gently. She could scarcely feel Stefan holding her.

She would have thought she'd be terrified. But she wasn't, not as long as Stefan was there.

"The people at the dance—they'll be all right now, won't they?" she said.

"They'll be all right now," Stefan whispered. "You saved them."

"I didn't get to say good-bye to Bonnie and Meredith. Or Aunt Judith. You have to tell them I love them."

"I'll tell them," Stefan said.

"You can tell them yourself," panted another voice, hoarse and unused-sounding. Damon had pulled himself across the floor behind Stefan. His face was ravaged, streaked with blood, but his dark eyes burned at her. "Use your will, Elena. Hold on. You have the strength—"

She smiled at him waveringly. She knew the truth. What was happening was only finishing what had been started two weeks ago. She'd had thirteen days to get things straight, to make amends with Matt and say good-bye to Margaret. To tell Stefan she loved him. But now the grace period was up.

Still, there was no point in hurting Damon. She loved Damon, too. "I'll try," she promised.

"We'll take you home," he said.

"But not yet," she told him gently. "Let's wait just a little while."

Something happened in the fathomless black eyes, and the burning spark went out. Then she saw that Damon knew, too.

"I'm not afraid," she said. "Well—only a little." A drowsiness had started, and she felt very comfortable, but as if she were falling asleep. Things were drifting away from her.

An ache rose in her chest. She was not much afraid, but she was sorry. There were so many things she would miss, so many things she wished she had done.

"Oh," she said softly. "How funny."

The walls of the crypt seemed to have melted. They were gray and cloudy and there was something like a doorway there, like the door that was the opening to the underground room. Only this was a doorway into a different light.

"How beautiful," she murmured. "Stefan? I'm so tired."

"You can rest now," he whispered.

"You won't let go of me?"

"No."

"Then I won't be afraid."

Something was shining on Damon's face. She reached toward it, touched it, and lifted her fingers away in wonder.

"Don't be sad," she told him, feeling the cool wetness on her fingertips. But a pang of worry disturbed her. Who was there to understand Damon now? Who would be there to push him, to try to see what was really inside him? "You have to take care of each other," she said, realizing it. A little strength came back to her, like a candle flaring in the wind. "Stefan, will you promise? Promise to take care of each other?"

"I promise," he said. "Oh, Elena . . ."

Waves of sleepiness were overcoming her. "That's good," she said. "That's good, Stefan."

The doorway was closer, so close she could touch it now. She wondered if her parents were somewhere behind it.

"Time to go home," she whispered.

And then the darkness and the shadows faded and there was nothing but light.

* * *

Stefan held her while her eyes closed. And then he just held her, the tears he'd been keeping back falling without restraint. It was a different pain than when he'd pulled her out of the river. There was no anger in this, and no hatred, but a love that seemed to go on and on forever.

It hurt even more.

He looked at the rectangle of sunlight, just a step or two away from him. Elena had gone into the light. She'd left him here alone.

Not for long, he thought.

His ring was on the floor. He didn't even glance at it as he rose, his eyes on the shaft of sunlight shining down.

A hand grabbed his arm and pulled him back.

Stefan looked into his brother's face.

Damon's eyes were dark as midnight, and he was holding Stefan's ring. As Stefan watched, unable to move, he forced the ring onto Stefan's finger and released him.

"Now," he said, sinking back painfully, "you can go wherever you want." He picked the ring Stefan had given to Elena off the ground and held it out. "This is yours, too. Take it. Take it and go." He turned his face away.

Stefan gazed at the golden circlet in his palm for a long time.

Then his fingers closed over it and he looked back at Damon. His brother's eyes were shut, his breathing labored. He looked exhausted and in pain.

And Stefan had made a promise to Elena.

"Come on," he said quietly, putting the ring in his pocket. "Let's get you someplace where you can rest."

He put an arm around his brother to help him up. And then, for a moment, he just held on.

16

December 16, Monday

Stefan gave this to me. He's given most of the things in his room away. I said I didn't want it at first, because I didn't know what to do with it. But now I think I have an idea.

People are starting to forget already. They're getting the details wrong, and adding things they just imagined. And, most of all, they're making up explanations. Why it wasn't really supernatural, why there's a rational reason for this or that. It's just silly, but there's no way to stop them, especially the adults.

They're the worst. They're saying the dogs were hydrophobic or something. The vet's come up with *a new name for it, some kind of rabies that's spread by bats. Meredith says that's ironic. I think it's just stupid.*

The kids are a little better, especially the ones who were at the dance. There are some I think we can rely on, like Sue Carson and Vickie. Vickie's changed so much in the last two days that it's like a miracle. She's not the way she's been for the last two and a half months, but she's not the way she used to be, either. She used to be pretty much of a bimbo, running around with the tough crowd. But now I think she's okay.

Even Caroline wasn't so bad today. She didn't talk at the other service, but she talked at this one. She said Elena was the real snow queen, which was kind of cribbing off of Sue's speech from before, but probably the best Caroline could do. It was a nice gesture.

Elena looked so peaceful. Not like a wax doll, but as if she were sleeping. I know everybody says that, but it's true. This time, it really is true.

But afterward people were talking about "her remarkable escape from drowning" and stuff like that. And saying she died of an embolism or something. Which is absolutely ridiculous. But that's what gave me the idea.

I'm going to get her other diary out of her closet. And then I'm going to ask Mrs. Grimesby to put them in the library, not in a case like Honoria Fell's, but where people can pick them up and read them. Because the truth is in here. This is where the real story is. And I don't want anybody to forget it.

I think maybe the kids will remember.

I suppose I should put what happened to the rest of the people around here; Elena would want that. Aunt Judith is okay, although she's one of the adults who can't deal with the truth. She needs a rational explanation. She and Robert are going to get married at Christmas. That should be good for Margaret.

Margaret's got the right idea. She told me at the service that she's going to go see Elena and her parents someday, but not now, because there were a lot of things she still had to do right here. I don't know what put that idea into her head. She's smart for a four-year-old.

Alaric and Meredith are also okay, of course. When they saw each other that horrible morning, after everything had quieted down and we were picking up the pieces, they practically fell into each other's arms. I think there's something going on there. Meredith says she'll discuss it when she's eighteen and she graduates.

Typical, absolutely typical. Everybody else gets the guys. I'm thinking of trying one of my grandmother's rituals, just to see if I'll ever get married at all. There isn't even anybody I want to marry around here.

Well, there's Matt. Matt's nice. But right now he's only got one girl on his mind. I don't know if that will ever change.

He punched Tyler in the nose after the service today, because Tyler said something off-color about her. Tyler is one person I know will never change, no matter what. He'll always be the mean, obnoxious jerk he is now.

But Matt—well, Matt's eyes are awfully blue. And he's got a terrific right hook.

Stefan couldn't hit Tyler because he wasn't there. There are still plenty of people in town who think he killed Elena. He must have, they say, because there was nobody else there. Katherine's ashes were scattered all over by the time the rescuers got to the crypt. Stefan says it's because she was so old that she flamed up like that. He says he should have realized the first time, when Katherine pretended to burn, that a young vampire wouldn't turn to ashes that way. She'd just die, like Elena.

Only the old ones crumble.

Some people—especially Mr. Smallwood and his friends—would probably blame Damon if they could get hold of him. But they can't. He wasn't there when they reached the tomb, because Stefan helped him get away. Stefan won't say where, but I think to someplace in the woods. Vampires must heal fast because today when I met him after the service, Stefan said that Damon had left Fell's Church. He wasn't happy about it; I think Damon didn't tell him. Now the question seems to be: What is Damon doing? Out biting innocent girls? Or is he reformed? I wouldn't lay bets on it either way. Damon was a strange guy.

But gorgeous. Definitely gorgeous.

Stefan won't say where he's going, either. But I have a sneaking suspicion Damon may get a surprise if he looks behind him. Apparently, Elena made Stefan promise to watch out for him or something. And Stefan takes promises very, very seriously.

I wish him luck. But he'll be doing what Elena wanted him to, which I think will make him happy. As happy as he can be here without her. He's wearing her ring on a chain around his neck now.

If you think any of this sounds frivolous or as

if I don't care about Elena, that just shows how wrong you are. ~~I dare anybody to say that to me.~~ *Meredith and I cried all day Saturday, and most of Sunday. And I was so angry I wanted to rip things apart and break them. I kept thinking, why Elena? Why? When there were so many other people who could have died that night. Out of the whole town, she was the only one.*

Of course, she did it to save them, but why did she have to give her life to do it? It isn't fair.

Oh, I'm starting to cry again. That's what happens when you think about life being fair. And I can't explain why it isn't. I'd like to go bang on Honoria Fell's tomb and ask her if she *can explain, but she wouldn't talk to me. I don't think it's something anybody knows.*

I loved Elena. And I'm going to miss her terribly. The whole school is. It's like a light that's gone out. Robert says that's what her name means in Latin, "light."

Now there'll always be a part of me where the light has gone away.

I wish I'd been able to say good-bye to her, but Stefan says she sent her love to me. I'm going to try to think of that as a light to take with me.

I'd better stop writing now, Stefan's leaving,

and Matt and Meredith and Alaric and I are going to see him off. I didn't mean to get so into this; I've never kept a journal myself. But I want people to know the truth about Elena. She wasn't a saint. She wasn't always sweet and good and honest and agreeable. But she was strong and loving and loyal to her friends, and in the end she did the most unselfish thing anybody could do. Meredith says it means she chose light over darkness. I want people to know that so they'll always remember.

I always will.

—Bonnie McCullough
12/16/91

1

"Things can be just like they were before," said Caroline warmly, reaching out to squeeze Bonnie's hand.

But it wasn't true. Nothing could ever be the way it had been before Elena died. Nothing. And Bonnie had serious misgivings about this party Caroline was trying to set up. A vague nagging in the pit of her stomach told her that for some reason it was a very, very bad idea.

"Meredith's birthday is already *over*," she pointed out. "It was last Saturday."

"But she didn't have a party, not a real party like this one. We've got all night; my parents won't be back until Sunday morning. Come on, Bonnie—just think how surprised she'll be."

Oh, she'll be surprised, all right, thought Bonnie. So

surprised she just might kill me afterward. "Look, Caroline, the reason Meredith didn't have a big party is that she still doesn't feel much like celebrating. It seems—disrespectful, somehow—"

"But that's *wrong*. Elena would want us to have a good time, you know she would. She loved parties. And she'd hate to see us sitting around and crying over her six months after she's gone." Caroline leaned forward, her normally feline green eyes earnest and compelling. There was no artifice in them now, none of Caroline's usual nasty manipulation. Bonnie could tell she really meant it.

"I want us to be friends again the way we used to be," Caroline said. "We always used to celebrate our birthdays together, just the four of us, remember? And remember how the guys would always try to crash our parties? I wonder if they'll try this year."

Bonnie felt control of the situation slipping away from her. This is a bad idea, this is a very bad idea, she thought. But Caroline was going on, looking dreamy and almost romantic as she talked about the good old days. Bonnie didn't have the heart to tell her that the good old days were as dead as disco.

"But there aren't even four of us anymore. Three doesn't make much of a party," she protested feebly when she could get a word in.

"I'm going to invite Sue Carson, too. Meredith gets

along with her, doesn't she?"

Bonnie had to admit Meredith did; everyone got along with Sue. But even so, Caroline had to understand that things couldn't be the way they had been before. You couldn't just substitute Sue Carson for Elena and say, There, everything is fixed now.

But how do I explain that to Caroline? Bonnie thought. Suddenly she knew.

"Let's invite Vickie Bennett," she said.

Caroline stared. "*Vickie Bennett*? You must be joking. Invite that bizarre little drip who undressed in front of half the school? After everything that happened?"

"*Because* of everything that happened," said Bonnie firmly. "Look, I know she was never in our crowd. But she's not in with the fast crowd anymore; they don't want her and she's scared to death of them. She needs friends. We need people. Let's invite her."

For a moment Caroline looked helplessly frustrated. Bonnie thrust her chin out, put her hands on her hips, and waited. Finally Caroline sighed.

"All right; you win. I'll invite her. But you have to take care of getting Meredith to my house Saturday night. And Bonnie—make sure she doesn't have any idea what's going on. I really want this to be a surprise."

"Oh, it will be," Bonnie said grimly. She was unprepared for the sudden light in Caroline's face or the impulsive warmth of Caroline's hug.

"I'm so glad you're seeing things my way," Caroline said. "And it'll be so good for us all to be together again."

She doesn't understand a thing, Bonnie realized, dazed, as Caroline walked off. What do I have to do to explain to her? Sock her?

And then: Oh, God, now I have to tell Meredith.

But by the end of the day she decided that maybe Meredith didn't need to be told. Caroline wanted Meredith surprised; well, maybe Bonnie should deliver Meredith surprised. That way at least Meredith wouldn't have to worry about it beforehand. Yes, Bonnie concluded, it was probably kindest to *not* tell Meredith anything.

And who knows, she wrote in her journal Friday night. *Maybe I'm being too hard on Caroline. Maybe she's really sorry about all the things she did to us, like trying to humiliate Elena in front of the whole town and trying to get Stefan put away for murder. Maybe Caroline's matured since then and learned to think about somebody besides herself. Maybe we'll actually have a good time at her party.*

And maybe aliens will kidnap me before tomorrow afternoon, she thought as she closed the diary. She could only hope.

The diary was an inexpensive drugstore blank book, with a pattern of tiny flowers on the cover. She'd only started keeping it since Elena had died, but she'd already become slightly addicted to it. It was the one place she could say anything she wanted without people looking shocked and saying, "Bonnie McCullough!" or "Oh, *Bonnie.*"

She was still thinking about Elena as she turned off the light and crawled under the covers.

She was sitting on lush, manicured grass that spread as far as she could see in all directions. The sky was a flawless blue, the air was warm and scented. Birds were singing.

"I'm so glad you could come," Elena said.

"Oh—yes," said Bonnie. "Well, naturally, so am I. Of course." She looked around again, then hastily back at Elena.

"More tea?"

There was a teacup in Bonnie's hand, thin and fragile as eggshell. "Oh—sure. Thanks."

Elena was wearing an eighteenth-century dress of gauzy white muslin, which clung to her, showing how slender she was. She poured the tea precisely, without spilling a drop.

"Would you like a mouse?"

"A *what?*"

"I said, would you like a sandwich with your tea?"

"Oh. A sandwich. Yeah. Great." It was thinly sliced cucumber with mayonnaise on a dainty square of white bread. Without the crust.

The whole scene was as sparkly and beautiful as a picture by Seurat. Warm Springs, that's where we are. The old picnic place, Bonnie thought. But surely we've got more important things to discuss than tea.

"Who does your hair these days?" she asked. Elena never had been able to do it herself.

"Do you like it?" Elena put a hand up to the silky, pale gold mass piled at the back of her neck.

"It's perfect," said Bonnie, sounding for all the world like her mother at a Daughters of the American Revolution dinner party.

"Well, hair is important, you know," Elena said. Her eyes glowed a deeper blue than the sky, lapis lazuli blue. Bonnie touched her own springy red curls self-consciously.

"Of course, blood is important too," Elena said.

"Blood? Oh—yes, of course," said Bonnie, flustered. She had no idea what Elena was talking about, and she felt as if she were walking on a tightrope over alligators. "Yes, blood's important, all right," she agreed weakly.

"Another sandwich?"

"Thanks." It was cheese and tomato. Elena selected one for herself and bit into it delicately. Bonnie watched her, feeling uneasiness grow by the minute inside her, and then—

And then she saw the mud oozing out of the edges of the sandwich.

"What—*what's that?*" Terror made her voice shrill. For the first time, the dream seemed like a dream, and she found that she couldn't move, could only gasp and stare. A thick glob of the brown stuff fell off Elena's sandwich onto the checkered tablecloth. It was mud, all right. "Elena . . . Elena, what—"

"Oh, we all eat this down here." Elena smiled at her with brown-stained teeth. Except that the voice wasn't Elena's; it was ugly and distorted and it was a man's voice. "You will too."

The air was no longer warm and scented; it was hot and sickly sweet with the odor of rotting garbage. There were black pits in the green grass, which wasn't manicured after all but wild and overgrown. This wasn't Warm Springs. She was in the old graveyard; how could she not have realized that? Only these graves were fresh.

"Another mouse?" Elena said, and giggled obscenely.

Bonnie looked down at the half-eaten sandwich she was holding and screamed. Dangling from one end was a ropy brown tail. She threw it as hard as she could against a headstone, where it hit with a wet slap. Then she stood, stomach heaving, scrubbing her fingers frantically against her jeans.

"You can't leave yet. The company is just arriving."

Elena's face was changing; she had already lost her hair, and her skin was turning gray and leathery. Things were moving in the plate of sandwiches and the freshly dug pits. Bonnie didn't want to see any of them; she thought she would go mad if she did.

"You're not Elena!" she screamed, and ran.

The wind blew her hair into her eyes and she couldn't see. Her pursuer was behind her; she could feel it right behind her. Get to the bridge, she thought, and then she ran into something.

"I've been waiting for you," said the thing in Elena's dress, the gray skeletal thing with long, twisted teeth. "Listen to me, Bonnie." It held her with terrible strength.

"You're not Elena! You're not Elena!"

"Listen to me, Bonnie!"

It was Elena's voice, Elena's real voice, not obscenely amused nor thick and ugly, but urgent. It came from somewhere behind Bonnie and it swept through the dream like a fresh, cold wind. "Bonnie, listen quickly—"

Things were melting. The bony hands on Bonnie's arms, the crawling graveyard, the rancid hot air. For a moment Elena's voice was clear, but it was broken up like a bad long-distance connection.

". . . He's twisting things, changing them. I'm not as strong as he is . . ." Bonnie missed some words. ". . . but this is important. You have to find . . . right now." Her voice was fading.

"Elena, I can't hear you! Elena!"

". . . an easy spell, only two ingredients, the ones I told you already . . ."

"Elena!"

Bonnie was still shouting as she sat bolt upright in bed.

2

"And that's all I remember," Bonnie concluded as she and Meredith walked down Sunflower Street between the rows of tall Victorian houses.

"But it was definitely Elena?"

"Yes, and she was trying to tell me something at the end. But that's the part that wasn't clear, except that it was important, terribly important. What do you think?"

"Mouse sandwiches and open graves?" Meredith arched an elegant eyebrow. "I think you're getting Stephen King mixed up with Lewis Carroll."

Bonnie thought she was probably right. But the dream still bothered her; it had bothered her all day, enough to put her earlier worries out of her mind. Now, as she and Meredith approached Caroline's house, the old worries returned with a vengeance.

She really should have told Meredith about this, she thought, casting an uneasy sideways glance at the taller girl. She shouldn't let Meredith just walk in there unprepared. . . .

Meredith looked up at the lighted windows of the Queen Anne House with a sigh. "Do you really *need* those earrings tonight?"

"Yes, I do; yes, absolutely." Too late now. Might as well make the best of it. "You'll love them when you see them," she added, hearing the note of hopeful desperation in her own voice.

Meredith paused and her keen dark eyes searched Bonnie's face curiously. Then she knocked on the door. "I just hope Caroline's not staying home tonight. We could end up stuck with her."

"Caroline staying home on a Saturday night? Don't be ridiculous." Bonnie had been holding her breath too long; she was starting to feel lightheaded. Her tinkling laughter came out brittle and false. "What a concept," she continued somewhat hysterically as Meredith said, "I don't think *anybody's* home," and tried the knob. Possessed by some crazy impulse Bonnie added, "Fiddle-dee-dee."

Hand on doorknob, Meredith stopped dead and turned to look at her.

"Bonnie," she said quietly, "have you gone completely through the ozone?"

"No." Deflated, Bonnie grabbed Meredith's arm and sought her eyes urgently. The door was opening on its own. "Oh, God, Meredith, please don't kill me . . ."

"*Surprise!*" shouted three voices.

"Smile," Bonnie hissed, shoving the suddenly resistant body of her friend through the door and into the bright room full of noise and showers of foil confetti. She beamed wildly herself and spoke through clenched teeth. "Kill me later—I deserve it—but for now just smile."

There were balloons, the expensive Mylar kind, and a cluster of presents on the coffee table. There was even a flower arrangement, although Bonnie noticed the orchids in it matched Caroline's pale green scarf exactly. It was a Hermès silk with a design of vines and leaves. She'll end up wearing one of those orchids in her hair, I'll bet, Bonnie thought.

Sue Carson's blue eyes were a little anxious, her smile wavering. "I hope you didn't have any big plans for tonight, Meredith," she said.

"Nothing I can't break with an iron crowbar," Meredith replied. But she smiled back with wry warmth and Bonnie relaxed. Sue had been a Homecoming Princess on Elena's court, along with Bonnie, Meredith, and Caroline. She was the only girl at school besides Bonnie and Meredith who'd stood by Elena when everyone else had turned against her. At Elena's funeral she'd said that Elena would always be the real queen of Robert E. Lee, and she'd given up her own nomination for Snow Queen in Elena's memory. Nobody could hate Sue. The worst was over now, Bonnie thought.

"I want to get a picture of us all on the couch," Caroline said, positioning them behind the flower arrangement. "Vickie, take it, will you?"

Vickie Bennett had been standing by quietly, unnoticed. Now she said, "Oh, sure," and nervously flicked long, light brown hair out of her eyes as she picked up the camera.

Just like she's some kind of servant, Bonnie thought, and then the flashbulb blinded her.

As the Polaroid developed and Sue and Caroline laughed and talked around Meredith's dry politeness, Bonnie noticed something else. It was a good picture; Caroline looked stunning as ever with her auburn hair gleaming and the pale green orchids in front of her. And there was Meredith, looking resigned and ironic and darkly beautiful without even trying, and there she was herself, a head shorter than the others, with her red curls tousled and a sheepish expression on her face. But the strange thing was the figure beside her on the couch. It was Sue, of course it was Sue, but for a moment the blond hair and blue eyes seemed to belong to someone else.

Someone looking at her urgently, on the verge of saying something important. Bonnie frowned at the photo, blinking rapidly. The image swam in front of her, and a chilling uneasiness ran up her spine.

No, it was just Sue in the picture. She must've gone crazy for a minute, or else she was letting Caroline's desire for them "all to be together again" affect her.

"I'll take the next one," she said, springing up. "Sit down, Vickie, and lean in. No, farther, farther—there!" All of Vickie's movements were quick and light and nervous. When the flashbulb went off, she started like a scared animal ready to bolt.

Caroline scarcely glanced at this picture, getting up and heading for the kitchen instead. "Guess what we're having instead of cake?" she said. "I'm making my own version of Death by Chocolate. Come on, you've got to help me melt the fudge." Sue followed her, and after an uncertain pause, so did Vickie.

The last traces of Meredith's pleasant expression evaporated and she turned to Bonnie. "You should have told me."

"I know." Bonnie lowered her head meekly a minute. Then she looked up and grinned. "But then you wouldn't have come and we wouldn't be having Death by Chocolate."

"And that makes it all worthwhile?"

"Well, it helps," Bonnie said, with an air of being reasonable. "And really, it probably won't be so bad. Caroline's actually trying to be nice, and it's good for Vickie to get out of the house for once . . ."

"It doesn't look like it's good for her," Meredith said bluntly. "It looks like she's going to have a heart attack."

"Well, she's probably just nervous." In Bonnie's opinion, Vickie had good reason to be nervous. She'd spent most of the previous fall in a trance, being slowly driven out of her mind by a power she didn't understand. Nobody had expected her to come out of it as well as she had.

Meredith was still looking bleak. "At least," Bonnie said consolingly, "it isn't your real birthday."

Meredith picked up the camera and turned it over and over. Still looking down at her hands, she said, "But it is."

"What?" Bonnie stared and then said louder, "*What* did you say?"

"I said, it is my real birthday. Caroline's mom must have told her; she and my mom used to be friends a long time ago."

"Meredith, what are you talking about? Your birthday was last week, May 30."

"No, it wasn't. It's today, June 6. It's true; it's on my driver's license and everything. My parents started celebrating it a week early because June 6 was too upsetting for them. It was the day my grandfather was attacked and went crazy." As Bonnie gasped, unable to speak, she added calmly, "He tried to kill my grandmother, you know. He tried to kill me, too." Meredith put the camera down carefully in the exact center of the coffee table. "We really should go in the kitchen," she said quietly. "I smell chocolate."

Bonnie was still paralyzed, but her mind was beginning to work again. Vaguely, she remembered Meredith speaking about this before, but she hadn't told her the full truth then. And she hadn't said when it had happened.

"Attacked—you mean like Vickie was attacked," Bonnie got out. She couldn't say the word *vampire*, but she knew Meredith understood.

"Like Vickie was attacked," Meredith confirmed. "Come on," she added, even more quietly. "They're waiting for us. I didn't mean to upset you."

Meredith doesn't want me to be upset, so I *won't* be upset, Bonnie thought, pouring hot fudge over the chocolate cake and chocolate ice cream. Even though we've been friends since first grade and she never told me this secret before.

For an instant her skin chilled and words came floating out of the dark corners of her mind. *No one is what they seem.* She'd been warned that last year by the voice of Honoria Fell speaking through her, and the prophecy had turned out to be horrifyingly true. What if it wasn't over yet?

Then Bonnie shook her head determinedly. She couldn't think about this right now; she had a *party* to think about. And I'll make sure it's a *good* party and we all get along somehow, she thought.

Strangely, it wasn't even that hard. Meredith and Vickie didn't talk much at first, but Bonnie went out of her way to be nice to Vickie, and even Meredith couldn't resist the pile of brightly wrapped presents on the coffee table. By the time she'd opened the last one they were all talking and laughing. The mood of truce and toleration continued as they moved up into Caroline's bedroom to examine her clothes and CDs and photo albums. As it got near midnight they flopped on sleeping bags, still talking.

"What's going on with Alaric these days?" Sue asked Meredith.

Alaric Saltzman was Meredith's boyfriend—sort of. He was a graduate student from Duke University who'd majored in parapsychology and had been called to Fell's Church last year when the vampire attacks began. Though he'd started out an enemy, he'd ended up an ally—and a friend.

"He's in Russia," Meredith said. "Perestroika, you know? He's over there finding out what they were doing with psychics during the Cold War."

"What are you going to tell him when he gets back?" asked Caroline.

It was a question Bonnie would have liked to ask Meredith herself. Because Alaric was almost four years older, Meredith had told him to wait until after she graduated to talk about their future. But now Meredith was eighteen—today, Bonnie reminded herself—and graduation was in two weeks. What was going to happen after that?

"I haven't decided," Meredith said. "Alaric wants me to go to Duke, and I've been accepted there, but I'm not sure. I have to think."

Bonnie was just as glad. She wanted Meredith to go to Boone Junior College with *her*, not go off and get married, or even engaged. It was stupid to decide on one guy so young. Bonnie herself was notorious for playing the field, going from boy to boy as she pleased. She got crushes easily, and got over them just as easily.

"I haven't seen the guy so far worth remaining faithful to," she said now.

Everyone looked at her quickly. Sue's chin was resting on her fists as she asked, "Not even Stefan?"

Bonnie should have known. With the only light the dim bedside lamp and the only sound the rustle of new leaves on the weeping willows outside, it was inevitable that the conversation would turn to Stefan—and to Elena.

Stefan Salvatore and Elena Gilbert were already a sort of legend in the town, like Romeo and Juliet. When Stefan had first come to Fell's Church, every girl had wanted him. And Elena, the most beautiful, most popular, most unapproachable girl at school, had wanted him too. It was only after she'd gotten him that she realized the danger. Stefan wasn't what he seemed—he had a secret far darker than anyone could have guessed. And he had a brother, Damon, even more mysterious and dangerous than himself. Elena had been caught between the two brothers, loving Stefan but drawn irresistibly to Damon's wildness. In the end she had died to save them both, and to redeem their love.

"Maybe Stefan—if you're Elena," Bonnie murmured, yielding the point. The atmosphere had changed. It was hushed now, a little sad, just right for late-night confidences.

"I still can't believe she's gone," Sue said quietly, shaking her head and shutting her eyes. "She was so much more alive than other people."

"Her flame burned brighter," said Meredith, gazing at the patterns the rose-and-gold lamp made on the ceiling. Her voice was soft but intense, and it seemed to Bonnie that those words described Elena better than anything she'd ever heard.

"There were times when I hated her, but I could never

ignore her," Caroline admitted, her green eyes narrowed in memory. "She wasn't a person you could ignore."

"One thing I learned from her death," Sue said, "is that it could happen to any of us. You can't waste any of life because you never know how long you've got."

"It could be sixty years or sixty minutes," Vickie agreed in a low voice. "Any of us could die tonight."

Bonnie wriggled, disturbed. But before she could say anything, Sue repeated, "I still can't believe she's really gone. Sometimes I feel as if she's somewhere near."

"Oh, so do I," said Bonnie, distracted. An image of Warm Springs flashed through her mind, and for a moment it seemed more vivid than Caroline's dim room. "Last night I dreamed about her, and I had the feeling it really *was* her and that she was trying to tell me something. I still have that feeling," she said to Meredith.

The others gazed at her silently. Once, they would all have laughed if Bonnie hinted at anything supernatural, but not now. Her psychic powers were undisputed, awesome, and a little scary.

"Do you really?" breathed Vickie.

"What do you think she was trying to say?" asked Sue.

"I don't know. At the end she was trying so hard to stay in contact with me, but she couldn't."

There was another silence. At last Sue said hesitantly, with the faintest catch in her voice, "Do you think . . . do you think *you* could contact *her*?"

It was what they'd all been wondering. Bonnie looked toward Meredith. Earlier, Meredith had dismissed the dream, but now she met Bonnie's eyes seriously.

"I don't know," Bonnie said slowly. Visions from the nightmare kept swirling around her. "I don't want to go into a trance and open myself up to whatever else might be out there, that's for sure."

"Is that the only way to communicate with dead people? What about a Ouija board or something?" Sue asked.

"My parents have a Ouija board," Caroline said a little too loudly. Suddenly the hushed, low-key mood was broken and an indefinable tension filled the air. Everyone sat up straighter and looked at each other with speculation. Even Vickie looked intrigued on top of her scaredness.

"Would it work?" Meredith said to Bonnie.

"Should we?" Sue wondered aloud.

"Do we dare? That's really the question," Meredith said. Once again Bonnie found everyone looking at her. She hesitated a final instant, and then shrugged. Excitement was stirring in her stomach.

"Why not?" she said. "What have we got to lose?"

Caroline turned to Vickie. "Vickie, there's a closet at the bottom of the stairs. The Ouija board should be inside, on the top shelf with a bunch of other games."

She didn't even say, "Please, will you get it?" Bonnie

frowned and opened her mouth, but Vickie was already out the door.

"You could be a little more gracious," Bonnie told Caroline. "What is this, your impression of Cinderella's evil stepmother?"

"Oh, come on, Bonnie," Caroline said impatiently. "She's lucky just to be invited. *She* knows that."

"And here I thought she was just overcome by our collective splendor," Meredith said dryly.

"And besides—" Bonnie started when she was interrupted. The noise was thin and shrill and it fell off weakly at the end, but there was no mistaking it. It was a scream. It was followed by dead silence and then suddenly peal after peal of piercing shrieks.

For an instant the girls in the bedroom stood transfixed. Then they were all running out into the hallway and down the stairs.

"Vickie!" Meredith, with her long legs, reached the bottom first. Vickie was standing in front of the closet, arms outstretched as if to protect her face. She clutched at Meredith, still screaming.

"Vickie, what is it?" Caroline demanded, sounding more angry than afraid. There were game boxes scattered across the floor and Monopoly markers and Trivial Pursuit cards strewn everywhere. "What are you yelling about?"

"It grabbed me! I was reaching up to the top shelf and

something grabbed me around the waist!"

"From behind?"

"No! From inside the closet."

Startled, Bonnie looked inside the open closet. Winter coats hung in an impenetrable layer, some of them reaching the floor. Gently disengaging herself from Vickie, Meredith picked up an umbrella and began poking the coats.

"Oh, don't—" Bonnie began involuntarily, but the umbrella encountered only the resistance of cloth. Meredith used it to push the coats aside and reveal the bare cedarwood of the closet wall.

"You see? Nobody there," she said lightly. "But you know what *is* there are these coat sleeves. If you leaned in far enough between them, I'll bet it could feel like somebody's arms closing around you."

Vickie stepped forward, touched a dangling sleeve, then looked up at the shelf. She put her face in her hands, long silky hair falling forward to screen it. For an awful moment Bonnie thought she was crying, then she heard the giggles.

"Oh, God! I really thought—oh, I'm so stupid! I'll clean it up," Vickie said.

"Later," said Meredith firmly. "Let's go in the living room."

Bonnie threw one last look at the closet as they went.

When they were all gathered around the coffee table, with several lights turned off for effect, Bonnie put her fingers lightly on the small plastic planchette. She'd never actually used a Ouija board, but she knew how it was done. The planchette moved to point at letters and spell out a message—if the spirits were willing to talk, that is.

"We all have to be touching it," she said, and then watched as the others obeyed. Meredith's fingers were long and slender, Sue's slim and tapering with oval nails. Caroline's nails were painted burnished copper. Vickie's were bitten.

"Now we close our eyes and concentrate," Bonnie said softly. There were little hisses of anticipation as the girls obeyed; the atmosphere was getting to all of them.

"Think of Elena. Picture her. If she's out there, we want to draw her here."

The big room was silent. In the dark behind her closed lids Bonnie saw pale gold hair and eyes like lapis lazuli.

"Come, on, Elena," she whispered. "Talk to me."

The planchette began to move.

None of them could be guiding it; they were all applying pressure from different points. Nevertheless, the little triangle of plastic was sliding smoothly, confidently. Bonnie kept her eyes shut until it stopped and then looked. The planchette was pointing to the word *Yes.*

Vickie gave something like a soft sob.

Bonnie looked at the others. Caroline was breathing fast, green eyes narrowed. Sue, the only one of all of them, still had her eyes resolutely closed. Meredith looked pale.

They all expected her to know what to do.

"Keep concentrating," Bonnie told them. She felt unready and a little stupid addressing the empty air directly. But she was the expert; she had to do it.

"Is that you, Elena?" she said.

The planchette made a little circle and returned to *Yes*.

Suddenly Bonnie's heart was beating so hard she was afraid it would shake her fingers. The plastic underneath her fingertips felt different, electrified almost, as if some supernatural energy was flowing through it. She no longer felt stupid. Tears came to her eyes, and she could see that Meredith's eyes were glistening too. Meredith nodded at her.

"How can we be sure?" Caroline was saying, loudly, suspiciously. Caroline doesn't feel it, Bonnie realized; she doesn't sense anything I do. Psychically speaking, she's a dud.

The planchette was moving again, touching letters now, so quickly that Meredith barely had time to spell out the message. Even without punctuation it was clear.

CAROLINE DONT BE A JERK, it said. YOURE LUCKY IM TALKING TO YOU AT ALL

"That's Elena, all right," Meredith said dryly.

"It sounds like her, but—"

"Oh, shut up, Caroline," Bonnie said. "Elena, I'm just so glad . . ." Her throat locked up and she tried again.

BONNIE THERES NO TIME   STOP SNIVELING AND GET DOWN TO BUSINESS

And *that* was Elena too, Bonnie sniffed and went on. "I had a dream about you last night."

TEA

"Yes." Bonnie's heart was thudding faster than ever. "I wanted to talk to you, but things got weird and then we kept losing contact—"

BONNIE DONT TRANCE   NO TRANCE   NO TRANCE

"All right." That answered her question, and she was relieved to hear it.

CORRUPTING INFLUENCES DISTORTING OUR COMMUNI-CATION   THERE ARE BAD THINGS VERY BAD THINGS OUT HERE

"Like what?" Bonnie leaned closer to the board. "Like what?"

NO TIME! The planchette seemed to add the exclamation point. It was jerking violently from letter to letter as if Elena could barely contain her impatience. HES BUSY SO I CAN TALK NOW BUT THERES NOT MUCH TIME   LISTEN WHEN WE STOP GET OUT OF THE HOUSE FAST   YOURE IN DANGER

"Danger?" Vickie repeated, looking as if she might jump off the chair and run.

WAIT   LISTEN FIRST   THE WHOLE TOWN IS IN DANGER

"What do we do?" said Meredith instantly.

YOU NEED HELP   HES OUT OF YOUR LEAGUE   UNBE-LIEVABLY STRONG   NOW LISTEN AND FOLLOW INSTRUC-TIONS   YOU HAVE TO DO A SUMMONING SPELL AND THE FIRST INGREDIENT IS H—

Without warning, the planchette jerked away from the letters and flew around the board wildly. It pointed at the stylized picture of the moon, then at the sun, then at the words *Parker Brothers, Inc.*

"Elena!"

The planchette bobbed back to the letters.

ANOTHER MOUSE ANOTHER MOUSE ANOTHER MOUSE

"What's happening?" Sue cried, eyes wide open now.

Bonnie was frightened. The planchette was pulsing with energy, a dark and ugly energy like boiling black tar that stung her fingers. But she could also feel the quivering silver thread that was Elena's presence fighting it. "Don't let go!" she cried desperately. "Don't take your hands off it!"

MOUSEMUDKILLYOU, the board reeled off. BLOOD-BLOODBLOOD. And then . . . BONNIE GET OUT RUN HES HERE RUN RUN RU—

The planchette jerked furiously, whipping out from

under Bonnie's fingers and beyond her reach, flying across the board and through the air as if someone had thrown it. Vickie screamed. Meredith started to her feet.

And then all the lights went out, plunging the house into darkness.

3

Vickie's screams went out of control. Bonnie could feel panic rising in her chest.

"Vickie, stop it! Come on; we've got to get out of here!" Meredith was shouting to be heard. "It's your house, Caroline. Everybody grab hands and you lead us to the front door."

"Okay," Caroline said. She didn't sound as frightened as everybody else. That was the advantage to having no imagination, Bonnie thought. You couldn't picture the terrible things that were going to happen to you.

She felt better with Meredith's narrow, cold hand grasping hers. She fumbled on the other side and caught Caroline's, feeling the hardness of long fingernails.

She could see nothing. Her eyes should have been adjusting to the dark by now, but she couldn't make out even a glimmer of light or shadow as Caroline started leading them. There was no light coming through the windows from the street; the power seemed to be out everywhere. Caroline cursed, running into some piece of furniture, and Bonnie stumbled against her.

Vickie was whimpering softly from the back of the line. "Hang on," whispered Sue. "Hang on, Vickie, we'll make it."

They made slow, shuffling progress in the dark. Then Bonnie felt tile under her feet. "This is the front hall," Caroline said. "Stay here a minute while I find the door." Her fingers slipped out of Bonnie's.

"Caroline! Don't let go—where are you? Caroline, give me your hand!" Bonnie cried, groping frantically like a blind person.

Out of the darkness something large and moist closed around her fingers. It was a hand. It wasn't Caroline's.

Bonnie screamed.

Vickie immediately picked it up, shrieking wildly. The hot, moist hand was dragging Bonnie forward. She kicked out, struggling, but it made no difference. Then she felt Meredith's arms around her waist, both arms, wrenching her back. Her hand came free of the big one.

And then she was turning and running, just running, only dimly aware that Meredith was beside her. She wasn't at all aware that she was still screaming until she slammed into a large armchair that stopped her progress, and she heard herself.

"Hush! Bonnie, hush, stop!" Meredith was shaking her. They had slid down the back of the chair to the floor.

"Something had me! Something grabbed me, Meredith!"

"I know. Be quiet! It's still around," Meredith said. Bonnie jammed her face into Meredith's shoulder to keep from screaming again. What if it was here in the room with them?

Seconds crawled past, and the silence pooled around them. No matter how Bonnie strained her ears, she could hear no sound except their own breathing and the dull thudding of her heart.

"Listen! We've got to find the back door. We must be in the living room now. That means the kitchen's right behind us. We have to get there," Meredith said, her voice low.

Bonnie started to nod miserably, then abruptly lifted her head. "Where's Vickie?" she whispered hoarsely.

"I don't know. I had to let go of her hand to pull you away from that thing. Let's move."

Bonnie held her back. "But why isn't she screaming?"

A shudder went through Meredith. "I don't know."

"Oh, God. Oh, God. We can't leave her, Meredith."

"We *have* to."

"We *can't*. Meredith, I made Caroline invite her. She wouldn't be here except for me. We have to get her out."

There was a pause, and then Meredith hissed, "All right! But you pick the strangest times to turn noble, Bonnie."

A door slammed, causing both of them to jump. Then there was a crashing, like feet on stairs, Bonnie thought. And briefly, a voice was raised.

"Vickie, where are you? Don't—Vickie, no! No!"

"That was Sue," gasped Bonnie, jumping up. "From upstairs!"

"Why don't we have a *flashlight*?" Meredith was raging.

Bonnie knew what she meant. It was too dark to go running blindly around this house; it was too frightening. There was a primitive panic hammering in her brain. She needed light, any light.

She couldn't go fumbling into that darkness again, exposed on all sides. She couldn't *do* it.

Nevertheless, she took one shaky step away from the chair.

"Come on," she gasped, and Meredith came with her, step by step, into the blackness.

Bonnie kept expecting that moist, hot hand to reach out and grab her again. Every inch of her skin tingled in anticipation of its touch, and especially her own hand, which she had outstretched to feel her way.

Then she made the mistake of remembering the dream.

Instantly, the sickly sweet smell of garbage overwhelmed her. She imagined things crawling out of the group and then remembered Elena's face, gray and hairless, with lips shriveled back from grinning teeth. If *that thing* grabbed hold of her . . .

I can't go any farther; I can't, I can't, she thought. I'm sorry for Vickie, but I can't go on. Please, just let me stop here.

She was clinging to Meredith, almost crying. Then from upstairs came the most horrifying sound she had ever heard.

It was a whole series of sounds, actually, but they all came so close together that they blended into one terrible swell of noise. First there was screaming, Sue's voice screaming, "Vickie! Vickie! No!" Then a resonant crash, the sound of glass shattering, as if a hundred windows were breaking at once. And over that a sustained scream, on a note of pure, exquisite terror.

Then it all stopped.

"*What was it?* What happened, Meredith?"

"Something bad." Meredith's voice was taut and choked. "Something very bad. Bonnie, let go. I'm going to see."

"Not alone, you're not," Bonnie said fiercely.

They found the staircase and made their way up it. When they reached the landing, Bonnie could hear a strange and oddly sickening sound, the tinkle of glass shards falling.

And then the lights went on.

It was too sudden; Bonnie screamed involuntarily. Turning to Meredith she almost screamed again. Meredith's dark hair was disheveled and her cheekbones looked too sharp; her face was pale and hollow with fear.

Tinkle, tinkle.

It was *worse* with the lights on. Meredith was walking toward the last door down the hall, where the noise was coming from. Bonnie followed, but she knew suddenly, with all her heart, that she didn't want to see inside that room.

Meredith pulled the door open. She froze for a minute in the doorway and then lunged quickly inside. Bonnie started for the door.

"Oh, my God, don't come any farther!"

Bonnie didn't even pause. She plunged into the doorway and then pulled up short. At first glance it looked as if the whole side of the house was gone. The French windows that connected the master bedroom to the balcony seemed to have exploded outward, the wood splintered, the glass shattered. Little pieces of glass were hanging precariously here and there from the remnants of the wood frame. They tinkled as they fell.

Diaphanous white curtains billowed in and out of the gaping hole in the house. In front of them, in silhouette, Bonnie could see Vickie. She was standing with her hands at her sides, as motionless as a block of stone.

"Vickie, are you okay?" Bonnie was so relieved to see her alive that it was painful. "Vickie?"

Vickie didn't turn, didn't answer. Bonnie maneuvered around her cautiously, looking into her face. Vickie was staring straight ahead, her pupils pinpoints. She was sucking in little whistling breaths, chest heaving.

"I'm next. It said I'm next," she whispered over and over, but she didn't seem to be talking to Bonnie. She didn't seem to see Bonnie at all.

Shuddering, Bonnie reeled away. Meredith was on the balcony. She turned as Bonnie reached the curtains and tried to block the way.

"Don't look. Don't look down there," she said.

Down *where*? Suddenly Bonnie understood. She shoved past Meredith, who caught her arm to stop her on the edge of a dizzying drop. The balcony railing had been blasted out like the French windows and Bonnie could see straight down to the lighted yard below. On the ground there was a twisted figure like a broken doll, limbs askew, neck bent at a grotesque angle, blond hair fanned on the dark soil of the garden. It was Sue Carson.

And throughout all the confusion that raged afterward, two thoughts kept vying for dominance in Bonnie's mind. One was that Caroline would never have her foursome now. And the other was that it wasn't fair for this to happen on Meredith's birthday. It just wasn't fair.

"I'm sorry, Meredith. I don't think she's up to it right now."

Bonnie heard her father's voice at the front door as she listlessly stirred sweetener into a cup of chamomile tea. She put the spoon down at once. What she wasn't up to was sitting in this kitchen one minute longer. She needed out.

"I'll be right there, Dad."

Meredith looked almost as bad as she had last night, face peaked, eyes shadowed. Her mouth was set in a tight line.

"We'll just go out driving for a little while," Bonnie said to her father. "Maybe see some of the kids. After all, you're the one who said it isn't dangerous, right?"

What could he say? Mr. McCullough looked down at his petite daughter, who stuck out the stubborn chin she'd inherited from him and met his gaze squarely. He lifted his hands.

"It's almost four o'clock now. Be back before dark," he said.

"They want it both ways," Bonnie said to Meredith on the way to Meredith's car. Once inside, both girls immediately locked their doors.

As Meredith put the car in gear she gave Bonnie a glance of grim understanding.

"Your parents didn't believe you, either."

"Oh, they believe everything I told them—except anything important. How can they be so *stupid*?"

Meredith laughed shortly. "You've got to look at it from their point of view. They find one dead body without a mark on it except those caused by the fall. They find that the lights were off in the neighborhood because of a malfunction at Virginia Electric. They find us, hysterical, giving answers to their questions that must have seemed pretty weird. Who did it? Some monster with sweaty hands. How do we know? Our dead friend Elena told us through a Ouija board. Is it any wonder they have their doubts?"

"If they'd never seen anything like it *before*," Bonnie said, hitting the car door with her fist. "But they *have*. Do they think we made up those dogs that attacked at the Snow Dance last year? Do they think Elena was killed by a fantasy?"

"They're forgetting already," Meredith replied softly. "You predicted it yourself. Life has gone back to normal, and everybody in Fell's Church feels safer that way. They all feel like they've woken up from a bad dream, and the last thing they want is to get sucked in again."

Bonnie just shook her head.

"And so it's easier to believe that a bunch of teenage girls got riled up playing with a Ouija board, and that when the lights went out they just freaked and ran. And one of them got so scared and confused she ran right out a window."

There was a silence and then Meredith added, "I wish Alaric were here."

Normally, Bonnie would have given her a dig in the ribs and answered, "So do *I*," in a lecherous voice. Alaric was one of the handsomest guys she'd ever seen, even if he was a doddering twenty-two years old. Now, she just gave Meredith's arm a disconsolate squeeze. "Can't you call him somehow?"

"In Russia? I don't even know *where* in Russia he is now."

Bonnie bit her lip.

Then she sat up. Meredith was driving down Lee Street, and in the high school parking lot they could see a crowd.

She and Meredith exchanged glances, and Meredith nodded. "We might as well," she said. "Let's see if they're any smarter than their parents."

Bonnie could see startled faces turning as the car

cruised slowly into the lot. When she and Meredith got out, people moved back, making a path for them to the center of the crowd.

Caroline was there, clutching her elbows with her hands and shaking back her auburn hair distractedly.

"We're not going to sleep in that house again until it's repaired," she was saying, shivering in her white sweater. "Daddy says we'll take an apartment in Heron until it's over."

"What difference does that make? He can follow you to Heron, I'm sure," said Meredith.

Caroline turned, but her green cat's eyes wouldn't quite meet Meredith's. "Who?" she said vaguely.

"Oh, Caroline, not you too!" Bonnie exploded.

"I just want to get out of here," Caroline said. Her eyes came up and for an instant Bonnie saw how frightened she was. "I can't take anymore." As if she had to prove her words that minute, she pushed her way through the crowd.

"Let her go, Bonnie," Meredith said. "It's no use."

"*She's* no use," said Bonnie furiously. If Caroline, who *knew*, was acting this way, what about the other kids?

She saw, the answer in the faces around her. Everybody looked scared, as scared as if she and Meredith had brought some loathsome disease with them. As if she and Meredith were the problem.

"I don't believe this," Bonnie muttered.

"I don't believe it either," said Deanna Kennedy, a friend of Sue's. She was in the front of the crowd, and she didn't look as uneasy as the others. "I talked with Sue yesterday afternoon and she was so up, so happy. She *can't* be dead." Deanna began to sob. Her boyfriend put an arm around her, and several other girls began to cry. The guys in the crowd shifted, their faces rigid.

Bonnie felt a little surge of hope. "And she's not going to be the only one dead," she added. "Elena told us that the whole town is in danger. Elena said . . ." Despite herself Bonnie heard her voice failing. She could see it in the way their eyes glazed up when she mentioned Elena's name. Meredith was right; they'd put everything that had happened last winter behind them. They didn't believe anymore.

"What's *wrong* with you all?" she said helplessly, wanting to hit something. "You don't really think Sue threw herself off that balcony!"

"People are saying—" Deanna's boyfriend started and then shrugged defensively. "Well—you told the police Vickie Bennett was in the room, right? And now she's off her head again. And just a little bit earlier you'd heard Sue shouting, 'No, Vickie, no!'?"

Bonnie felt as if the wind had been knocked out of her. "You think that *Vickie*—oh, God, you're out of your mind!

Listen to me. Something grabbed my hand in that house, and it *wasn't* Vickie. And Vickie had nothing to do with throwing Sue off that balcony."

"She's hardly strong enough, for one thing," Meredith said pointedly. "She weighs about ninety-five pounds soaking wet."

Somebody from the back of the crowd muttered about insane people having superhuman strength. "Vickie has a psychiatric record—"

"Elena told us it was a guy!" Bonnie almost shouted, losing her battle with self-control. The faces tilted toward her were shuttered, unyielding. Then she saw one that made her chest loosen. "Matt! Tell them you believe us."

Matt Honeycutt was standing on the fringe with his hands in his pockets and his blond head bowed. Now he looked up, and what Bonnie saw in his blue eyes made her draw in her breath. They weren't hard and shuttered like everyone else's, but they were full of a flat despair that was just as bad. He shrugged without taking his hands from his pockets.

"For what it's worth, I believe you," he said. "But what difference does it make? It's all going to turn out the same anyway."

Bonnie, for one of the first times in her life, was speechless. Matt had been upset ever since Elena died, but this . . .

"He does believe it, though," Meredith was saying quickly, capitalizing on the moment. "Now what have we got to do to convince the rest of you?"

"Channel Elvis for us, maybe," said a voice that immediately set Bonnie's blood boiling. Tyler. Tyler Smallwood. Grinning like an ape in his overexpensive Perry Ellis sweater, showing a mouthful of strong white teeth.

"It's not as good as psychic e-mail from a dead Homecoming Queen, but it's a start," Tyler added.

Matt always said that grin was asking for a punch in the nose. But Matt, the only guy in the crowd with close to Tyler's physique, was staring dully at the ground.

"Shut up, Tyler! You don't know what happened in that house," Bonnie said.

"Well, neither do you, apparently. Maybe if you hadn't been hiding in the living room, you'd have seen what happened. Then somebody might believe you."

Bonnie's retort died on her tongue. She stared at Tyler, opened her mouth, and then closed it. Tyler waited. When she didn't speak, he showed his teeth again.

"For my money, Vickie did it," he said, winking at Dick Carter, Vickie's ex-boyfriend. "She's a strong little babe, right, Dick? She *could* have done it." He turned and added deliberately over his shoulder, "Or else that Salvatore guy is back in town."

"You creep!" shouted Bonnie. Even Meredith cried out

in frustration. Because of course at the very mention of Stefan pandemonium ensued, as Tyler must have known it would. Everyone was turning to the person next to them and exclaiming in alarm, horror, excitement. It was primarily the girls who were excited.

Effectively, it put an end to the gathering. People had been edging away surreptitiously before, and now they broke up into twos and threes, arguing and hastening off.

Bonnie gazed after them angrily.

"Supposing they did believe you. What did you want them to do, anyway?" Matt said. She hadn't noticed him beside her.

"I don't know. Something besides just standing around waiting to be picked off." She tried to look him in the face. "Matt, are you all right?"

"I don't know. Are you?"

Bonnie thought. "No. I mean, in one way I'm surprised I'm doing as well as I am, because when Elena died, I just couldn't deal. At all. But then I wasn't as close to Sue, and besides . . . I don't know!" She wanted to hit something again. "It's just all too much!"

"You're mad."

"*Yes*, I'm mad." Suddenly Bonnie understood the feelings she'd been having all day. "Killing Sue wasn't just wrong, it was *evil*. Truly evil. And whoever did it isn't going to get away with it. That would be—if the world is

like that, a place where that can happen and go unpun-
ished . . . if that's the truth . . ." She found she didn't have
a way to finish.

"Then what? You don't want to live here anymore?
What if the world *is* like that?"

His eyes were so lost, so bitter. Bonnie was shaken. But
she said staunchly, "I won't *let* it be that way. And you
won't either."

He simply looked at her as if she were a kid insisting
there was so a Santa Claus.

Meredith spoke up. "If we expect other people to take
us seriously, we'd better take ourselves seriously. Elena
did communicate with us. She wanted us to do something.
Now if we really believe that, we'd better figure out what
it is."

Matt's face had flexed at the mention of Elena. You
poor guy, you're still as much in love with her as ever,
thought Bonnie. I wonder if anything could make you forget her? She said, "Are you going to help us, Matt?"

"I'll help," Matt said quietly. "But I still don't know
what it is you're doing."

"We're going to stop that murdering creep before he
kills anybody else," said Bonnie. It was the first time she'd
fully realized herself that this was what she meant to do.

"Alone? Because you are alone, you know."

"*We* are alone," Meredith corrected. "But that's what

Elena was trying to tell us. She said we had to do a summoning spell to call for help."

"An easy spell with only two ingredients," Bonnie remembered from her dream. She was getting excited. "And she said she'd already told me the ingredients—but she hadn't."

"Last night she said there were corrupting influences distorting her communication," Meredith said. "Now to me that sounds like what was happening in the dream. Do you think it really *was* Elena you were drinking tea with?"

"Yes," Bonnie said positively. "I mean, I know we weren't really having a mad tea party at Warm Springs, but I think Elena was sending that message into my brain. And then partway through something else took over and pushed her out. But she fought, and for a minute at the end she got back control."

"Okay. Then that means we have to concentrate on the beginning of the dream, when it was still Elena communicating with you. But if what she was saying was already being distorted by other influences, then maybe it came out weird. Maybe it wasn't something she actually said, maybe it was something she did . . ."

Bonnie's hand flew up to touch her curls. "Hair!" she cried.

"What?"

"Hair! I asked her who did hers, and we talked about

it, and she said, 'Hair is very important.' And Meredith—when she was trying to tell us the ingredients last night, the first letter of one of them was *H*!"

"That's it!" Meredith's dark eyes were flashing. "Now we just have to think of the other one."

"But I know that too!" Bonnie's laughter bubbled up exuberantly. "She told me right after we talked about hair, and I thought she was just being strange. She said, 'Blood is important too.'"

Meredith shut her eyes in realization. "And last night, the Ouija board said 'Bloodbloodblood.' I thought it was the other thing threatening us, but it wasn't," she said. She opened her eyes. "Bonnie, do you think that's really it? Are those the ingredients, or do we have to start worrying about mud and sandwiches and mice and tea?"

"Those are the ingredients," Bonnie said firmly. "They're the kind of ingredients that make sense for a summoning spell. I'm sure I can find a ritual to do with them in one of my Celtic magic books. We just have to figure out the person we're supposed to summon . . ." Something struck her, and her voice trailed off in dismay.

"I was wondering when you'd notice," Matt said, speaking for the first time in a long while. "You don't know who it is, do you?"

eredith tilted an ironic glance at Matt. "Hmm," she said. "Now, who do you *think* Elena would call in time of trouble?"

Bonnie's grin gave way to a twinge of guilt at Matt's expression. It wasn't fair to tease him about this. "Elena said that the killer is too strong for us and that's why we need help," she told Matt. "And I can think of only one person Elena knows who could fight off a psychic killer."

Slowly, Matt nodded. Bonnie couldn't tell what he was feeling. He and Stefan had been best friends once, even after Elena had chosen Stefan over Matt. But that had been before Matt found out what Stefan was, and what kind of violence he was capable of. In his rage and grief over Elena's death Stefan had nearly killed Tyler Smallwood and five other guys. Could Matt really forget that?

Could he even deal with Stefan coming back to Fell's Church?

Matt's square-jawed face gave no sign now, and Meredith was talking again. "So all we need to do is let some blood and cut some hair. You won't miss a curl or two, will you, Bonnie?"

Bonnie was so abstracted that she almost missed this. Then she shook her head. "No, no, no. It isn't *our* blood and hair we need. We need it from the person we want to summon."

"What? But that's ridiculous. If we had *Stefan's* blood and hair we wouldn't *need* to summon him, would we?"

"I didn't think of that," Bonnie admitted. "Usually with a summoning spell you get the stuff beforehand and use it when you want to call a person back. What are we going to do, Meredith? It's impossible."

Meredith's brows were drawn together. "Why would Elena ask it if it were impossible?"

"Elena asked lots of impossible things," Bonnie said darkly. "Don't look like that, Matt; you know she did. She wasn't a saint."

"Maybe, but this one isn't impossible," Matt said. "I can think of one place where Stefan's blood has got to be, and if we're lucky some of his hair, too. In the crypt."

Bonnie flinched, but Meredith simply nodded. "Of course," she said. "While Stefan was tied up there, he must have bled all over the place. And in that kind of fight he might have lost some hair. If only everything down there has been left undisturbed . . ."

"I don't think anybody's been down there since Elena died," Matt said. "The police investigated and then left it. But there's only one way to find out."

I was wrong, Bonnie thought. I was worrying about whether Matt could deal with Stefan coming back, and here he is doing everything he can to help us summon him. "Matt, I could kiss you!" she said.

For an instant something she couldn't identify flickered in Matt's eyes. Surprise, certainly, but there was more than that. Suddenly Bonnie wondered what he would do if she *did* kiss him.

"All the girls say that," he replied calmly at last, with a shrug of mock resignation. It was as close as he'd gotten to lightheartedness all day.

Meredith, however, was serious. "Let's go. We've got a lot to do, and the last thing we want is to get stuck in the crypt after dark."

The crypt was beneath the ruined church that stood on a hill in the cemetery. It's only late afternoon, plenty of light left, Bonnie kept telling herself as they walked up the hill, but gooseflesh broke out on her arms anyway. The modern cemetery on one side was bad enough, but the old graveyard on the other side was downright spooky even in daylight. There were so many crumbling head-stones tilting crazily in the overgrown grass, representing so many young men killed in the Civil War. You didn't have to be psychic to feel their presence.

"Unquiet spirits," she muttered.

"Hmm?" said Meredith as she stepped over the pile of rubble that was one wall of the ruined church. "Look, the lid of the tomb's still off. That's good news; I don't think we would have been able to lift it."

Bonnie's eyes lingered wistfully on the white marble statues carved on the displaced lid. Honoria Fell lay there with her husband, hands folded on her breast, looking as gentle and sad as ever. But Bonnie knew there would be no more help from that quarter. Honoria's duties as pro-tector of the town she'd founded were done.

Leaving Elena holding the bag, Bonnie thought grimly, looking down into the rectangular hole that led to the crypt. Iron rungs disappeared into darkness.

Even with the help of Meredith's flashlight it was hard to climb down into that underground room. Inside, it was dank and silent, the walls faced with polished stone. Bonnie tried not to shiver.

"Look," said Meredith quietly.

Matt had the flashlight trained on the iron gate that separated the anteroom of the crypt from its main chamber. The stone below was stained black with blood in several places. Looking at the puddles and rivulets of dried gore made Bonnie feel dizzy.

"We know Damon was hurt the worst," Meredith said, moving forward. She sounded calm, but Bonnie could hear the tight control in her voice. "So he must have been on this side where there's the most blood. Stefan said Elena was in the center. That means Stefan himself must have been . . . here." She bent down.

"I'll do it," Matt said gruffly. "You hold the light." With a plastic picnic knife from Meredith's car he scraped at the encrusted stone. Bonnie swallowed, glad she'd had only tea for lunch. Blood was all right in the abstract, but when you were actually confronted with so much of it—especially when it was the blood of a friend who'd been tortured . . .

Bonnie turned away, looking at the stone walls and thinking about Katherine. Both Stefan and his older brother, Damon, had been in love with Katherine, back in fifteenth-century Florence. But what they hadn't known was that the girl they loved wasn't human. A vampire in her own German village had changed her to save her life when she was ill. Katherine in her turn had made both the boys vampires.

And then, thought Bonnie, she faked her own death to get Stefan and Damon to stop fighting over her. But it didn't work. They hated each other more than ever, and she hated both of them for *that*. She'd gone back to the vampire who made her, and over the years she'd turned as evil as he was. Until at last all she wanted to do was destroy the brothers she had once loved. She'd lured them both to Fell's Church to kill them, and this room was where she'd almost succeeded in doing it. Elena had died stopping her.

"There," Matt said, and Bonnie blinked and came back to herself. Matt was standing with a paper napkin that now held flakes of Stefan's blood in its folds. "Now the hair," he said.

They swept the floor with their fingers, finding dust and bits of leaves and fragments of things Bonnie didn't want to identify. Among the detritus were long strands of pale gold hair. Elena's—or Katherine's, Bonnie thought. They had looked much alike. There were also shorter strands of dark hair, crisp with a slight wave. Stefan's.

It was slow, finicky work sorting through it all and putting the right hairs in another napkin. Matt did most of it. When they were through, they were all tired and the light sifting down through the rectangular opening in the ceiling was dim blue. But Meredith smiled tigerishly.

"We've got it," she said. "Tyler wants Stefan back; well, we'll *give* him Stefan back."

And Bonnie, who had been only half paying attention

to what she was doing, still lost in her own thoughts, froze.

She'd been thinking about other things entirely, nothing to do with Tyler, but at the mention of his name something had winked on in her mind. Something she'd realized in the parking lot and then forgotten afterward in the heat of arguing. Meredith's words had triggered it and now it was suddenly all clear again. How had he *known*? she wondered, heart racing.

"Bonnie? What's the matter?"

"Meredith," she said softly, "did you tell the police specifically that we were in the living room when everything was going on upstairs with Sue?"

"No, I think I just said we were downstairs. Why?"

"Because I didn't either. And Vickie couldn't have told them because she's gone catatonic again, and Sue's dead and Caroline was outside by that time. *But Tyler knew.* Remember, he said, 'If you hadn't been hiding in the living room, you'd have seen what happened.' How could he know?"

"Bonnie, if you're trying to suggest Tyler was the murderer, it just won't wash. He's not smart enough to organize a killing spree, for one thing," Meredith said.

"But there's something else. Meredith, last year at the Junior Prom, Tyler touched me on my bare shoulder. I'll never forget it. His hand was big, and meaty, and hot, and damp." Bonnie shivered at the recollection. "Just like the hand that grabbed me last night."

But Meredith was shaking her head, and even Matt looked unconvinced.

"Elena's sure wasting her time asking us to bring back Stefan, then," he said. "I could take care of Tyler with a couple of right hooks."

"Think about it, Bonnie," Meredith added. "Does Tyler have the psychic power to move a Ouija board or come into your dreams? *Does* he?"

He didn't. Psychically speaking, Tyler was as much a dud as Caroline. Bonnie couldn't deny it. But she couldn't deny her intuition, either. It didn't make sense, but she still felt Tyler had been in the house last night.

"We'd better get moving," Meredith said. "It's dark, and your father's going to be furious."

They were all silent on the ride home. Bonnie was still thinking about Tyler. Once at her house they smuggled the napkins upstairs and began looking through Bonnie's books on Druids and Celtic magic. Ever since she'd discovered that she was descended from the ancient race of magic workers, Bonnie had been interested in the druids. And in one of the books she found a ritual for a summoning spell.

"We need to buy candles," she said. "And pure water—better get some bottled," she said to Meredith. "And chalk to draw a circle on the floor, and something to make a small fire in. I can find those in the house. There's no hurry; the spell has to be done at midnight."

Midnight was a long time coming. Meredith bought the necessary items at a grocery store and brought them back. They ate dinner with Bonnie's family, though no one had much of an appetite. By eleven o'clock Bonnie had the circle drawn on the hardwood floor of her bedroom and all the other ingredients on a low bench inside the circle. On the stroke of twelve she started.

With Matt and Meredith watching, she made a small fire in an earthenware bowl. Three candles were burning behind the bowl; she stuck a pin halfway down the one in the center. Then she unfolded a napkin and carefully stirred the dried flakes of blood into a wineglass of water. It turned rusty pink.

She opened the other napkin. Three pinches of dark hair went into the fire, sizzling with a terrible smell. Then three drops of the stained water, hissing.

Her eyes went to the words in the open book.

Swift on the heel thou comest,
Thrice summoned by my spell,
Thrice troubled by my burning.
Come to me without delay.

She read the words aloud slowly, three times. Then she sat back on her heels. The fire went on burning smokily.

The candle flames danced.

"And now what?" Matt said.

"I don't know. It just says wait for the middle candle to burn down to the pin."

"And what then?"

"I guess we'll find out when it happens."

In Florence, it was dawn.

Stefan watched the girl move down the stairway, one hand resting lightly on the banister to keep her balance. Her movements were slow and slightly dreamlike, as if she were floating.

Suddenly, she swayed and clutched at the banister more tightly. Stefan moved quickly behind her and put a hand under her elbow.

"Are you all right?"

She looked up at him with the same dreaminess. She was very pretty. Her expensive clothes were the latest fashion and her stylishly disarrayed hair was blond. A tourist. He knew she was American before she spoke.

"Yes . . . I think . . ." Her brown eyes were unfocused.

"Do you have a way to get home? Where are you staying?"

"On Via dei Conti, near the Medici chapel. I'm with the Gonzaga in Florence program."

Damn! Not a tourist, then; a student. And that meant

she'd be carrying this story back with her, telling her classmates about the handsome Italian guy she'd met last night. The one with night-dark eyes. The one who took her back to his exclusive place on Via Tornabuoni and wined her and dined her and then, in the moonlight, maybe, in his room or out in the enclosed courtyard, leaned close to look into her eyes and . . .

Stefan's gaze slid away from the girl's throat with its two reddened puncture wounds. He'd seen marks like that so often—how could they still have the power to disturb him? But they did; they sickened him and set a slow burning in his gut.

"What's your name?"

"Rachael. With an *a*." She spelled it.

"All right, Rachael. Look at me. You will go back to your *pensione* and you won't remember anything about last night. You don't know where you went or who you saw. And you've never seen *me* before, either. Repeat."

"I don't remember anything about last night," she said obediently, her eyes on his. Stefan's Powers were not as strong as they would have been if he'd been drinking human blood, but they were strong enough for this. "I don't know where I went or who I saw. I haven't seen you."

"Good. Do you have money to get back? Here." Stefan pulled a fistful of crumpled lire—mostly 50,000 and

100,000 notes—out of his pocket and led her outside.

When she was safely in a cab, he went back inside and made straight for Damon's bedroom.

Damon was lounging near the window, peeling an orange, not even dressed yet. He looked up, annoyed, as Stefan entered.

"It's customary to knock," he said.

"Where'd you meet her?" said Stefan. And then, when Damon turned a blank stare on him, he added, "That girl. Rachael."

"Was that her name? I don't think I bothered to ask. At Bar Gilli. Or perhaps it was Bar Mario. Why?"

Stefan struggled to contain his anger. "That's not the only thing you didn't bother to do. You didn't bother to influence her to forget you, either. Do you *want* to get caught, Damon?"

Damon's lips curved in a smile and he twisted off a curlicue of orange peel. "I am *never* caught, little brother," he said.

"So what are you going to do when they come after you? When somebody realizes, 'My God, there's a blood-sucking monster on Via Tornabuoni'? Kill them all? Wait until they break down the front door and then melt away into darkness?"

Damon met his gaze directly, challengingly, that faint smile still clinging about his lips.

"Why not?" he said.

"*Damn* you!" said Stefan. "Listen to me, Damon. This has got to stop."

"I'm touched at your concern for my safety."

"It isn't fair, Damon. To take an unwilling girl like that—"

"Oh, she was willing, brother. She was very, very willing."

"Did you tell her what you were going to do? Did you warn her about the consequences of exchanging blood with a vampire? The nightmares, the psychic visions? Was she willing for *that*?" Damon clearly wasn't going to reply, so he went on. "You know it's wrong."

"As a matter of fact, I do." With that, Damon gave one of his sudden, unnerving smiles, turning it on and off instantly.

"And you don't care," Stefan said dully, looking away.

Damon tossed away the orange. His tone was silky, persuasive. "Little brother, the world is full of what you call 'wrong,'" he said. "Why not relax and join the winning side? It's much more fun, I assure you."

Stefan felt himself go hot with anger. "How can you even say that?" he flashed back. "Didn't you learn anything from Katherine? *She* chose 'the winning side.'"

"Katherine died too quickly," said Damon. He was smiling again, but his eyes were cold.

"And now all you can think about is revenge." Looking at his brother, Stefan felt a crushing weight settle on his own chest. "That and your own pleasure," he said.

"What else is there? Pleasure is the only reality, little brother—pleasure and power. And you're a hunter by nature, just as much as I am," Damon said. He added, "I don't remember inviting you to come to Florence with me, anyway. Since you're not enjoying yourself, why don't you just leave?"

The weight in Stefan's chest tightened suddenly, unbearably, but his gaze, locked with Damon's, did not waver. "You know why," he said quietly. And at last he had the satisfaction of seeing Damon's eyes drop.

Stefan himself could hear Elena's words in his mind. She'd been dying then, and her voice had been weak, but he'd heard her clearly. *You have to take care of each other. Stefan, will you promise? Promise to take care of each other?* And he had promised, and he would keep his word. No matter what.

"You know why I don't leave," he said again to Damon, who wouldn't look at him. "You can pretend you don't care. You can fool the whole world. But *I* know differently." It would have been kindest at this point to leave Damon alone, but Stefan wasn't in a kind mood. "You know that girl you picked up, Rachael?" he added. "The hair was all right, but her eyes were the wrong color.

Elena's eyes were blue."

With that he turned, meaning to leave Damon here to think it over—if Damon would do anything so constructive, of course. But he never made it to the door.

"It's there!" said Meredith sharply, her eyes on the candle flame and the pin.

Bonnie sucked in her breath. Something was opening in front of her like a silver thread, a silver tunnel of communication. She was rushing along it, with no way to stop herself or check her speed. Oh, God, she thought, when I reach the end and hit—

The flash in Stefan's head was soundless, lightless, and powerful as a thunderclap. At the same time he felt a violent, wrenching tug. An urge to follow—something. This was not like Katherine's sly subliminal nudging to go somewhere; this was a psychic shout. A command that could not be disobeyed.

Inside the flash he sensed a presence, but he could scarcely believe who it was.

Bonnie?

Stefan! It's you! It worked!

Bonnie, what have you done?

Elena told me to. Honestly, Stefan, she did. We're in trouble and we need—

And that was it. The communication collapsed, caving in on itself, dwindling to a pinpoint. It was gone, and in its aftermath the room vibrated with Power.

Stefan and his brother were left staring at each other.

Bonnie let out a long breath she hadn't realized she'd been holding and opened her eyes, though she didn't remember closing them. She was lying on her back. Matt and Meredith were crouched over her, looking alarmed.

"What happened? Did it work?" Meredith demanded.

"It worked." She let them help her up. "I made contact with Stefan. I talked to him. Now all we can do is wait and see if he's coming or not."

"Did you mention Elena?" Matt asked.

"Yes."

"Then he's coming."

5

Monday, June 8, 11:15 p.m.

Dear Diary,
    I don't seem to be sleeping very well tonight, so I might as well write you. All day today I've been waiting for something to happen. You don't do a spell like that and have it work like that and then have nothing happen.

    But nothing has. I stayed home from school because Mom thought I should. She was upset about Matt and Meredith staying so late Sunday night, and she said I needed to get some rest. But every time I lie down I see Sue's face.

    Sue's dad did the eulogy at Elena's funeral. I wonder who's going to do it for Sue on Wednesday?

I've got to stop thinking about things like this.
Maybe I'll try to go to sleep again. Maybe if I
lie down with my headphones on, I won't see Sue.

Bonnie put the diary back in her nightstand drawer and took out her Walkman. She flipped through the channels as she stared at the ceiling with heavy eyes. Through the crackle and sputter of static a D.J.'s voice sounded in her ear.

"And here's a golden oldie for all you fabulous fifties fans. 'Goodnight Sweetheart' on the Vee Jay label by The Spaniels . . ."

Bonnie drifted away on the music.

The ice cream soda was strawberry, Bonnie's favorite. The jukebox was playing 'Goodnight Sweetheart' and the counter was squeaky clean. But Elena, Bonnie decided, would never have really worn a poodle skirt.

"No poodles," she said, gesturing at it. Elena looked up from her hot fudge sundae. Her blond hair was pulled back in a ponytail. "Who thinks of these things anyway?" Bonnie asked.

"You do, silly. I'm only visiting."

"Oh." Bonnie took a pull at the soda. Dreams. There was a reason to be afraid of dreams, but she couldn't think of it just now.

"I can't stay long," Elena said. "I think he already knows I'm here. I just came to tell you . . ." She frowned.

Bonnie looked at her sympathetically. "Can't you remember either?" She drank more soda. It tasted odd.

"I died too young, Bonnie. There was so much I was supposed to do, to accomplish. And now I have to help you."

"Thanks," Bonnie said.

"This isn't easy, you know. I don't have that much power. It's hard getting through and it's hard keeping everything together."

"Gotta keep it together," Bonnie agreed, nodding. She was feeling strangely lightheaded. What was *in* this soda?

"I don't have much control, and things turn out strange somehow. He's doing it, I guess. He's always fighting me. He watches you. And every time we try to communicate, he comes."

"Okay." The room was floating.

"Bonnie, are you listening to me? He can use your fear against you. It's the way he gets in."

"Okay . . ."

"But *don't let him in*. Tell everyone that. And tell Stefan . . ." Elena stopped and put a hand to her mouth. Something fell onto the hot fudge sundae.

It was a tooth.

"He's here." Elena's voice was strange, indistinct.

Bonnie stared at the tooth in mesmerized horror. It was lying in the middle of the whipped cream, among the slivered almonds. "Bonnie, tell Stefan . . ."

Another tooth plunked down, and another. Elena sobbed, both her hands at her mouth now. Her eyes were terrified, helpless. "Bonnie, don't go . . ."

But Bonnie was stumbling back. Everything was whirling around. The soda was bubbling out of the glass, but it wasn't soda; it was blood. Bright red and frothy, like something you coughed up when you died. Bonnie's stomach convulsed.

"Tell Stefan I love him!" It was the voice of a toothless old woman, and it ended in hysterical sobs. Bonnie was glad to fall into darkness and forget everything.

Bonnie nibbled at the end of her felt pen, her eyes on the clock, her mind on the calendar. Eight and a half more days of school to survive. And it looked as if every minute was going to be misery.

Some guy had said it outright, backing away from her on the stairs. "No offense, but your friends keep turning up dead." Bonnie had gone into the bathroom and cried.

But now all she wanted was to be out of school, away from the tragic faces and accusing eyes—or worse, the *pitying* eyes. The principal had given a speech over the P.A. about "this new misfortune" and "this terrible loss," and Bonnie had felt the eyes on her back as if they were boring holes there.

When the bell rang, she was the first person out the door. But instead of going to her next class she went to the bathroom again, where she waited for the next bell. Then, once the halls were empty, she hurried toward the foreign language wing. She passed bulletins and banners for end-of-the-year events without glancing at them. What did SATs matter, what did graduation matter, what did any-thing matter anymore? They might all be dead by the end of the month.

She nearly ran into the person standing in the hall. Her gaze jerked up, off her own feet, to take in fashionably ratty deck shoes, some foreign kind. Above that were jeans, body hugging, old enough to look soft over hard muscles. Narrow hips. Nice chest. Face to drive a sculptor crazy: sensuous mouth, high cheekbones. Dark sunglasses. Slightly tousled black hair. Bonnie stood gaping a moment.

Oh, my God, I forgot how gorgeous he is, she thought. Elena, forgive me; I'm going to grab him.

"Stefan!" she said.

Then her mind wrenched her back into reality again and she cast a hunted look around. No one was in eyeshot. She grabbed his arm.

"Are you crazy, showing up here? Are you *nuts*?"

"I had to find you. I thought it was urgent."

"It is, but—" He looked so incongruous, standing there in the high school hallway. So exotic. Like a zebra in a flock of sheep. She started pushing him toward a broom closet.

He wasn't going. And he was stronger than she was. "Bonnie, you said you'd talked to—"

"You have to hide! I'll go get Matt and Meredith and bring them back here and then we can talk. But if anybody sees you, you're probably going to get lynched. There's been another murder."

Stefan's face changed, and he let her push him toward the closet. He started to say something, then clearly decided not to.

"I'll wait," he said simply.

It took only a few minutes to find Matt in auto tech and Meredith in economics class. They hurried back to the broom closet and bustled Stefan out of school as inconspicuously as possible, which wasn't very.

Someone's bound to have seen us, Bonnie thought. It all depends on *who*, and how much of a blab they are.

"We have to get him someplace safe—not to any of our houses," Meredith was saying. They were all walking as fast as they could through the high school parking lot.

"Fine, but *where*? Wait a minute, what about the boardinghouse . . . ?" Bonnie's voice trailed off. There was a little black car in the parking slot in front of her. An Italian car, sleek, svelte, and sexy looking. All the windows were tinted illegally dark; you couldn't even see inside. Then Bonnie made out the stallion emblem on the back.

"Oh, my *God*."

Stefan glanced at the Ferrari distractedly. "It's Damon's."

Three sets of eyes turned to him in shock. *"Damon's?"* Bonnie said, hearing the squeak in her own voice. She hoped Stefan meant Damon had just loaned it to him.

But the car window was rolling down to reveal black hair as sleek and liquidy as the car's paint job, mirrored glasses, and a very white smile. *"Buon giorno,"* said Damon smoothly. "Anybody need a ride?"

"Oh, my God," Bonnie said again, faintly. But she didn't back away.

Stefan was visibly impatient. "We'll head for the boardinghouse. You follow. Park behind the barn so nobody sees your car."

Meredith had to lead Bonnie away from the Ferrari. It wasn't that Bonnie liked Damon or that she was ever going to let him kiss her again as he had at Alaric's party. She knew he was dangerous; not as bad as Katherine had been, maybe, but bad. He'd killed wantonly, just for the fun of it. He'd killed Mr. Tanner, the history teacher, at the Haunted House fund-raiser last Halloween. He might kill again at any time. Maybe that was why Bonnie felt like a mouse staring at a shining black snake when she looked at him.

In the privacy of Meredith's car Bonnie and Meredith exchanged glances.

"Stefan shouldn't have brought him," said Meredith.

"Maybe he just came," Bonnie offered. She didn't think Damon was the sort of person who got *brought* anywhere.

"Why should he? Not to help us, that's for sure."

Matt said nothing. He didn't even seem to notice the tension in the car. He just stared through the windshield, lost in himself.

The sky was clouding up.

"Matt?"

"Just leave it alone, Bonnie," said Meredith.

Wonderful, thought Bonnie, depression settling like a dark blanket over her. Matt and Stefan and Damon, all together, all thinking about Elena.

They parked behind the old barn, next to the low black car. When they went inside, Stefan was standing alone. He turned and Bonnie saw that he'd taken off his sunglasses. The faintest chill went through her, just the lightest prickling of the hairs on her arms and neck. Stefan wasn't like any other guy she'd ever met. His eyes were so green; green as oak leaves in the spring. But just now they had shadows underneath.

There was a moment of awkwardness; the three of

them standing on one side and looking at Stefan without a word. No one seemed to know what to say.

Then Meredith went over to him and took his hand. "You look tired," she said.

"I came as soon as I could." He put an arm around her in a brief, almost hesitant hug. He never would have done that in the old days, Bonnie thought. He used to be so reserved.

She came forward for her own hug. Stefan's skin was cool under the T-shirt, and she had to make herself not shiver. When she pulled back, her eyes were swimming. What did she feel now that Stefan Salvatore was back in Fell's Church? Relief? Sadness for the memories he brought with him? Fear? All she could tell was that she wanted to cry.

Stefan and Matt were looking at each other. Here we go, thought Bonnie. It was almost funny; the same expression was on both their faces. Hurt and tired, and trying not to show it. No matter what, Elena would always be between them.

At last, Matt stuck out his hand and Stefan shook it. They both stepped back, looking glad to have it over with.

"Where's Damon?" said Meredith.

"Poking around. I thought we might want a few minutes without him."

"We want a few *decades* without him," Bonnie said before she could stop herself, and Meredith said, "He can't be trusted, Stefan."

"I think you're wrong," Stefan said quietly. "He can be a big help if he puts his mind to it."

"In between killing a few of the locals every other night?" Meredith said, her eyebrows up. "You shouldn't have brought him, Stefan."

"But he didn't." The voice came from behind Bonnie, behind and frighteningly close. Bonnie jumped and made an instinctive lunge for Matt, who gripped her shoulder.

Damon smiled briefly, just one corner of his mouth up. He'd taken off his sunglasses, but his eyes weren't green. They were black as the spaces between the stars. He's almost better looking than Stefan, Bonnie thought wildly, finding Matt's fingers and hanging on to them.

"So she's yours now, is she?" Damon said to Matt casually.

"No," Matt said, but his grip on Bonnie didn't loosen.

"Stefan didn't bring you?" prompted Meredith from the other side. Of all of them, she seemed least affected by Damon, least afraid of him, least susceptible to him.

"No," Damon said, still looking at Bonnie. He doesn't *turn* like other people, she thought. He goes on looking at whatever he wants no matter who's talking. "You did," he said.

"Me?" Bonnie shrank a little, uncertain who he meant.

"You. You did the spell, didn't you?"

"The . . ." Oh, *hell*. A picture blossomed in Bonnie's mind, of black hair on a white napkin. Her eyes went to Damon's hair, finer and straighter than Stefan's but just as dark. Obviously Matt had made a mistake in the sorting.

Stefan's voice was impatient. "You sent for us, Bonnie. We came. What's going on?"

They took seats on the decaying bales of hay, all except Damon, who remained standing. Stefan was leaning forward, hands on knees, looking at Bonnie.

"You told me—you said that Elena spoke to you." There was a perceptible pause before he got the name out. His face was tense with control.

"Yes." She managed a smile for him. "I had this dream, Stefan, this very strange dream . . ."

She told him about it, and about what had happened after. It took a long time. Stefan listened intently, his green eyes flaring every time she mentioned Elena. When she told about the end of Caroline's party and how they had found Sue's body in the backyard, the blood drained from his face, but he said nothing.

"The police came and said she was dead, but we knew that already," Bonnie finished. "And they took Vickie away—poor Vickie was just raving. They wouldn't let us talk to her, and her mother hangs up if we call. Some people are even saying Vickie *did* it, which is insane. But they won't believe that Elena talked to us, so they won't believe anything she said."

"And what she said was 'he,'" Meredith interrupted. "Several times. It's a man; someone with a lot of psychic power."

"And it was a man who grabbed my hand in the hallway," said Bonnie. She told Stefan about her suspicion of Tyler, but as Meredith pointed out, Tyler didn't fit the rest of the description. He had neither the brains nor the psychic power to be the one Elena was warning them about.

"What about Caroline?" Stefan asked. "Could she have seen anything?"

"She was out front," Meredith said. "She found the door and got out while we were all running. She heard the screams, but she was too frightened to go back in the house. And to be honest, I don't blame her."

"So nobody actually saw what happened except Vickie."

"No. And Vickie's not telling." Bonnie picked up the story where she had left off. "Once we realized nobody would believe us, we remembered Elena's message about the summoning spell. We figured it must have been you she wanted to summon, because she thought you could do something to help. So . . . can you?"

"I can try," Stefan said. He got up and walked a little

distance away, turning his back on them. He stood like that in silence awhile, unmoving. At last he turned back and looked Bonnie in the eyes. "Bonnie," he said, quiet but intense, "in your dreams you actually spoke to Elena face to face. Do you think if you went into a trance you could do it again?"

Bonnie was a little frightened by what she saw in his eyes. They were blazing emerald green in his pale face. All at once it was as if she could see behind the mask of control he wore. Underneath was so much pain, so much longing—so much of that intensity that she could hardly bear to look at it.

"I *could*, maybe . . . but Stefan—"

"Then we'll do it. Right here, right now. And we'll see if you can take me with you." Those eyes were mesmerizing, not with any hidden Power, but with the sheer force of his will. Bonnie wanted to do it for him—he made her want to do anything for him. But the memory of that last dream was too much. She couldn't face that horror again; she *couldn't*.

"Stefan, it's too dangerous. I could be opening myself up to anything—and I'm *scared*. If that thing gets hold of my mind, I don't know what might happen. I *can't*, Stefan. Please. Even with a Ouija board, it's just inviting him to come."

For a moment she thought he was going to try to make

her do it. His mouth tightened in an obstinate line, and his eyes blazed even brighter. But then, slowly, the fire died out of them.

Bonnie felt her heart tear. "Stefan, I'm sorry," she whispered.

"We'll just have to do it on our own," he said. The mask was back on, but his smile looked stiff, as if it hurt him. Then he spoke more briskly. "First we have to find out who this killer is, what he wants here. All we know now is that something evil has come to Fell's Church again."

"But *why*?" said Bonnie. "Why would anything evil just happen to pick here? Haven't we been through enough?"

"It does seem a bit of a strange coincidence," Meredith said drolly. "Why should we be so singularly blessed?"

"It's not coincidence," said Stefan. He got up and lifted his hands as if unsure how to start. "There are some places on this earth that are . . . different," he said. "That are full of psychic energy, either positive or negative, good or evil. Some of them have always been that way, like the Bermuda Triangle and Salisbury Plain, the place where they built Stonehenge. Others *become* that way, especially where a lot of blood has been shed." He looked at Bonnie.

"Unquiet spirits," she whispered.

"Yes. There was a battle here, wasn't there?"

"In the Civil War," Matt said. "That's how the church

in the cemetery got ruined. It was a slaughter on both sides. Nobody won, but almost everyone who fought got killed. The woods are full of their graves."

"And the ground was soaked with blood. A place like that draws the supernatural to it. It draws evil to it. That's why Katherine was attracted to Fell's Church in the first place. I felt it too, when I first came here."

"And now something else has come," Meredith said, perfectly serious for once. "But how are we supposed to fight it?"

"We have to know what we're fighting first. I think . . ." But before he could finish, there was a creak, and pale, dusty sunlight fell across the bales of hay. The barn door had opened.

Everyone tensed defensively, ready to jump up and run or fight. The figure nudging the huge door back with one elbow, however, was anything but menacing.

Mrs. Flowers, who owned the boardinghouse, smiled at them, her little black eyes crinkling into wrinkles. She was carrying a tray.

"I thought you children might like something to drink while you're talking," she said comfortably.

Everyone exchanged disconcerted glances. How had she known they were out here? And how could she be so calm about it?

"Here you go," Mrs. Flowers continued. "This is grape

juice, made from my own Concord grapes." She put a paper cup beside Meredith, then Matt, then Bonnie. "And here are some gingersnap cookies. Fresh." She held the plate around. Bonnie noticed she didn't offer any to Stefan or Damon.

"You two can come round to the cellar if you like and try some of my blackberry wine," she said to them, with what Bonnie would swear was a wink.

Stefan took a deep, wary breath. "Uh, look, Mrs. Flowers . . ."

"And your old room's just like you left it. Nobody's been up there since you went. You can use it when you want; it won't put me out a bit."

Stefan seemed at a loss for words. "Well—thank you. Thank you very much. But—"

"If you're worried I'll say something to somebody you can set your mind at ease. I don't tend to run off at the mouth. Never have, never will. How's that grape juice?"—turning suddenly on Bonnie.

Bonnie hastily took a gulp. "Good," she said truthfully.

"When you finish, throw the cups in the trash. I like things kept tidy." Mrs. Flowers cast a look about the barn, shaking her head and sighing. "Such a shame. Such a pretty girl." She looked at Stefan piercingly with eyes like onyx beads. "You've got your work cut out for you this time, boy," she said, and left, still shaking her head.

"Well!" said Bonnie, staring after her, amazed. Everyone else just looked at each other blankly.

"'Such a pretty girl'—but which?" said Meredith at last. "Sue or Elena?" Elena had actually spent a week or so in this very barn last winter—but Mrs. Flowers wasn't supposed to know that. "Did *you* say something to her about us?" Meredith asked Damon.

"Not a word." Damon seemed amused. "She's an old lady. She's batty."

"She's sharper than any of us gave her credit for," Matt said. "When I think of the days we spent watching her potter around that basement—do you think she *knew* we were watching?"

"I don't know what to think," Stefan said slowly. "I'm just glad she seems to be on our side. And she's given us a safe place to stay."

"And grape juice, don't forget that." Matt grinned at Stefan. "Want some?" He proffered the leaky cup.

"Yeah, you can take your grape juice and . . ." But Stefan was almost smiling himself. For an instant Bonnie saw the two of them the way they used to be, before Elena had died. Friendly, warm, as comfortable together as she and Meredith were. A pang went through her.

But Elena isn't dead, she thought. She's more here than ever. She's directing everything we say and do.

Stefan had sobered again. "When Mrs. Flowers came

in, I was about to say that we'd better get started. And I think we should start with Vickie."

"She won't see us," Meredith replied instantly. "Her parents are keeping everyone away."

"Then we'll just have to bypass her parents," Stefan said. "Are you coming with us, Damon?"

"A visit to yet another pretty girl? I wouldn't miss it."

Bonnie turned to Stefan in alarm, but he spoke reassuringly as he guided her out of the barn. "It'll be all right. I'll keep an eye on him."

Bonnie hoped so.

6

ickie's house was on a corner, and they approached it from the side street. By now the sky was filled with heavy purple clouds. The light had an almost underwater quality.

"Looks like it's going to storm," Matt said.

Bonnie glanced at Damon. Neither he nor Stefan liked bright light. And she could feel the Power emanating from him, like a low thrum just under the surface of his skin. He smiled without looking at her and said, "How about snow in June?"

Bonnie clamped down on a shiver.

She had looked Damon's way once or twice in the barn and found him listening to the story with an air of detached indifference. Unlike Stefan, his expression hadn't changed in the slightest when she mentioned Elena—or when she told about Sue's death. What did he really feel for Elena? He'd called up a snowstorm once and left her to freeze in it. What was he feeling now? Did he even care about catching the murderer?

"That's Vickie's bedroom," said Meredith. "The bay window in the back."

Stefan looked at Damon. "How many people in the house?"

"Two. Man and woman. The woman's drunk."

Poor Mrs. Bennett, thought Bonnie.

"I need them both asleep," Stefan said.

In spite of herself, Bonnie was fascinated by the surge of Power she felt from Damon. Her psychic abilities had never been strong enough to sense its raw essence before, but now they were. Now she could feel it as clearly as she could see the fading violet light or smell the honeysuckle outside Vickie's window.

Damon shrugged. "They're asleep."

Stefan tapped lightly on the glass.

There was no response, or at least none Bonnie could see. But Stefan and Damon looked at each other.

"She's half tranced already," Damon said.

"She's scared. I'll do it; she knows me," said Stefan. He put his fingertips on the window. "Vickie, it's Stefan Salvatore," he said. "I'm here to help you. Come let me in."

His voice was quiet, nothing that should have been

heard on the other side of the glass. But after a moment the curtains stirred and a face appeared.

Bonnie gasped aloud.

Vickie's long, light brown hair was disheveled, and her skin was chalky. There were huge black rings under her eyes. The eyes themselves were fixed and glassy. Her lips were rough and chapped.

"She looks like she's dressed up to do Ophelia's mad scene," Meredith said under her breath. "Nightgown and all."

"She looks *possessed*," Bonnie whispered back, unnerved.

Stefan just said, "Vickie, open the window."

Mechanically, like a windup doll, Vickie cranked one of the side panels of the bay window open, and Stefan said, "Can I come in?"

Vickie's glazed eyes swept over the group outside. For a moment Bonnie thought she didn't recognize any of them. But then she blinked and said slowly, "Meredith . . . Bonnie . . . Stefan? You're back. What are you doing here?"

"Ask me in, Vickie." Stefan's voice was hypnotic.

"Stefan . . ." There was a long pause and then: "Come in."

She stepped back as he put a hand on the sill and vaulted through. Matt followed him, then Meredith.

Bonnie, who was wearing a mini, remained outside with Damon. She wished she'd worn jeans to school today, but then she hadn't known she'd be going on an expedition.

"You shouldn't be here," Vickie said to Stefan, almost calmly. "He's coming to get me. He'll get you too."

Meredith put an arm around her. Stefan just said, "Who?"

"Him. He comes to me in my dreams. He killed Sue." Vickie's matter-of-fact tone was more frightening than any hysteria could have been.

"Vickie, we've come to help you," Meredith said gently. "Everything's going to be all right now. We won't let him hurt you, I promise."

Vickie swung around to stare at her. She looked Meredith up and down as if Meredith had suddenly changed into something unbelievable. Then she began to laugh.

It was awful, a hoarse burst of mirth like a hacking cough. It went on and on until Bonnie wanted to cover her ears. Finally Stefan said, "Vickie, stop it."

The laughter died into something like sobs, and when Vickie lifted her head again, she looked less glassy eyed but more genuinely upset. "You're all going to die, Stefan," she said, shaking her head. "No one can fight him and live."

"We need to know about him so we *can* fight him. We

need your help," Stefan said. "Tell me what he looks like."

"I can't see him in my dreams. He's just a shadow without a face." Vickie whispered it, her shoulders hunching.

"But you saw him at Caroline's house," Stefan said insistently. "Vickie, listen to me," he added as the girl turned away sharply. "I know you're frightened, but this is important, more important than you can understand. We can't fight him unless we know what we're up against, and you are the only one, the *only* one right now who has the information we need. You have to help us."

"I can't *remember*—"

Stefan's voice was unyielding. "I have a way to help you remember," he said. "Will you let me try?"

Seconds crawled by, then Vickie gave a long, bubbling sigh, her body sagging. "Do whatever you want," she said indifferently. "I don't care. It won't make any difference."

"You're a brave girl. Now look at me, Vickie. I want you to relax. Just look at me and relax." Stefan's voice dropped to a lulling murmur. It went on for a few minutes, and then Vickie's eyes drooped shut.

"Sit down." Stefan guided her to sit on the bed. He sat beside her, looking into her face. "Vickie, you feel calm and relaxed now. Nothing you remember will hurt you," he said, his voice soothing. "Now, I need you to go back to Saturday night. You're upstairs, in the master bedroom of Caroline's house. Sue Carson is with you, and someone else. I need you to see—"

"No!" Vickie twisted back and forth as if trying to escape something. "No! I can't—"

"Vickie, calm down. He won't hurt you. He can't see you, but you can see him. Listen to me."

As Stefan spoke, Vickie's whimpers quieted. But she still thrashed and writhed.

"You *need* to see him, Vickie. Help us fight him. What does he look like?"

"He looks like the devil!"

It was almost a scream. Meredith sat on Vickie's other side and took her hand. She looked out through the window at Bonnie who looked back wide eyed and shrugged slightly. Bonnie had no idea what Vickie was talking about.

"Tell me more," Stefan said evenly.

Vickie's mouth twisted. Her nostrils were flared as if she were smelling something awful. When she spoke, she got out each word separately as if they were making her sick.

"He wears . . . an old raincoat. It flaps around his legs in the wind. He makes the wind blow. His hair is blond. Almost white. It stands up all over his head. His eyes are so blue—electric blue." Vickie licked her lips and swallowed, looking nauseated. "Blue is the color of death."

Thunder rumbled and cracked in the sky. Damon glanced up quickly, then frowned, eyes narrowed.

"He's tall. And he's laughing. He's reaching for me, laughing. But Sue screams, 'No, no' and tries to pull me away. So he takes her instead. The window's broken, and the balcony is right there. Sue's crying, 'No, please.' And then I watch him—I watch him throw her . . ." Vickie's breath was hitching, her voice rising hysterically.

"Vickie, it's all right. You're not really there. You're safe."

"Oh, please, no—Sue! *Sue! Sue!*"

"Vickie, stay with me. Listen. I need just one more thing. Look at him. Tell me if he's wearing a blue jewel—"

But Vickie was whipping her head back and forth, sobbing, more hysterical each second. "No! No! I'm next! I'm next!" Suddenly, her eyes sprang open as she came out of the trance by herself, choking and gasping. Then her head jerked around.

On the wall, a picture was rattling.

It was picked up by the bamboo-framed mirror, then by perfume bottles and lipsticks on the dresser below. With a sound like popcorn, earrings began bursting from an earring tree. The rattling got louder and louder. A straw hat fell off a hook. Photos were showering down from the mirror. Tapes and CDs sprayed out of a rack and onto the floor like playing cards being dealt.

Meredith was on her feet and so was Matt, fists clenched.

"Make it stop! Make it stop!" Vickie cried wildly.

But it didn't stop. Matt and Meredith looked around as new objects joined the dance. Everything movable was shaking, jittering, swaying. It was as if the room were caught in an earthquake.

"Stop! Stop!" shrieked Vickie, her hands over her ears.

Directly above the house thunder exploded.

Bonnie jumped violently as she saw the zigzag of lightning shoot across the sky. Instinctively she grabbed for something to hang on to. As the lightning bolt flared a poster on Vickie's wall tore diagonally as if slashed by a phantom knife. Bonnie choked back a scream and clutched tighter.

Then, as quickly as if someone had flicked a power switch off, all the noise stopped.

Vickie's room was still. The fringe on the bedside lamp swayed slightly. The poster had curled up in two irregular pieces, top and bottom. Slowly, Vickie lowered her hands from her ears.

Matt and Meredith looked around rather shakily.

Bonnie shut her eyes and murmured something like a prayer. It wasn't until she opened them again that she realized what she had been hanging on to. It was the supple coolness of a leather jacket. It was Damon's arm.

He hadn't moved away from her, though. He didn't move now. He was leaning forward slightly, eyes narrowed, watching the room intently.

"Look at the mirror," he said.

Everyone did, and Bonnie drew in her breath, fingers clenching again. She hadn't seen it, but it must have happened while everything in the room was going berserk.

On the glass surface of the bamboo mirror two words were scrawled in Vickie's hot coral lipstick.

Goodnight, Sweetheart.

"Oh, God," Bonnie whispered.

Stefan turned from the mirror to Vickie. There was something different about him, Bonnie thought—he was holding himself relaxed but poised, like a soldier who's just gotten confirmation of a battle. It was as if he'd accepted a personal challenge of some kind.

He took something out of his back pocket and unfolded it, revealing sprigs of a plant with long green leaves and tiny lilac flowers.

"This is vervain, fresh vervain," he said quietly, his voice even and intense. "I picked it outside Florence; it's blooming there now." He took Vickie's hand and pressed the packet into it. "I want you to hold on to this and keep it. Put some in every room of the house, and hide pieces somewhere in your parents' clothes if you can, so they'll have it near them. As long as you have this with you, he can't take over your mind. He can scare you, Vickie, but he can't make you do anything, like open a window or door for him. And listen, Vickie, because this is important."

Vickie was shivering, her face crumpled. Stefan took both her hands and made her look at him, speaking slowly and distinctly.

"If I'm right, Vickie, *he can't get in unless you let him*. So talk to your parents. Tell them it's important that they don't ask any stranger inside the house. In fact, I can have Damon put that suggestion in their mind right now." He glanced at Damon, who shrugged slightly and nodded, looking as if his attention was somewhere else. Self-consciously, Bonnie removed her hand from his jacket.

Vickie's head was bent over the vervain. "He'll get in somehow," she said softly, with terrible certainty.

"No. Vickie, listen to me. From now on, we're going to watch your house; we're going to be waiting for him."

"It doesn't *matter*," Vickie said. "You can't stop him." She began to laugh and cry at the same time.

"We're going to try," Stefan said. He looked at Meredith and Matt, who nodded. "Right. From this moment on, you will never be alone. There will always be one or more of us outside watching you."

Vickie just shook her bent head. Meredith gave her

arm a squeeze and stood as Stefan tilted his head toward the window.

When she and Matt joined him there, Stefan spoke to all of them in a low voice. "I don't want to leave her unguarded, but I can't stay myself right now. There's something I have to do, and I need one of the girls with me. On the other hand, I don't want to leave either Bonnie or Meredith alone here." He turned to Matt. "Matt, will you . . ."

"I'll stay," said Damon.

Everyone looked at him, startled.

"Well, it's the logical solution, isn't it?" Damon seemed amused. "After all, what do you expect one of *them* to do against him anyway?"

"They can call for *me*. I can monitor their thoughts that far," Stefan said, not giving one inch.

"Well," Damon said whimsically, "I can call for you too, little brother, if I get into trouble. I'm getting bored with this investigation of yours anyway. I might as well stay here as anywhere."

"Vickie needs to be protected, not abused," Stefan said.

Damon's smile was charming. "*Her?*" He nodded toward the girl who sat on the bed, rocking over the vervain. From disheveled hair to bare feet, Vickie was not a pretty picture. "Take my word for it, brother, I can do better than that." For just an instant Bonnie thought those dark eyes flicked sideways toward her. "You're always saying how you'd like to trust me, anyway," Damon added. "Here's your chance to prove it."

Stefan looked as if he wanted to trust, as if he were tempted. He also looked suspicious. Damon said nothing, merely smiled in that taunting, enigmatic way. Practically asking to be *mistrusted*, Bonnie thought.

The two brothers stood looking at each other while the silence and the tension stretched out between them. Just then Bonnie could see the family resemblance in their faces, one serious and intense, the other bland and faintly mocking, but both inhumanly beautiful.

Stefan let his breath out slowly. "All right," he said quietly at last. Bonnie and Matt and Meredith were all staring at him, but he didn't seem to notice. He spoke to Damon as if they were the only two people there. "You stay here, outside the house where you won't be seen. I'll come back and take over when I'm finished with what I'm doing."

Meredith's eyebrows were in her hair, but she made no comment. Neither did Matt. Bonnie tried to quell her own feelings of unease. Stefan must know what he's doing, she told herself. Anyway, he'd *better*.

"Don't take too long," Damon said dismissively.

And that was how they left it, with Damon blending in

with the darkness in the shadow of the black walnut trees in Vickie's backyard and Vickie herself in her room, rocking endlessly.

In the car, Meredith said, "Where next?"

"I need to test a theory," said Stefan briefly.

"That the killer is a vampire?" Matt said from the back, where he sat with Bonnie.

Stefan glanced at him sharply. "Yes."

"That's why you told Vickie not to invite anyone in," Meredith added, not to be outdone in the reasoning department. Vampires, Bonnie remembered, couldn't enter a place where humans lived and slept unless they were invited. "And that's why you asked if the man was wearing a blue stone."

"An amulet against daylight," Stefan said, spreading his right hand. On the third finger there was a silver ring set with lapis lazuli. "Without one of these, direct exposure to the sun kills us. If the murderer *is* a vampire he keeps a stone like this somewhere on him." As if by instinct, Stefan reached up to briefly touch something under his T-shirt. After a moment Bonnie realized what it must be.

Elena's ring. Stefan had given it to her in the first place, and after she died he'd taken it to wear on a chain around his neck. So that part of her would be with him always, he'd said.

When Bonnie looked at Matt beside her, she saw his eyes were closed.

"So how can we tell if he's a vampire?" Meredith asked.

"There's only one way I can think of, and it isn't very pleasant. But it's got to be done."

Bonnie's heart sank. If Stefan thought it wasn't very pleasant, she was sure she was going to find it even less so. "What is it?" she said unenthusiastically.

"I need to get a look at Sue's body."

There was dead silence. Even Meredith, normally so unflappable, looked appalled. Matt turned away, leaning his forehead against the window glass.

"You've got to be kidding," Bonnie said.

"I wish I were."

"But—for God's sake, Stefan. We *can't*. They won't let us. I mean, what are we going to say? 'Excuse me while I examine this corpse for holes'?"

"Bonnie, stop it," Meredith said.

"I can't help it," Bonnie snapped back shakily. "It's an *awful* idea. And besides, the police already checked her body. There wasn't a mark on it except the cuts she got in the fall."

"The police don't know what to look for," Stefan said. His voice was steely. Hearing it brought something home to Bonnie, something she tended to forget. Stefan was one of *them*. One of the hunters. He'd seen dead people before. He might even have killed some.

He drinks *blood*, she thought, and shuddered.

"Well?" said Stefan. "Are you still with me?"

Bonnie tried to make herself small in the backseat. Meredith's hands were tight on the steering wheel. It was Matt who spoke, turning back from the window.

"We don't have a choice, do we?" he said tiredly.

"There's a viewing of the body from seven to ten at the funeral home," Meredith added, her voice low.

"We'll have to wait until after the viewing, then. After they close the funeral home, when we can be alone with her," said Stefan.

"This is the most gruesome thing I've ever had to do," Bonnie whispered wretchedly. The funeral chapel was dark and cold. Stefan had sprung the locks on the outside door with a thin piece of flexible metal.

The viewing room was thickly carpeted, its walls covered with somber oak panels. It would have been a depressing place even with the lights on. In the dark it seemed close and suffocating and crowded with grotesque shapes. It looked as if someone might be crouching behind each of the many standing flower arrangements.

"I don't want to *be* here," Bonnie moaned.

"Let's just get it over with, okay?" Matt said through his teeth.

When he snapped the flashlight on, Bonnie looked anywhere but where it was pointing. She didn't want to see the coffin, she *didn't*. She stared at the flowers, at a heart made of pink roses. Outside, thunder grumbled like a sleeping animal.

"Let me get this open—here," Stefan was saying. In spite of her resolve not to, Bonnie looked.

The casket was white, lined with pale pink satin. Sue's blond hair shone against it like the hair of a sleeping princess in a fairy tale. But Sue didn't look as if she were sleeping. She was too pale, too still. Like a waxwork.

Bonnie crept closer, her eyes fixed on Sue's face.

That's why it's so cold in here, she told herself staunchly. To keep the wax from melting. It helped a little.

Stefan reached down to touch Sue's high-necked pink blouse. He undid the top button.

"For God's *sake*," Bonnie whispered, outraged.

"What do you think we're here for?" Stefan hissed back. But his fingers paused on the second button.

Bonnie watched a minute and then made her decision. "Get out of the way," she said, and when Stefan didn't move immediately, she gave him a shove. Meredith drew up close to her and they formed a phalanx between Sue and the boys. Their eyes met with understanding. If they had to actually remove the blouse, the guys were going out.

Bonnie undid the small buttons while Meredith held the light. Sue's skin felt as waxy as it looked, cool against her fingertips. Awkwardly, she folded the blouse back to reveal a lacy white slip. Then she made herself push Sue's shining gold hair off the pale neck. The hair was stiff with spray.

"No holes," she said, looking at Sue's throat. She was proud that her voice was almost steady.

"No," said Stefan oddly. "But there's something else. Look at this." Gently, he reached around Bonnie to point out a cut, pale and bloodless as the skin around it, but visible as a faint line running from collarbone to breast. Over the heart. Stefan's long finger traced the air above it and Bonnie stiffened, ready to smack the hand away if he touched.

"What is it?" asked Meredith, puzzled.

"A mystery," Stefan said. His voice was still odd. "If I saw a mark like that on a vampire, it would mean the vampire was giving blood to a human. That's how it's done. Human teeth can't pierce our skin, so we cut ourselves if we want to share blood. But Sue wasn't a vampire."

"She certainly wasn't!" said Bonnie. She tried to fight off the image her mind wanted to show her, of Elena bending to a cut like that on Stefan's chest and sucking, drinking . . .

She shuddered and realized her eyes were shut. "Is there anything else you need to see?" she said, opening them.

"No. That's all."

Bonnie did up the buttons. She rearranged Sue's hair. Then, while Meredith and Stefan eased the lid of the casket back down, she walked quickly out of the viewing room and to the outside door. She stood there, arms wrapped around herself.

A hand touched her elbow lightly. It was Matt.

"You're tougher than you look," he said.

"Yes, well . . ." She tried to shrug. And then suddenly she was crying, crying hard. Matt put his arms around her.

"I know," he said. Just that. Not "Don't cry" or "Take it easy" or "Everything's going to be all right." Just "I know." His voice was as desolate as she felt.

"They've got hair spray in her hair," she sobbed. "Sue *never* used hair spray. It's awful." Somehow, just then, this seemed the worst thing of all.

He simply held her.

After a while Bonnie got her breath. She found she was holding on to Matt almost painfully tightly and loosened her arms. "I got your shirt all wet," she said apologetically, sniffling.

"It doesn't matter."

Something in his voice made her step back and look at him. He looked the way he had in the high school parking lot. So lost, so . . . hopeless.

"Matt, what is it?" she whispered. "Please."

"I told you already," he said. He was looking away into some immeasurable distance. "Sue's lying in there dead, and she shouldn't be. You said it yourself, Bonnie. What kind of world is it that lets a thing like that happen? That lets a girl like Sue get murdered for kicks, or kids in Afghanistan starve, or baby seals get skinned alive? If that's what the world is like, what does anything matter? It's all over anyway." He paused and seemed to come back to himself. "Do you understand what I'm talking about?"

"I'm not so sure." Bonnie didn't even think she wanted to. It was too scary. But she was overwhelmed by an urge to comfort him, to wipe that lost look from his eyes. "Matt, I—"

"We're finished," Stefan said from behind them.

As Matt looked toward the voice the lost look seemed to intensify. "Sometimes I think we're *all* finished," Matt said, moving away from Bonnie, but he didn't explain what he meant by that. "Let's go."

Stefan approached the corner house reluctantly, almost afraid of what he might find. He half expected that Damon would have abandoned his post by now. He'd probably been an idiot to rely on Damon in the first place.

But when he reached the backyard, there was a shimmer of motion among the black walnut trees. His eyes, sharper than a human's because they were adapted for hunting, made out the darker shadow leaning against a trunk.

"You took your time getting back."

"I had to see the others home safe. And I had to eat."

"Animal blood," Damon said contemptuously, eyes fixed on a tiny round stain on Stefan's T-shirt. "Rabbit, from the smell of it. That seems appropriate somehow, doesn't it?"

"Damon—I've given Bonnie and Meredith vervain too."

"A wise precaution," Damon said distinctly, and showed his teeth.

A familiar surge of irritation welled up in Stefan. Why did Damon always have to be so difficult? Talking with him was like walking between land mines.

"I'll be going now," Damon continued, swinging his jacket over one shoulder. "I've got business of my own to take care of." He tossed a devastating grin over his shoulder. "Don't wait up.

"Damon." Damon half turned, not looking but listening. "The last thing we need is some girl in this town screaming 'Vampire!'" Stefan said. "Or showing the signs, either. These people have been through it before; they're not ignorant."

"I'll bear that in mind." It was said ironically, but it was the closest thing to a promise Stefan had ever gotten from his brother in his life.

"And, Damon?"

"Now what?"

"Thank you."

It was too much. Damon whipped around, his eyes cold and uninviting, a stranger's eyes.

"Don't expect anything of me, little brother," he said dangerously. "Because you'll be wrong every time. And don't think you can manipulate me, either. Those three humans may follow you, but I won't. I'm here for reasons of my own."

He was gone before Stefan could gather words for a reply. It wouldn't have mattered anyway. Damon never listened to anything he said. Damon never even called him by name. It was always the scornful "little brother."

And now Damon was off to prove how unreliable he was, Stefan thought. Wonderful. He'd do something particularly vicious just to show Stefan he was capable of it.

Wearily, Stefan found a tree to lean against and slid down it to look at the night sky. He tried to think about the problem at hand, about what he'd learned tonight. The description Vickie had given of the killer. Tall, blond hair and blue eyes, he thought—that seemed to remind him of someone. Not someone he'd met, but someone he'd heard about . . .

It was no use. He couldn't keep his mind on the puzzle. He was tired and lonely and in desperate need of comfort. And the stark truth was that there was no comfort to be had.

Elena, he thought, you lied to me.

It was the one thing she'd insisted on, the one thing she'd always promised. "Whatever happens, Stefan, I'll be with you. Tell me you believe that." And he had answered, helpless in her spell, "Oh, Elena, I believe it.

Whatever happens, we'll be together."

But she had left him. Not by choice maybe, but what did that matter in the end? She had left him and gone away.

There were times when all he wanted was to follow her.

Think about something else, anything else, he told himself, but it was too late. Once unleashed, the images of Elena swirled around him, too painful to bear, too beautiful to push away.

The first time he'd kissed her. The shock of dizzy sweetness when his mouth met hers. And after that, shock after shock, but at some deeper level. As if she were reaching down to the core of himself, a core he'd almost forgotten.

Frightened, he'd felt his defenses tear away. All his secrets, all his resistance, all the tricks he used to keep other people at arm's length. Elena had ripped through them all, exposing his vulnerability.

Exposing his soul.

And in the end, he found that it was what he wanted. He wanted Elena to see him without defenses, without walls. He wanted her to know him for what he was.

Terrifying? Yes. When she'd discovered his secret at last, when she'd found him feeding on that bird, he had cringed in shame. He was sure that she'd turn away from the blood on his mouth in horror. In disgust.

But when he looked into her eyes that night, he saw understanding. Forgiveness. Love.

Her love had healed him.

And that was when he knew they could never be apart.

Other memories surged up and Stefan held on to them, even though the pain tore into him like claws. Sensations. The feel of Elena against him, supple in his arms. The brush of her hair on his cheek, light as a moth's wing. The curve of her lips, the taste of them. The impossible midnight blue of her eyes.

All lost. All beyond his reach forever.

But Bonnie had reached Elena. Elena's spirit, her soul, was still somewhere near.

Of anyone, he should be able to summon it. He had Power at his command. And he had more right than anyone to seek her.

He knew how it was done. Shut your eyes. Picture the person you want to draw near. That was easy. He could see Elena, feel her, smell her. Then call them, let your longing reach out into the emptiness. Open yourself and let your need be felt.

Easier still. He didn't give a damn about the danger. He gathered all his yearning, all his pain, and sent it out searching like a prayer.

And felt . . . nothing.

Only void and his own loneliness. Only silence.

His Power wasn't the same as Bonnie's. He couldn't reach the one thing he loved most, the one thing that mattered to him.

He had never felt so alone in his life.

"You want *what*?" Bonnie said.

"Some sort of records about the history of Fell's Church. Particularly about the founders," Stefan said. They were all sitting in Meredith's car, which was parked a discreet distance behind Vickie's house. It was dusk of the next day and they had just returned from Sue's funeral—all but Stefan.

"This has something to do with Sue, doesn't it?" Meredith's dark eyes, always so level and intelligent, probed Stefan's. "You think you've solved the mystery."

"Possibly," he admitted. He had spent the day thinking. He'd put the pain of last night behind him, and once again he was in control. Although he could not reach Elena, he could justify her faith in him—he could do what she wanted done. And there was a comfort in work, in concentration. In keeping all emotion away. He added, "I have an idea about what might have happened, but it's a long shot and I don't want to talk about it until I'm sure."

"Why?" demanded Bonnie. Such a contrast to Meredith, Stefan thought. Hair as red as fire and a spirit to go with it. That delicate heart-shaped face and fair, translucent skin were deceptive, though. Bonnie was smart and resourceful—even if she was only beginning to find that out herself.

"Because if I'm wrong, an innocent person might get hurt. Look, at this point it's just an idea. But I promise if I find any evidence tonight to back it up, I'll tell you all about it."

"You could talk with Mrs. Grimesby," Meredith suggested. "She's the town librarian, and she knows a lot about the founding of Fell's Church."

"Or there's always Honoria," Bonnie said. "I mean, she *was* one of the founders."

Stefan looked at her quickly. "I thought Honoria Fell had stopped communicating with you," he said carefully.

"I don't mean talk to *her*. She's gone, *pfft*, kaput," Bonnie said disgustedly. "I mean her journal. It's right there in the library with Elena's; Mrs. Grimesby has them on display near the circulation desk."

Stefan was surprised. He didn't entirely like the idea of Elena's journal on display. But Honoria's records might be exactly what he was looking for. Honoria had not just been a wise woman; she had been well versed in the supernatural. A witch.

"The library's closed by now, though," Meredith said.

"That's even better," said Stefan. "No one will know

what information we're interested in. Two of us can go down there and break in, and the other two can stay here. Meredith, if you'll come with me—"

"I'd like to stay here, if you don't mind," she said. "I'm tired," she added in explanation, seeing his expression. "And this way I can get my watch over with and get home earlier. Why don't you and Matt go and Bonnie and I stay here?"

Stefan was still looking at her. "Okay," he said slowly. "Fine. If it's all right with Matt." Matt shrugged. "That's it, then. It might take us a couple of hours or more. You two stay in the car with the doors locked. You should be safe enough that way." If he was right in his suspicions, there wouldn't be any more attacks for a while—a few days at least. Bonnie and Meredith *should* be safe. But he couldn't help wonder what was behind Meredith's suggestion. Not simple tiredness, he was sure.

"By the way, where's Damon?" Bonnie asked as he and Matt started to leave.

Stefan felt his stomach muscles tighten. "I don't know." He had been waiting for someone to ask that. He hadn't seen his brother since last night, and he had no idea what Damon might be doing.

"He'll show up eventually," he said, and closed the door on Meredith's, "That's what I'm afraid of."

He and Matt walked to the library in silence, keeping

to the shadows, skirting areas of light. He couldn't afford to be seen. Stefan had come back to help Fell's Church, but he felt sure Fell's Church didn't want his help. He was a stranger again, an intruder here. They would hurt him if they caught him.

The library lock was easy to pick, just a simple spring mechanism. And the journals were right where Bonnie had said they would be.

Stefan forced his hand away from Elena's journal. Inside was the record of Elena's last days, in her own handwriting. If he started thinking about that now . . .

He concentrated on the leather-bound book beside it. The faded ink on the yellowing pages was hard to read, but after a few minutes his eyes got accustomed to the dense, intricate writing with its elaborate curlicues.

It was the story of Honoria Fell and her husband, who with the Smallwoods and a few other families had come to this place when it was still virgin wilderness. They had faced not only the dangers of isolation and hunger but of native wildlife. Honoria told the story of their battle to survive simply and clearly, without sentimentality.

And in those pages Stefan found what he was looking for.

With a prickling at the back of his neck, he reread the entry carefully. At last he leaned back and shut his eyes.

He'd been right. There was no longer any doubt in his mind. And that meant he must also be right about what was going on in Fell's Church now. For an instant, bright sickness washed over him, and an anger that made him want to rip and tear and hurt something. Sue. Pretty Sue who had been Elena's friend had died for . . . that. A blood ritual, an obscene initiation. It made him want to *kill*.

But then the rage faded, replaced by a fierce determination to stop what was happening and set things right.

I promise you, he whispered to Elena in his own mind. I *will* stop it somehow. No matter what.

He looked up to find Matt looking at him.

Elena's journal was in Matt's hand, closing itself over his thumb. Just then Matt's eyes looked as dark a blue as Elena's. Too dark, full of turmoil and grief and something like bitterness.

"You found it," Matt said. "And it's bad."

"Yes."

"It would be." Matt pushed Elena's journal back into the case and stood. There was a ring almost of satisfaction in his voice. Like somebody who's just proved a point.

"I could have saved you the trouble of coming here." Matt surveyed the darkened library, jingling change in his pocket. A casual observer might have thought he was relaxed, but his voice betrayed him. It was raw with strain. "You just think of the worst thing you can imagine and that's always the truth," he said.

"Matt . . ." Sudden concern stabbed at Stefan. He'd

been too preoccupied since coming back to Fell's Church to look at Matt properly. Now he realized that he'd been unforgivably stupid. Something was terribly wrong. Matt's whole body was rigid with tension lying just under the surface. And Stefan could sense the anguish, the desperation in his mind.

"Matt, what is it?" he said quietly. He got up and crossed to the other boy. "Is it something I did?"

"I'm fine."

"You're shaking." It was true. Fine tremors were running through the taut muscles.

"I said I'm fine!" Matt swung away from him, shoulders hunched defensively. "Anyway, what could *you* have done to upset me? Besides taking my girl and getting her killed, I mean?"

This stab was different, it was somewhere around Stefan's heart and it went straight through. Like the blade that had killed him once upon a time. He tried to breathe around it, not trusting himself to speak.

"I'm sorry." Matt's voice was leaden, and when Stefan looked, he saw that the tense shoulders had slumped. "That was a lousy thing to say."

"It was the truth." Stefan waited a moment and then added, levelly, "But it's not the whole problem, is it?"

Matt didn't answer. He stared at the floor, pushing something invisible with the side of one shoe. Just when

Stefan was about to give up, he turned with a question of his own.

"What's the world really like?"

"What's . . . what?"

"The world. You've seen a lot of it, Stefan. You've got four or five centuries on the rest of us, right? So what's the deal? I mean, is it basically the kind of place worth saving or is it essentially a pile of crap?"

Stefan shut his eyes. "Oh."

"And what about people, huh, Stefan? The human race. Are we the disease or just a symptom? I mean, you take somebody like—like Elena." Matt's voice shook briefly, but he went on. "Elena died to keep the town safe for girls like Sue. And now Sue's dead. And it's all happening again. It's never over. We can't win. So what does that tell you?"

"Matt."

"What I'm really asking is, what's the point? Is there some cosmic joke I'm not getting? Or is the whole thing just one big freaking mistake? Do you understand what I'm trying to say here?"

"I understand, Matt." Stefan sat down and ran his hands through his hair. "If you'll shut up a minute, I'll try to answer you."

Matt drew up a chair and straddled it. "Great. Take your best shot." His eyes were hard and challenging, but underneath Stefan saw the bewildered hurt that had been festering there.

"I've seen a lot of evil, Matt, more than you can imagine," Stefan said. "I've even lived it. It's always going to be a part of me, no matter how I fight it. Sometimes I think the whole human race is evil, much less my kind. And sometimes I think that enough of both our races is evil that it doesn't matter what happens to the rest.

"When you get down to it, though, I don't know any more than you do. I can't tell you if there's a point or if things are ever going to turn out all right." Stefan looked straight into Matt's eyes and spoke deliberately. "But I've got another question for you. So what?"

Matt stared. "So what?"

"Yeah. So what."

"So what if the universe is evil and if nothing we do to try and change it can really make any difference?" Matt's voice was gaining volume with his disbelief.

"Yeah, so what?" Stefan leaned forward. "So what are you going to do, Matt Honeycutt, if every bad thing you've said is true? What are you going to do personally? Are you going to stop fighting and swim with the sharks?"

Matt was grasping the back of his chair. "What are you talking about?"

"You can do that, you know. Damon says so all the time. You can join up with the evil side, the winning side.

And nobody can really blame you, because if the universe is that way, why shouldn't you be that way too?"

"Like hell!" Matt exploded. His blue eyes were searing and he had half risen from his chair. "That's Damon's way, maybe! But just because it's hopeless doesn't mean it's all right to stop fighting. Even if I *knew* it was hopeless, I'd still have to try. I have to try, damn it!"

"I know." Stefan settled back and smiled faintly. It was a tired smile, but it showed the kinship he felt right then with Matt. And in a moment he saw by Matt's face that Matt understood.

"I know because I feel the same way," Stefan continued. "There's no excuse for giving up just because it looks like we're going to lose. We have to try—because the other choice is to surrender."

"I'm not ready to surrender *anything*," Matt said through his teeth. He looked as if he'd fought his way back to a fire inside him that had been burning all along. "Ever," he said.

"Yeah, well, 'ever' is a long time," Stefan said. "But for what it's worth, I'm going to try not to either. I don't know if it's possible, but I'm going to try."

"That's all anybody can do," Matt said. Slowly, he pushed himself off the chair and stood straight. The tension was gone from his muscles, and his eyes were the clear, almost piercing blue eyes Stefan remembered.

"Okay," he said quietly. "If you found what you came for, we'd better get back to the girls."

Stefan thought, his mind switching gears. "Matt, if I'm right about what's going on, the girls should be okay for a while. But you go ahead and take over the watch from them. As long as I'm here there's something I'd like to read up on—by a guy named Gervase of Tilbury, who lived in the early 1200s."

"Even before your time, eh?" Matt said, and Stefan gave him the ghost of a smile. They stood for a moment, looking at each other.

"All right. I guess I'll see you at Vickie's." Matt turned to the door, then hesitated. Abruptly, he turned again and held out his hand. "Stefan—I'm glad you came back."

Stefan gripped it. "I'm glad to hear it" was all he said, but inside he felt a warmth that took away the stabbing pain.

And some of the loneliness, too.

8

From where Bonnie and Meredith sat in the car, they could just see Vickie's window. It would have been better to be closer, but then someone might have discovered them.

Meredith poured the last of the coffee out of the Thermos and drank it. Then she yawned. She caught herself guiltily and looked at Bonnie.

"You having trouble sleeping at night too?"

"Yes. I can't imagine why," Meredith said.

"Do you think the guys are having a little talk?"

Meredith glanced at her quickly, obviously surprised, then smiled. Bonnie realized Meredith hadn't expected her to catch on. "I hope so," Meredith said. "It might do Matt some good."

Bonnie nodded and relaxed back into the seat.

Meredith's car had never seemed so comfortable before.

When she looked at Meredith again, the dark-haired girl was asleep.

Oh, great. Terrific. Bonnie stared into the dregs of her coffee mug, making a face. She didn't dare relax again; if they *both* fell asleep, it could be disastrous. She dug her nails into her palms and stared at Vickie's lighted window.

When she found the image blurring and doubling on her, she knew something had to be done.

Fresh air. That would help. Without bothering to be too quiet about it, she unlocked the door and pulled the handle up. The door clicked open, but Meredith went on breathing deeply.

She must really be tired, Bonnie thought, getting out. She shut the door more gently, locking Meredith inside. It was only then that she realized she herself didn't have a key.

Oh, well, she'd wake Meredith to let her back in. Meanwhile she'd go check on Vickie. Vickie was probably still awake.

The sky was brooding and overcast, but the night was warm. Behind Vickie's house the black walnut trees stirred very faintly. Crickets sang, but their monotonous chirping only seemed like part of a larger silence.

The scent of honeysuckle filled Bonnie's nostrils. She tapped on Vickie's window lightly with her fingernails, peering through the crack in the curtains.

No answer. On the bed she could make out a lump of blankets with unkempt brown hair sticking out the top. Vickie was asleep too.

As Bonnie stood there, the silence seemed to thicken around her. The crickets weren't singing anymore, and the trees were still. And yet it was as if she was straining to hear something she *knew* was there.

I'm not alone, she realized.

None of her ordinary senses told her this. But her sixth sense, the one that sent chills up her arms and ice down her spine, the one that was newly awakened to the presence of Power, was certain. There was . . . something . . . near. Something . . . watching her.

She turned slowly, afraid to make a sound. If she didn't make any noise, maybe whatever it was wouldn't get her. Maybe it wouldn't notice her.

The silence had become deadly, menacing. It hummed in her ears with the beat of her own blood. And she couldn't help imagining what might come screaming out of it at any minute.

Something with hot, moist hands, she thought, staring into the darkness of the backyard. Black on gray, black on black was all she could see. Every shape might be anything, and all the shadows seemed to be moving. Something with hot, sweaty hands and arms strong enough to crush her—

The snap of a twig exploded through her like gunfire.

She spun toward it, eyes and ears straining. But there was only darkness and silence.

Fingers touched the back of her neck.

Bonnie whirled again, almost falling, almost fainting. She was too frightened to scream. When she saw who it was, shock robbed all her senses and her muscles collapsed. She would have ended up in a heap on the ground if he hadn't caught her and held her straight.

"You look frightened," Damon said softly.

Bonnie shook her head. She didn't have any voice yet. She thought she still might faint. But she tried to pull away just the same.

He didn't tighten his grip, but he didn't let go. And struggling did about as much good as trying to break a brick wall with bare hands. She gave up and tried to calm her breathing.

"Are you frightened of *me*?" Damon said. He smiled reprovingly, as if they shared a secret. "You don't need to be."

How had Elena managed to deal with this? But Elena hadn't, of course, Bonnie realized. Elena had succumbed to Damon in the end. Damon had won and had his way.

He released one of her arms to trace, very lightly, the curve of her upper lip. "I suppose I should go away," he said, "and not scare you anymore. Is that what you want?"

Like a rabbit with a snake, Bonnie thought. This is

how the rabbit feels. Only I don't suppose he'll kill me. I might just die on my own, though. She felt as if her legs might melt away at any minute, as if she might collapse. There was a warmth and a trembling inside her.

Think of something . . . fast. Those unfathomable black eyes were filling the universe now. She thought she could see stars inside them. *Think*. Quickly.

Elena wouldn't like it, she thought, just as his lips touched hers. Yes, that was it. But the problem was, she didn't have the strength to say it. The warmth was growing, rushing out to all parts of her, from her fingertips to the soles of her feet. His lips were cool, like silk, but everything else was so warm. She didn't need to be afraid; she could just let go and float on this. Sweetness rushed through her . . .

"What the *hell* is going on?"

The voice broke the silence, broke the spell. Bonnie started and found herself able to turn her head. Matt was standing at the edge of the yard, his fists clenched, his eyes like chips of blue ice. Ice so cold it burned.

"Get away from her," Matt said.

To Bonnie's surprise, the grip on her arms eased. She stepped back, straightening her blouse, a little breathless. Her mind was working again.

"It's okay," she said to Matt, her voice almost normal. "I was just—"

"Go back to the car and stay there."

Now *wait* a minute, thought Bonnie. She was glad Matt had come; the interruption had been very conveniently timed. But he was coming on a little heavy with the protective older brother bit.

"Look, Matt—"

"Go on," he said, still staring at Damon.

Meredith wouldn't have let herself be ordered around this way. And Elena certainly wouldn't. Bonnie opened her mouth to tell Matt to go sit in the car himself when she suddenly realized something.

This was the first time in months she'd seen Matt really *care* about anything. The light was back in those blue eyes—that cold flash of righteous anger that used to make even Tyler Smallwood back down. Matt was alive right now, and full of energy. He was himself again.

Bonnie bit her lip. For a moment she struggled with her pride. Then she conquered it and lowered her eyes.

"Thanks for rescuing me," she murmured, and left the yard.

Matt was so angry he didn't dare move closer to Damon for fear he might take a swing at him. And the chilling darkness in Damon's eyes told him that wouldn't be a very good idea.

But Damon's voice was smooth, almost dispassionate. "My taste for blood isn't just a whim, you know. It's a necessity you're interfering with here. I'm only doing what I have to."

This callous indifference was too much for Matt. They think of us as food, he remembered. They're the hunters, we're the prey. And he had his claws in Bonnie, Bonnie who couldn't wrestle a kitten.

Contemptuously he said, "Why don't you pick on somebody your own size, then?"

Damon smiled and the air went colder. "Like you?"

Matt just stared at him. He could feel muscles clench in his jaw. After a moment he said tightly, "You can try."

"I can do more than try, Matt." Damon took a single step toward him like a stalking panther. Involuntarily, Matt thought of jungle cats, of their powerful spring and their sharp, tearing teeth. He thought of what Tyler had looked like in the Quonset hut last year when Stefan was through with him. Red meat. Just red meat and blood.

"What was that history teacher's name?" Damon was saying silkily. He seemed amused now, enjoying this. "Mr. Tanner, wasn't it? I did more than try with him."

"You're a murderer."

Damon nodded, unoffended, as if he'd just been introduced. "Of course, he stuck a knife in me. I wasn't planning to drain him quite dry, but he annoyed me and I changed my mind. You're annoying me now, Matt."

Matt had his knees locked to keep from running. It was more than the catlike stalking grace, it was more than those unearthly black eyes fastened on his. There was something *inside* Damon that whispered terror to the human brain. Some menace that spoke directly to Matt's blood, telling him to do anything to get away.

But he wouldn't run. His conversation with Stefan was blurred in his mind right now, but he knew one thing from it. Even if he died here, he wouldn't run.

"Don't be stupid," Damon said, as if he'd heard every word of Matt's thoughts. "You've never had blood taken from you by force, have you? It hurts, Matt. It hurts a lot."

Elena, Matt remembered. That first time when she'd taken his blood he'd been scared, and the fear had been bad enough. But he'd been doing it of his own volition then. What would it be like when he was unwilling?

I will not run. I will not look away.

Aloud he said, still looking straight at Damon, "If you're going to kill me, you'd better stop talking and do it. Because maybe you can make me die, but that's all you can make me do."

"You're even stupider than my brother," Damon said. With two steps he crossed the distance to Matt. He grabbed Matt by his T-shirt, one hand on either side of the throat. "I guess I'll have to teach you the same way."

Everything was frozen. Matt could smell his own fear, but he wouldn't move. He couldn't move now.

It didn't matter. He hadn't given in. If he died right now, he died knowing that.

Damon's teeth were a white glitter in the dark. Sharp as carving knives. Matt could almost feel the razor bite of them before they touched him.

I will not surrender anything, he thought, and closed his eyes.

The shove took him completely off balance. He stumbled and fell backward, his eyes flying open. Damon had let go and pushed him away.

Expressionless, those black eyes looked down at him where he sat in the dirt.

"I'll try to put this in a way you can understand," Damon said. "You don't want to mess with me, Matt. I am more dangerous than you can possibly imagine. Now get out of here. It's my watch."

Silently, Matt got up. He rubbed at his shirt where Damon's hands had crumpled it. And then he left, but he didn't run and he didn't flinch from Damon's eyes.

I won, he thought. I'm still alive, so I won.

And there had been a kind of grim respect in those black eyes in the end. It made Matt wonder about some things. It really did.

* * *

Bonnie and Meredith were sitting in the car when he got back. They both looked concerned.

"You were gone a long time," Bonnie said. "Are you okay?"

Matt wished people would stop asking him that. "I'm fine," he said, and then added, "Really." After a moment's thought he decided there was something else he should say. "Sorry if I yelled at you back there, Bonnie."

"That's all right," Bonnie said coolly. Then, thawing, she said, "You really do look better, you know. More like your old self."

"Yeah?" He rubbed at his crumpled T-shirt again, looking around. "Well, tangling with vampires is obviously a great warm-up exercise."

"What'd you guys do? Lower your heads and run at each other from opposite sides of the yard?" asked Meredith.

"Something like that. He says he's going to watch Vickie now."

"Do you think we can trust him?" Meredith said soberly.

Matt considered. "As a matter of fact, I do. It's weird, but I don't think he's going to hurt her. And if the killer comes along, I think he's in for a surprise. Damon's spoiling for a fight. We might as well go back to the library for Stefan."

Stefan wasn't visible outside the library, but when the

car had cruised up and down the street once or twice he materialized out of the darkness. He had a thick book with him.

"Breaking and entering and grand theft, library book," Meredith remarked. "I wonder what you get for that these days?"

"I borrowed it," Stefan said, looking aggrieved. "That's what libraries are for, right? And I copied what I needed out of the journal."

"You mean you found it? You figured it out? Then you can tell us everything, like you promised," Bonnie said. "Let's go to the boardinghouse."

Stefan looked slightly surprised when he heard that Damon had turned up and stationed himself at Vickie's, but he made no comment. Matt didn't tell him exactly *how* Damon had turned up, and he noticed Bonnie didn't either.

"I'm almost positive about what's going on in Fell's Church. And I've got half the puzzle solved, anyway," Stefan said once they were all settled in his room in the boardinghouse attic. "But there's only one way to prove it, and only one way to solve the other half. I need help, but it isn't something I'm going to ask lightly." He was looking at Bonnie and Meredith as he said it.

They looked at each other, then back at him. "This guy killed one of our friends," said Meredith. "And he's driving another one crazy. If you need our help, you've got it."

"Whatever it takes," Bonnie added.

"It's something dangerous, isn't it?" Matt demanded. He couldn't restrain himself. As if Bonnie hadn't been through enough . . .

"It's dangerous, yes. But it's their fight too, you know."

"Darn right it is," said Bonnie. Meredith was obviously trying to repress a smile. Finally she had to turn away and grin.

"Matt's back," she said when Stefan asked her what the joke was.

"We missed you," added Bonnie. Matt couldn't understand why they were all smiling at him, and it made him feel hot and uncomfortable. He went over to stand by the window.

"It *is* dangerous; I won't try to kid you about that," Stefan said to the girls. "But it's the only chance. The whole thing's a little complicated, and I'd better start at the beginning. We have to go back to the founding of Fell's Church . . ."

He talked on late into the night.

Thursday, June 11, 7:00 a.m.

Dear Diary,

I couldn't write last night, because I got in too late. Mom was upset again. She'd have been hysterical if she'd known what I was actually doing. Hanging out with vampires and planning something that may get me killed. That may get us all killed.

Stefan has a plan to trap the guy who murdered Sue. It reminds me of some of Elena's plans—and that's what worries me. They always sounded wonderful, but lots of the time they went wrong.

We talked about who gets the most dangerous job and decided it should be Meredith. Which is fine with me—I mean, she is stronger and more athletic, and she always keeps calm in emergencies. But it bugs me just a little that everybody was so quick *about choosing her, especially Matt. I mean, it's not like I'm totally incompetent. I know I'm not as smart as the others, and I'm certainly not as good at sports or as cool under pressure, but I'm not a total dweeb. I'm good for* something.

Anyway, we're going to do it after graduation. We're all in on it except Damon, who'll be watching Vickie. It's strange, but we all trust him now. Even me. Despite what he did to me last night, I don't think he'll let Vickie get hurt.

I haven't had any more dreams about Elena. I think if I do, I will go absolutely screaming berserk. Or never go to sleep again. I just can't take any more of that.

All right. I'd better go. Hopefully, by Sunday we'll have the mystery solved and the killer caught. I trust Stefan.

I just hope I can remember my part.

9

"... *A*nd so, ladies and gentlemen, I give you the class of '92!"

Bonnie threw her cap into the air along with everyone else. We made it, she thought. Whatever happens tonight, Matt and Meredith and I made it to graduation. There had been times this last school year when she had seriously doubted they would.

Considering Sue's death, Bonnie had expected the graduation ceremony to be listless or grim. Instead, there was a sort of frenzied excitement about it. As if everyone was celebrating being alive—before it was too late.

It turned into rowdiness as parents surged forward and the senior class of Robert E. Lee fragmented in all directions, whooping and acting up. Bonnie retrieved her cap and then looked up into her mother's camera lens.

Act normal, that's what's important, she told herself. She caught a glimpse of Elena's aunt Judith and Robert Maxwell, the man Aunt Judith had recently married, standing on the sidelines. Robert was holding Elena's little sister, Margaret, by the hand. When they saw her, they smiled bravely, but she felt uncomfortable when they came her way.

"Oh, Miss Gilbert—I mean, Mrs. Maxwell—you shouldn't have," she said as Aunt Judith handed her a small bouquet of pink roses.

Aunt Judith smiled through the tears in her eyes. "This would have been a very special day for Elena," she said. "I want it to be special for you and Meredith, too."

"Oh, Aunt Judith." Impulsively, Bonnie threw her arms around the older woman. "I'm so sorry," she whispered. "You know how much."

"We all miss her," Aunt Judith said. Then she pulled back and smiled again and the three of them left. Bonnie turned from looking at them with a lump in her throat to look at the madly celebrating crowd.

There was Ray Hernandez, the boy she'd gone to Homecoming with, inviting everybody to a party at his house that night. There was Tyler's friend Dick Carter, making a fool of himself as usual. Tyler was smiling brazenly as his father took picture after picture. Matt was listening, with an unimpressed look, to some football recruiter from James Mason University. Meredith was standing nearby, holding a bouquet of red roses and looking pensive.

Vickie wasn't there. Her parents had kept her home, saying she was in no state to go out. Caroline wasn't there either. She was staying in the apartment in Heron. Her mother had told Bonnie's mother she had the flu, but Bonnie knew the truth. Caroline was scared.

And maybe she's right, Bonnie thought, moving toward Meredith. Caroline may be the only one of us to make it through next week.

Look normal, act normal. She reached Meredith's group. Meredith was wrapping the red-and-black tassel from her cap around the bouquet, twisting it between elegant, nervous fingers.

Bonnie threw a quick glance around. Good. This was the place. And now was the time.

"Be careful with that; you'll ruin it," she said aloud.

Meredith's look of thoughtful melancholy didn't change. She went on staring at the tassel, kinking it up. "It doesn't seem fair," she said, "that we should get these and Elena shouldn't. It's wrong."

"I know; it's awful," Bonnie said. But she kept her tone light. "I wish there was something we could do about it, but we can't."

"It's all *wrong*," Meredith went on, as if she hadn't

heard. "Here we are out in the sunlight, graduating, and there she is under that—stone."

"I know, I know," Bonnie said in a soothing tone. "Meredith, you're getting yourself all upset. Why don't you try to think about something else? Look, after you go out to dinner with your parents, do you want to go to Raymond's party? Even if we're not invited, we can crash it."

"No!" Meredith said with startling vehemence. "I don't want to go to any party. How can you even think of that, Bonnie? How can you be so shallow?"

"Well, we've got to do *something* . . ."

"I'll tell you what *I'm* doing. I'm going up to the cemetery after dinner. I'm going to put *this* on Elena's grave. She's the one who deserves it." Meredith's knuckles were white as she shook the tassel in her hand.

"Meredith, don't be an idiot. You can't go up there, especially at night. That's crazy. Matt would say the same thing."

"Well, I'm not asking Matt. I'm not asking anybody. I'm going by myself."

"You can't. God, Meredith, I always thought you had some brains—"

"And I always thought you had some sensitivity. But obviously you don't even want to think about Elena. Or is it just because you want her old boyfriend for yourself?"

Bonnie slapped her.

It was a good hard slap, with plenty of energy behind it. Meredith drew in a sharp breath, one hand to her reddening cheek. Everyone around them was staring.

"That's it for you, Bonnie McCullough," Meredith said after a moment, in a voice of deadly quiet. "I don't ever want to speak to you again." She turned on her heel and walked away.

"Never would be too soon for me!" Bonnie shouted at her retreating back.

Eyes were hastily averted as Bonnie looked around her. But there was no question that she and Meredith had been the center of attention for several minutes past. Bonnie bit the inside of her cheek to keep a straight face and walked over to Matt, who had lost the recruiter.

"How was that?" she murmured.

"Good."

"Do you think the slap was too much? We didn't really plan that; I was just sort of going with the moment. Maybe it was too obvious . . ."

"It was fine, just fine." Matt was looking preoccupied. Not that dull, apathetic, turned-in look of the last few months, but distinctly abstracted.

"What is it? Something wrong with the plan?" Bonnie said.

"No, no. Listen, Bonnie, I've been thinking. You were the one to discover Mr. Tanner's body in the Haunted

House last Halloween, right?"

Bonnie was startled. She gave an involuntary shiver of distaste. "Well, I was the first one to know he was dead, really dead, instead of just playing his scene. Why on earth do you want to talk about that now?"

"Because maybe you can answer this question. Could Mr. Tanner have got a knife in Damon?"

"*What?*"

"Well, could he?"

"I . . ." Bonnie blinked and frowned. Then she shrugged. "I suppose so. Sure. It was a druid sacrifice scene, remember, and the knife we used was a real knife. We talked about using a fake one, but since Mr. Tanner was going to be lying right there beside it, we figured it was safe enough. As a matter of fact . . ." Bonnie's frown deepened. "I think when I found the body, the knife was in a different place from where we'd set it in the beginning. But then, some kid could have moved it. Matt, why are you asking?"

"Just something Damon said to me," Matt said, staring off into the distance again. "I wondered if it could be the truth."

"Oh." Bonnie waited for him to say more, but he didn't. "Well," she said finally, "if it's all cleared up, can you come back to Earth, please? And don't you think you should maybe put your arm around me? Just to show you're on my side and there's no chance *you're* going to show up at Elena's grave tonight with Meredith?"

Matt snorted, but the faraway look disappeared from his eyes. For just a brief instant he put his arm around her and squeezed.

Déjà vu, Meredith thought as she stood at the gate to the cemetery. The problem was, she couldn't remember exactly which of her previous experiences in the graveyard this night reminded her of. There had been so many.

In a way, it had all started here. It had been here that Elena had sworn not to rest until Stefan belonged to her. She'd made Bonnie and Meredith swear to help her, too—in blood. How suitable, Meredith thought now.

And it had been here that Tyler had assaulted Elena the night of the Homecoming dance. Stefan had come to the rescue, and that had been the beginning for them. This graveyard had seen a lot.

It had even seen the whole group of them file up the hill to the ruined church last December, looking for Katherine's lair. Seven of them had gone down into the crypt: Meredith herself, Bonnie, Matt, and Elena, with Stefan, Damon, and Alaric. But only six of them had come out all right. When they took Elena out of there, it was to bury her.

This graveyard had been the beginning, and the end as

well. And maybe there would be another end tonight.

Meredith started walking.

I wish you were here now, Alaric, she thought. I could use your optimism and your savvy about the supernatural—and I wouldn't mind your muscles, either.

Elena's headstone was in the new cemetery, of course, where the grass was still tended and the graves marked with wreaths of flowers. The stone was very simple, almost plain looking, with a brief inscription. Meredith bent down and placed her bouquet of roses in front of it. Then, slowly, she added the red-and-black tassel from her cap. In this dim light, both colors looked the same, like dried blood. She knelt and folded her hands quietly. And she waited.

All around her the cemetery was still. It seemed to be waiting with her, breath held in anticipation. The rows of white stones stretched on either side of her, shining faintly. Meredith listened for any sound.

And then she heard one. Heavy footsteps.

With her head down, she stayed quiet, pretending she noticed nothing.

The footsteps sounded closer, not even bothering to be stealthy.

"Hi, Meredith."

Meredith looked around quickly. "Oh—Tyler," she said. "You scared me. I thought you were—never mind."

"Yeah?" Tyler's lips skinned back in an unsettling grin. "Well, I'm sorry you're disappointed. But it's me, just me and nobody else."

"What are you doing here, Tyler? No good parties?"

"I could ask you the same question." Tyler's eyes dropped to the headstone and the tassel and his face darkened. "But I guess I already know the answer. You're here for *her*. Elena Gilbert, A Light in Darkness," he read sarcastically.

"That's right," Meredith said evenly. "'Elena' means light, you know. And she was certainly surrounded by darkness. It almost beat her, but she won in the end."

"Maybe," Tyler said, and worked his jaw meditatively, squinting. "But you know, Meredith, it's a funny thing about darkness. There's always more of it waiting in the wings."

"Like tonight," Meredith said, looking up at the sky. It was clear and dotted with faint stars. "It's very dark tonight, Tyler. But sooner or later the sun will come up."

"Yeah, but the moon comes up first." Tyler chuckled suddenly, as if at some joke only he could see. "Hey, Meredith, you ever see the Smallwood family plot? Well, come on and I'll show you. It's not far."

Just like he showed Elena, Meredith thought. In a way she was enjoying this verbal fencing, but she never lost sight of what she had come here for. Her cold fingers dipped into her jacket pocket and found the tiny sprig of vervain there. "That's all right, Tyler. I think I'd prefer to stay here."

"You sure about that? A cemetery's a dangerous place to be alone."

Unquiet spirits, Meredith thought. She looked right at him. "I know."

He was grinning again, displaying teeth like tombstones. "Anyway, you can see it from here if you have good eyes. Look that way, toward the old graveyard. Now, do you see something sort of shining red in the middle?"

"No." There was a pale luminosity over the trees in the east. Meredith kept her eyes on it.

"Aw, come on, Meredith. You're not trying. Once the moon's up you'll see it better."

"Tyler, I can't waste any more time here. I'm going."

"No, you're not," he said. And then, as her fingers tightened on the vervain, encompassing it in her fist, he added in a wheedling voice, "I mean, you're not going until I tell you the story of that headstone, are you? It's a great story. See, the headstone is made of red marble, the only one of its kind in the whole graveyard. And that ball on top—see it?—that must weigh about a ton. But it moves. It turns whenever a Smallwood is going to die. My grandfather didn't believe that; he put a scratch on it right down the front. He used to come out and check it every month or so. Then one day he came and found the scratch in the rear. The ball had turned completely backward. He did everything he could to turn it around, but he couldn't. It was too heavy. And that night, in bed, he died. They buried him under it."

"He probably had a heart attack from overexertion," Meredith said caustically, but her palms were tingling.

"You're funny, aren't you? Always so cool. Always so together. Takes a lot to make you scream, doesn't it?"

"I'm leaving, Tyler. I've had enough."

He let her walk a few paces, then said, "You screamed that night at Caroline's, though, didn't you?"

Meredith turned back. "How do you know that?"

Tyler rolled his eyes. "Give me credit for a little intelligence, okay? I know a lot, Meredith. For instance, I know what's in your pocket."

Meredith's fingers stilled. "What do you mean?"

"Vervain, Meredith. *Verbena officinalis.* I've got a friend who's into these things." Tyler was focused now, his smile growing, watching her face as if it were his favorite TV show. Like a cat tired of playing with a mouse, he was moving in. "And I know what it's for, too." He cast an exaggerated glance around and put a finger to his lips. "Shh. Vampires," he whispered. Then he threw back his head and laughed loudly.

Meredith backed away a step.

"You think that's going to help you, don't you? But I'm going to tell you a secret."

Meredith's eyes measured the distance between herself and the path. She kept her face calm, but a violent shaking was beginning inside her. She didn't know if she was going to be able to pull this off.

"You're not going anywhere, babe," Tyler said, and a large hand clasped Meredith's wrist. It was hot and damp where she could feel it below her jacket cuff. "You're going to stay right here for your surprise." His body was hunched now, his head thrust forward, and there was an exultant leer on his lips.

"Let me go, Tyler. You're hurting me!" Panic flashed down all Meredith's nerves at the feel of Tyler's flesh against hers. But the hand only gripped harder, grinding tendon against bone in her wrist.

"This is a secret, baby, that nobody else knows," Tyler said, pulling her close, his breath hot in her face. "You came here all decked out against vampires. But I'm not a vampire."

Meredith's heart was pounding. "Let *go*!"

"First I want you to look over there. You can see the headstone now," he said, turning her so that she couldn't help but look. And he was right; she *could* see it, like a red monument with a shining globe on top. Or—not a globe. That marble ball looked like . . . it looked like . . .

"Now look east. What do you see there, Meredith?" Tyler went on, his voice hoarse with excitement.

It was the full moon. It had risen while he'd been talking to her, and now it hung above the hills, perfectly round and enormously distended, a huge and swollen red ball.

And that was what the headstone looked like. Like a full moon dripping with blood.

"You came here protected against vampires, Meredith," Tyler said from behind her, even more hoarsely. "But the Smallwoods aren't vampires at all. We're something else."

And then he growled.

No human throat could have made the sound. It wasn't an imitation of an animal; it was *real*. A vicious guttural snarl that went up and up, snapping Meredith's head around to look at him, to stare in disbelief. What she was seeing was so horrible her mind couldn't accept it . . .

Meredith screamed.

"I told you it was a surprise. How do you like it?" Tyler said. His voice was thick with saliva, and his red tongue lolled among the rows of long canine teeth. His face wasn't a face anymore. It jutted out grotesquely into a muzzle, and his eyes were yellow, with slitlike pupils. His reddish-sandy hair had grown over his cheeks and down the back of his neck. A pelt. "You can scream all you want up here and nobody's going to hear you," he added.

Every muscle in Meredith's body was rigid, trying to get away from him. It was a visceral reaction, one she couldn't have helped if she wanted to. His breath was so hot, and it smelled feral, like an animal. The nails he was digging into her wrist were stumpy blackened claws. She didn't have the strength to scream again.

"There's other things besides vampires with a taste for blood," Tyler said in his new slurping voice. "And I want to taste yours. But first we're going to have some fun."

Although he still stood on two feet, his body was humped and strangely distorted. Meredith's struggles were feeble as he forced her to the ground. She was a strong girl, but he was far stronger, his muscles bunching under his shirt as he pinned her.

"You've always been too good for me, haven't you? Well, now you're going to find out what you've been missing."

I can't breathe, Meredith thought wildly. His arm was across her throat, blocking her air. Gray waves rolled through her brain. If she passed out now . . .

"You're going to wish you died as fast as Sue." Tyler's face floated above her, red as the moon, with that long tongue lolling. His other hand held her arms above her head. "You ever hear the story of Little Red Riding Hood?"

The gray was turning into blackness, speckled with

little lights. Like stars, Meredith thought. I'm falling in the stars . . .

"Tyler, take your hands off her! Let go of her, now!" Matt's voice shouted.

Tyler's slavering snarl broke off into a surprised whine. The arm against Meredith's throat released pressure, and air rushed into her lungs.

Footsteps were pounding around her. "I've been waiting a long time to do this, Tyler," Matt said, jerking the sandy-red head back by the hair. Then Matt's fist smashed into Tyler's newly grown muzzle. Blood spurted from the wet animal nose.

The sound Tyler made froze Meredith's heart in her chest. He sprang at Matt, twisting in midair, claws outstretched. Matt fell back under the assault and Meredith, dizzy, tried to push herself up off the ground. She couldn't; all her muscles were trembling uncontrollably. But someone else picked Tyler off Matt as if Tyler weighed no more than a doll.

"Just like old times, Tyler," Stefan said, setting Tyler on his feet and facing him.

Tyler stared a minute, then tried to run.

He was fast, dodging with animal agility between the rows of graves. But Stefan was faster and cut him off.

"Meredith, are you hurt? Meredith?" Bonnie was kneeling beside her. Meredith nodded—she still couldn't speak—and let Bonnie support her head. "I knew we should have stopped him sooner, I knew it," Bonnie went on worriedly.

Stefan was dragging Tyler back. "I always knew you were a jerk," he said, shoving Tyler against a headstone, "but I didn't know you were this stupid. I'd have thought you would have learned not to jump girls in graveyards, but no. And you had to brag about what you did to Sue, too. That wasn't smart, Tyler."

Meredith looked at them as they faced each other. So different, she thought. Even though they were both creatures of darkness in some way. Stefan was pale, his green eyes blazing with anger and menace, but there was a dignity, almost a purity about him. He was like some stern angel carved in unyielding marble. Tyler just looked like a trapped animal. He was crouched, breathing hard, blood and saliva mingling on his chest. Those yellow eyes glittered with hate and fear, and his fingers worked as if he'd like to claw something. A low sound came out of his throat.

"Don't worry, I'm not going to beat you up this time," Stefan said. "Not unless you try to get away. We're all going up to the church to have a little chat. You like to tell stories, Tyler; well, you're going to tell me one now."

Tyler sprang at him, vaulting straight from the ground for Stefan's throat. But Stefan was ready for him.

Meredith suspected that both Stefan and Matt enjoyed the next few minutes, working off their accumulated aggressions, but she didn't, so she looked away.

In the end, Tyler was trussed up with nylon cord. He could walk, or shuffle at least, and Stefan held the back of his shirt and guided him ungently up the path to the church.

Inside, Stefan pushed Tyler onto the ground near the open tomb. "Now," he said, "we are going to talk. And you're going to cooperate, Tyler, or you're going to be very, very sorry."

eredith sat down on the knee-high wall of the ruined church. "You said it was going to be dangerous, Stefan, but you didn't say you were going to let him strangle me."

"I'm sorry. I was hoping he'd give some more information, especially after he admitted to being there when Sue died. But I shouldn't have waited."

"I haven't admitted anything! You can't prove anything," Tyler said. The animal whine was back in his voice, but on the walk up his face and body had returned to normal. Or rather, they'd returned to human, Meredith thought. The swelling and bruises and dried blood weren't normal.

"This isn't a court of law, Tyler," she said. "Your father can't help you now."

"But if it were, we'd have a pretty good case," Stefan added. "Enough to put you away on conspiracy to commit murder, I think."

"That's if somebody doesn't melt down their grandma's teaspoons to make a silver bullet," Matt put in.

Tyler looked from one to another of them. "I won't tell you anything."

"Tyler, you know what you are? You're a bully," Bonnie said. "And bullies always talk."

"You don't mind pinning a girl down and threatening her," said Matt, "but when her friends turn up you're scared spitless."

Tyler just glared at all of them.

"Well, if you don't want to talk, I guess *I'll* have to," Stefan said. He leaned down and picked up the thick book he'd gotten from the library. One foot on the lip of the tomb, he rested the book on his knee and opened it. In that moment, Meredith thought, he looked frighteningly like Damon.

"This is a book by Gervase of Tilbury, Tyler," he said. "It was written around the year 1210 A.D. One of the things it talks about is werewolves."

"You can't prove anything! You don't have any evidence—"

"Shut up, Tyler!" Stefan looked at him. "I don't need to prove it. I can *see* it, even now. Have you forgotten what

I am?" There was a silence, and then Stefan went on. "When I got here a few days ago, there was a mystery. A girl was dead. But who killed her? And why? All the clues I could see seemed contradictory.

"It wasn't an ordinary killing, not some human psycho off the street. I had the word of somebody I trusted on that—and independent evidence, too. An ordinary killer can't work a Ouija board by telekinesis. An ordinary killer can't cause fuses to blow in a power plant hundreds of miles away.

"No, this was somebody with tremendous physical and psychic power. From everything Vickie told me, it sounded like a vampire.

"Except that Sue Carson still had her blood. A vampire would have drained at least some of it. No vampire could resist that, especially not a killer. That's where the high comes from, and the high's the reason to kill. But the police doctor found no holes in her veins, and only a small amount of bleeding. It didn't make sense.

"And there was another thing. *You* were in that house, Tyler. You made the mistake of grabbing Bonnie that night, and then you made the mistake of shooting off your mouth the next day, saying things you couldn't have known unless you were there.

"So what did we have? A seasoned vampire, a vicious killer with Power to spare? Or a high school bully who couldn't organize a trip to the toilet without falling over his own feet? Which? The evidence pointed both ways, and I couldn't make up my mind.

"Then I went to see Sue's body myself. And there it was, the biggest mystery of all. A cut *here*." Stefan's finger sketched a sharp line down from his collarbone. "Typical, traditional cut—made by vampires to share their own blood. But Sue *wasn't* a vampire, and she didn't make that cut herself. Someone made it for her as she lay there dying on the ground."

Meredith shut her eyes, and she heard Bonnie swallow hard beside her. She put out a hand and found Bonnie's and held tight, but she went on listening. Stefan had not gone into this kind of detail in his explanation to them before.

"Vampires don't need to cut their victims like that; they use their teeth," Stefan said. His upper lip lifted slightly to show his own teeth. "But if a vampire wanted to draw blood *for somebody else to drink*, he might cut instead of biting. If a vampire wanted to give someone else the first and only taste, he might do that.

"And *that* started me thinking about blood. Blood is important, you see. For vampires, it gives life, Power. It's all we need for survival, and there are times when needing it drives us crazy. But it's good for other things, too. For instance . . . initiation.

"Initiation and Power. Now I was thinking about those two things, putting them together with what I'd seen of *you*, Tyler, when I was in Fell's Church before. Little things I hadn't really focused on. But I remembered something Elena had told me about your family history, and I decided to check it out in Honoria Fell's journal."

Stefan lifted a piece of paper from between the pages of the book he held. "And there it was, in Honoria's handwriting. I Xeroxed the page so I could read it to you. The Smallwoods' little family secret—if you can read between the lines."

Looking down at the paper, he read:

"*November 12. Candles made, flax spun. We are short on cornmeal and salt, but we will get through the winter. Last night an alarm; wolves attacked Jacob Smallwood as he returned from the forest. I treated the wound with whortleberry and sallow bark, but it is deep and I am afraid. After coming home I cast the runes. I have told no one but Thomas the results.*

"Casting the runes is divining," Stefan added, looking up. "Honoria was what we'd call a witch. She goes on here to talk about 'wolf trouble' in various other parts of the settlement—it seems that all of a sudden there were frequent attacks, especially on young girls. She tells how she and her husband became more and more concerned. And finally, this:

"*December 20. Wolf trouble at the Smallwoods' again. We*

heard the screams a few minutes ago, and Thomas said it was time. He made the bullets yesterday. He has loaded his rifle and we will walk over. If we are spared, I will write again.

"*December 21. Went over to Smallwoods' last night. Jacob sorely afflicted. Wolf killed.*

"*We will bury Jacob in the little graveyard at the foot of the hill. May his soul find peace in death.*

"In the official history of Fell's Church," Stefan said, "that's been interpreted to mean that Thomas Fell and his wife went over to the Smallwoods' to find Jacob Smallwood being attacked by a wolf again, and that the wolf killed him. But that's wrong. What it really says is *not* that the wolf killed Jacob Smallwood but that Jacob Smallwood, *the wolf,* was killed."

Stefan shut the book. "He was a werewolf, your great-great-great-whatever grandfather, Tyler. He got that way by being attacked by a werewolf himself. And he passed his werewolf virus on to the son who was born eight and a half months after he died. Just the way your father passed it on to you."

"I always knew there was something about you, Tyler," Bonnie said, and Meredith opened her eyes. "I never could tell what it was, but at the back of my mind something was telling me you were creepy."

"We used to make jokes about it," Meredith said, her voice still husky. "About your 'animal magnetism' and your big white teeth. We just never knew how close to the mark we were."

"Sometimes psychics can sense that kind of thing," Stefan conceded. "Sometimes even ordinary people can. *I* should have seen it, but I was preoccupied. Still, that's no excuse. And obviously somebody else—the psychic killer—saw it right away. Didn't he, Tyler? A man wearing an old raincoat came to you. He was tall, with blond hair and blue eyes, and he made some kind of a deal with you. In exchange for—*something*—he'd show you how to reclaim your heritage. How to become a real werewolf.

"Because according to Gervase of Tilbury"—Stefan tapped the book on his knee—"a werewolf who hasn't been bitten himself needs to be initiated. That means you can have the werewolf virus all your life but never even know it because it's never activated. Generations of Smallwoods have lived and died, but the virus was dormant in them because they didn't know the secret of waking it up. But the man in the raincoat knew. He knew that you have to kill and taste fresh blood. After that, at the first full moon you can change." Stefan glanced up, and Meredith followed his gaze to the white disk of the moon in the sky. It looked clean and two-dimensional now, no longer a sullen red globe.

A look of suspicion passed over Tyler's fleshy features,

and then a look of renewed fury. "You tricked me! You planned this!"

"Very clever," said Meredith, and Matt said, "No kidding." Bonnie wet her finger and marked an imaginary 1 on an invisible scoreboard.

"I knew you wouldn't be able to resist following one of the girls here if you thought she'd be alone," said Stefan. "You'd think that the graveyard was the perfect place to kill; you'd have complete privacy. And I knew you wouldn't be able to resist bragging about what you'd done. I was hoping you'd tell Meredith more about the other killer, the one who actually threw Sue out the window, the one who cut her so you could drink fresh blood. The vampire, Tyler. Who is he? Where is he hiding?"

Tyler's look of venomous hatred changed to a sneer. "You think I'd tell you that? He's my friend."

"He is not your friend, Tyler. He's using you. And he's a murderer."

"Don't get in any deeper, Tyler," Matt added.

"You're already an accessory. Tonight you tried to kill Meredith. Pretty soon you're not going to be able to go back even if you want to. Be smart and stop this now. Tell us what you know."

Tyler bared his teeth. "I'm not telling you *anything*. How're you going to make me?"

The others exchanged glances. The atmosphere

changed, became charged with tension as they all turned back to Tyler.

"You really don't understand, do you?" Meredith said quietly. "Tyler, you helped *kill* Sue. She died for an obscene ritual so that you could change into that *thing* I saw. You were planning to kill me, and Vickie and Bonnie too, I'm sure. Do you think we have any pity for you? Do you think we brought you up here to be nice to you?"

There was a silence. The sneer was fading from Tyler's lips. He looked from one face to another.

They were all implacable. Even Bonnie's small face was unforgiving.

"Gervase of Tilbury mentions one interesting thing," Stefan said, almost pleasantly. "There's a cure for werewolves besides the traditional silver bullet. Listen." By moonlight, he read from the book on his knee. "*It is commonly reported and held by grave and worthy doctors that if a werewolf be shorn of one of his members, he shall surely recover his original body*. Gervase goes on to tell the story of Raimbaud of Auvergne, a werewolf who was cured when a carpenter cut off one of his hind paws. Of course, that was probably hideously painful, but the story goes that Raimbaud thanked the carpenter 'for ridding him forever of the accursed and damnable form.'" Stefan raised his head. "Now, I'm thinking that if Tyler won't help us with information, the least we can do is make sure he doesn't go out and kill again. What do the rest of you say?"

Matt spoke up. "I think it's our duty to cure him."

"All we have to do is relieve him of one of his members," Bonnie agreed.

"I can think of one right off," Meredith said under her breath.

Tyler's eyes were starting to bulge. Under the dirt and blood his normally ruddy face had gone pale. "You're bluffing!"

"Get the ax, Matt," said Stefan. "Meredith, you take off one of his shoes."

Tyler kicked when she did, aiming for her face. Matt came and got his head in a hammerlock. "Don't make it any worse on yourself, Tyler."

The bare foot Meredith exposed was big, the sole as sweaty as Tyler's palms. Coarse hair sprouted from the toes. It made Meredith's skin crawl.

"Let's get this over with," she said.

"You're joking!" Tyler howled, thrashing so that Bonnie had to come and grab his other leg and kneel on it. "You can't do this! You can't!"

"Keep him still," Stefan said. Working together, they stretched Tyler out, his head locked in Matt's arm, his legs spread and pinned by the girls. Making sure Tyler could see what he was doing, Stefan balanced a branch perhaps two inches thick on the lip of the tomb. He raised the ax and then brought it down hard, severing the stick with one blow.

"It's sharp enough," he said. "Meredith, roll his pants leg up. Then tie some of that cord just above his ankle as tight as you can for a tourniquet. Otherwise he'll bleed out."

"You can't do this!" Tyler was screaming. *"You can't dooooooo this!"*

"Scream all you want, Tyler. Up here, nobody's going to hear you, right?" Stefan said.

"You're no better than I am!" Tyler yelled in a spray of spittle. "You're a killer too!"

"I know exactly what I am," Stefan said. "Believe me, Tyler. I know. Is everybody ready? Good. Hold on to him; he's going to jump when I do it."

Tyler's screams weren't even words anymore. Matt was holding him so that he could see Stefan kneel and take aim, hefting the ax blade above Tyler's ankle to gauge force and distance.

"Now," said Stefan, raising the ax high.

"No! No! I'll talk to you! I'll talk!" shrieked Tyler.

Stefan glanced at him. "Too late," he said, and brought the ax down.

It rebounded off the stone floor with a clang and a spark, but the noise was drowned by Tyler's screaming. It seemed to take Tyler several minutes to realize that the blade hadn't touched his foot. He paused for breath only when he choked, and turned wild, bulging eyes on Stefan.

"Start talking," Stefan said, his voice wintry, remorseless.

Little whimpers were coming from Tyler's throat and there was foam on his lips. "I don't know his name," he gasped out. "But he looks like you said. And you're right; he's a vampire, man! I saw him drain a ten-point buck while it was still kicking. He *lied* to me," Tyler added, the whine creeping back into his voice. "He told me I'd be stronger than anybody, as strong as him. He said I could have any girl I wanted, any way I wanted. The creep lied."

"He told you that you could kill and get away with it," Stefan said.

"He said I could do Caroline that night. She had it coming after the way she ditched me. I wanted to make her beg—but she got out of the house somehow. I could have Caroline and Vickie, he said. All he wanted was Bonnie and Meredith."

"But you just tried to kill Meredith."

"That was *now*. Things are different now, stupid. He said it was all right."

"Why?" Meredith asked Stefan in an undertone.

"Maybe because you'd served your purpose," he said. "You'd brought me here." Then he went on. "All right,

Tyler, show us you're cooperating. Tell us how we can get this guy."

"*Get* him? You're nuts!" Tyler burst into ugly laughter, and Matt tightened the arm around his throat. "Hey, choke me all you want; it's still the truth. He told me he's one of the Old Ones, one of the Originals, whatever that means. He said he's been making vampires since before the pyramids. He said he's made a bargain with the devil. You could stick a stake in his heart and it wouldn't do *anything*. You can't kill him." The laughter became uncontrolled.

"Where's he hiding, Tyler?" Stefan rapped out. "Every vampire needs a place to sleep. Where is it?"

"He'd kill me if I told you that. He'd *eat* me, man. God, if I told you what he did to that buck before it died . . ." Tyler's laughter was turning into something like sobs.

"Then you'd better help us destroy him before he can find you, hadn't you? What's his weak point? How's he vulnerable?"

"God, that poor buck . . ." Tyler was blubbering.

"What about Sue? Did you cry over *her*?" Stefan said sharply. He picked up the ax. "I think," he said, "that you're wasting our time."

The ax lifted.

"No! No! I'll talk to you; I'll tell you something. Look, there's one kind of wood that can hurt him—not kill him, but hurt him. He admitted that but didn't tell me what it was! I swear to you that's the truth!"

"Not good enough, Tyler," said Stefan.

"For God's sake—I'll tell you where he's going tonight. If you get over there fast enough, maybe you can stop him."

"What do you mean, where he's going tonight? Talk fast, Tyler!"

"He's going to Vickie's, okay? He said tonight we get one each. That's helpful, isn't it? If you hurry, maybe you can get there!"

Stefan had frozen, and Meredith felt her heart racing. Vickie. They hadn't even thought about an attack on Vickie.

"Damon's guarding her," Matt said. "Right, Stefan? Right?"

"He's supposed to be," Stefan said. "I left him there at dusk. If something happened, he should have called me . . ."

"You guys," Bonnie whispered. Her eyes were big and her lips were trembling. "I think we'd better get over there *now*."

They stared at her a moment and then everyone was moving. The ax clanged on the floor as Stefan dropped it.

"Hey, you can't leave me like this! I can't drive! He's gonna come back for me! Come back and untie my hands!" Tyler shrieked. None of them answered.

They ran all the way down the hill and piled into Meredith's car. Meredith took off speeding, rounding corners dangerously fast and gliding through stop signs, but there was a part of her that didn't want to get to Vickie's house. That wanted to turn around and drive the other way.

I'm calm; I'm the one who's always calm, she thought. But that was on the outside. Meredith knew very well how calm you could look on the outside when inside everything was breaking up.

They rounded the last corner onto Birch Street and Meredith hit the brakes.

"Oh, God!" Bonnie cried from the backseat. "No! No!"

"Quick," Stefan said. "There may still be a chance." He wrenched open the door and was out even before the car had stopped. But in back, Bonnie was sobbing.

11

The car skidded in behind one of the police cars that was parked crookedly in the street. There were lights everywhere, lights flashing blue and red and amber, lights blazing from the Bennett house.

"Stay here," Matt snapped, and he plunged outside, following Stefan.

"No!" Bonnie's head jerked up; she wanted to grab him and drag him back. The dizzy nausea she'd felt ever since Tyler had mentioned Vickie was overwhelming her. It was too late; she'd known in the first instant that it was too late. Matt was only going to get himself killed too.

"You stay, Bonnie—keep the doors locked. I'll go after them." That was Meredith.

"No! I'm sick of having everybody tell me to *stay*!"

Bonnie cried, struggling with the seat belt, finally getting it unlocked. She was still crying, but she could see well enough to get out of the car and start toward Vickie's house. She heard Meredith right behind her.

The activity all seemed concentrated at the front: people shouting, a woman screaming, the crackling voices of police radios. Bonnie and Meredith headed straight for the back, for Vickie's window. What is wrong with this picture? Bonnie thought wildly as they approached. The wrongness of what she was looking at was undeniable, yet hard to put a finger on. Vickie's window was open—but it *couldn't* be open; the middle pane of a bay window never opens, Bonnie thought. But then how could the curtains be fluttering out like shirttails?

Not open, broken. Glass was all over the gravel pathway, grinding underfoot. There were shards like grinning teeth left in the bare frame. Vickie's house had been broken into.

"She asked him *in*," Bonnie cried in agonized fury. "Why did she *do* that? Why?"

"Stay here," Meredith said, trying to moisten dry lips.

"*Stop telling me that*. I can take it, Meredith. I'm *mad*, that's all. I *hate* him." She gripped Meredith's arm and went forward.

The gaping hole got closer and closer. The curtains

rippled. There was enough space between them to see inside.

At the last moment, Meredith pushed Bonnie away and looked through first herself. It didn't matter. Bonnie's psychic senses were awake and already telling her about this place. It was like the crater left in the ground after a meteor has hit and exploded, or like the charred skeleton of a forest after a wildfire. Power and violence were still thrumming in the air, but the main event was over. This place had been violated.

Meredith spun away from the window, doubling over, retching. Clenching her fists so that the nails bit into her palms, Bonnie leaned forward and looked in.

The smell was what struck her first. A wet smell, meaty and coppery. She could almost taste it, and it tasted like an accidentally bitten tongue. The stereo was playing something she couldn't hear over the screaming out front and the drumming-surf sound in her own ears. Her eyes, adjusting from the darkness outside, could see only red. Just red.

Because that was the new color of Vickie's room. The powder blue was gone. Red wallpaper, red comforter. Red in great gaudy splashes across the floor. As if some kid had gotten a bucket of red paint and gone crazy.

The record player clicked and the stylus swung back to

the beginning. With a shock, Bonnie recognized the song as it started over.

It was "Goodnight Sweetheart."

"You monster," Bonnie gasped. Pain shot through her stomach. Her hand gripped the window frames, tighter, tighter. "You monster, I *hate* you! I hate you!"

Meredith heard and straightened up, turning. She shakily pushed back her hair and managed a few deep breaths, trying to look as if she could cope. "You're cutting your hand," she said. "Here, let me see it."

Bonnie hadn't even realized she was gripping broken glass. She let Meredith take the hand, but instead of letting her examine it, she turned it over and clasped Meredith's own cold hand tightly. Meredith looked terrible: dark eyes glazed, lips blue-white and shaking. But Meredith was still trying to take care of her, still trying to keep it together.

"Go on," she said, looking at her friend intently. "Cry, Meredith. Scream, if you want to. But get it out somehow. You don't have to be cool now and keep it all inside. You have every right to lose it today."

For a moment Meredith just stood there, trembling, but then she shook her head with a ghastly attempt at a smile. "I can't. I'm just not made that way. Come on, let me look at the hand."

Bonnie might have argued, but just then Matt came

around the corner. He started violently to see the girls standing there.

"What are you doing—?" he began. Then he saw the window.

"She's dead," Meredith said flatly.

"I know." Matt looked like a bad photograph of himself, an overexposed one. "They told me up front. They're bringing out . . ." He stopped.

"We blew it. Even after we promised her . . ." Meredith stopped too. There was nothing more to say.

"But the police will have to believe us now," Bonnie said, looking at Matt, then Meredith, finding one thing to be grateful for. "They'll *have* to."

"No," Matt said, "they won't, Bonnie. Because they're saying it's a suicide."

"A *suicide*? Have they seen that room? They call *that* a suicide?" Bonnie cried, her voice rising.

"They're saying she was mentally unbalanced. They're saying she—got hold of some scissors . . ."

"Oh, my God," Meredith said, turning away.

"They think maybe she was feeling guilty for having killed Sue."

"Somebody broke into this house," Bonnie said fiercely. "They've got to admit that!"

"No." Meredith's voice was soft, as if she were very tired. "Look at the window here. The glass is all outside.

Somebody from the inside broke it." And that's the rest of what's wrong with the picture, Bonnie thought.

"*He* probably did, getting out," Matt said. They looked at each other silently, in defeat.

"Where's Stefan?" Meredith asked Matt quietly. "Is he out front where everyone can see him?"

"No, once we found out she was dead he headed back this way. I was coming to look for him. He must be around somewhere . . ."

"Sh!" said Bonnie. The shouting from the front had stopped. So had the woman's screaming. In the relative stillness they could hear a faint voice from beyond the black walnut trees in the back of the yard.

"—while *you* were supposed to be watching her!"

The tone made Bonnie's skin break out in goose-flesh. "That's him!" Matt said. "And he's with Damon. Come on!"

Once they were among the trees Bonnie could hear Stefan's voice clearly. The two brothers were facing each other in the moonlight.

"I trusted you, Damon. I trusted you!" Stefan was saying. Bonnie had never seen him so angry, not even with Tyler in the graveyard. But it was more than anger.

"And you just let it happen," Stefan went on, without glancing at Bonnie and the others as they appeared, without giving Damon a chance to reply. "Why didn't you do *something*? If you were too much of a coward to fight him, you could at least have called for me. But you just stood there!"

Damon's face was hard, closed. His black eyes glittered, and there was nothing lazy or casual about his posture now. He looked as unbending and brittle as a pane of glass. He opened his mouth, but Stefan interrupted.

"It's my own fault. I should have known better. I *did* know better. *They* all knew, they warned me, but I wouldn't listen."

"Oh, did *they*?" Damon snapped a glance toward Bonnie on the sidelines. A chill went through her.

"Stefan, wait," Matt said. "I think—"

"I should have listened!" Stefan was raging on. He didn't even seem to hear Matt. "I should have stayed with her myself. I promised her she would be safe—and I lied! She died thinking I betrayed her." Bonnie could see it in his face now, the guilt eating into him like acid. "If I had stayed here—"

"You would be dead too!" Damon hissed. "This isn't an ordinary vampire you're dealing with. He would have broken you in two like a dry twig—"

"*And that would have been better!*" Stefan cried. His chest was heaving. "I would rather have died with her than stood by and watched it! What happened, Damon?" He had gotten hold of himself now, and he was calm, too calm; his green eyes were burning feverishly in his pale face, his voice vicious, poisonous, as he spoke. "Were you too busy chasing some other girl through the bushes? Or just too uninterested to interfere?"

Damon said nothing. He was just as pale as his brother, every muscle tense and rigid. Waves of black fury were rising from him as he watched Stefan.

"Or maybe you enjoyed it," Stefan was continuing, moving another half step forward so that he was right in Damon's face. "Yes, that was probably it; you liked it, being with another killer. Was it good, Damon? Did he let you watch?"

Damon's fist jerked back and he hit Stefan.

It happened too fast for Bonnie's eye to follow. Stefan fell backward onto the soft ground, long legs sprawling. Meredith cried out something, and Matt jumped in front of Damon.

Brave, Bonnie thought dazedly, but stupid. The air was crackling with electricity. Stefan raised a hand to his mouth and found blood, black in the moonlight. Bonnie lurched over to his side and grabbed his arm.

Damon was coming after him again. Matt fell back before him, but not all the way. He dropped to his knees beside Stefan, sitting on his heels, one hand upraised.

"Enough, you guys! Enough, all right?" he shouted.

Stefan was trying to get up. Bonnie held on to his arm

more firmly. "No! Stefan, don't! Don't!" she begged. Meredith grabbed his other arm.

"Damon, leave it alone! Just leave it!" Matt was saying sharply.

We're all crazy, getting in the middle of this, Bonnie thought. Trying to break up a fight between two angry vampires. They're going to kill us just to shut us up. Damon's going to swat Matt like a fly.

But Damon had stopped, with Matt blocking his way. For a long moment the scene remained frozen, nobody moving, everybody rigid with strain. Then, slowly, Damon's stance relaxed.

His hands lowered and unclenched. He drew a slow breath. Bonnie realized she'd been holding her own breath, and she let it out.

Damon's face was cold as a statue carved in ice. "All right, have it your way," he said, and his voice was cold too. "But I'm through here. I'm leaving. And this time, *brother*, if you follow me, I'll kill you. Promise or no promise."

"I won't follow you," Stefan said from where he sat. His voice sounded as if he'd been swallowing ground glass.

Damon hitched up his jacket, straightening it. With a glance at Bonnie that scarcely seemed to see her, he turned to go. Then he turned back and spoke clearly and precisely, each word an arrow aimed at Stefan.

"I warned you," he said. "About what I am, and about which side would win. You should have listened to *me*, little brother. Maybe you'll learn something from tonight."

"I've learned what trusting you is worth," Stefan said. "Get out of here, Damon. I never want to see you again."

Without another word, Damon turned and walked away into the darkness.

Bonnie let go of Stefan's arm and put her head in her hands.

Stefan got up, shaking himself like a cat that had been held against its will. He walked a little distance from the others, his face averted from them. Then he simply stood there. The rage seemed to have left him as quickly as it had come.

What do we say now? Bonnie wondered, looking up. What *can* we say? Stefan was right about one thing: they had warned him about Damon and he hadn't listened. He'd truly seemed to believe that his brother could be trusted. And then they'd all gotten careless, relying on Damon because it was easy and because they needed the help. No one had argued against letting Damon watch Vickie tonight.

They were all to blame. But it was Stefan who would tear himself apart with guilt over this. She knew that was behind his out-of-control fury at Damon: his own shame and remorse. She wondered if Damon knew that, or cared. And she wondered what had really happened tonight. Now that Damon had left, they would probably never know.

No matter what, she thought, it was better he was gone.

Outside noises were reasserting themselves: cars being started in the street, the short burst of a siren, doors slamming. They were safe in the little grove of trees for the moment, but they couldn't stay here.

Meredith had one hand pressed to her forehead, her eyes shut. Bonnie looked from her to Stefan, to the lights of Vickie's silent home beyond the trees. A wave of sheer exhaustion passed through her body. All the adrenaline that had been supporting her throughout this evening seemed to have drained away. She didn't even feel angry anymore at Vickie's death; only depressed and sick and very, very tired. She wished she could crawl into her bed at home and pull the blankets over her head.

"Tyler," she said aloud. And when they all turned to look at her, she said, "We left him in the ruined church. And he's our last hope now. We've got to make him help us."

That roused everyone. Stefan turned around silently, not speaking and not meeting anyone's eyes as he followed them back to the street. The police cars and ambulance were gone, and they drove to the cemetery without incident.

But when they reached the ruined church, Tyler wasn't there.

"We left his feet untied," Matt said heavily, with a grimace of self-disgust. "He must have walked away since his car's still down there." Or he could have been taken, Bonnie thought. There was no mark on the stone floor to show which.

Meredith went to the knee-high wall and sat down, one hand pinching the bridge of her nose.

Bonnie sagged against the belfry.

They'd failed completely. That was the long and short of it tonight. They'd lost and *he* had won. Everything they'd done today had ended in defeat.

And Stefan, she could tell, was taking the whole responsibility on his own shoulders.

She glanced at the dark, bowed head in the front seat as they drove back to the boardinghouse. Another thought occurred to her, one that sent thrills of alarm down her nerves. Stefan was all they had to protect them now that Damon was gone. And if Stefan himself was weak and exhausted . . .

Bonnie bit her lip as Meredith pulled up to the barn. An idea was forming in her mind. It made her uneasy, even frightened, but another look at Stefan put steel in her resolve.

The Ferrari was still parked behind the barn—

apparently Damon had abandoned it. Bonnie wondered how he planned to get about the countryside, and then thought of wings. Velvety soft, strong black crow's wings that reflected rainbows in their feathers. Damon didn't need a car.

They went into the boardinghouse just long enough for Bonnie to call her parents and say she was spending the night at Meredith's. This was her idea. But after Stefan had climbed the stairs to his attic room, Bonnie stopped Matt on the front porch.

"Matt? Can I ask you a favor?"

He swung around, blue eyes widening. "That's a loaded phrase. Every time Elena said those particular words . . ."

"No, no, this is nothing terrible. I just want you to take care of Meredith, see she's okay once she gets home and all." She gestured toward the other girl, who was already walking toward the car.

"But you're coming with us."

Bonnie glanced at the stairs through the open door. "No. I think I'll stay a few minutes. Stefan can drive me home. I just want to talk to him about something."

Matt looked bewildered. "Talk to him about what?"

"Just something. I can't explain now. Will you, Matt?"

"But . . . oh, all right. I'm too tired to care. Do what you want. I'll see you tomorrow." He walked off, seeming baffled and a little angry.

Bonnie was baffled herself at his attitude. Why *should* he care, tired or not, if she talked to Stefan? But there was no time to waste puzzling over it. She faced the stairs and, squaring her shoulders, went up them.

The bulb in the attic ceiling lamp was missing, and Stefan had lighted a candle. He was lying haphazardly on the bed, one leg off and one leg on, his eyes shut. Maybe asleep. Bonnie tiptoed up and fortified herself with a deep breath.

"Stefan?"

His eyes opened. "I thought you'd left."

"They did. I didn't." God, he's pale, thought Bonnie. Impulsively, she plunged right in.

"Stefan, I've been thinking. With Damon gone, you're the only thing between us and the killer. That means you've got to be strong, as strong as you can be. And, well, it occurred to me that maybe . . . you know . . . you might need . . ." Her voice faltered. Unconsciously she'd begun fiddling with the wad of tissues forming a makeshift bandage on her palm. It was still bleeding sluggishly from where she'd cut it on the glass.

His gaze followed hers down to it. Then his eyes lifted quickly to her face, reading the confirmation there. There was a long moment of silence.

Then he shook his head.

"But why? Stefan, I don't want to get personal, but frankly you don't look so good. You're not going to be much help to anybody if you collapse on us. And . . . I don't mind, if you only take a little. I mean, I'm never going to miss it, right? And it can't hurt all that much. And . . ." Once again her voice trailed off. He was just looking at her, which was very disconcerting. "Well, why *not*?" she demanded, feeling slightly let down.

"Because," he said softly, "I made a promise. Maybe not in so many words, but—a promise just the same. I won't take human blood as food, because that means *using* a person, like livestock. And I won't exchange it with any-one, because that means love, and—" This time he was the one who couldn't finish. But Bonnie understood.

"There won't ever be anyone else, will there?" she said.

"No. Not for me." Stefan was so tired that his control was slipping and Bonnie could see behind the mask. And again she saw that pain and need, so great that she had to look away from him.

A strange little chill of premonition and dismay trick-led through her heart. Before, she had wondered if Matt would ever get over Elena, and he had, it seemed. But Stefan—

Stefan, she realized, the chill deepening, was different. No matter how much time passed, no matter what he did, he would never truly heal. Without Elena he would always be half himself, only half alive.

She had to think of something, do something, to push this awful feeling of dread away. Stefan needed Elena; he couldn't be whole without her. Tonight he'd started to crack up, swinging between dangerously tight control and violent rage. If only he could see Elena for just a minute and talk to her . . .

She'd come up here to give Stefan a gift that he didn't want. But there was something else he did want, she realized, and only she had the power to give it to him.

Without looking at him, her voice husky, she said, "Would you like to see Elena?"

Dead silence from the bed. Bonnie sat, watching the shadows in the room sway and flicker. At last, she chanced a look at him out of the corner of her eye.

He was breathing hard, eyes shut, body taut as a bowstring. Trying, Bonnie diagnosed, to work up the strength to resist temptation.

And losing. Bonnie saw that.

Elena always had been too much for him.

When his eyes met hers again, they were grim, and his mouth was a tight line. His skin wasn't pale anymore but flushed with color. His body was still trembling-taut and keyed up with anticipation.

"You might get hurt, Bonnie."

"I know."

"You'd be opening yourself up to forces beyond your control. I can't guarantee that I can protect you from them."

"I know. How do you want to do it?"

Fiercely, he took her hand. "Thank you, Bonnie," he whispered.

She felt the blood rise to her face. "That's all right," she said. Good *grief*, he was gorgeous. Those eyes . . . in a minute she was either going to jump him or melt into a puddle on his bed. With a pleasurably agonizing feeling of virtue she removed her hand from his and turned to the candle.

"How about if I go into a trance and try to reach her, and then, once I make contact, try to find you and draw you in? Do you think that would work?"

"It might, if I'm reaching for you too," he said, withdrawing that intensity from her and focusing it on the candle. "I can touch your mind . . . when you're ready, I'll feel it."

"Right." The candle was white, its wax sides smooth and shining. The flame drew itself up and then fell back. Bonnie stared until she became lost in it, until the rest of the room blacked out around her. There was only the flame, herself and the flame. She was going into the flame.

Unbearable brightness surrounded her. Then she passed through it into the dark.

The funeral home was cold. Bonnie glanced around uneasily, wondering how she had gotten here, trying to gather her thoughts. She was all alone, and for some reason that bothered her. Wasn't somebody else supposed to be here too? She was looking for someone.

There was light in the next room. Bonnie moved toward it and her heart began pounding. It was a visitation room, and it was filled with tall candelabras, the white candles glimmering and quivering. In the midst of them was a white coffin with an open lid.

Step by step, as if something were pulling her, Bonnie approached the casket. She didn't want to look in. She had to. There was something in that coffin waiting for her.

The whole room was suffused with the soft white light of the candles. It was like floating in an island of radiance. But she didn't want to look . . .

Moving as if in slow motion, she reached the coffin, stared at the white satin lining inside. It was empty.

Bonnie closed it and leaned against it, sighing.

Then she caught motion in her peripheral vision and whirled.

It was Elena.

"Oh, God, you scared me," Bonnie said.

"I thought I told you not to come here," Elena answered.

This time her hair was loose, flowing over her shoulders and down her back, the pale golden white of a flame. She was wearing a thin white dress that glowed softly in the candlelight. She looked like a candle herself, luminous, radiant. Her feet were bare.

"I came here to . . ." Bonnie floundered, some concept teasing around the edges of her mind. This was *her* dream, her trance. She had to remember. "I came here to let you see Stefan," she said.

Elena's eyes widened, her lips parting. Bonnie recognized the look of yearning, of almost irresistible longing. Not fifteen minutes ago she'd seen it on Stefan's face.

"Oh," Elena whispered. She swallowed, her eyes clouding. "Oh, Bonnie . . . but I *can't*."

"Why not?"

Tears were shining in Elena's eyes now, and her lips were trembling. "What if things start to change? What if *he* comes, and . . ." She put a hand to her mouth and Bonnie remembered the last dream, with teeth falling like rain. Bonnie met Elena's eyes with understanding horror.

"Don't you see? I couldn't stand it if something like that happened," Elena whispered. "If he saw me like that . . . And I can't control things here; I'm not strong enough. Bonnie, please don't let him through. Tell him how sorry I am. Tell him—" She shut her eyes, tears spilling.

"All right." Bonnie felt as if she might cry too, but Elena was right. She reached for Stefan's mind to explain to him, to help him bear the disappointment. But the instant she touched it she knew she'd made a mistake.

"Stefan, no! Elena says—" It didn't matter. His mind was stronger than hers, and the instant she'd made contact he had taken over. He'd sensed the gist of her conversation with Elena, but he wasn't going to take no for an answer. Helplessly, Bonnie felt herself being overridden, felt his mind come closer, closer to the circle of light formed by the candelabras. She felt his presence there, felt it taking shape. She turned and saw him, dark hair, tense face, green eyes fierce as a falcon's. And then, knowing there was nothing more she could do, she stepped back to allow them to be alone.

tefan heard a voice whisper, soft with pain, "Oh, no."

A voice that he'd never thought to hear again, that he would never forget. Ripples of chills poured over his skin, and he could feel a shaking start inside him. He turned toward the voice, his attention fixing instantly, his mind almost shutting down because it couldn't cope with so many sudden driving emotions at once.

His eyes were blurred and could only discern a wash of radiance like a thousand candles. But it didn't matter. He could *feel* her there. The same presence he had sensed the very first day he'd come to Fell's Church, a golden white light that shone into his consciousness. Full of cool beauty and searing passion and vibrant life. Demanding that he move toward it, that he forget everything else.

Elena. It was really Elena.

Her presence pervaded him, filling him to his fingertips. All his hungry senses were fixed on that wash of luminance, searching for her. Needing her.

Then she stepped out.

She moved slowly, hesitantly. As if she could barely make herself do it. Stefan was caught in the same paralysis.

Elena.

He saw her every feature as if for the first time. The pale gold hair floating about her face and shoulders like a halo. The fair, flawless skin. The slender, supple body just now canted away from him, one hand raised in protest.

"Stefan," the whisper came, and it was *her* voice. Her voice saying his name. But there was such pain in it that he wanted to run to her, hold her, promise her that everything would be all right. "Stefan, please . . . I *can't* . . ."

He could see her eyes now. The dark blue of lapis lazuli, flecked in this light with gold. Wide with pain and wet with unshed tears. It shredded his guts.

"You don't want to see me?" His voice was dry as dust.

"I don't want *you* to see *me*. Oh, Stefan, he can make anything happen. And he'll find us. He'll come here . . ."

Relief and aching joy flooded through Stefan. He could scarcely concentrate on her words, and it didn't matter. The way she said his name was enough. That

"Oh, Stefan" told him everything he cared about.

He moved toward her quietly, his own hand coming up to reach for hers. He saw the protesting shake of her head, saw that her lips were parted with her quickening breath. Up close, her skin had an inner glow, like a flame shining through translucent candle wax. Droplets of wetness were caught on her eyelashes like diamonds.

Although she kept shaking her head, kept protesting, she did not move her hand away. Not even when his out-spread fingers touched it, pressing against her cool finger-tips as if they were on opposite sides of a pane of glass.

And at this distance her eyes could not evade his. They were looking at each other, looking and not turning aside. Until at last she stopped whispering "Stefan, no" and only whispered his name.

He couldn't think. His heart was threatening to come through his chest. Nothing mattered except that she was here, that they were here together. He didn't notice the strange surroundings, didn't care who might be watching.

Slowly, so slowly, he closed his hand around hers, inter-twining their fingers, the way they were meant to be. His other hand lifted to her face.

Her eyes closed at the touch, her cheek leaning into it. He felt the moisture on his fingers and a laugh caught in his throat. Dream tears. But they were real, *she* was real. Elena.

Sweetness pierced him. A pleasure so sharp it was a pain, just to stroke the tears away from her face with his thumb.

All the frustrated tenderness of the last six months, all the emotion he'd kept locked in his heart that long, came cascading out, submerging him. Drowning both of them. It took such a little movement and then he was holding her.

An angel in his arms, cool and thrilling with life and beauty. A being of flame and air. She shivered in his embrace; then, eyes still shut, put up her lips.

There was nothing cool about the kiss. It struck sparks from Stefan's nerves, melting and dissolving everything around it. He felt his control unraveling, the control he'd worked so hard to preserve since he'd lost her. Everything inside him was being jarred loose, all knots untied, all floodgates opened. He could feel his own tears as he held her to him, trying to fuse them into one flesh, one body. So that nothing could ever separate them again.

They were both crying without breaking the kiss. Elena's slender arms were around his neck now, every inch of her fitting to him as if she had never belonged anywhere else. He could taste the salt of her tears on his lips and it drenched him with sweetness.

He knew, vaguely, that there was something else he should be thinking about. But the first electric touch of her cool skin had driven reason from his mind. They were in the center of a whirlwind of fire; the universe could explode or crumble or burn to ashes for all he cared, as long as he could keep her safe.

But Elena was trembling.

Not just from emotion, from the intensity that was making him dizzy and drunk with pleasure. From fear. He could feel it in her mind and he wanted to protect her, to shield her and to cherish her and to *kill* anything that dared frighten her. With something like a snarl he raised his face to look around.

"What is it?" he said, hearing the predator's rasp in his own voice. "Anything that tries to hurt you—"

"Nothing can hurt me." She still clung to him, but she leaned back to look into his face. "I'm afraid for *you*, Stefan, for what he might do to you. And for what he might make you see . . ." Her voice quavered. "Oh, Stefan, go now, before he comes. He can find you through me. Please, please, go . . ."

"Ask me anything else and I'll do it," Stefan said. The killer would have to shred him nerve from nerve, muscle from muscle, cell from cell to make him leave her.

"Stefan, it's only a dream," Elena said desperately, new tears falling. "We can't really touch, we can't be together. It's not allowed."

Stefan didn't care. It didn't seem like a dream. It felt

real. And even in a dream he was not going to give up Elena, not for anyone. No force in heaven or hell could make him . . .

"Wrong, sport. Surprise!" said a new voice, a voice Stefan had never heard. He recognized it instinctively, though, as the voice of a killer. A hunter among hunters. And when he turned, he remembered what Vickie, poor Vickie, had said.

He looks like the devil.

If the devil was handsome and blond.

He wore a threadbare raincoat, as Vickie had described. Dirty and tattered. He looked like any street person from any big city, except that he was so tall and his eyes were so clear and penetrating. Electric blue, like razor-frosted sky. His hair was almost white, standing straight up as if blown by a blast of chilly wind. His wide smile made Stefan feel sick.

"Salvatore, I presume," he said, scraping a bow. "And of course the beautiful Elena. The beautiful *dead* Elena. Come to join her, Stefan? You two were just meant to be together."

He looked young, older than Stefan, but still young. He wasn't.

"Stefan, leave now," Elena whispered. "He can't hurt me, but you're different. He can make something happen that will follow you out of the dream."

Stefan's arm stayed locked around her.

"Bravo!" the man in the raincoat applauded, looking around as if to encourage an invisible audience. He staggered slightly, and if he'd been human, Stefan would have thought he was drunk.

"Stefan, *please*," Elena whispered.

"It would be rude to leave before we've even been properly introduced," the blond man said. Hands in coat pockets, he strode a step or two closer. "Don't you want to know who I am?"

Elena shook her head, not in negation but in defeat, and dropped it to Stefan's shoulder. He cupped a hand around her hair, wanting to shield every part of her from this madman.

"I want to know," he said, looking at the blond man over her head.

"I don't see why you didn't ask me in the first place," the man replied, scratching his cheek with his middle finger. "Instead of going to everybody else. *I'm* the only one who can tell you. I've been around a long time."

"How long?" said Stefan, unimpressed.

"A *long* time . . ." The blond man's gaze turned dreamy, as if looking back over the years. "I was tearing pretty white throats when your ancestors were building the Colosseum. I killed with Alexander's army. I fought in the Trojan War. I'm old, Salvatore. I'm one of the Originals. In my earliest memories I carried a bronze ax."

Slowly, Stefan nodded.

He'd heard of the Old Ones. They were whispered about among vampires, but no one Stefan had ever known had actually met one. Every vampire was made by another vampire, changed by the exchange of blood. But somewhere, back in time, had been the Originals, the ones who *hadn't* been made. They were where the line of continuity stopped. No one knew how they'd gotten to be vampires themselves. But their Powers were legendary.

"I helped bring the Roman Empire down," the blond man continued dreamily. "They called us barbarians—they just didn't understand! War, Salvatore! There's nothing like it. Europe was exciting then. I decided to stick around the countryside and enjoy myself. Strange, you know, people never really seemed comfortable around me. They used to run or hold up crosses." He shook his head. "But one woman came and asked my help. She was a maid in a baron's household, and her little mistress was sick. Dying, she said. She wanted me to do something about it. And so . . ." The smile returned and broadened, getting wider and impossibly wider. "I did. She was a pretty little thing."

Stefan had turned his body to hold Elena away from the blond man, and now, for a moment, he turned his head away too. He should have known, should have guessed. And so it all came back to him. Vickie's death, and Sue's, were ultimately to be laid at his door. He had started the chain of events that ended here.

"Katherine," he said, lifting his head to look at the man. "You're the vampire who changed Katherine."

"To *save* her *life*," the blond man said, as if Stefan were stupid at learning a lesson. "Which your little sweetheart here took."

A name. Stefan was searching for a name in his mind, knowing that Katherine had told it to him, just as she must have described this man to him once. He could hear Katherine's words in his mind: *I woke in the middle of the night and I saw the man that Gudren, my maid, had brought. I was frightened. His name was Klaus and I'd heard the people in the village say he was evil . . .*

"Klaus," the blond man said mildly, as if agreeing with something. "That was what *she* called me, anyway. She came back to me after two little Italian boys jilted her. She'd done everything for them, changed them into vampires, given them eternal life, but they were ungrateful and threw her out. Very strange."

"That isn't how it happened," Stefan said through his teeth.

"What was even stranger was that she never got over you, Salvatore. You especially. She was always drawing unflattering comparisons between us. I tried to beat some sense into her, but it never really worked. Maybe I should have just killed her myself, I don't know. But by then I'd gotten used to having her around. She never was the brightest. But she was good to look at, and she knew how to have fun. I showed her that, how to enjoy the killing. Eventually her brain turned a little, but so what? It wasn't her brains I was keeping her for."

There was no longer any vestige of love for Katherine in Stefan's heart, but he found he could still hate the man who had made her what she was in the end.

"Me? *Me*, sport?" Klaus pointed to his own chest in unbelief. "*You* made Katherine into what she is right now, or rather your little girlfriend did. *Right now*, she's dust. Worm's meat. But your sweetie is just slightly beyond my reach at present. Vibrating on a higher plane, isn't that what the mystics say, Elena? Why don't you vibrate down here with the rest of us?"

"If only I could," whispered Elena, lifting her head and looking at him with hatred.

"Oh, well. Meanwhile I've got your friends. Sue was such a *sweet* girl, I hear." He licked his lips. "And Vickie was delectable. Delicate but full bodied, with a nice bouquet. More like a nineteen-year-old than seventeen."

Stefan lunged one step forward, but Elena caught him. "Stefan, don't! This is his territory, and his mental powers are stronger than ours. He controls it."

"Precisely. This is my territory. Unreality." Klaus grinned, his staring psychotic grin again. "Where your wildest nightmares come true, free of charge. For instance," he said, looking at Stefan, "how'd you like to see what your sweetheart really looks like right now? Without her makeup?"

Elena made a soft sound, almost a moan. Stefan held her tighter.

"It's been how long since she died? About six months? Do you know what happens to a body once it's been in the ground six months?" Klaus licked his lips again, like a dog.

Now Stefan understood. Elena shivered, head bent, and tried to move away from him, but he locked his arms around her.

"It's all right," he said to her softly. And to Klaus: "You're forgetting yourself. I'm not a human who jumps at shadows and the sight of blood. I know about death, Klaus. It doesn't frighten me."

"No, but does it thrill you?" Klaus's voice dropped, low, intoxicating. "Isn't it exciting, the stench, the rot, the fluids of decomposing flesh? Isn't it a *kick*?"

"Stefan, let me go. *Please*." Elena was shaking, pushing at him with her hands, all the time keeping her head twisted away so he couldn't see her face. Her voice sounded close to tears. *"Please."*

"The only Power you have here is the power of illusion,"

Stefan said to Klaus. He held Elena to him, cheek pressed to her hair. He could feel the changes in the body he embraced. The hair under his cheek seemed to coarsen and Elena's form to shrink on itself.

"In certain soils the skin can tan like leather," Klaus assured him, bright eyed, grinning.

"Stefan, I don't want you to look at me—"

Eyes on Klaus, Stefan gently pushed the coarsened white hair away and stroked the side of Elena's face, ignoring the roughness against his fingertips.

"But of course most of the time it just decomposes. What a way to go. You lose everything, skin, flesh, muscles, internal organs—all back into the ground. . . ."

The body in Stefan's arms was dwindling. He shut his eyes and held tighter, hatred for Klaus burning inside him. An illusion, it was all an illusion . . .

"Stefan . . ." It was a dry whisper, faint as the scratch of paper blown down a sidewalk. It hung on the air a minute and then vanished, and Stefan found himself holding a pile of bones.

"And finally it ends up like that, in over two hundred separate, easy-to-assemble pieces. Comes with its own handy-dandy carrying case . . ." On the far side of the circle of light there was a creaking sound. The white coffin there was opening by itself, the lid lifting. "Why don't you do the honors, Salvatore? Go put Elena where she belongs."

Stefan had dropped to his knees, shaking, looking at the slender white bones in his hands. It was all an illusion—Klaus was merely controlling Bonnie's trance and showing Stefan what he wanted Stefan to see. He hadn't really hurt Elena, but the hot, protective fury inside Stefan wouldn't recognize that. Carefully, Stefan laid the fragile bones on the ground and touched them once, gently. Then he looked up at Klaus, lips curled with contempt.

"*That* is not Elena," he said.

"Of course it is. I'd recognize her anywhere." Klaus spread his hands and declaimed, "'*I knew a woman, lovely in her bones . . .*'"

"No." Sweat was beading on Stefan's forehead. He shut out Klaus's voice and concentrated, fists clenched, muscles cracking with effort. It was like pushing a boulder uphill, fighting Klaus's influence. But where they lay, the delicate bones began trembling, and a faint golden light shone around them.

"'*A rag and a bone and a hank of hair . . . the fool he called them his lady fair . . .*'"

The light was shimmering, dancing, linking the bones together. Warm and golden it folded about them, clothing them as they rose in the air. What stood there now was a featureless form of soft radiance. Sweat ran into Stefan's eyes and he felt as if his lungs would burst.

"'*Clay lies still, but blood's a rover . . .*'"

Elena's hair, long and silky gold, arranged itself over glowing shoulders. Elena's features, blurred at first and then clearly focused, formed on the face. Lovingly, Stefan reconstructed every detail. Thick lashes, small nose, parted lips like rose petals. White light swirled around the figure, creating a thin gown.

"'*And the crack in the teacup opens a lane to the land of the dead . . .*'"

"No." Dizziness swept over Stefan as he felt the last surge of Power sigh out of him. A breath lifted the figure's breast and eyes blue as lapis lazuli opened.

Elena smiled, and he felt the blaze of her love arc to meet him. "Stefan." Her head was high, proud as any queen's.

Stefan turned to Klaus, who had stopped speaking and was glaring mutely.

"This," Stefan said distinctly, "is Elena. Not whatever empty shell she's left behind in the ground. This is Elena, and nothing you do can ever touch her."

He held out his hand, and Elena took it and stepped to him. When they touched, he felt a jolt, and then felt her Powers flowing into him, sustaining him. They stood together, side by side, facing the blond man. Stefan had never felt as fiercely victorious in his life, or as strong.

Klaus stared at them for perhaps twenty seconds and then went berserk.

His face twisted in loathing. Stefan could feel waves of malignant Power battering against him and Elena, and he used all his strength to resist it. The maelstrom of dark fury was trying to tear them apart, howling through the room, destroying everything in its path. Candles snuffed out and flew into the air as if caught in a tornado. The dream was breaking up around them, shattering.

Stefan clung to Elena's other hand. The wind blew her hair, whipping it around her face.

"Stefan!" She was shouting, trying to make herself heard. Then he heard her voice in his mind. *"Stefan, listen to me! There is one thing you can do to stop him. You need a victim, Stefan—find one of his victims. Only a victim will know—"*

The noise level was unbearable, as if the very fabric of space and time was tearing. Stefan felt Elena's hands ripped from his. With a cry of desperation, he reached out for her again, but he could feel nothing. He was already drained by the effort of fighting Klaus, and he couldn't hold on to consciousness. The darkness took him spinning down with it.

Bonnie had seen everything.

It was strange, but once she stepped aside to let Stefan go to Elena, she seemed to lose physical presence in the dream. It was as if she were no longer a player but the stage the action was being played upon. She could watch, but she couldn't do anything else.

In the end, she'd been afraid. She wasn't strong enough to hold the dream together, and the whole thing finally exploded, throwing her out of the trance, back into Stefan's room.

He was lying on the floor and he looked dead. So white, so still. But when Bonnie tugged at him, trying to get him on the bed, his chest heaved and she heard him suck in a gasping breath.

"Stefan? Are you okay?"

He looked wildly around the room as if trying to find something. "Elena!" he said, and then he stopped, memory clearly returning.

His face twisted. For one dreadful instant Bonnie thought he was going to cry, but he only shut his eyes and dropped his head into his hands.

"I lost her. I couldn't hold on."

"I know." Bonnie watched him a moment, then, gathering her courage, knelt in front of him, touching his shoulders. "I'm sorry."

His head lifted abruptly, his green eyes dry but so dilated they looked black. His nostrils were flared, his lips drawn back from his teeth.

"Klaus!" He spat the name as if it were a curse. "Did you see him?"

"Yes," Bonnie said, pulling back. She gulped, her

stomach churning. "He's crazy, isn't he, Stefan?"

"Yes." Stefan got up. "And he must be stopped."

"But how?" Since seeing Klaus, Bonnie was more frightened than ever, more frightened and less confident. "What could stop him, Stefan? I've never felt anything like that Power."

"But didn't you—?" Stefan turned to her quickly. "Bonnie, didn't you hear what Elena said at the end?"

"No. What do you mean? I couldn't hear anything; there was a slight hurricane going on at the time."

"Bonnie . . ." Stefan's eyes went distant with speculation and he spoke as if to himself. "That means that *he* probably didn't hear it either. So he doesn't know, and he won't try to stop us."

"From what? Stefan, what are you talking about?"

"From finding a victim. Listen, Bonnie, Elena told me that if we can find a surviving victim of Klaus's, we can find a way to stop him."

Bonnie was in completely over her head. "But . . . why?"

"Because vampires and their donors—their prey— share minds briefly while the blood is being exchanged. Sometimes the donor can learn things about the vampire that way. Not always, but occasionally. That's what must have happened, and Elena knows it."

"That's all very well and good—except for one small thing," Bonnie said tartly. "Will you please tell me who on *earth* could have survived an attack by Klaus?"

She expected Stefan to be deflated, but he wasn't. "A vampire," he said simply. "A human Klaus made into a vampire would qualify as a victim. As long as they've exchanged blood, they've touched minds."

"Oh. *Oh*. So . . . if we can find a vampire he's made . . . but *where*?"

"Maybe in Europe." Stefan began to pace around the room, his eyes narrowed. "Klaus has a long history, and some of his vampires are bound to be there. I may have to go and look for one."

Bonnie was utterly dismayed. "But Stefan, you can't leave *us*. You can't!"

Stefan stopped where he was, across the room, and stood very still. Then at last, he turned to face her. "I don't want to," he said quietly. "And we'll try to think of another solution first—maybe we can get hold of Tyler again. I'll wait a week, until next Saturday. But I may have to leave, Bonnie. You know that as well as I do."

There was a long, long silence between them. Bonnie fought the heat in her eyes, determined to be grown up and mature. She wasn't a baby and she would prove that now, once and for all. She caught Stefan's gaze and slowly nodded.

13

June 19, Friday, 11:45 p.m.

ear Diary,

    Oh, God, what are we going to do?
This has been the longest week of
my life. Today was the last day of school and
tomorrow Stefan is leaving. He's going to Europe
to search for a vampire who got changed by Klaus.
He says he doesn't want to leave us unprotected.
But he's going to go.

    We can't find Tyler. His car disappeared from
the cemetery, but he hasn't turned up at school. He's
missed every final this week. Not that the rest of us
are doing much better. I wish Robert E. Lee was
like the schools that have all their finals before

> *graduation. I don't know whether I'm writing English or Swahili these days.*
>
> *I hate Klaus. From what I saw he's as crazy as Katherine—and even crueler. What he did to Vickie —but I can't even talk about that or I'll start crying again. He was just playing with us at Caroline's party, like a cat with a mouse. And to do it on Meredith's birthday, too—although I suppose he couldn't have known that. He seems to know a lot, though. He doesn't talk like a foreigner, not like Stefan did when he first came to America, and he knows all about American things, even songs from the fifties. Maybe he's been over here for a while . . .*

Bonnie stopped writing. She thought desperately. All this time, they had been thinking of victims in Europe, of vampires. But from the way Klaus talked, he had obviously been in America a long time. He didn't sound foreign at all. And he'd chosen to attack the girls on Meredith's birthday . . .

Bonnie got up, reached for the telephone, and called Meredith's number. A sleepy male voice answered.

"Mr. Sulez, this is Bonnie. Can I speak to Meredith?"

"Bonnie! Don't you know what time it is?"

"Yes." Bonnie thought quickly. "But it's about—about a final we had today. Please, I have to talk with her."

There was a long pause, then a heavy sigh. "Just a minute."

Bonnie tapped her fingers impatiently as she waited. At last there was the click of another phone being picked up.

"Bonnie?" came Meredith's voice. "What's wrong?"

"Nothing. I mean—" Bonnie was excruciatingly conscious of the open line, of the fact that Meredith's father hadn't hung up. He might be listening. "It's about—that German problem we've been working on. *You* remember. The one we couldn't figure out for the final. You know how we've been looking for the one person who can help us solve it? Well, I think I know who it is."

"You *do?*" Bonnie could sense Meredith scrambling for the right words. "Well—who is it? Does it involve any long-distance calls?"

"No," Bonnie said, "it doesn't. It hits a lot closer to home, Meredith. A lot. In fact, you could say it's right in your own backyard, hanging on your family tree."

The line was silent so long Bonnie wondered if Meredith was still there. "Meredith?"

"I'm thinking. Does this solution have anything to do with coincidence?"

"Nope." Bonnie relaxed and smiled slightly, grimly. Meredith had it now. "Not a thing to do with coincidence. It's more a case of history repeating itself. Deliberately repeating itself, if you see what I mean."

"Yes," Meredith said. She sounded as if she were recovering from a shock, and no wonder. "You know, I think you just may be right. But there's still the matter of persuading—this person—to actually help us."

"You think that may be a problem?"

"I think it could. Sometimes people get very rattled—about a test. Sometimes they even kind of lose their minds."

Bonnie's heart sank. This was something that hadn't occurred to her. What if he *couldn't* tell them? What if he were that far gone?

"All we can do is try," she said, making her voice as optimistic as possible. "Tomorrow we'll have to try."

"All right. I'll pick you up at noon. Good night, Bonnie."

"Night, Meredith." Bonnie added, "I'm sorry."

"No, I think it may be for the best. So that history doesn't continue to repeat itself forever. Good-bye."

Bonnie pressed the disconnect button on the handset, clicking it off. Then she just sat for a few minutes, her finger on the button, staring at the wall. Finally she replaced the handset in its cradle and picked up her diary again. She put a period on the last sentence and added a new one.

We are going to see Meredith's grandfather tomorrow.

"I'm an idiot," Stefan said in Meredith's car the next day. They were going to West Virginia, to the institution where Meredith's grandfather was a patient. It was going to be a fairly long drive.

"We're all idiots. Except Bonnie," Matt said. Even in the midst of her anxiety Bonnie felt a warm glow at that.

But Meredith was shaking her head, eyes on the road. "Stefan, you couldn't have realized, so stop beating up on yourself. You didn't know that Klaus attacked Caroline's party on the anniversary of the attack on my grandfather. And it didn't occur to Matt or me that Klaus could have been in America for so long because we never saw Klaus or heard him speak. We were thinking of people he could have attacked in Europe. Really, Bonnie was the only one who *could* have put it all together, because she had all the information."

Bonnie stuck out her tongue. Meredith caught it in the rearview mirror and arched an eyebrow. "Just don't want you getting too cocky," she said.

"I won't; modesty is one of my most charming qualities," Bonnie replied.

Matt snorted, but then he said, "I still think it was pretty smart," which started the glow all over again.

The institution was a terrible place. Bonnie tried as hard as she could to conceal her horror and disgust, but she knew Meredith could sense it. Meredith's shoulders were stiff with defensive pride as she walked down the halls in front of them. Bonnie, who had known her for so many years, could see the humiliation underneath that pride. Meredith's parents considered her grandfather's condition such a blot that they never allowed him to be mentioned to outsiders. It had been a shadow over the entire family.

And now Meredith was showing that secret to strangers for the first time. Bonnie felt a rush of love and admiration for her friend. It was so like Meredith to do it without fuss, with dignity, letting nobody see what it cost her. But the institution was still terrible.

It wasn't filthy or filled with raving maniacs or anything like that. The patients looked clean and well cared for. But there was something about the sterile hospital smells and the halls crowded with motionless wheelchairs and blank eyes that made Bonnie want to run.

It was like a building full of zombies. Bonnie saw one old woman, her pink scalp showing through thin white hair, slumped with her head on the table next to a naked plastic doll. When Bonnie reached out desperately, she found Matt's hand already reaching for hers. They followed Meredith that way, holding on so hard it hurt.

"This is his room."

Inside was another zombie, this one with white hair that still showed an occasional fleck of black like Meredith's. His face was a mass of wrinkles and lines, the eyes rheumy and rimmed with scarlet. They stared vacantly.

"Granddad," Meredith said, kneeling in front of his wheelchair. "Granddad, it's me, Meredith. I've come to visit you. I've got something important to ask you."

The old eyes never flickered.

"Sometimes he knows us," Meredith said quietly, without emotion. "But mostly these days he doesn't."

The old man just went on staring.

Stefan dropped to his heels. "Let me try," he said. Looking into the wrinkled face he began to speak, softly, soothingly, as he had to Vickie.

But the filmy dark eyes didn't so much as blink. They just went on staring aimlessly. The only movement was a slight, continuous tremor in the knotted hands on the arms of the wheelchair.

And no matter what Meredith or Stefan did, that was all the response they could elicit.

Eventually Bonnie tried, using her psychic powers. She could sense *something* in the old man, some spark of life trapped in the imprisoning flesh. But she couldn't reach it.

"I'm sorry," she said, sitting back and pushing hair out of her eyes. "It's no use. I can't do anything."

"Maybe we can come another time," Matt said, but Bonnie knew it wasn't true. Stefan was leaving tomorrow; there would never be another time. And it had seemed like such a good idea. . . . The glow that had warmed her earlier was ashes now, and her heart felt like a lump of lead. She turned away to see Stefan already starting out of the room.

Matt put a hand under her elbow to help her up and guide her out. And after standing for a minute with her head bent in discouragement, Bonnie let him. It was hard to summon up enough energy to put one foot in front of the other. She glanced back dully to see whether Meredith was following—

And *screamed*. Meredith was standing in the center of the room, facing the door, discouragement written on her face. But behind her, the figure in the wheelchair had stirred at last. In a silent explosion of movement, it had reared above her, the rheumy old eyes open wide and the mouth open wider. Meredith's grandfather looked as if he had been caught in the act of leaping—arms flung out, mouth forming a silent howl. Bonnie's screams rang from the rafters.

Everything happened at once then. Stefan came charging back in, Meredith spun around, Matt grabbed for her. But the old figure didn't leap. He stood towering above all of them, staring over their heads, seeming to see something none of them could. Sounds were coming from his mouth at last, sounds that formed one ululating word.

"*Vampire! Vampiiiire!*"

Attendants were in the room, crowding Bonnie and

the others away, restraining the old man. Their shouts added to the pandemonium.

"*Vampire! Vampire!*" Meredith's grandfather caterwauled, as if warning the town. Bonnie felt panicked—was he looking at Stefan? Was it an accusation?

"Please, you'll have to leave now. I'm sorry, but you'll have to go," a nurse was saying. They were being whisked out. Meredith fought as she was forced out into the hall.

"Granddaddy—!"

"*Vampire!*" that unearthly voice wailed on.

And then: "White ash wood! Vampire! White ash wood—"

The door slammed shut.

Meredith gasped, fighting tears. Bonnie had her nails dug into Matt's arm. Stefan turned to them, green eyes wide with shock.

"I *said*, you'll have to leave now," the harassed nurse was repeating impatiently. The four of them ignored her. They were all looking at each other, stunned confusion giving way to realization in their faces.

"Tyler said there was only one kind of wood that could hurt him—" Matt began.

"*White ash wood,*" said Stefan.

"We'll have to find out where he's hiding," Stefan said on the way home. He was driving, since Meredith had dropped the keys at the car door. "That's the first thing. If we rush this, we could warn him off."

His green eyes were shining with a queer mixture of triumph and grim determination, and he spoke in a clipped and rapid voice. They were all on the ragged edge, Bonnie thought, as if they'd been gulping uppers all night. Their nerves were frayed so thin that anything could happen.

She had a sense, too, of impending cataclysm. As if everything were coming to a head, all the events since Meredith's birthday party gathering to a conclusion.

Tonight, she thought. Tonight it all happens. It seemed strangely appropriate that it should be the eve of the solstice.

"The eve of what?" Matt said.

She hadn't even realized she'd spoken aloud. "The eve of the solstice," she said. "That's what today is. The day before the summer solstice."

"Don't tell me. Druids, right?"

"They celebrated it," Bonnie confirmed. "It's a day for magic, for marking the change of the seasons. And . . ." she hesitated. "Well, it's like all other feast days, like Halloween or the winter solstice. A day when the line between the visible world and the invisible world is thin. When you can see ghosts, they used to say. When things happen."

"Things," Stefan said, turning onto the main highway that headed back toward Fell's Church, "are going to happen."

None of them realized how soon.

Mrs. Flowers was in the back garden. They had driven straight to the boardinghouse to look for her. She was pruning rosebushes, and the smell of summer surrounded her.

She frowned and blinked when they all crowded around her and asked her in a rush where to find a white ash tree.

"Slow down, slow down now," she said, peering at them from under the brim of her straw hat. "What is it you want? White ash? There's one just down beyond those oak trees in back. Now, wait a minute—" she added as they all scrambled off again.

Stefan ringed a branch of the tree with a jackknife Matt produced from his pocket. I wonder when he started carrying *that*? Bonnie thought. She also wondered what Mrs. Flowers thought of them as they came back, the two boys carrying the leafy six-foot bough between them on their shoulders.

But Mrs. Flowers just looked without saying anything. As they neared the house, though, she called after them,

"A package came for you, boy."

Stefan turned his head, the branch still on his shoulder. "For *me*?"

"It had your name on it. A package and a letter. I found them on the front porch this afternoon. I put them upstairs in your room."

Bonnie looked at Meredith, then at Matt and Stefan, meeting their bewildered, suspicious gazes in turn. The anticipation in the air heightened suddenly, almost unbearably.

"But who could it be from? Who could even know you're here—" she began as they climbed the stairs to the attic. And then she stopped, dread fluttering between her ribs. Premonition was buzzing around inside her like a nagging fly, but she pushed it away. Not now, she thought, not now.

But there was no way to keep from seeing the package on Stefan's desk. The boys propped the white ash branch against the wall and went to look at it, a longish, flattish parcel wrapped in brown paper, with a creamy envelope on top.

On the front, in familiar crazy handwriting, was scrawled *Stefan*.

The handwriting from the mirror.

They all stood staring down at the package as if it were a scorpion.

"Watch out," Meredith said as Stefan slowly reached for it. Bonnie knew what she meant. She felt as if the whole thing might explode or belch poisonous gas or turn into something with teeth and claws.

The envelope Stefan picked up was square and sturdy, made of good paper with a fine finish. Like a prince's invitation to the ball, Bonnie thought. But incongruously, there were several dirty fingerprints on the surface and the edges were grimy. Well—Klaus hadn't looked any too clean in the dream.

Stefan glanced at front and back and then tore the envelope open. He pulled out a single piece of heavy stationery. The other three crowded around, looking over his shoulder as he unfolded it. Then Matt gave an exclamation.

"What the . . . it's blank!"

It was. On both sides. Stefan turned it over and examined each. His face was tense, shuttered. Everyone else relaxed, though, making noises of disgust. A stupid practical joke. Meredith had reached for the package, which looked flat enough to be empty as well, when Stefan suddenly stiffened, his breath hissing in. Bonnie glanced quickly over and jumped. Meredith's hand froze on the package, and Matt swore.

On the blank paper, held tautly between Stefan's two hands, letters were appearing. They were black with long downstrokes, as if each were being slashed by an invisible knife while Bonnie watched. As she read them, the dread inside her grew.

> *Stefan—*
> *Shall we try to solve this like gentlemen? I have the*
> *girl. Come to the old farmhouse in the woods after*
> *dark and we'll talk, just the two of us. Come alone*
> *and I'll let her go. Bring anyone else and she dies.*

There was no signature, but at the bottom the words appeared: *This is between you and me.*

"What girl?" Matt was demanding, looking from Bonnie to Meredith as if to make sure they were still there. "What girl?"

With a sharp motion, Meredith's elegant fingers tore the package open and pulled out what was inside. A pale green scarf with a pattern of vines and leaves. Bonnie remembered it perfectly, and a vision came to her in a rush. Confetti and birthday presents, orchids and chocolate.

"Caroline," she whispered, and shut her eyes.

These last two weeks had been so strange, so different from ordinary high school life that she had almost forgotten Caroline existed. Caroline had gone off to an apartment in another town to escape, to be safe—but Meredith had said it to her in the beginning. *He can follow you to Heron, I'm sure.*

"He was just playing with us again," Bonnie mur- mured. "He let us get this far, even going to see your grandfather, Meredith, and then . . ."

"He must have known," Meredith agreed. "He must have known all along we were looking for a victim. And now he's checkmated us. Unless—" Her dark eyes lit with sudden hope. "Bonnie, you don't think Caroline could have dropped this scarf the night of the party? And that he just picked it up?"

"No." The premonition was buzzing closer and Bonnie swatted at it, trying to keep it away. She didn't *want* it, didn't want to know. But she felt certain of one thing: this wasn't a bluff. Klaus had Caroline.

"What are we going to do?" she said softly.

"I know what we're *not* going to do, and that's listen to *him*," Matt said. "'Try to solve it like gentlemen'—he's scum, not a gentleman. It's a trap."

"Of course it's a trap," Meredith said impatiently. "He waited until we found out how to hurt him and now he's trying to separate us. But it won't work!"

Bonnie had been watching Stefan's face with growing dismay. Because while Matt and Meredith were indignantly talking, he had been quietly folding up the letter and put- ting it back in its envelope. Now he stood gazing down at it, his face still, untouched by anything that was going on around him. And the look in his green eyes scared Bonnie.

"We can make it backfire on him," Matt was saying. "Right, Stefan? Don't you think?"

"I think," said Stefan carefully, concentrating on each word, "that I am going out to the woods after dark."

Matt nodded, and like the quarterback he was, began to chart out a plan. "Okay, you go distract him. And meanwhile, the three of us—"

"The three of you," Stefan continued just as deliberately, looking right at him, "are going home. To bed."

There was a pause that seemed endless to Bonnie's taut nerves. The others just stared at Stefan.

At last Meredith said lightly, "Well, it's going to be hard to catch him while we're in bed unless he's kind enough to come visiting."

That broke the tension and Matt said, drawing a long-suffering breath, "All right, Stefan, I understand how you feel about this—" But Stefan interrupted.

"I'm dead serious, Matt. Klaus is right; this is between him and me. And he says to come alone or he'll hurt Caroline. So I'm going alone. It's my decision."

"It's your *funeral*," Bonnie blurted out, almost hysterically. "Stefan, you're crazy. You *can't*."

"Watch me."

"We won't *let* you—"

"Do you think," Stefan said, looking at her, "that you could stop me if you tried?"

This silence was acutely uncomfortable. Staring at him, Bonnie felt as if Stefan had changed somehow before her eyes. His face seemed sharper, his posture different, as if to remind her of the lithe, hard predator's muscles under his clothes. All at once he seemed distant, alien. Frightening.

Bonnie looked away.

"Let's be reasonable about this," Matt was saying, changing tactics. "Let's just stay calm and talk this over—"

"There's nothing to talk over. I'm going. You're not."

"You owe us more than that, Stefan," Meredith said, and Bonnie felt grateful for her cool voice. "Okay, so you can tear us all limb from limb; fine, no argument. We get the point. But after all we've been through together, we deserve more of a thorough discussion before you go running off."

"You said it was the girls' fight too," Matt added. "When did you decide it wasn't?"

"When I found out who the killer was!" Stefan said. "It's because of me that Klaus is here."

"No, it isn't!" Bonnie cried. "Did you make Elena kill Katherine?"

"I made Katherine go back to Klaus! *That's* how this got started. And I got Caroline involved; if it wasn't for me, she would never have hated Elena, never have gotten in with Tyler. I have a responsibility toward her."

"You just *want* to believe that," Bonnie almost yelled. "Klaus hates all of us! Do you really think he's going to let you walk out of there? Do you think he plans to leave the rest of us alone?"

"No," Stefan said, and picked up the branch leaning against the wall. He took Matt's knife out of his own pocket and began to strip the twigs off, making it into a straight white spear.

"Oh, great, you're going off for single combat!" Matt said, furious. "Don't you see how stupid that is? You're walking right into his trap!" He advanced a step on Stefan. "You may not think that the three of us can stop you—"

"No, Matt." Meredith's low, level voice cut across the room. "It won't do any good." Stefan looked at her, the muscles around his eyes hardening, but she just looked back, her face set and calm. "So you're determined to meet Klaus face to face, Stefan. All right. But before you go, at least be sure you have a fighting chance." Coolly, she began to unbutton the neck of her tailored blouse.

Bonnie felt a jolt, even though she'd offered the same thing only a week earlier. But that had been in private, for God's sake, she thought. Then she shrugged. Public or private, what difference did it make?

She looked at Matt, whose face reflected his consternation. Then she saw Matt's brow crease and the beginning of that stubborn, bullheaded expression that used to terrify the coaches of opposing football teams. His blue eyes turned to hers and she nodded, thrusting out her chin. Without a word, she unzipped the light windbreaker she was wearing and Matt pulled off his T-shirt.

Stefan stared from one to another of the three people grimly disrobing in his room, trying to conceal his own shock. But he shook his head, the white spear in front of him like a weapon. "No."

"Don't be a jerk, Stefan," Matt snapped. Even in the confusion of this terrible moment something inside Bonnie paused to admire his bare chest. "There's three of us. You should be able to take plenty without hurting any one of us."

"I said, no! Not for revenge, and not to fight evil with evil! Not for any reason. I thought *you* would understand that." Stefan's look at Matt was bitter.

"I understand that you're going to die out there!" Matt shouted.

"He's right!" Bonnie pressed her knuckles against her lips. The premonition was getting through her defenses. She didn't want to let it in, but she didn't have the strength to resist anymore. With a shudder, she felt it stab through and heard the words in her mind.

"No one can fight him and live," she said painfully. "That's what Vickie said, and it's true. I *feel* it, Stefan. No one can fight him and live!"

For a moment, just a moment, she thought he might listen to her. Then his face went hard again and he spoke coldly.

"It isn't your problem. Let me worry about it."

"But if there's no way to win—" Matt began.

"That isn't what Bonnie said!" Stefan replied tersely.

"Yes, it is! What the hell are you talking about?" Matt shouted. It was hard to make Matt lose his temper, but once lost it wasn't easily gotten back. "Stefan, I've had enough—"

"And so have I!" Stefan shot back in a roar. In a tone Bonnie had never heard him use before. "I'm sick of you all, sick of your bickering and your spinelessness—and your premonitions, too! This is *my* problem."

"I thought we were a team—" Matt cried.

"We are not a *team. You* are a bunch of stupid humans! Even with everything that's happened to you, deep down you just want to live your safe little lives in your safe little houses until you go to your safe little graves! I'm nothing like you and I don't want to be! I've put up with you this long because I had to, but this is the end." He looked at each of them and spoke deliberately, emphasizing each word. "I don't need any of you. I don't want you with me, and I don't want you following me. You'll only spoil my strategy. Anyone who *does* follow me, I'll kill."

And with one last smoldering glance, he turned on his heel and walked out.

14

"He's gone round the bend," Matt said, staring at the empty doorway through which Stefan had disappeared.

"No, he hasn't," said Meredith. Her voice was rueful and quiet, but there was a kind of helpless laugh in it too. "Don't you see what he's doing, Matt?" she said when he turned to her. "Yelling at us, making us hate him to try and chase us away. Being as nasty as possible so we'll stay mad and let him do this alone." She glanced at the doorway and raised her eyebrows. "'Anyone who does follow me, I'll kill' *was* going a bit overboard, though."

Bonnie giggled suddenly, wildly, in spite of herself. "I think he borrowed it from Damon. 'Get this straight, I don't need any of you!'"

"'You bunch of stupid humans,'" Matt added. "But I

still don't understand. You just had a premonition, Bonnie, and Stefan doesn't usually discount those. If there's no way to fight and win, what's the point of going?"

"Bonnie didn't say there was no way to fight and win. She said there was no way to fight and *survive*. Right, Bonnie?" Meredith looked at her.

The fit of giggles dissolved away. Startled herself, Bonnie tried to examine the premonition, but she knew no more than the words that had sprung into her mind. *No one can fight him and live.*

"You mean Stefan thinks—" Slow, thunderous outrage was smoldering in Matt's eyes. "He thinks he's going to go and stop Klaus even though he gets killed himself? Like some sacrificial lamb?"

"More like Elena," Meredith said soberly. "And maybe—so he can be with her."

"Huh-uh." Bonnie shook her head. She might not know more about the prophecy, but *this* she knew. "He doesn't think that, I'm sure. Elena's special. She is what she is because she died too young; she left so much unfinished in her own life, and—well, she's a special case. But Stefan's been a vampire for five hundred years, and he certainly wouldn't be dying young. There's no guarantee he'd end up with Elena. He might go to another place or—or just *go out*. And he knows that. I'm sure he knows that. I think he's just keeping his promise to her, to stop Klaus no matter what it costs."

"To try, at least," Matt said softly, and it sounded as if he were quoting. "Even if you know you're going to lose." He looked up at the girls suddenly. "I'm going after him."

"Of course," said Meredith patiently.

Matt hesitated. "Uh—I don't suppose I could convince you two to stay here?"

"After all that inspiring talk about teamwork? Not a chance."

"I was afraid of that. So . . ."

"So," said Bonnie, "we're out of here."

They gathered what weapons they could. Matt's pocketknife that Stefan had dropped, the ivory-hilted dagger from Stefan's dresser, a carving knife from the kitchen.

Outside, there was no sign of Mrs. Flowers. The sky was pale purple, shading to apricot in the west. Twilight of the solstice eve, Bonnie thought, and hairs on her arms tried to lift.

"Klaus said the old farmhouse in the woods—that must mean the Francher place," Matt said. "Where Katherine dumped Stefan in the abandoned well."

"That makes sense. He's probably been using Katherine's tunnel to get back and forth under the river," Meredith said. "Unless Old Ones are so powerful they can cross running water without harming themselves."

That's right, Bonnie remembered, evil things couldn't cross running water, and the more evil you were, the harder it was. "But we don't know anything about the Originals," she said aloud.

"No, and that means we've got to be careful," Matt said. "I know these woods pretty well, and I know the path Stefan will probably use. I think we should take a different one."

"So Stefan won't see us and kill us?"

"So *Klaus* won't see us, or not all of us. So maybe we'll have a chance of getting to Caroline. Somehow or other we've got to get Caroline out of the equation; as long as Klaus can threaten to hurt her he can make Stefan do anything he wants. And it's always best to plan ahead, to get a jump on the enemy. Klaus said meet there after dark; well, we'll be there *before* dark and maybe we can surprise him."

Bonnie was deeply impressed by this strategy. No wonder he's a quarterback, she was thinking. I would have just rushed in, yelling.

Matt picked out an almost invisible path between the oak trees. The undergrowth was especially lush this time of year, with mosses, grasses, flowering plants, and ferns. Bonnie had to trust that Matt knew where he was going, because *she* certainly didn't. Above, birds were giving one last burst of song before seeking out a roost for the night.

It got dimmer. Moths and lacewings fluttered past

Bonnie's face. After stumbling through a patch of toad-stools covered with feeding slugs, she was intensely grateful that this time she'd worn jeans.

At last Matt stopped them. "We're getting close," he said, his voice low. "There's a sort of bluff where we can look down and Klaus might not see us. Be quiet and careful."

Bonnie had never taken so much trouble placing her feet before. Fortunately the leaf litter was wet and not crackly. After a few minutes Matt dropped to his stomach and gestured for them to follow. Bonnie kept telling herself, fiercely, that she didn't mind the centipedes and earthworms her sliding fingers dug up, that she had no feelings one way or another about cobwebs in the face. This was life and death, and she was *competent*. No dweeb, no baby, but *competent*.

"Here," Matt whispered, his voice barely audible. Bonnie scooted on her stomach up to him and looked.

They were gazing down on the Francher homestead—or what was left of it. It had crumbled into the earth long ago, taken back by the forest. Now it was only a foundation, building stones covered with flowering weeds and prickly brambles, and one tall chimney like a lonely monument.

"There she is. Caroline," Meredith breathed in Bonnie's other ear.

Caroline was a dim figure sitting against the chimney.

Her pale green dress showed up in the gathering dark, but her auburn hair just looked black. Something white shone across her face, and after a moment Bonnie realized it was a gag. Tape or a bandage. From her strange posture—arms behind her, legs stretched straight out in front—Bonnie also guessed she was tied.

Poor Caroline, she thought, forgiving the other girl all the nasty, petty, selfish things she'd ever done, which was a pretty considerable amount when you got down to it. But Bonnie couldn't imagine anything worse than being abducted by a psycho vampire who'd already killed two of your classmates, dragged out here to the woods and bound, and then left to wait, with your life depending on another vampire who had fairly good reason to hate you. After all, Caroline had wanted Stefan in the beginning, and had hated and tried to humiliate Elena for getting him. Stefan Salvatore was the last person who should feel kindly toward Caroline Forbes.

"Look!" said Matt. "Is that him? Klaus?"

Bonnie had seen it too, a ripple of movement on the opposite side of the chimney. As she strained her eyes he appeared, his light tan raincoat flapping ghostlike around his legs. He glanced down at Caroline and she shrank from him, trying to lean away. His laughter sounded so clearly in the quiet air that Bonnie flinched.

"That's him," she whispered, dropping down behind

the screening ferns. "But where's Stefan? It's almost dark now."

"Maybe he got smart and decided not to come," said Matt.

"No such luck," said Meredith. She was looking though the ferns to the south. Bonnie glanced that way herself and started.

Stefan was standing at the edge of the clearing, having materialized there as if out of thin air. Not even Klaus had seen him coming, Bonnie thought. He stood silently, making no attempt to hide himself or the white ash spear he was carrying. There was something in his stance and the way he looked over the scene before him that made Bonnie remember that in the fifteenth century he'd been an aristocrat, a member of the nobility. He said nothing, waiting for Klaus to notice him, refusing to be rushed.

When Klaus did turn south he went still, and Bonnie got the feeling he was surprised Stefan had sneaked up on him. But then he laughed and spread his arms.

"Salvatore! What a coincidence; I was just thinking about you!"

Slowly, Stefan looked Klaus up and down, from the tails of his tattered raincoat to the top of his windblown head. What Stefan said was:

"You asked for me. I'm here. Let the girl go."

"Did I say that?" Looking genuinely surprised, Klaus

pressed two hands to his chest. Then he shook his head, chuckling. "I don't think so. Let's talk first."

Stefan nodded, as if Klaus had confirmed something bitter he'd been expecting. He took the spear from his shoulder and held it in front of him, handling the unwieldy length of wood deftly, easily. "I'm listening," he said.

"Not as dumb as he looks," Matt murmured from behind the ferns, a note of respect in his voice. "And he's not as anxious to get killed as I thought," Matt added. "He's being careful."

Klaus gestured toward Caroline, the tips of his fingers brushing her auburn hair. "Why don't you come here so we don't have to shout?" But he didn't threaten to hurt his prisoner, Bonnie noticed.

"I can hear you just fine," Stefan replied.

"Good," Matt whispered. "That's it, Stefan!"

Bonnie, though, was studying Caroline. The captive girl was struggling, tossing her head back and forth as if she were frantic or in pain. But Bonnie got a strange feeling about Caroline's movements, especially those violent jerks of the head, as if the girl was straining to reach the sky. The sky . . . Bonnie's gaze lifted up to it, where full darkness had fallen and a waning moon shone over the trees. That was why she could see that Caroline's hair was auburn now: the moonlight, she thought. Then, with a shock, her eyes dropped to the tree just above Stefan, whose branches were rustling slightly in the absence of any wind. "Matt?" she whispered, alarmed.

Stefan was focused on Klaus, every sense, every muscle, every atom of his Power honed and turned toward the Old One before him. But in that tree directly above him . . .

All thoughts of strategy, of asking Matt what to do, fled from Bonnie's mind. She bolted up from her place of concealment and shouted.

"Stefan! Above you! It's a trap!"

Stefan leaped aside, neat as a cat, just as something plunged down on the exact place he'd been standing an instant before. The moon lit the scene perfectly, enough for Bonnie to see the white of Tyler's bared teeth.

And to see the white flash of Klaus's eyes as he whirled on her. For one stunned instant she stared at him, and then lightning crackled.

From an empty sky.

It was only later that Bonnie would realize the strangeness—the fearsomeness—of this. At the time she scarcely noted that the sky was clear and star swept and that the jagged blue bolt that forked down struck the palm of Klaus's upraised hand. The next sight she saw was so terrifying as to black everything else out: Klaus folding his hand over that lightning, *gathering* it somehow, and throwing it at her.

Stefan was yelling, telling her to get away, *get away!* Bonnie heard him while she stared, paralyzed, and then something grabbed her and wrenched her aside. The bolt snapped over her head, with a sound like a giant whip cracking and a smell like ozone. She landed facedown in moss and rolled over to grasp Meredith's hand and thank Meredith for saving her, only to find that it was Matt.

"Stay here! Right here!" he shouted, and bounded away.

Those dreaded words. They catapulted Bonnie right up, and she was running after him before she knew what she was doing.

And then the world turned into chaos.

Klaus had whirled back on Stefan, who was grappling with Tyler, beating him. Tyler, in his wolf form, was making terrible sounds as Stefan threw him to the ground.

Meredith was running toward Caroline, approaching from behind the chimney so Klaus wouldn't spot her. Bonnie saw her reach Caroline and saw the flash of Stefan's silver dagger as Meredith cut the cords around Caroline's wrists. Then Meredith was half carrying half dragging Caroline behind the chimney to work on her feet.

A sound like antlers clashing made Bonnie spin around. Klaus had come at Stefan with a tall branch of his own— it must have been lying flat on the ground before. It looked just as sharp as Stefan's, making it a serviceable lance. But Klaus and Stefan weren't just stabbing at each other; they were using the sticks as quarterstaffs. Robin Hood, Bonnie thought dazedly. Little John and Robin. That was what it looked like: Klaus was that much taller and heavier boned than Stefan.

Then Bonnie saw something else and cried out wordlessly. Behind Stefan, Tyler had gotten up again and was crouching, just as he had in the graveyard before lunging for Stefan's throat. Stefan's back was to him. And Bonnie couldn't warn him in time.

But she'd forgotten about Matt. Head down, ignoring claws and fangs, he was charging at Tyler, tackling him like a first-rate linebacker before he could leap. Tyler went flying sideways, with Matt on top of him.

Bonnie was overwhelmed. So much was happening. Meredith was sawing through Caroline's ankle cords; Matt was pummeling Tyler in a way that certainly would have gotten him disqualified on the football field; Stefan was whirling that white ash staff as if he'd been trained for it. Klaus was laughing deliriously, seeming exhilarated by the exercise, as they traded blows with deadly speed and accuracy.

But Matt seemed to be in trouble now. Tyler was gripping him and snarling, trying to get a hold on his throat. Wildly, Bonnie looked around for a weapon, entirely forgetting the carving knife in her pocket. Her eye fell on a dead oak branch. She picked it up and ran to where Tyler and Matt were struggling.

Once there, though, she faltered. She didn't dare use the stick for fear she'd hit Matt with it. He and Tyler were rolling over and over in a blur of motion.

Then Matt was on top of Tyler again, holding Tyler's head down, holding himself clear. Bonnie saw her chance and aimed the stick. But Tyler saw *her*. With a burst of supernatural strength, he gathered his legs and sent Matt soaring off him backward. Matt's head struck a tree with a sound Bonnie would never forget. The dull sound of a rotten melon bursting. He slid down the front of the tree and was still.

Bonnie was gasping, stunned. She might have started toward Matt, but Tyler was there in front of her, breathing hard, bloody saliva running down his chin. He looked even more like an animal than he had in the graveyard. As if in a dream, Bonnie raised her stick, but she could feel it shaking in her hands. Matt was so still—was he breathing? Bonnie could hear the sob in her own breath as she faced Tyler. This was ridiculous; this was a boy from her own school. A boy she'd danced with last year at the Junior Prom. How could he be keeping her away from Matt, how could he be trying to hurt them all? How could he be *doing* this?

"Tyler, please—" she began, meaning to reason with him, to beg him . . .

"All alone in the woods, little girl?" he said, and his voice was a thick and guttural growl, shaped at the last minute into words. In that instant Bonnie knew that this was not the boy she'd gone to school with. This was an *animal*. Oh, God, he's ugly, she thought. Ropes of red spit hung out of his mouth. And those yellow eyes with the slitted pupils—in them she saw the cruelty of the shark, and the crocodile, and the wasp that lays its eggs in a caterpillar's living body. All the cruelty of animal nature in those two yellow eyes.

"Somebody should have warned you," Tyler said, dropping his jaw to laugh the way a dog does. "Because if you go out in the woods alone, you might meet the Big Bad—"

"Jerk!" a voice finished for him, and with a feeling of gratitude that bordered on the religious, Bonnie saw Meredith beside her. Meredith, holding Stefan's dagger, which shone liquidly in the moonlight.

"Silver, Tyler," Meredith said, brandishing it. "I wonder what silver does to a werewolf's members? Want to see?" All Meredith's elegance, her standoffishness, her cool observer's dispassion were gone. This was the essential Meredith, a warrior Meredith, and although she was smiling, she was *mad*.

"*Yes!*" shouted Bonnie gleefully, feeling power rush through her. Suddenly she could move. She and Meredith, together, were strong. Meredith was stalking Tyler from one side, Bonnie held her stick ready on the other. A longing she'd never felt before shot through her, the longing to hit Tyler so hard his head would come flying off. She could feel the strength to do it surging in her arm.

And Tyler, with his animal instinct, could sense it, could sense it from both of them, closing in on either side. He recoiled, caught himself, and turned to try and get away from them. They turned too. In a minute they were all three orbiting like a mini solar system: Tyler turning around and around in the middle; Bonnie and Meredith circling him, looking for a chance to attack.

One, two, *three*. Some unspoken signal flashed from Meredith to Bonnie. Just as Tyler leaped at Meredith, trying to knock the knife aside, Bonnie hit. Remembering the advice of a distant boyfriend who'd tried to teach her to play baseball, she imagined not just hitting Tyler's head but *through* his head, hitting something on the opposite side. She put the whole weight of her small body behind the blow, and the shock of connecting nearly jarred her teeth loose. It jolted her arms agonizingly and it shattered the stick. But Tyler fell like a bird shot out of the sky.

"I did it! *Yes! All right! Yes!*" Bonnie shouted, flinging the stick away. Triumph erupted from her in a primal shout. "*We did it!*" She grabbed the heavy body by the back of the mane and pulled it off Meredith, where it had fallen. *"We—"*

Then she broke off, her words freezing in her throat. *"Meredith!"* she cried.

"It's all right," Meredith gasped, her voice tight with pain. And weakness, Bonnie thought, chilled as if doused with ice water. Tyler had clawed her leg to the bone. There were huge, gaping wounds in the thigh of Meredith's jeans and in the white skin that showed clearly through the torn cloth. And to Bonnie's absolute horror, she could see inside the skin too, could see flesh and muscle ripped and red blood pouring out.

"Meredith—" she cried frantically. They had to get Meredith to a doctor. Everyone had to stop now; everyone must understand that. They had an injury here; they needed to get an ambulance, to call 911. "Meredith," she gasped, almost weeping.

"Tie it up with something." Meredith's face was white. Shock. Going into shock. And so much blood; so much blood coming out. Oh, God, thought Bonnie, please help me. She looked for something to tie it up with, but there was nothing.

Something dropped on the ground beside her. A length of nylon cord like the cord they'd used to tie up Tyler, with frayed edges. Bonnie looked up.

"Can you use that?" asked Caroline uncertainly, her

teeth chattering.

She was wearing the green dress, her auburn hair straggling and stuck to her face with sweat and blood. Even as she spoke she swayed, and fell to her knees beside Meredith.

"Are *you* hurt?" Bonnie gasped.

Caroline shook her head, but then she bent forward, racked with nausea, and Bonnie saw the marks in her throat. But there was no time to worry about Caroline now. Meredith was more important.

Bonnie tied the cord above Meredith's wounds, her mind running desperately over things she'd learned from her sister Mary. Mary was a nurse. Mary said—a tourniquet couldn't be too tight or left on too long or gangrene set in. But she had to stop the gushing blood. Oh, Meredith.

"Bonnie—help Stefan," Meredith was gasping, her voice almost a whisper. "He's going to need it. . . ." She sagged backward, her breathing stertorous, her slitted eyes looking up at the sky.

Wet. Everything was wet. Bonnie's hands, her clothes, the ground. Wet with Meredith's blood. And Matt was still lying under the tree, unconscious. She couldn't leave them, especially not with Tyler there. He might wake up.

Dazed, she turned to Caroline, who was shivering and retching, sweat beading her face. Useless, Bonnie thought. But she had no other choice.

"Caroline, listen to me," she said. She picked up the largest piece of the stick she'd used on Tyler and put it into Caroline's hands. "You stay with Matt and Meredith. Loosen that tourniquet every twenty minutes or so. And if Tyler starts to wake up, if he even *twitches*, you hit him as hard as you can with this. Understand? Caroline," she added, "this is your big chance to prove you're good for something. That you're not useless. All right?" She caught the furtive green eyes and repeated, "All right?"

"But what are *you* going to do?"

Bonnie looked toward the clearing.

"No, Bonnie." Caroline's hand grasped her, and Bonnie noted with some part of her mind the broken nails, the rope burns on the wrists. "Stay here where it's safe. Don't go to them. There's nothing you can do—"

Bonnie shook her off and made for the clearing before she lost her resolve. In her heart, she knew Caroline was right. There was nothing she could do. But something Matt had said before they left was ringing in her mind. To try at least. She had to try.

Still, in those next few horrible minutes all she could do was look.

So far, Stefan and Klaus had been trading blows with such violence and accuracy that it had been like a beautiful, lethal dance. But it had been an equal, or almost equal, match. Stefan had been holding his own.

Now she saw Stefan bearing down with his white ash lance, pressing Klaus to his knees, forcing him backward, farther and farther back, like a limbo dancer seeing how low he could go. And Bonnie could see Klaus's face now, mouth slightly open, staring up at Stefan with what looked like astonishment and fear.

Then everything changed.

At the very bottom of his descent, when Klaus had bent back as far as he could go, when it seemed that he must be about to collapse or break, something happened.

Klaus smiled.

And then he started pushing back.

Bonnie saw Stefan's muscles knot, saw his arms go rigid, trying to resist. But Klaus, still grinning madly, eyes wide open, just kept coming. He unfolded like some terrible jack-in-the-box, only slowly. Slowly. Inexorably. His grin getting wider until it looked as if it would split his face. Like the Cheshire cat.

A cat, thought Bonnie.

Cat with a mouse.

Now Stefan was the one grunting and straining, teeth clenched, trying to hold Klaus off. But Klaus and his stick bore down, forcing Stefan backward, forcing him to the ground.

Grinning all the time.

Until Stefan was lying on his back, his own stick pressing into his throat with the weight of Klaus's lance across it. Klaus looked down at him and beamed. "I'm tired of playing, little boy," he said, and he straightened and threw his own stick down. "Now it's dying time."

He took Stefan's staff away from him as easily as if he were taking it from a child. Picked it up with a flick of his wrist and broke it over his knee, showing how strong he was, how strong he had always been. How cruelly he had been playing with Stefan.

One of the halves of the white ash stick he tossed over his shoulder across the clearing. The other he jabbed at Stefan. Using not the pointed end but the splintered one, broken into a dozen tiny points. He jabbed down with a force that seemed almost casual, but Stefan screamed. He did it again and again, eliciting a scream each time.

Bonnie cried out, soundlessly.

She had never heard Stefan scream before. She didn't need to be told what kind of pain must have caused it. She didn't need to be told that white ash might be the only wood deadly to Klaus, but that any wood was deadly to Stefan. That Stefan was, if not dying now, about to die. That Klaus, with his hand now raised, was going to finish it with one more plunging blow. Klaus's face was tilted to the moon in a grin of obscene pleasure, showing that *this* was what he liked, where he got his thrills. From killing.

And Bonnie couldn't move, couldn't even cry. The world swam around her. It had all been a mistake, she wasn't competent; she was a baby after all. She didn't want to see that final thrust, but she couldn't look away. And all this couldn't be happening, but it was. It was.

Klaus flourished the splintered stake and with a smile of pure ecstasy started to bring it down.

And a spear shot across the clearing and struck him in the middle of the back, landing and quivering like a giant arrow, like half a giant arrow. It made Klaus's arms fling out, dropping the stake; it shocked the ecstatic grin right off his face. He stood, arms extended, for a second, and then turned, the white ash stick in his back wobbling slightly.

Bonnie's eyes were too dazzled by waves of gray dots to see, but she heard the voice clearly as it rang out, cold and arrogant and filled with absolute conviction. Just five words, but they changed everything.

"Get away from my brother."

15

Klaus screamed, a scream that reminded Bonnie of ancient predators, of the sabertooth cat and the bull mammoth. Blood frothed out of his mouth along with the scream, turning that handsome face into a twisted mask of fury.

His hands scrabbled at his back, trying to get a grip on the white ash stake and pull it out. But it was buried too deep. The throw had been a good one.

"Damon," Bonnie whispered.

He was standing at the edge of the clearing, framed by oak trees. As she watched, he took a step toward Klaus, and then another; lithe stalking steps filled with deadly purpose.

And he was angry. Bonnie would have run from the look on his face if her muscles hadn't been frozen. She had never seen such menace so barely held in check.

"Get . . . away . . . from my brother," he said, almost breathing it, with his eyes never leaving Klaus's as he took another step.

Klaus screamed again, but his hands stopped their frantic scrabbling. "You idiot! We don't have to fight! I told you that at the house! We can ignore each other!"

Damon's voice was no louder than before. "Get away from my brother." Bonnie could feel it inside him, a swell of Power like a tsunami. He continued, so softly that Bonnie had to strain to hear him, "Before I tear your heart out."

Bonnie could move after all. She stepped backward.

"I told you!" screamed Klaus, frothing. Damon didn't acknowledge the words in any way. His whole being seemed focused on Klaus's throat, on his chest, on the beating heart inside that he was going to tear out.

Klaus picked up the unbroken lance and rushed him.

In spite of all the blood, the blond man seemed to have plenty of strength left. The rush was sudden, violent, and almost inescapable. Bonnie saw him thrust the lance at Damon and shut her eyes involuntarily, and then opened them an instant later as she heard the flurry of wings.

Klaus had plunged right through the spot where Damon had been, and a black crow was soaring upward while a single feather floated down. As Bonnie stared,

Klaus's rush took him into the darkness beyond the clearing and he disappeared.

Dead silence fell in the wood.

Bonnie's paralysis broke slowly, and she first stepped, and then ran to where Stefan lay. He didn't open his eyes at her approach; he seemed unconscious. She knelt beside him. And then she felt a sort of horrible calm creep over her, like someone who has been swimming in ice water and at last feels the first undeniable signs of hypothermia. If she hadn't had so many successive shocks already, she might have fled screaming or dissolved into hysterics. But as it was, this was simply the last step, the last little slide into unreality. Into a world that couldn't be, but was.

Because it was bad. Very bad. As bad as it could be.

She'd never seen anybody hurt like this. Not even Mr. Tanner, and he had died of his wounds. Nothing Mary had ever said could help fix this. Even if they'd had Stefan on a stretcher outside an operating room, it wouldn't have been enough.

In that state of dreadful calm she looked up to see a flutter of wings blur and shimmer in the moonlight. Damon stood beside her, and she spoke quite collectedly and rationally.

"Will giving him blood help?"

He didn't seem to hear her. His eyes were all black, all pupil. That barely leashed violence, that sense of ferocious energy held back, was gone. He knelt and touched the dark head on the ground.

"Stefan?"

Bonnie shut her eyes.

Damon's scared, she thought. Damon's scared—*Damon!*—and oh, God, I don't know what to do. There's *nothing* to do—and it's all over and we're all lost and *Damon* is scared for Stefan. He isn't going to take care of things and he hasn't got a solution and somebody's got to fix this. And oh, God, please help me because I'm so frightened and Stefan's dying and Meredith and Matt are hurt and Klaus is going to come back.

She opened her eyes to look at Damon. He was white, his face looking terrifyingly young at that moment, with those dilated black eyes.

"Klaus is coming back," Bonnie said quietly. She wasn't afraid of him anymore. They weren't a centuries-old hunter and a seventeen-year-old human girl, sitting here at the edge of the world. They were just two people, Damon and Bonnie, who had to do the best they could.

"I know," Damon said. He was holding Stefan's hand, looking completely unembarrassed about it, and it seemed quite logical and sensible. Bonnie could feel him sending

Power into Stefan, could also feel that it wasn't enough.

"Would blood help him?"

"Not much. A little, maybe."

"Anything that helps at all we've got to try."

Stefan whispered, "No."

Bonnie was surprised. She'd thought he was unconscious. But his eyes were open now, open and alert and smoldering green. They were the only alive thing about him.

"Don't be stupid," Damon said, his voice hardening. He was gripping Stefan's hand until his knuckles whitened. "You're badly hurt."

"I won't break my promise." That immovable stubbornness was in Stefan's voice, in his pale face. And when Damon opened his mouth again, undoubtedly to say that Stefan would break it and like it or Damon would break his neck, Stefan added, "Especially when it won't do any good."

There was a silence while Bonnie fought with the raw truth of this. Where they were now, in this terrible place beyond all ordinary things, pretense or false reassurance seemed wrong. Only the truth would do. And Stefan was telling the truth.

He was still looking at his brother, who was looking back, all that fierce, furious attention focused on Stefan as it had been focused on Klaus earlier. As if somehow that would help.

"I'm not badly hurt, I'm dead," Stefan said brutally, his eyes locked on Damon's. Their last and greatest struggle of wills, Bonnie thought. "And you need to get Bonnie and the others out of here."

"We won't leave you," Bonnie intervened. That was the truth; she could say that.

"You *have* to!" Stefan didn't glance aside, didn't look away from his brother. "Damon, you know I'm right. Klaus will be here any minute. Don't throw your life away. Don't throw *their* lives away."

"I don't give a damn about their lives," Damon hissed. The truth also, Bonnie thought, curiously unoffended. There was only one life Damon cared about here, and it wasn't his own.

"Yes, you do!" Stefan flared back. He was hanging on to Damon's hand with just as fierce a grip, as if this was a contest and he could force Damon to concede that way. "Elena had a last request; well, this is mine. You have Power, Damon. I want you to use it to help them."

"Stefan . . ." Bonnie whispered helplessly.

"*Promise me,*" Stefan said to Damon, and then a spasm of pain twisted his face.

For uncountable seconds Damon simply looked down

at him. Then he said, "I promise," quick and sharp as the stroke of a dagger. He let go of Stefan's hand and stood, turning to Bonnie. "Come on."

"We can't *leave* him . . ."

"Yes, we can." There was nothing young about Damon's face now. Nothing vulnerable. "You and your human friends are leaving here, permanently. *I* am coming back."

Bonnie shook her head. She knew, dimly, that Damon wasn't betraying Stefan, that it was some case of Damon putting Stefan's ideals above Stefan's life, but it was all too abstruse and incomprehensible to her. She didn't understand it and she didn't want to. All she knew was that Stefan couldn't be left lying there.

"You're coming *now*," Damon said, reaching for her, the steely ring back in his voice. Bonnie prepared herself for a fight, and then something happened that made all their debating meaningless. There was a crack like a giant whip and a flash like daylight, and Bonnie was blinded. When she could see through the afterimage, her eyes flew to the flames that were licking up from a newly blackened hole at the base of a tree.

Klaus had returned. With lightning.

Bonnie's eye darted to him next, as the only other thing moving in the clearing. He was waving the bloody white ash stake he'd pulled out of his own back like a gory trophy.

Lightning rod, thought Bonnie illogically, and then there was another crash.

It stabbed down from an empty sky, in huge blue-white forks that lit everything like the sun at noon. Bonnie watched as one tree and then another was hit, each one closer than the last. Flames licked up like hungry red goblins among the leaves.

Two trees on either side of Bonnie exploded, with cracks so loud that she felt rather than heard it, a piercing in her eardrums. Damon, whose eyes were more sensitive, threw up a hand to protect them.

Then he shouted, "Klaus!" and sprang toward the blond man. He wasn't stalking now; this was the deadly race of attack. The burst of killing speed of the hunting cat or the wolf.

Lightning caught him in midspring.

Bonnie screamed as she saw it, jumping to her feet. There was a blue flash of superheated gases and a smell of burning, and then Damon was down, lying motionless on his face. Bonnie could see tiny wisps of smoke rise from him, just as they did from the trees.

Speechless with horror, she looked at Klaus.

He was swaggering through the clearing, holding his

bloody stick like a golf club. He bent down over Damon as he passed, and smiled. Bonnie wanted to scream again, but she didn't have the breath. There didn't seem to be any air left to breathe.

"I'll deal with *you* later," Klaus told the unconscious Damon. Then his face tipped up toward Bonnie.

"You," he said, "I'm going to deal with right now."

It was an instant before she realized he was looking at Stefan, and not her. Those electric blue eyes were fixed on Stefan's face. They moved to Stefan's bloody middle.

"I'm going to *eat* you now, Salvatore."

Bonnie was all alone. The only one left standing. And she was afraid.

But she knew what she had to do.

She let her knees collapse again, dropping to the ground beside Stefan.

And this is how it ends, she thought. You kneel beside your knight and then you face the enemy.

She looked at Klaus and moved so that she was shielding Stefan. He seemed to notice her for the first time, and frowned as if he'd found a spider in his salad. Firelight flickered orange-red on his face.

"Get out of the way."

"No."

And this is how the ending starts. Like this, so simply, with one word, and you're going to die on a summer night.

A summer night when the moon and stars are shining and bonfires burn like the flames the druids used to summon the dead.

"Bonnie, go," Stefan said painfully. "Get out while you can."

"No," Bonnie said. I'm sorry, Elena, she thought. I can't save him. This is all I can do.

"Get out of the way," Klaus said through his teeth.

"No." She could wait and let Stefan die this way, instead of with Klaus's teeth in his throat. It might not seem like much of a difference, but it was the most she could offer.

"Bonnie . . ." Stefan whispered.

"Don't you know who I am, girl? I've walked with the devil. If you move, I'll let you die quickly."

Bonnie's voice had given out. She shook her head.

Klaus threw back his own head and laughed. A little more blood trickled out, too. "All right," he said. "Have it your own way. Both of you go together."

Summer night, Bonnie thought. The solstice eve. When the line between worlds is so thin.

"Say good night, sweetheart."

No time to trance, no time for anything. Nothing except one desperate appeal.

"*Elena!*" Bonnie screamed. "*Elena! Elena!*"

Klaus recoiled.

For an instant, it seemed as if the name alone had the power to alarm him. Or as if he expected something to respond to Bonnie's cry. He stood, listening.

Bonnie drew on her powers, putting everything she had into it, throwing her need and her call out into the void.

And felt . . . nothing.

Nothing disturbed the summer night except the crackling sound of flames. Klaus turned back to Bonnie and Stefan, and grinned.

Then Bonnie saw the mist creeping along the ground.

No—it couldn't be mist. It must be smoke from the fire. But it didn't behave like either. It was swirling, rising in the air like a tiny whirlwind or dust devil. It was gathering into a shape roughly the size of a man.

There was another one a little distance away. Then Bonnie saw a third. The same thing was happening all over.

Mist was flowing out of the ground, between the trees. Pools of it, each separate and distinct. Bonnie, staring mutely, could see through each patch, could see the flames, the oak trees, the bricks of the chimney. Klaus had stopped smiling, stopped moving, and was watching too.

Bonnie turned to Stefan, unable to even frame the question.

"Unquiet spirits," he whispered huskily, his green eyes intent. "The solstice."

And then Bonnie understood.

They were coming. From across the river, where the old cemetery lay. From the woods, where countless make-shift graves had been dug to dump bodies in before they rotted. The unquiet spirits, the soldiers who had fought here and died during the Civil War. A supernatural host answering the call for help.

They were forming all around. There were hundreds of them.

Bonnie could actually see faces now. The misty out-lines were filling in with pale hues like so many runny watercolors. She saw a flash of blue, a glimmer of gray. Both Union and Confederate troops. Bonnie glimpsed a pistol thrust into a belt, the glint of an ornamented sword. Chevrons on a sleeve. A bushy dark beard; a long, well-tended white one. A small figure, child size, with dark holes for eyes and a drum hanging at thigh level.

"Oh, my God," she whispered. "Oh, *God*." It wasn't swearing. It was something like a prayer.

Not that she wasn't frightened of them, because she was. It was every nightmare she'd ever had about the cemetery come true. Like her first dream about Elena, when things came crawling out of the black pits in the earth; only these things weren't crawling, they were *flying*, skimming and floating until they swirled into human form. Everything that Bonnie had ever felt about the old graveyard—that it was alive and full of watching eyes, that there was some Power lurking behind its waiting still-ness—was proving true. The earth of Fell's Church was giving up its bloody memories. The spirits of those who'd died here were walking again.

And Bonnie could feel their anger. It frightened her, but another emotion was waking up inside her, making her catch her breath and clench tighter on Stefan's hand. Because the misty army had a leader.

One figure was floating in front of the others, closest to the place where Klaus stood. It had no shape or definition as yet, but it glowed and scintillated with the pale golden light of a candle flame. Then, before Bonnie's eyes, it seemed to take on substance from the air, shining brighter and brighter every minute with an unearthly light. It was brighter than the circle of fire. It was so bright that Klaus leaned back from it and Bonnie blinked, but when she turned at a low sound, she saw Stefan staring straight into it, fearlessly, with wide-open eyes. And smiling, so faintly, as if glad to have this be the last thing he saw.

Then Bonnie was sure.

Klaus dropped the stake. He had turned away from Bonnie and Stefan to face the being of light that hung in the clearing like an avenging angel. Golden hair stream-ing back in an invisible wind, Elena looked down on him.

"She came," Bonnie whispered.

"You asked her to," Stefan murmured. His voice trailed off into a labored breath, but he was still smiling. His eyes were serene.

"Stand away from them," Elena said, her voice coming simultaneously to Bonnie's ears and her mind. It was like the chiming of dozens of bells, distant and close up at once. "It's over now, Klaus."

But Klaus rallied quickly. Bonnie saw his shoulders swell with a breath, noticed for the first time the hole in the back of the tan raincoat where the white ash stake had pierced him. It was stained dull red, and new blood was flowing now as Klaus flung out his arms.

"You think I'm afraid of you?" he shouted. He spun around, laughing at all the pallid forms. "You think I'm afraid of any of you? You're dead! Dust on the wind! You can't touch me!"

"You're wrong," Elena said in her wind-chime voice.

"I'm one of the Old Ones! An Original! Do you know what that means?" Klaus turned again, addressing all of them, his unnaturally blue eyes seeming to catch some of the red glow of the fire. *"I've never died.* Every one of you has died, you gallery of spooks! But not me. Death can't touch me. I am *invincible!"*

The last word came in a shout so loud it echoed among the trees. *Invincible . . . invincible . . . invincible.* Bonnie heard it fading into the hungry sound of the fire.

Elena waited until the last echo had died. Then she said, very simply, "Not quite." She turned to look at the misty shapes around her. "He wants to spill more blood here."

A new voice spoke up, a hollow voice that ran like a trickle of cold water down Bonnie's spine. "There's been enough killing, I say." It was a Union soldier with a double row of buttons on his jacket.

"More than enough," said another voice, like the boom of a faraway drum. A Confederate holding a bayonet.

"It's time somebody stopped it"—an old man in home-dyed butternut cloth.

"We can't let it go on"—the drummer boy with the black holes for eyes.

"No more blood spilled!" Several voices took it up at once. "No more killing!" The cry passed from one to another until the swell of sound was louder than the roar of the fire. "No more blood!"

"*You can't touch me!* You can't kill me!"

"Let's take 'im, boys!"

Bonnie never knew who gave that last command. But he was obeyed by all, Confederate and Union soldiers alike. They were rising, flowing, dissolving into mist again, a dark mist with a hundred hands. It bore down on Klaus like an ocean wave, dashing itself on him and engulfing him. Each hand took hold, and although Klaus was fighting and thrashing with arms and legs, they were too many for him. In seconds he was obscured by them, surrounded, swallowed by the dark mist. It rose, whirling like a tornado from which screams could be heard only faintly.

"You can't kill me! I'm immortal!"

The tornado swept away into the darkness beyond Bonnie's sight. Following it was a trail of ghosts like a comet's tail, shooting off into the night sky.

"Where are they taking him?" Bonnie didn't mean to say it aloud; she just blurted it out before she thought. But Elena heard.

"Where he won't do any harm," she said, and the look on her face stopped Bonnie from asking any other questions.

There was a squealing, bleating sound from the other side of the clearing. Bonnie turned and saw Tyler, in his terrible part-human, part-animal shape, on his feet. There was no need for Caroline's club. He was staring at Elena and the few remaining ghostly figures and gibbering.

"Don't let them take me! Don't let them take me too!"

Before Elena could speak, he had spun around. He regarded the fire, which was higher than his own head, for an instant, then plunged right through it, crashing into the forest beyond. Through a parting of the flames, Bonnie saw him drop to the ground, beating out flames on himself, then rise and run again. Then the fire flared up and she couldn't see anything more.

But she'd remembered something: Meredith—and Matt. Meredith was lying propped up, her head in Caroline's lap, watching. Matt was still on his back. Hurt, but not so badly hurt as Stefan.

"Elena," Bonnie said, catching the bright figure's attention, and then she simply looked at him.

The brightness came closer. Stefan didn't blink. He looked into the heart of the light and smiled. "He's been stopped now. Thanks to you."

"It was Bonnie who called us. And she couldn't have done it at the right place and the right time without you and the others."

"I tried to keep my promise."

"I know, Stefan."

Bonnie didn't like the sound of this at all. It sounded too much like a farewell—a permanent one. Her own words floated back to her: *He might go to another place or— or just go out.* And she didn't want Stefan to go *anywhere.* Surely anyone who looked that much like an angel . . .

"Elena," she said, "can't you—do something? Can't you help him?" Her voice was shaking.

And Elena's expression as she turned to look at Bonnie, gentle but so sad, was even more distressing. It reminded her of someone, and then she remembered.

Honoria Fell. Honoria's eyes had looked like that, as if she were looking at all the inescapable wrongs in the world. All the unfairness, all the things that shouldn't have been, but were.

"I can do something," she said. "But I don't know if it's the kind of help he wants." She turned back to Stefan. "Stefan, I can cure what Klaus did. Tonight I have that much Power. But I can't cure what Katherine did."

Bonnie's numbed brain struggled with this for a while. What Katherine did—but Stefan had recovered months ago from Katherine's torture in the crypt. Then she understood. What Katherine had done was make Stefan a vampire.

"It's been too long," Stefan was saying to Elena. "If you *did* cure it, I'd be a pile of dust."

"Yes." Elena didn't smile, just went on looking at him steadily. "Do you want my help, Stefan?"

"To go on living in this world in the shadows . . ." Stefan's voice was a whisper now, his green eyes distant. Bonnie wanted to shake him. *Live,* she thought to him, but she didn't dare say it for fear she'd make him decide just the opposite. Then she thought of something else.

"To go on trying," she said, and both of them looked at her. She looked back, chin thrust out, and saw the beginning of a smile on Elena's bright lips. Elena turned to Stefan, and that tiny hint of a smile passed to him.

"Yes," he said quietly, and then, to Elena, "I want your help."

She bent and kissed him.

Bonnie saw the brightness flow from her to Stefan, like a river of sparkling light engulfing him. It flooded over him the way the dark mist had surrounded Klaus, like a cascade of diamonds, until his entire body glowed like Elena's. For an instant Bonnie imagined she could see the blood inside him turned molten, flowing out to each vein, each capillary, healing everything it touched. Then the glow faded to a golden aura, soaking back into Stefan's skin. His shirt was still demolished, but underneath the flesh was smooth and firm. Bonnie, feeling her own eyes wide with wonder, couldn't help reaching out to touch.

It felt just like any skin. The horrible wounds were gone.

She laughed aloud with sheer excitement, and then looked up, sobering. "Elena—there's Meredith, too—"

The bright being that was Elena was already moving across the clearing. Meredith looked up at her from Caroline's lap.

"Hello, Elena," she said, almost normally except that her voice was so weak.

Elena bent and kissed her. The brightness flowed again, encompassing Meredith. And when it faded, Meredith stood up on her own two feet.

Then Elena did the same thing with Matt, who woke up, looking confused but alert. She kissed Caroline too, and Caroline stopped shaking and straightened.

Then she went to Damon.

He was still lying where he had fallen. The ghosts had passed over him, taking no notice of him. Elena's brightness hovered over him, one shining hand reaching to touch his hair. Then she bent and kissed the dark head on the ground.

As the sparkling light faded, Damon sat up and shook his head. He saw Elena and went still, then, every movement careful and self-contained, stood up. He didn't say anything, only looked as Elena turned back to Stefan.

He was silhouetted against the fire. Bonnie had scarcely noticed how the red glow had grown so that it almost eclipsed Elena's gold. But now she saw it and felt a thrill of alarm.

"My last gift to you," Elena said, and it began to rain.

Not a thunder-and-lightning storm, but a thorough pattering rain that soaked everything—Bonnie included—and doused the fire. It was fresh and cool, and it seemed to wash all the horror of the last hours away, cleansing the glade of everything that had happened there. Bonnie tilted her face up to it, shutting her eyes, wanting to stretch out her arms and embrace it. At last it slackened and she looked again at Elena.

Elena was looking at Stefan, and there was no smile on her lips now. The wordless sorrow was back in her face.

"It's midnight," she said. "And I have to go."

Bonnie knew instantly, at the sound of it, that "go" didn't just mean for the moment. "Go" meant forever. Elena was going somewhere that no trance or dream could reach.

And Stefan knew it too.

"Just a few more minutes," he said, reaching for her.

"I'm sorry—"

"Elena, wait—I need to tell you—"

"I can't!" For the first time the serenity of that bright face was destroyed, showing not only gentle sadness but tearing grief. "Stefan, I can't wait. I'm so sorry." It was as if she were being pulled backward, retreating from them into some dimension that Bonnie could not see. Maybe the same place Honoria went when her task was finished, Bonnie thought. To be at peace.

But Elena's eyes didn't look as if she were at peace. They clung to Stefan, and she reached out her hand toward his, hopelessly. They didn't touch. Wherever Elena was being pulled was too far away.

"Elena—*please!*" It was the voice Stefan had called her with in his room. As if his heart was breaking.

"Stefan," she cried, both hands held out to him now.

But she was diminishing, vanishing. Bonnie felt a sob swell in her own chest, close her own throat. It wasn't fair. All they had ever wanted was to be together. And now Elena's reward for helping the town and finishing her task was to be separated from Stefan irrevocably. It just wasn't *fair*.

"Stefan," Elena called again, but her voice came as if from a long distance. The brightness was almost gone. Then, as Bonnie stared through helpless tears, it winked out.

Leaving the clearing silent once again. They were all gone, the ghosts of Fell's Church who had walked for one night to keep more blood from being spilled. The bright spirit that had led them had vanished without a trace, and even the moon and stars were covered by clouds.

Bonnie knew that the wetness on Stefan's face wasn't due to the rain that was still splashing down.

He was standing, chest heaving, looking at the last place where Elena's brightness had been seen. And all the longing and the pain Bonnie had glimpsed on his face at times before was nothing to what she saw now.

"It isn't fair," she whispered. Then she shouted it to the sky, not caring who she was addressing. "It isn't fair!"

Stefan had been breathing more and more quickly. Now he lifted his face too, not in anger but in unbearable pain. His eyes were searching the clouds as if he might find some last trace of golden light, some flicker of brightness there. He couldn't. Bonnie saw the spasm go through him, like the agony of Klaus's stake. And the cry that burst out of him was the most terrible thing she'd ever heard.

"*Elena!*"

onnie never could quite remember how the next few seconds went. She heard Stefan's cry that almost seemed to shake the earth beneath her. She saw Damon start toward him. And then she saw the flash.

A flash like Klaus's lightning, only not blue-white. This one was gold.

And so bright Bonnie felt that the sun had exploded in front of her eyes. All she could make out for several seconds were whirling colors. And then she saw something in the middle of the clearing, near the chimney stack. Something white, shaped like the ghosts, only more solid looking. Something small and huddled that had to be anything but what her eyes were telling her it looked like.

Because it looked like a slender naked girl trembling

on the forest floor. A girl with golden hair.

It looked like Elena.

Not the glowing, candle-lit Elena of the spirit world and not the pale, inhumanly beautiful girl who had been Elena the vampire. This was an Elena whose creamy skin was blotching pink and showing gooseflesh under the spatter of the rain. An Elena who looked bewildered as she slowly raised her head and gazed around her, as if all the familiar things in the clearing were unfamiliar to her.

It's an illusion. Either that or they gave her a few minutes to say good-bye. Bonnie kept telling herself that, but she couldn't make herself believe it.

"Bonnie?" said a voice uncertainly. A voice that wasn't like wind chimes at all. The voice of a frightened young girl.

Bonnie's knees gave out. A wild feeling was growing inside her. She tried to push it away, not daring to even examine it yet. She just watched Elena.

Elena touched the grass in front of her. Hesitantly at first, then more and more firmly, quicker and quicker. She picked up a leaf in fingers that seemed clumsy, put it down, patted the ground. Snatched it up again. She grabbed a whole handful of wet leaves, held them to her, smelled them. She looked up at Bonnie, the leaves scattering away.

For a moment, they just knelt and stared at each other

from the distance of a few feet. Then, tremulously, Bonnie stretched out her hand. She couldn't breathe. The feeling was growing and growing.

Elena's hand came up in turn. Reached toward Bonnie's. Their fingers touched.

Real fingers. In the real world. Where they both were.

Bonnie gave a kind of scream and threw herself on Elena.

In a minute she was patting her everywhere in a frenzy, with wild, disbelieving delight. And Elena was solid. She was wet from the rain and she was shivering and Bonnie's hands didn't go through her. Bits of damp leaf and crumbs of soil were clinging to Elena's hair.

"You're here," she sobbed. "I can touch you, Elena!"

Elena gasped back, "I can touch you! I'm here!" She grabbed the leaves again. "I can touch the ground!"

"I can see you touching it!" They might have kept this up indefinitely, but Meredith interrupted. She was standing a few steps away, staring, her dark eyes enormous, her face white. She made a choking sound.

"Meredith!" Elena turned to her and held out handfuls of leaves. She opened her arms.

Meredith, who had been able to cope when Elena's body was found in the river, when Elena had appeared at her window as a vampire, when Elena had materialized in the clearing like an angel, just stood there, shaking.

She looked about to faint.

"Meredith, she's solid! You can touch her! See?" Bonnie pummeled Elena again joyfully.

Meredith didn't move. She whispered, "It's impossible—"

"It's true! See? It's true!" Bonnie was getting hysterical. She knew she was, and she didn't care. If anyone had a right to get hysterical, it was her. "It's true, it's true," she caroled. "Meredith, come *see*."

Meredith, who had been staring at Elena all this while, made another choked sound. Then, with one motion, she flung herself down on Elena. She touched her, found that her hand met the resistance of flesh. She looked into Elena's face. And then she burst into uncontrollable tears.

She cried and cried, her head on Elena's naked shoulder.

Bonnie gleefully patted both of them.

"Don't you think she'd better put something on?" said a voice, and Bonnie looked up to see Caroline taking off her dress. Caroline did it rather calmly, standing in her beige polyester slip afterward as if she did this sort of thing all the time. No imagination, Bonnie thought again, but without malice. Clearly there were times when no imagination was an advantage.

Meredith and Bonnie pulled the dress over Elena's head. She looked small inside it, wet and somehow unnatural, as if she wasn't used to clothing anymore. But it was some protection from the elements, anyway.

Then Elena whispered, "Stefan."

She turned. He was standing there, with Damon and Matt, a little apart from the girls. He was just watching her. As if not only his breath, but his life was held, waiting.

Elena got up and took a tottery step to him, and then another and another. Slim and newly fragile inside her borrowed dress, she wavered as she moved toward him. Like the little mermaid learning how to use her legs, Bonnie thought.

He let her get almost all the way there, just staring, before he stumbled toward her. They ended in a rush and then fell to the ground together, arms locked around each other, each holding on as tightly as possible. Neither of them said a word.

At last Elena pulled back to look at Stefan, and he cupped her face between his hands, just gazing back at her. Elena laughed aloud for sheer joy, opening and closing her own fingers and looking at them in delight before burying them in Stefan's hair. Then they kissed.

Bonnie watched unabashedly, feeling some of the heady joy spill over into tears. Her throat ached, but these were sweet tears, not the salt tears of pain, and she was still smiling. She was filthy, she was soaking wet, she had never been so happy in her life. She felt as if she wanted to dance and sing and do all sorts of crazy things.

Some time later Elena looked up from Stefan to all of them, her face almost as bright as when she'd floated in the clearing like an angel. Shining like starlight. No one will ever call her Ice Princess again, Bonnie thought.

"My friends," Elena said. It was all she said, but it was enough, that and the queer little sob she gave as she held out a hand to them. They were around her in a second, swarming her, all trying to embrace at once. Even Caroline.

"Elena," Caroline said, "I'm sorry . . ."

"It's all forgotten now," Elena said, and hugged her as freely as anyone else. Then she grasped a sturdy brown hand and held it briefly to her cheek. "Matt," she said, and he smiled at her, blue eyes swimming. But not with misery at seeing her in Stefan's arms, Bonnie thought. Just now Matt's face expressed only happiness.

A shadow fell over the little group, coming between them and the moonlight. Elena looked up, and held out her hand again.

"Damon," she said.

The clear light and shining love in her face was irresistible. Or it should have been irresistible, Bonnie thought. But Damon stepped forward unsmiling, his black eyes as bottomless and unfathomable as ever. None of the starlight that shone from Elena was reflected back from them.

Stefan looked up at him fearlessly, as he'd looked into

the painful brilliance of Elena's golden brightness. Then, never looking away, he held out his hand as well.

Damon stood gazing down at them, the two open, fearless faces, the mute offer of their hands. The offer of connection, warmth, humanity. Nothing showed in his own face, and he was utterly motionless himself.

"Come on, Damon," Matt said softly. Bonnie looked at him quickly, and saw that the blue eyes were intent now as they looked at the shadowed hunter's face.

Damon spoke without moving. "I'm not like you."

"You're not as different from us as you want to think," Matt said. "Look," he added, an odd note of challenge in his voice, "I know you killed Mr. Tanner in self-defense, because you told me. And I know you didn't come here to Fell's Church because Bonnie's spell dragged you here, because I sorted the hair and I didn't make any mistakes. You're more like us than you admit, Damon. The only thing I *don't* know is why you didn't go into Vickie's house to help her."

Damon snapped, almost automatically, "Because I wasn't invited!"

Memory swept over Bonnie. Herself standing outside Vickie's house, Damon standing beside her. Stefan's voice: *Vickie, invite me in.* But no one had invited Damon.

"But how did *Klaus* get in, then—?" she began, following her own thoughts.

"That was Tyler's job, I'm sure," Damon said tersely. "What Tyler did for Klaus in return for learning how to reclaim his heritage. And he must have invited Klaus in before we ever started guarding the house—probably before Stefan and I came to Fell's Church. Klaus was well prepared. That night he was in the house and the girl was dead before I knew what was happening."

"Why didn't you call for Stefan?" Matt said. There was no accusation in his voice. It was a simple question.

"Because there was nothing he could have done! *I* knew what you were dealing with as soon as I saw it. An Old One. Stefan would only have gotten himself killed and the girl was past caring, anyway."

Bonnie heard the thread of coldness in his voice, and when Damon turned back to Stefan and Elena, his face had hardened. It was as if some decision had been made.

"You see, I'm not like you," he said.

"It doesn't matter." Stefan had still not withdrawn his hand. Neither had Elena.

"And sometimes the good guys *do* win," Matt said quietly, encouragingly.

"Damon—" Bonnie began. Slowly, almost reluctantly, he turned toward her. She was thinking about that moment when they had been kneeling over Stefan and he had looked so young. When they had been just Damon and Bonnie at the edge of the world.

She thought, for just one instant, that she saw stars in those black eyes. And she could sense in him something—some ferment of feelings like longing and confusion and fear and anger all mixed. But then it was all smoothed over again and his shields were back up and Bonnie's psychic senses told her nothing. And those black eyes were simply opaque.

He turned back to the couple on the ground. Then he removed his jacket and stepped behind Elena. He draped it over her shoulders without touching her.

"It's a cold night," he said. His eyes held Stefan's a moment as he settled the black jacket around her.

And then he turned to walk into the darkness between the oak trees. In an instant Bonnie heard the rush of wings.

Stefan and Elena wordlessly joined hands again, and Elena's golden head dropped to Stefan's shoulder. Over her hair Stefan's green eyes were turned toward the patch of night where his brother had disappeared.

Bonnie shook her head, feeling a catch in her throat. It was eased as something touched her arm and she looked up at Matt. Even soaking wet, even covered with bits of moss and fern, he was a beautiful sight. She smiled at him, feeling her wonder and joy come back. The giddy, dizzy excitement as she thought about what had happened tonight. Meredith and Caroline were smiling too, and in an impulsive burst Bonnie seized Matt's hands and whirled him into a dance. In the middle of the clearing they kicked up wet leaves and spun and laughed. They were alive, and they were young, and it was the summer solstice.

"You wanted us all back together again!" Bonnie shouted at Caroline, and pulled the scandalized girl into the dance. Meredith, her dignity forgotten, joined them too.

And for a long time in the clearing there was only rejoicing.

June 21, 7:30 a.m.
The Summer Solstice

Dear Diary,
   Oh, it's all too much to explain and you wouldn't believe it anyway. I'm going to bed.
                                                   Bonnie